Hall x 3

D0355584

_M_

COLLECTED TALES

AND FANTASIES

ALSO BY LORD BERNERS

First Childhood

A Distant Prospect

The Girls of Radcliff Hall

Collected Tales

AND

Fantasies

of

Lord Berners

INCLUDING

Percy Wallingford

The Camel ✠ *Mr. Pidger*

Count Omega

The Romance of a Nose

Far from the Madding War

TURTLE POINT PRESS
AND
HELEN MARX BOOKS
NEW YORK

Collected Tales and Fantasies of Lord Berners

Turtle Point Press
and
Helen Marx Books
1999

Copyright © Lord Berners c/o The Berners Trust

All rights reserved, including the right
to reproduce this book or portions thereof in any form.

LIBRARY OF CONGRESS CATALOGING-IN-PUBLICATION DATA

Berners, Gerald Hugh Tyrwhitt-Wilson, Baron, 1883–1950.
 Collected tales and fantasies of Lord Berners : including
Far from the madding war, Count Omega, The camel,
The romance of a nose, Percy Wallingford and Mr. Pidger.
—1st ed.
  p. cm.
 LIBRARY OF CONGRESS NUMBER: 98-61036
 ISBN: 1-885983-38-7
 1. World War, 1939–1945—Fiction. 2. Trombone—
Fiction. 3. Camels—Fiction. 4. Cleopatra, Queen of
Egypt, d. 30 B.C.—Fiction. 5. Dogs—Fiction. I. Title.
II. Title: Far from the madding war.
PR6003.E7425A15 1999   823'.912
              QBI98-1335

DESIGN AND COMPOSITION BY MELISSA EHN AT
WILSTED & TAYLOR PUBLISHING SERVICES.

Contents

COLLECTED TALES

AND FANTASIES

PERCY WALLINGFORD

(1914)

Percy Wallingford

Lord Berners

TO

Clarissa Churchill

1

A Paragon

Mrs. Pontefract's house parties were considered by many people not to be a wholly unmixed pleasure.

Some indeed found them so lacking in pleasurable aspects that, after one visit, they never returned. Such recusants, however, were rare, and Mrs. Pontefract never had any difficulty in filling her house whenever she wished to do so. In the first decade of the twentieth century her week-end parties had come to be almost a national institution.

Mrs. Pontefract was rich, fashionable and eccentric. Her eccentricity consisted in a passion for economy. Meanness is not generally looked upon as a particularly amiable trait, yet it was precisely this that, in spite of all they had to suffer from it, endeared her to her friends.

There was nothing mean about her meanness. As grandiose as it was diverting, it gave people a great deal to talk and laugh about. It had become the subject of innumerable anecdotes and amusing stories, and placed her among the ranks of famous and eccentric great ladies of social history.

She inherited her economical disposition from her father, Lord Saxifrage, a miser in the ordinary sense of the word, who had gained no credit in the eyes of the world. His position was that of the "father of the Great Mozart," and his daughter had invested a mere talent with genius.

She had contracted what was considered in those days a misalliance with a wealthy Birmingham manufacturer whom she had completely dominated. She had forced him to go in for politics, for which he had no very marked capacity. However, having spent a great deal of money in the course of his political career, he was on the point of being ennobled, when unfortunately he died.

Mrs. Pontefract was now in control of a gigantic fortune which she was employing in the paradoxical combination of entertainment and economy. In some ways, however, she was generous enough. She was helpful to the poor. She was always ready to subscribe to public charities, but she never allowed her name to appear on a subscription list for fear of encouraging expectations in other quarters.

It was only with regard to herself and her friends that she exercised a rigid and painful parsimony. Her household presented a strange combination of Spartan frugality and Edwardian grandeur. So did her mode of life.

Attired in the costliest of furs, wearing jewels that were worth a king's or at least a crown prince's ransom, she invariably travelled third class, and if there had been a fourth class she would have travelled in that. She sat in cold rooms to economize fuel. She starved herself, and when she entertained, the food was barely sufficient to go round. People who took too liberal a helping were shouted at by their hostess, and if her eagle eye failed to observe, those who were served last went hungry. Although she was fond of animals, she allowed no pets in the house. A cat was kept solely for the purpose of putting down mice and the cat itself was the subject of innumerable economical ingenuities. Picking up a dead bird in the park, she would race home to tell the butler to countermand the cat's meat, and once, when a member of the royal family was visiting her and had asked for a glass of milk, she had said to the footman "Bring the cat's milk. The cat can have water."

For Mrs. Pontefract economy seemed to be something in the nature of an exciting game. Picking up a penny stamp on the floor, getting someone to pay her cab fare, she felt she had scored a point. She was quite frank about her stinginess, even boastful of it. In fact she was so cheerful, so jolly about it, that one was completely disarmed. She had a hearty, slap-back amiability and, in her rather arrogant manner, was at times very amusing. She was completely devoid of affectation or fantasy; hers was a humour that everyone could understand, and she was extremely popular.

It was in her country house, Pontefract Hall, built by her late husband at the end of the nineteenth century, that the incidence of her Spartan régime was felt to the full.

The bedrooms were, for the most part, small and uncomfortable and the beds gave the impression that they had been designed primarily as instruments of torture. The bathrooms were situated in a distant wing, and the bath water was apt to be tepid. One had to get out of one's bed to turn out the light and stumble back again in the dark, and the light itself was switched off at the main at midnight, so that, reading your novel or undressing, you were suddenly plunged in darkness. Even in the coldest weather there was never a fire in a bedroom. Such minor amenities as would be available in the humblest homes were absent at Pontefract Hall.

Notwithstanding the hardships they had to endure, people accustomed to every form of comfort and luxury, flocked to Mrs. Pontefract's house parties. Not impecunious or snobbish folk, who might under any conditions have accepted an invitation from a rich and fashionable hostess, but the élite of the aristocracy, ambassadors, rising politicians, American millionaires, smart society women, and persons famous in the world of art or literature.

What was the lure that attracted such people time after time in the face of fearful odds to this Gehenna of discomfort? Was it the personality of the hostess? The certainty that you would meet interesting people? Or the feeling that penance was sometimes necessary, a latent masochism that lurks unexpectedly in the background of the proudest spirits?

My first impulse, on receiving an invitation from Mrs. Pontefract, was to refuse. But the final sentence of her letter "Percy Wallingford and his wife are coming" decided me to change my mind.

It would seem as if the powers who guide our destiny were sometimes bent on giving us friends we should not of our own free will have selected, and it is certain that if these capricious powers had not thrust Percy Wallingford upon me at an early age, I should never have presumed to aim so high, for, in so far as human perfection on this earth can go, he was as near to it as mortal man can be, and to one riddled with doubts and indecisions his presence was a constant reproach.

The first time Percy Wallingford entered majestically into my life was at my private school. He had been deputed by his parents, who were friends of my father, to look after me. Otherwise I do not imagine that, dim and uninteresting small boy as I was, he would ever have deigned to notice me.

I can still recall my emotion when, on the day of my arrival at school, timid and bewildered, I was accosted by one of the heroes of my childish reading. But it was not from the pages of Dean Farrer, Hughes or Henty this glamorous being sprang. Not from *Eric, Tom Brown* or *The Knight of the White Cross*, but from Kingsley's *Heroes*, from the *Tanglewood Tales*, from Lemprière; a mythological figure of classical beauty, radiant and semi-divine. At the same time he had a more homely amiability than one might expect to find in such characters as Perseus, Jason or Theseus, and it was a proof of the inherent kindliness of his nature, a quality as rare among schoolboys as among Greek heroes, that he should have taken so much trouble about me. He helped me through many a difficulty, allayed many a terror, throughout a period full of difficulties and terrors. Naturally I idolized him and it was perhaps my blind idolatry, as well as his sense of obligation to parental instructions, that kept alive his patience with one who must have seemed to him a very unsatisfactory protégé. For this I felt that I owed him eternal gratitude. Yet later I was sometimes tempted ungratefully to wonder whether perhaps it would not have been better for my character if I had been left to fend for myself.

Percy was a favourite both with the masters and the boys. Even with the Headmaster, that horrible old demon who appeared to be animated with so violent a hatred for small boys that one often wondered why he had not adopted some other profession.

Percy was nearly always top of his class, and in cricket and football he excelled. His superiority both in work and games was effortless. One never caught him working out of hours, and for games he seemed to have an aptitude that required no practice.

During my school days his perfection, as it came to do in later years, never jarred on me. I just marvelled at it and accepted it as a glorious example I could never hope to follow. It may have perhaps aroused apprehensions in others. I remember once overhearing an assistant master saying to another, "Young Wallingford is the type of boy who, I fear, is apt to die young. One doubts if he will be able to keep it up."

Often during the term Percy was visited by his parents, and on one occasion I had the privilege of being introduced to them. His father was a general. My ideas of what a general should be, based on one or two military gentlemen who used to call on my mother, had up till then been very different. I had always believed that in order to be a general it was essential to be elderly, apoplectic, impressively foolish, with a stock of anecdotes about the old Duke of Cambridge. General Wallingford was of youthful appearance, tall and distinguished-looking, with an almost intellectual expression. It was from him that Percy had inherited his good looks, while from his mother he inherited his charming manners. Lady Wallingford had a sweet face and it looked as if her slightly prominent teeth had been inserted into it as an afterthought. Her charm was a little overwhelming and luckily it had been transmitted to her son in a diluted form.

At Eton I saw far less of Percy. He had preceded me by a year and by the time I arrived he had already become so important, so much of a public character, that the sense of my inferiority deterred me from deliberately seeking him out. We were in different houses and the segregation of age and hierarchy was more rigorous than it had been at the private school. However, when I did chance to meet him, he was as agreeable and friendly as ever, and the manner in which he conveyed to me that we were now in different social strata was so admirable that it left unwounded any susceptibilities I might have had.

Percy was going into the diplomatic service. It was my knowledge of this, more than anything else, that decided me to choose the same vocation.

It was customary in those days for aspirant diplomatists, instead of going to the University, to spend a year or two abroad in the study of foreign languages. There were a number of establishments on the continent reserved for the purpose. Monsieur Lansade's family pension in the Touraine was one of these.

When I went to Monsieur Lansade's on leaving Eton I knew that I should find Percy there. He was employing the last few weeks before going up for the diplomatic examination in polishing up his French.

The family consisted of an elderly couple and a middle-aged daughter. I never succeeded in discovering what exactly had been the nature of Monsieur Lansade's profession. You were given to understand that it had been something very important and was connected with diplomacy. Ignorant of the social nuances of a foreign country I thought it might have been anything, from a consul-general to the hall porter of an Embassy. Madame Lansade apparently belonged to an aristocratic family ruined by the Revolution. They both seemed bent on creating an impression of fallen grandeur and each of them hinted, in moments of confidence, that they had married beneath their station. The daughter, whose name was Jacqueline, was angular and plain. Her mind was also angular and plain and she was inclined to speak a little scornfully both to and about her parents. It was she who taught us French.

I was not long in discovering that she adored Percy with all the enthusiasm of her spinsterish nature. Her parents adored him too. He had made a complete conquest of the family.

There was another Englishman in the house, Mark Heneage by name. He was of the same age as Percy, a year older than myself. He was rather a cynical young man. He seemed to have made a special study of Percy's character and it was in some measure due to his influence that my admiration for my hero became infected with an insidious critical sense. I was also growing out of the hero-worshipping phase and I began to see his perfection in a less romantic light.

Mark Heneage said to me one day, "I have found out what is wrong with Percy. There is nothing wrong with him." The comment made me realize for the first time what it was in my erstwhile idol that was beginning vaguely to irritate me. It was precisely that his perfection was unassailable.

Approach to manhood had improved his looks. With his wavy golden hair and his pink and white complexion he might easily have given an impression of effeminacy or flashiness. But nobody could have accused him of either of these defects. He was a perfect specimen of clean, athletic youth. His appearance seemed to me to have become a little less ethereal. The Greek God had descended from Olympus but had lost nothing in his transition to earth.

His clothes were always exactly right. Yet one would never think of commenting on them. One took them as a matter of course. He achieved the aim of all successful tailoring; that people should notice that they didn't notice how well dressed you were.

His self-assurance was amazing. He wore it as unconsciously as he wore his clothes; as unconsciously as, when consummate technique has been acquired in some art or sport, you are no longer conscious of the movements that have been so laboriously, so painstakingly learnt. With Percy, however, one felt there had been no learning. It had just come to him naturally, instinctively.

He was very sure of his mental attitude to all the problems of life. He would never enter into an argument and, if you attempted to do so, he would withdraw from it saying, "Well, you know what I think," leaving you high and dry with your own side of the question. And if it happened to be a matter that could be proved and you were proved wrong, he would never triumph. He would never say anything so vulgar as "I told you so" or "I knew I was right." His lofty complacence was often hard to bear.

It was no use trying to pretend to yourself that he wasn't always right. He had an extraordinary instinct for the right thing. He would hit upon it with the talent of a water diviner both in matters of the flesh and of the spirit. His instinct was almost uncanny. In a bookshop or a library he would, without previous information, choose the best book on any subject in which he was interested. When we went for expeditions on our bicycles and stopped for luncheon in some town or village—in those days the helpful indications of the Michelin Guide were not yet available—he would, among several restaurants whose exteriors were identical, invariably select the best. He never thrust the superiority of his judgment upon you. You always gave in to him because it always proved reliable.

Mark Heneage described him as a crypto-egoist, and it was true that his egoism was so concealed that by most people it was not noticed, and such was his inherent good fortune that, if ever he saw fit to indulge in some altruistic action, it inevitably turned out to his own advantage. On the pretext that you would be better without them, he would often slyly deprive you of things in order to enjoy them himself. He managed, without undue emphasis, to give the impression that everything he did was done with the highest ends in view.

Percy had nothing of the arrogance of the superman. His manner was polite and disarming. Over his solid ethical foundation, as over the marble slabs of a paved waterway, there flowed a gentle current of charm that bore you along with it, floating pleasantly on its surface, a buoyant stream that prevented you bruising your feet on the hard surface below.

In proof of the infallibility of Percy's judgment there was the matter of his French accent. Although he had a thorough grammatical and idiomatic grasp of the language, he spoke it with a markedly English accent. I thought that, as everything seemed to come so easily to him, he would have had little difficulty, had he wished it, in acquiring a more perfect pronunciation. When one day, I took the liberty of chaffing him about it he said, "An Englishman should not speak French too well." Later on I came to appreciate the truth of his observation. Except for purposes of secret service, a too perfect French accent is inadvisable and is apt to disconcert the English and the French alike. It was obvious that the Lansade family preferred Percy's way of speaking their language to that of Mark Heneage which was far more like the real thing.

This period marks the decline and fall of Percy's empire over me. Instead of being grateful to him for providing me with an ideal, an example to be followed, my admiration and my affection gave place to a feeling of annoyance that at times almost amounted to dislike. With the advent of psychoanalysis I am enabled to recognize the workings of the "Diable de nos jours," the inferiority complex, and the effects of envy and discouragement such as an unsuccessful creative artist might feel in the presence of a perfect work of art.

After a couple of months Percy and Mark returned to England for the diplomatic examination. Percy passed triumphantly. Mark, who had just scraped through, wrote to me that, after the oral examination in

French, the examiner had said to Percy, "Monsieur, je vous felicite." "This was only natural," Mark added, "as it is Percy's rôle in life to be congratulated." I was reminded of the accent question and thought that if Percy's pronunciation had been more perfect, the examiner might not have been so impressed by the excellence of his syntax. I decided to follow his example and thenceforward took no more trouble with my accent. With me, however, it was less successful and, when the time came, I failed in French.

Before taking up a post abroad, Percy, as was the rule, spent a year in London at the Foreign Office. There I heard it was just as it had been at school. Everyone from the humblest clerk to the head of his department adored him. In the fashionable world it was the same. He was invited everywhere and mothers of marriageable daughters had their eyes on him. His father had recently died and he was now very well off. In London society he seemed to be having the same kind of glamorous success as one of the heroes of Lord Beaconsfield's novels.

I saw him once or twice when I went to London and, although it would have given me a malicious satisfaction to find him a little spoilt by his success, to find that he had grown fatuous, snobbish or arrogant, I had to admit that he was unaltered. The same superiority was still sugared by the same charm; the proportions were unchanged. The only difference that I noticed was in his appearance, and to a slight extent also, in his manner. The golden sparkle of his hair was a little dulled, the pink and white of his complexion had resolved itself into a more uniform tint and his deportment was moving towards a more official dignity.

After a year in London he was appointed to the Embassy in Paris. In the country of Balzac he was as popular and as successful as he had been in that of Disraeli. He merely exchanged the rôle of Endymion for that of Rastignac or Henri de Marsay, except that he had, of course, nothing in him of the arriviste.

After Paris he went to Vienna and after Vienna to St. Petersburg. Deaths and retirements came to accelerate promotion and, in an unusually short time, he was appointed as first secretary to Constantinople. Discussing his meteoric progress with Mark Heneage, we wondered how long it would be before he became an ambassador, and decided that this would most certainly not be the end of his career. He would not be the kind of ambassador who retired. "He will finally be made Viceroy of India," Mark suggested, "or Foreign Minister. After which, one presumes, he will be translated to heaven."

Having failed twice in the diplomatic examination, I applied for an honorary attachéship as the next best thing, and was sent to the embassy in Rome. It was here that I heard the news that Percy was to be married.

The name of his fiancée, Vera Mansfield, conveyed nothing to me, and on making inquiries I learnt that she was an orphan, about twenty-five years of age, and that she was a protégée of Mrs. Pontefract. Miss Mansfield had been living somewhere abroad with an aunt. Mrs. Pontefract had made her acquaintance at some foreign watering place. The aunt had died suddenly and Mrs. Pontefract had befriended the girl and brought her back to England with her, where for some time she employed her as secretary and companion. Poor girl, I thought. What a time she must have had contending with or abetting Mrs. Pontefract's economies. Percy had met her at one of Mrs. Pontefract's house parties and became engaged to her.

Percy never indulged very much in confidences and he never revealed his intimate thoughts. Possibly because he had none. For although he had a solid, matter of fact intelligence, he never gave me the impression that he thought very much. He never dreamt of confronting an abstract problem and would have considered it a waste of time.

Only on one occasion—because of its uniqueness it remains fixed in my memory—after a good luncheon in a restaurant at Amboise, he became a little more expansive than usual and disclosed his views on love and marriage. In his mind the two things were inseparable.

"I don't believe," he said, "that I shall ever fall violently in love. But if I do I'm determined not to lose my head."

He went on to speak of the kind of woman he intended to marry. "She needn't be rich, because, you see, when my father dies I shall have lots of money. And she needn't be very beautiful either, not the society beauty kind, though of course I should never think of marrying a fright or a frump. A rather ordinary sort of girl would suit me best, the sort of girl who would fit in with my way of living whatever it is going to be."

I understood that by this he meant the type of woman who would make a good diplomat's wife, a good ambassadress, but who would be at the same time completely under his thumb.

Percy always got everything he wanted and it was to be foreseen that such a type would float automatically into his arms. If Miss Vera Mansfield had proved an efficient secretary and companion to Mrs. Pontefract she would probably have been well broken in and would be an equally suitable wife for Percy. Although my affection and my esteem for him had diminished I was still very interested in him as a specimen and I was curious to see to what extent this young woman corresponded to his ideal. I might, of course, have become acquainted with her under more favourable circumstances than at Mrs. Pontefract's house party and it was probable that I should have done so. But my curiosity led me to seize the first opportunity.

2

—⌐*ⱺ/ⱺ/ⱺ*⌐—

A House Party

A certain nervousness besets me on approaching a large house party, an anxiety I have never succeeded in living down. It may be that the state of mind in which I first went to school has left so deep and painful an impression on my mind that it recurs each time I have occasion to penetrate into an assembly of fellow creatures among whom there may be unknown or hostile elements.

However, the prospect of meeting Percy and his chosen bride was worth it, and I likened myself to a horticultural explorer about to face discomfort and difficulties for the sake of some rare plant.

I contrived to defer my arrival at Pontefract Hall until the last possible moment, so as to avoid that dreadful period of hanging about and making desultory conversation before the time comes to go upstairs and dress for dinner. I knew from previous experience that it was better to face the ordeal in its entirety at dinner-time.

When I arrived I found Mrs. Pontefract in the entrance hall shouting directions to a scared-looking footman.

"You're late," she said to me, "dinner is in twenty minutes and please be on time."

I was taken to the small cubicle that had been allotted to me and proceeded to change for dinner as rapidly as the exiguities of space and accommodation permitted. The coldness of my room was intense, and the water in a can labelled Hot Water was tepid. In a mortified frame of mind I hurried down to dinner.

Most of the guests were already assembled. It was the usual kind of party. The Italian Ambassador and his wife, Colonel Smart, the well-known racehorse owner, Lady Mary Motley, the society beauty who photographed well but whose appearance in the flesh was a little disappointing, Mr. Lullaby the popular novelist, a Cabinet Minister whose face I knew but whose name I had forgotten, and many other people of whom I knew neither the names nor the faces. In a further corner of the room I saw Percy and made straight for him.

"Oh hulloa," he said, "I didn't know you were going to be here."

His way of looking pleased to see one always gave an agreeable thrill.

"Thank you so much for your present," he went on. "Forgive me for not writing, but I've been so frightfully busy. It was just what I wanted. I know it's the usual thing to say, but when you give a present it's always true."

Dinner was announced. I scanned the throng but could see no one I thought likely to be Mrs. Wallingford. When I found my place at the dinner table I saw the name on a card next to mine.

At the first glance I saw that Percy had not departed from the ideal he had described to me. She was about as ordinary-looking a young woman as anyone could be. She was small, fair-haired and well proportioned, almost pretty in rather a dull fashion. Her features were such as might be described on a passport as "normal." In the way of ordinariness she was without a flaw. She was well, and I should think, expensively dressed. The jewels she wore, a diamond necklace and ear-rings, had a superimposed look and gave the impression of being worn more from sense of duty than for ornament.

I set about to investigate what hidden qualities this mouse-like exterior might conceal and found it no easy task.

I opened the conversation by telling her that I was one of her husband's oldest friends.

"Fancy that!" she replied.

It seemed that Percy had not mentioned my name to her, but afterwards I thought that perhaps he might have done so and that she had forgotten, as she seemed quite unconcerned with human personalities. She was acquainted with most of the people at the dinner table but, beyond knowing their names and their attributes, she appeared to be completely uninterested in them.

She discouraged the attempts I made to speak to her about her husband and seemed unwilling to discuss him with a stranger.

I tried to find out in what direction her tastes lay. She seemed to know a certain amount about politics, art and sport, but over every subject we discussed there lay a delicate veneer of indifference that rendered conversation futile. My efforts were met with ejaculations of "No, really," "You don't say so," "Well, I never." Her outlook on life seemed to be that of a bewildered housemaid. But at the same time a conscientious housemaid. She would, one felt, dust every object carefully and never break a single thing. She would use the same precautions with a kitchen tumbler as with a Sèvres vase.

No doubt Percy had been, as usual, right in his selection and she would make an excellent ambassadress. In spite of a mediocrity of verbal expression that might seem to indicate a rather limited culture, she was well-bred, and would probably grace any position she might be called upon to occupy with adequate distinction. She had even a certain charm, the kind of charm that is to be found sometimes in commonplace things, a basket, a handbag, an inkpot; utilitarian rather than ornamental and not the kind that leads you to expect that you may find more of it by looking inside.

All the same, I couldn't help being a little surprised at Percy's choice. I felt that, in the pursuit of his ideal, he had gone further than he need have done. Many of his friends possessing a less intimate knowledge of Percy's matrimonial views must, I thought, have been considerably more surprised. He could have had the picking of anything he chose. I remembered that there had been rumours at one time of an attachment to Lady Mary Motley who was sitting on my other side, and I thought it might be interesting to hear what she might have to say.

As soon as Mrs. Wallingford had been engaged in conversation by her neighbour, I turned to Lady Mary and broached the subject in undertones.

"I know," she said. "Isn't she frightful?"

The adjective was so wildly inappropriate that I feared she would be unlikely to throw any very instructive psychological light on the matter.

"I met her here before," she continued, "when she was Mrs. Pontefract's secretary. She's a perfect fool."

People had said the same thing of Lady Mary and as there was, at the moment, only one topic I was anxious to pursue, the conversation flagged. After a few minutes she resumed her flirtation with the young man next to her. Mrs. Wallingford was still talking with her neighbour, or rather he was talking to her, and I had the embarrassment that so often occurs to me at dinner-parties of being odd man out.

I have seen it happen to people who are known to be brilliant conversationalists and it is, more often than not, a matter of chance. Still it is a slightly humiliating experience and I have learnt to carry it off by assuming an air of nonchalant reverie.

I glanced across the table at Percy. The two women on either side of him were hanging eagerly on his words. To be odd man out was not the kind of thing that was ever likely to happen to him.

As I looked at the scene before me I thought how little an uninitiated observer would have guessed that he was in the presence of a whited sepulchre. Contemplating the distinguished personages gathered round the table, the table itself with its elaborate centre of flowers and fruit grown in Mrs. Pontefract's hothouses, the rare porcelain, the cut glass, the gold plate, the three fat butlers and the tall footmen, how could he have imagined the discomforts the distinguished personages were made to suffer? Or that the fruit was never handed round and, together with the flowers, was sent up to London early on Monday morning to be sold, that the gold dishes when they reached the last person to be served often contained just one tiny scrap of food and sometimes none at all, that the three fat butlers, in spite of their well-fed appearance, practically subsisted on their tips, and that most of the tall footmen were hired for the occasion?

After dinner, when the gentlemen rejoined the ladies, the guests were dispatched with military precision to the various recreation units, bridge, poker, baccarat or billiards, customary in country house parties to avoid the horrors of conversation.

Like the British Government in war-time Mrs. Pontefract had a tendency to disregard individual aptitudes. She concerned herself only with the necessity of her guests being engaged in some activity, and those who prided themselves on their superior skill at bridge were often made to play baccarat or billiards and vice-versa. It was useless to protest. Theirs was not to reason why.

There were sometimes two or three of the party left over, people who like myself had no talent or inclination for card-games or billiards. In the strenuous private school atmosphere that prevailed I felt, on such occasions, rather like the boy who didn't care for games. The ignominious residue gathered together and conversed in undertones until it was time to go to bed. To play chess or any other game, to read a book, would have been considered at Pontefract Hall an eccentricity that verged on indecency.

Mrs. Pontefract herself rarely took part in these recreations and when everyone had been settled at different tables she would move about from one group to another keeping a watchful eye for minor delinquencies, such as carelessness in disposing of cigarette ends, excessive consumption of whisky and soda or the setting down of wet glasses on varnished tables.

Marooned on a sofa sat Mr. Lullaby and Miss Stork, also a writer. Knowing how much they disliked one another, I thought their conversation might prove entertaining, and joined them.

Mr. Lullaby and Miss Stork both wrote about the poor, but from widely different angles. They both wrote of mining districts, factories and slums but while Mr. Lullaby invested the sufferings of the poor with a delicate poetic melancholy, Miss Stork referred to them as the Proletariat and her books were frankly propaganda.

It was, perhaps, surprising to find the authoress of *The Rising of the Masses* and other revolutionary works in this stronghold of capitalism, but Miss Stork, although a Marxist holding violently subversive views, had at the same time a weakness for high society. She meant to make the most of capitalism while it lasted and her solicitude for the idle rich almost equalled her concern for the down-trodden workers; a Tricoteuse knitting scarves for the Aristocrats to keep them cosy on their way to execution. Mrs. Pontefract was at times a little unconventional in her choice of guests and had no hesitation in introducing an occasional wolf into the sheepfold, as long as the wolf was sufficiently in the public eye.

Miss Stork and Mr. Lullaby were discussing literature from a professional point of view. They discoursed at length on contracts, royalties, serial rights and other technicalities of the book market. On the subject of the iniquity of publishers they seemed, for once in a way, to be in perfect harmony. The conversation was not as spicy as I had hoped, and I welcomed a beckon from Mrs. Pontefract who, having satisfied herself that her guests were, for the moment, behaving properly, was taking a rest from her watch patrol on a sofa. I went over and sat down beside her.

"She's a nice girl, isn't she?" Mrs. Pontefract remarked.

"Who, Miss Stork?"

"No, silly. Percy's wife, of course. I put you next to her at dinner as I remembered you were an old friend of Percy Wallingford's. What did you think of her?"

I hesitated for a moment and Mrs. Pontefract continued, "Now don't tell me you think she is a bore. She isn't, of course, smart and fashionable, the kind of woman you snobs admire. But she has sterling worth and that is more than one can say of most of the scatter-brained minxes one sees knocking around."

"I don't know why you should take it for granted that I thought her a bore," I protested.

"It enrages me," Mrs. Pontefract went on, "when people come and tell me that they're surprised at Percy's choice, or that they think her unsuitable, because it was I who arranged the marriage, and I take credit to myself for having done so. Percy is one of the few men of all that gang who is worth anything. He has a great future before him and I was determined to see that he got the right kind of wife."

It was all very well, I thought, for Mrs. Pontefract to talk in this managing way. She would never have brought it off, I knew, if Percy, like Barkis, had not been "willin'."

"Yes," said Mrs. Pontefract. "It was a great sacrifice on my part. Vera was invaluable to me. But I felt that it was worth while making the sacrifice to prevent Percy throwing himself away on some trivial creature."

"She certainly doesn't give the impression," I remarked, "of being the sort of woman who would wreck a man's career. I hope Percy is in love with her."

"He is very fond of her," Mrs. Pontefract replied, "and there is no doubt that Vera is very much in love with him. What is of far more importance is that she is steady, sensible and tactful. The three things don't always go together and Percy is lucky. It is a perfect marriage."

"A perfect 'mariage de raison'?" I hazarded.

"Yes, if you like. They are both of them perfectly reasonable people. Damnation!" she suddenly exclaimed. One of the guests had upset a glass of barley-water over a card table and she hurried away to mop and scold.

As I watched her go, I thought how admirably Mrs. Pontefract fitted in with the Edwardian decorations of her house. It was almost a case of zoological mimicry. Though there was nothing from which she needed protection, she had grown to look exactly like her furniture. Her presence, a little overwhelming near at hand, seemed, when seen in the distance, to merge completely into the creations of Waring and Gillow, the rich brocades of the upholstery, the gilt chairs, the occasional tables bristling with photographs in silver frames, the general environment of tasteless opulence.

Next morning, as the protestant and, in some cases, protesting guests were being lined up for church, I crept off down a passage to hide in a remote sitting-room until the danger of the devotional press-gang was over. The room was known as "the Library," because it contained bookcases filled with bound volumes of *Punch*, the *Illustrated London News* and a quantity of Victorian novels. Here I found Percy, ensconced in a leather armchair, reading a Sunday paper.

"Hulloa," he said. "You've escaped."

"And you too, I see."

"Yes. Vera has sacrificed herself. One of us, I thought, was enough. As long as a couple of pews are filled the old girl is satisfied. As you know, she hates any kind of waste, even of pew-space in a church."

"I always get the impression here of being back at school. Do you remember how awful it used to be? Getting up in the morning, with all the day before one, I always used to think the worst moment. I wonder if your bath water this morning was as cold as mine?"

"No," said Percy, "mine was all right. Vera locked the bathroom in our passage so I got the first look-in."

"I sat next to her last night at dinner."

"I know. She told me."

He left it at that. He seemed as unwilling to speak of Vera as she had been to speak of him, and the attempts I made to lead the conversation in her direction were effectively repulsed. When Percy held a conversational bridge his efficiency was equal to that of Horatius Cocles.

We went on talking until distant noises announced the return of the house party from church. It was just such a conversation as might take place between two people whose relationship rested more on community of circumstances than on natural sympathy. We discussed our respective posts, Rome and Constantinople. We spoke of the other guests.

"The Italian Ambassador seems a bit of an ass," Percy remarked.

"I don't agree," I said. "I thought he seemed unusually intelligent."

"Yes," Percy acquiesced. "Perhaps you are right. He is quite intelligent."

I could hardly believe my ears. A volte-face of this kind was unprecedented.

As our talk proceeded I began to notice that Percy was in some way slightly changed. It seemed to me as if he had lost a little of his terrible self-assurance. The change was just sufficient to be noticeable, and it was welcome. Never since my school-days had I found him so much to my liking. I wondered if marriage could have effected this tiny rift in his perfection, if it had opened a few minute chinks in his armour-plated ego. But I feared that it could not be permanent and was probably only a temporary matter of health or the effect of Sunday morning which, in English country houses, often tends to be lowering. I was afraid that the next time I met him I should find the rift gone, the chinks in the armour soldered up again and his perfection once more invulnerable.

For someone who had made a study of his personality it was an interesting phenomenon. There was nobody in the house party, however, with whom I could discuss it.

Mrs. Pontefract was hardly a person with whom one could debate upon subtle psychological changes in the characters of her guests.

During the rest of the week-end I had no further occasion to speak with Percy alone. The afternoon had its strenuous programme. The routine was invariable. After luncheon the entire house party was made to pose for a group out of doors no matter how inclement the weather. Chairs were brought out on to the lawn in front of the house. The group was arranged by Mrs. Pontefract and the photograph was taken by one of the butlers. It was always a lengthy proceeding. There was a great deal of arranging, adjustment of facial expression, pulling down of skirts.

"A little brighter, please," Mrs. Pontefract called to the Italian Ambassadress, a woman who looked like a tragic crow. "Stop grinning," to

Lady Mary Motley. "You're not at a charity bazaar." One of the women was told to remove her large picture-hat as it impeded the view, and some of the humbler guests were forced to sit cross-legged on the damp grass.

When this was over, we were sent off to play various games: tennis, golf, squash rackets. Some of the older people were allowed to play bridge indoors and a favoured few were taken round the home farm by their hostess.

In the less active interval between tea and dinner I had some further talk with Percy's wife. I suspected that he had told her to make herself agreeable to me and I found her more forthcoming than she had been at dinner on the previous night. Her ejaculations of bewilderment, I discovered were a mannerism. In reality she was not at all bewildered, and although she had little critical sense of the differentiation of values she seemed to have a good practical knowledge of what was what.

She told me that she was looking forward to accompanying her husband to Constantinople in a week or two. "Percy has taken a house on the Bosphorus near Therapia for the summer," she said. "If you would care to do so, I hope you will come and stay with us there. I am sure Percy would enjoy showing you the place. The climate, Percy tells me, is quite pleasant and it never gets too hot." She continued to speak of Constantinople in her curiously impersonal way and I thought that any anticipations she may have had would have been the same if the place were Berlin or Washington.

Now that my claims to her husband's friendship had been properly confirmed, she seemed disposed to talk about him, and here at last was a subject on which she spoke with animation. She was obviously very much in love with him. She referred to his physical attractions in terms that were almost voluptuous and I began to suspect that Percy might find her a little over-exacting. His was not, I imagined, a very passionate nature and it amused me to think of him coping with excessive manifestations of temperament.

There was another thing, besides this hint of temperament, that seemed a trifle out of place in this very colourless little person and it was only after talking with her for some time that I noticed it. There was a peculiar look in her eyes. She had an odd way of staring at you as if she didn't see you quite clearly. At the same time you had the sensation that, in different lighting or by a greater effort of will, she would be able to see you more distinctly than you might perhaps desire. It may have been due to short-sightedness or astigmatism but it made a queer impression on me and I always remembered it whenever I thought about her.

The rest of my visit to Pontefract Hall was uneventful, except for a curious little incident that took place later in the evening.

Just before going to bed I remembered that I had left a cigarette case in the room where I had held my conversation with Percy that morning. I went to retrieve it. The door was ajar and as I fumbled for the switch I realized that there was someone in the room. When I turned on the light I found Vera standing in front of one of the bookcases. She was replacing a book and when she turned and saw me she seemed embarrassed.

"Oh," she said, "I was afraid that it was Mrs. Pontefract. I was putting back a book that Percy had taken out to read in bed last night. It always annoys her when people take books out of the bookcases."

The explanation was plausible enough and it accounted for the guilty look she had when I discovered her. But afterwards, when I thought about the incident again, I wondered why she had omitted to turn on the light and what had been her reason for replacing the book in the dark. The thing puzzled me considerably. The strangest conjectures came into my mind and my detective curiosity was so far aroused that, before leaving next morning, I went back to the room to see whether there might be any indication of which book it was that she had replaced. But none of the titles gave me any clue and the mystery remained unsolved.

3

~~~

Change and Decay

I saw no more of Percy and his wife before they left for Constantinople. One day I came across Mark Heneage. I asked him if he had seen Percy since his marriage. He told me that he had and I was interested to hear from him that he, too, had noticed a subtle change in Percy's character.

"He didn't seem quite so damned superior as usual," was his comment. "One can only hope that marriage has humanized him a little, only it's difficult to think that that little woman can have had any effect on so tough a nut as Percy."

"Difficult indeed," I replied. "Did the marriage surprise you?"

"It's a waste of time to be surprised by anything Percy does. It always turns out not to be surprising."

"What did you think of her?"

"What did I think of her? Well, I just didn't, you know. She doesn't supply one with much to think about, does she?"

"No. There's nothing about her that encourages thought. All the same there's just one thing. Did you notice anything at all odd about her eyes?"

"I noticed nothing odd about her anywhere at all."

I spent the rest of my leave in London and returned to Rome at the end of May.

Rome, in those days, still retained a certain amount of the nineteenth century charm that has since been swept away by the depredations of progress. It was an easy place to live in. Social life had an agreeable, amateurish quality and had not yet been hustled into English and American standards of efficiency. The entertainments were magnificent and simple. There were moonlit nights and nightingales but no night-clubs, and in many quarters the grandeurs and curiosities of Papal Rome still continued to prevail. The Forum and the Palatine had not yet been spoilt by archæologists and the atmosphere of the city had not yet succumbed to unsuccessful attempts to achieve the ideals of the Weltstadt. Although, from the point of view of romantic poets and artists, the town itself had already begun to deteriorate. Many picturesque villas, gardens and cypress groves had been destroyed to make way for modern streets, and the Tiber had been deprived of its grassy banks and confined in tight embankments.

In the summer the Embassy moved southwards to the Villa Rosebery at Posillipo. I had thought at one time of responding to Vera Wallingford's invitation and going to stay with her and Percy in their house on the Bosphorus, but I found the life at Posillipo so exquisite that I was unable to tear myself away from it.

It was my first experience of the Bay of Naples in summer time and I hailed it as an earthly paradise. International politics as far as Italy was concerned seemed to be taking a siesta and there was very little work to do. My colleagues, with one exception, were charming, and we spent most of our time bathing, sailing, and sight-seeing.

The Villa Rosebery, with its terraced gardens sloping to the sea, looking out on to the panorama of Naples, Vesuvius and the opalescent cliffs of Sorrento, was the quintessence of Romantic Italy, the Italy of Goethe, Beckford and the Grand Tour. It was almost too nostalgic. The days passed in a nirvana of delight and some of the happiest moments of my life were spent in lazy amphibian existence, swimming in the sea or wandering about the hills with a sketch book. In spite of the unappetising objects that occasionally came floating into the bathing-pool I found perpetual inspiration in the clear blue waters and even the curious smells so frequently encountered, a mixture of drainage, orange-blossom and the sea, had an intoxicating pungency. I have often thought of asking some chemist to concoct for me reproductions of certain mixed aromas evocative of places I have loved.

The days passed rapidly and blissfully. Percy, Vera and the Bosphorus seemed very far away.

*

Towards the end of the summer when the Embassy returned to Rome I had disturbing news of Percy. It appeared that he had had a serious nervous breakdown and had resigned from the diplomatic service.

I made inquiries, but nobody seemed to know more than these bare facts. A little later I met one of the Secretaries from the Embassy in Constantinople who was passing through Rome and from him I had a more detailed account of what had happened.

"When Wallingford came back with his wife after his marriage," the young man told me, "I noticed that he seemed out of sorts. I liked his wife. She was a nice little woman. Not at all what we had expected. I gathered that the Ambassadress had not been looking forward to her arrival and had been agreeably surprised to find her so unpretentious. You know him well, I gather?"

"Very well indeed," I replied.

"Then you'll understand what a shock it gave me when, one day I heard him admitting himself to have been in the wrong. That was the first indication I had that there was something seriously the matter with him. In the Chancery, you know, his cocksuredness had become something of a joke. We used to laugh about it among ourselves. Even the Ambassador couldn't stand up to it. He had given up trying to do so, as Percy always proved to be right. Well, that was the first sign. After this it seemed almost as if a sort of internal rot had begun to set in. At first it was gradual, but soon it became so rapid that one seemed to see his character disintegrating before one's eyes. He lost all his buoyancy and self-assurance. His nerves went to pieces and he appeared to be falling into a state of mental depression. For a time he managed to put up a pretty good show, and I don't think that anyone outside the Embassy noticed anything. At first there were the usual sort of jokes (among ourselves, of course) about the effects of conjugal life, overdoing it and all that sort of thing. But we soon began to realize that it was something more serious than that and we hadn't the least idea what could possibly have been the cause of it. As you no doubt know, Percy is not the kind of man to welcome tender inquiries or manifestations of sympathy. He always hated people commenting on his looking tired or having a headache, and we thought it better to pretend we didn't notice."

"And what was his wife's attitude about it?"

"She went on as if she was completely unaware of what was happening. She never spoke to anyone about it and discouraged any kind of mention of it, but we could see that she was worried. In games as well as in other things he seemed to be losing his grip, and you know how good he was at tennis, polo and golf. He gave up playing bridge. He just mooned about looking miserable. It was really pathetic. One of the most curious things about his nervous condition was that he seemed terrified of the dark. You would hardly believe it. When he used to dine with us in the Secretary's mess, whenever we sat out in the garden after dinner he refused to join us and he would never walk home at night without a lantern. Once when, as a silly joke, someone turned out the light in the Chancery, he began yelling like a lunatic and when it was turned on again we saw that he was white and trembling just as if he had seen a ghost. It really was extraordinary. He grew worse and worse. It was difficult to keep on ignoring it. The Ambassador suggested his taking a holiday but this he refused to do. At last things came to such a pass that he was unable to write a report or interview the humblest foreign colleague and he had to give in. He left quite suddenly without saying good-bye to anyone and we heard that he had quit the service altogether."

"And where is he now?" I asked.

"In England, I suppose."

But when I returned to England a few weeks later I could find no trace of the Wallingfords. Nobody knew where they were.

I paid a call on Mrs. Pontefract, hoping that she might be able to supply me with the information I desired. She generally knew "where everybody was." I often suspected her of having an organized spy-service to keep her advised of people's movements so that she might know when they would be available for a house-party. However she knew no more than anyone else. She had heard of Percy's breakdown and of his leaving the diplomatic service, but she displayed little sympathy with regard to his illness and seemed to consider the step he had taken as a personal grievance.

Like many of her generation, Mrs. Pontefract had rigid social standards. She was interested in people as long as they were healthy, wealthy and worldly-wise. If they lost their health, their wealth, or departed from worldly wisdom, she was inclined to dissociate herself from them. She was not totally unsympathetic in a case of ill-health. She had been known to send grapes to an invalid. But any ailment connected with the mind she regarded with suspicion. From what she had heard of Percy's mental condition she obviously thought that he would hardly be likely to prove much of an asset to one of her house-parties and his leaving the diplomatic service was a distinct departure from worldly wisdom.

Towards her former secretary Mrs. Pontefract adopted an attitude of lofty aggrievement. "Since leaving England Vera has never written to me once. It is surprising after all I have done for her," Mrs. Pontefract complained. "If it is her idea to drop me now that she thinks I can be of no further use to her, I don't intend to break my heart about it."

I was, perhaps, to some extent influenced by Mrs. Pontefract's worldly indifference. After all, I reflected, Percy had never written to me nor had he endorsed his wife's invitation. I was rather glad now that I hadn't gone out to stay with them, and anyhow, if Percy wished to disappear for a while, it was none of my business to try to unearth his hiding place and thrust my sympathy upon him.

When I thought of Percy as I had known him, when I thought of his character, his physique, any kind of breakdown seemed to me incredible. Was it possible, I wondered, that, in his apparently invulnerable perfection there could have been secreted some microbe of decay? Some canker at the root such as causes the sudden unexpected withering of the plant? I was unable to believe that his affliction could be permanent. He would recover, I was convinced, and soon we should have him back among us, the same old Percy with all his irritating superiority. It puzzled me a little that he should have left the diplomatic service. However I had suffered, myself, from fits of acute depression and I knew that in such moments one is apt to take unnecessarily pessimistic decisions.

Other distractions drove the Wallingfords from my mind, until one day, in a newspaper, I came upon the headline, "Tragic death of diplo-

mat's wife." It was Vera. She had met her death by asphyxiation in a hotel bedroom in France. The place was given as Avallon and the account
was not very circumstantial. In the few newspapers that mentioned
it the details of the accident were conflicting, and there seemed to be
some doubt as to whether her death had been caused by the fumes of
gas or charcoal.

The event caused some sensation among Percy's friends but it was
the height of the season and nobody seemed inclined to bestir themselves on his behalf.

I sent a telegram to the hotel at Avallon but received no reply. I made
every effort to get into touch with Percy but my endeavours to communicate with him were vain. I was unable to trace any relations who
might have given me information, nor did I succeed in discovering the
identities of his banker and his lawyer. I wrote to his mother and my letter remained unanswered. This was explained later by the fact that she
was dead.

It seemed an extraordinary thing that a man who had been so much
of a figure in the social world should have succeeded in so completely
cutting himself off from society.

Mrs. Pontefract gave me the impression that she was rather relieved
at having lost sight of the Wallingfords, and that she felt herself to be
under no obligation to be unduly upset by what had happened. Lady
Mary Motley's point of view was more frankly cynical. "She was such a
frightful bore," was the humorous line she took. "I am not in the least
surprised at his doing her in."

There was no further mention of Vera's death in the newspapers,
and soon the matter ceased to be discussed at London luncheon parties.

I pondered sadly on the evanescence of human relationships. Then I
began to wonder if, after all, Percy had, in the course of his life, made
any real friends. He had always felt himself so secure in his superiority that, perhaps, friendship was unnecessary to him and to acquire it
would be something in the nature of a work of supererogation.

For some time I continued to have distressing visions of Percy wandering, disconsolate and lonely, about the continent or lying forlorn in
some foreign nursing home. However, I told myself, had he felt the need

of help and sympathy, he could easily have obtained it. I could hardly take it upon myself to advertise in the personal column of the *Times*, employ a detective agency or go out in search of him myself, and I continued to cherish the hope that one day Percy would write to me or return to England.

4

A Confession

A year elapsed. In the early spring of 1914 I was motoring through France on my way back to England. I made a slight deviation in my route in order to spend the night at Avignon. What attracted me to the place was not the charm of the town itself, the Palace of the Popes, the exquisite view from the garden on the summit of the hill over the river and the broken bridge, or the admirable restaurant, so much as the memory of a certain room in the Hôtel d'Europe. The tourist season had not yet begun and I expected that the room would be available, as indeed it was.

In any case it was not an apartment that would have appealed to everyone. I fancy that most English and American tourists would have preferred something more up-to-date. It had the appearance of having been left untouched since the days of Louis Philippe, and to people indifferent to period atmosphere it might have seemed melancholy, uncomfortable and stuffy.

The light from the windows overlooking the courtyard was almost excluded by curtains of crimson rep, draped and festooned in elaborate folds, with heavy tassels hanging in unexpected places. Curtains of the same material concealed the voluted mahogany bed standing in an alcove. The wallpaper was ochre-coloured and had a pattern of foliage in a deeper hue. Two indifferent oil-paintings hung on the wall, one of a military gentleman in uniform with a long drooping moustache; the other of an anæmic-looking lady dressed in grey with her dark hair parted in the middle and glossy bunching curls on either side of her face. In one corner of the room, upholstered in faded Indian cashmere, stood a sofa that looked as if it were so weighed down with weariness that it had little sympathy left for that of the human frame and, in front of it, a large table covered with a dull red cloth and, on the table, an old illustrated hotel guide and an elaborate blotting book but no blotting paper, pens, ink, or material for writing. From the ceiling hung a dilapidated fly-blown crystal chandelier and resting on the grey marble mantelpiece there was a tarnished gilt framed mirror. It was the kind of room that a modern hotel-keeper would have scrapped without hesitation, replacing the cumbrous decoration with tasteful modern Toile de Jouy and sham Louis Seize.

For me, however, the room had a peculiar charm. I was a great reader of Balzac and it was a perfect setting from a Balzac novel. I could imagine Lucien de Rubempré and the Abbé Carlos Herrera spending the night there in the course of their journey. I could visualize Lucien sitting languidly on the sofa while his mentor paced up and down proffering worldly counsel.

There was one material disadvantage, however, for which the literary value of the room could hardly compensate. It was a chilly evening. The iron screen of the fire-place was down and there seemed to be no heating. I rang the bell and an elderly waiter appeared. I remembered him from my previous visit. His name was Alphonse and he had been a member of the hotel staff for many years. He took a paternal interest in the visitors and was genuinely distressed by a complaint. He went off down the passage making a clucking noise that reminded me of a startled hen, returning shortly afterwards with an armful of firewood. In the twinkling of an eye he had kindled a cheerful fire and I sat before it reading *Illusions Perdues* in this atmosphere of illusion, until dinner time.

In the restaurant I noticed a man dining by himself at the further end of the room. For several minutes I hesitated as to whether it was

Percy Wallingford or not, so greatly altered was his appearance. At length I decided to cross the room and speak to him.

He glanced up at me and a momentary look of alarm passed over his face. Then he smiled and greeted me. I suggested that we should dine together, a suggestion he could hardly do otherwise than accept.

When a chair had been brought for me and I sat down at his table, I was overcome for a moment by a slight feeling of dismay. Conversation, I feared, was not going to be easy and I thought that he might be resenting the intrusion on his solitude. I was also a little disconcerted by the change that had taken place in his appearance. He had not exactly aged, but his features had shrunk and his body was unnaturally thin. It was in his expression that the change was chiefly noticeable. Formerly he looked you straight in the face with a fixity that was almost embarrassing. But now his look was shifty, evasive, and at times his eyes had that curious vacant stare that one associates with certain kinds of drug addicts.

Conversation, as I had expected, was at first difficult to manipulate. It had all the polite awkwardness of a reconciliation after a long-drawn-out quarrel. For a time, in order to stave off indiscreet inquiries and unwilling confessions, we spoke feverishly on such topics as the curiosities of Avignon, foreign hotels, continental travel and my own affairs. However this could not be kept up indefinitely and at last Percy himself took the initiative.

"You heard, no doubt, about my illness?"

"Yes," I answered, "and I tried several times to get into touch with you."

"That was kind of you. But I deliberately hid myself. I couldn't face the idea of meeting people."

"But you surely could have seen your friends?"

"It was my friends I dreaded seeing most of all. I felt I couldn't stand their pity."

"Why call it pity? You could have faced their sympathy."

"Sympathy is only to be got on equal terms. For anyone who is down and out it can only be pity."

"It's absurd for you to talk of being down and out," I protested, "I once had a spell of nervous depression myself. It's appalling while it lasts and makes one feel that nothing is worth living for. One loses hope and thinks that the joy of life will never return. But it does."

Percy shook his head.

"It will never return to me. You don't perhaps realize what a wreck I am. The instrument is damaged beyond repair."

"What do you mean?" I cried. "I don't want to ask you questions you'd perhaps rather not answer. But after all I'm an old friend of yours and, whatever it is, I implore you to confide in me and I promise you not to pity you."

"It's not insanity," he said, "if that's what you're thinking of. And yet I suppose, in a kind of way, it is. I don't know how to explain it so that you or anyone could understand. I can only tell you that something has happened to me that has made it impossible for me to continue my normal way of living. It is as if the keystone of the arch had been removed. The arch still continues to stand but it can support no weight."

"Your simile, I fear, conveys little to me. It was some kind of shock you had? And I gather it happened before your wife's death?"

He winced and I felt that it might be unkind to continue my inquiries.

"Anyhow," I said, "of one thing I am certain. You must come back to England. This lonely, migratory life can't possibly be doing you any good."

"It is the only kind of life I can bear. I can only be with strangers, with those who have not known me as I was. And there have been one or two people I have been able to help, poor people I have met in hotels. That has given me pleasure, the only pleasure that remains to me. No, I couldn't return to England. I have still a few dregs of pride left and it doesn't appeal to me to figure as a picturesque ruin in my native land."

After dinner I suggested that we should go upstairs to my room and continue our conversation there. In spite of what he had said about meeting friends, Percy seemed almost pathetically anxious for my company and I hoped to be able to persuade him to return with me, on the following day, to England.

Although the fire was still burning brightly, my room was cold and I rang for Alphonse. He brought in a charcoal brazier and set it down in a corner of the room.

"Voilà, Monsieur," he said, "that will help. Only be sure," he added, "that you put it outside in the passage before going to bed. Faites bien attention. We had an accident here last year——"

He suddenly became aware of Percy and started. "Oh pardon, Monsieur," he exclaimed, and hurriedly left the room.

I caught sight of Percy's face in the mirror. It was white and haggard, and when I turned I saw that he was trembling violently.

"It was in this hotel," he said, "that Vera died."

He sat down on the sofa and hid his face in his hands.

"But I thought it happened at Avallon."

"No, it was here. The newspapers mistook the name."

"Not in this very room?" the words came unconsciously from my lips, for all of a sudden the room seemed to have taken on a sinister air of tragedy. What mysterious horrors might not those crimson curtains have concealed? What strange happenings had been reflected in that tarnished mirror? The military gentleman's moustache gave him a criminal look and the pale lady had the air of a victim.

"No, no," Percy cried. "Not in this room."

He began to pace restlessly up and down. After a while he stopped and confronted me.

"Meeting you here to-night has made me feel that I can no longer go on keeping this thing to myself. I must speak. I must tell you everything there is to tell—if you want to hear. I had resolved to remain silent about it for ever, and when you have heard you will realize why. The story is so strange, so incredible that few people would believe it. I sometimes feel that I can hardly believe it myself.

"When I saw you at Mrs. Pontefract's soon after my marriage the thing had already happened. But I don't suppose you noticed anything then. Or perhaps you did. I remember you were always damned observant, that you used to talk about people's psychological peculiarities. Well, you'll find what I'm going to tell you peculiar enough.

"I may as well begin at the beginning, that is to say with my marriage to Vera. Some time before I met her, I had been thinking that I ought to get married and, as a matter of fact, I had got myself vaguely engaged to one or two girls. But it never came to anything. I was too cautious I suppose, and I was always being put off by discovering traits in their characters that I feared might lead to trouble. I mean I was afraid of marrying someone who might turn out to be too bossy. I never used to think very much about my own character, but I always felt I had a kind of superiority over other people. I never used to think very much about that either, and I suppose I looked upon it as something quite natural. I always had a kindly feeling for my fellow creatures and it was only when I suspected that they were trying to get the better of me or dominate me in any way that I took a dislike to them.

"Well, in Vera I realized that I had found someone who would never assert herself unduly. She had an essentially nice character. She was intelligent, practical and quite good-looking. As you may have noticed there was nothing very striking about her. I was attracted to her as one might be attracted to a house in which there was nothing very remarkable about its architecture, a pleasant unpretentious house without too definite a style that one could furnish as one pleased and live in agreeably. She was also very much in love with me and I was flattered and touched by it. Those are the reasons why I married Vera."

Percy became agitated again and began once more to pace the room.

"What I am going to tell you now is so fantastic and unbelievable that I may not be able to make the account of my reactions sound very convincing. You may perhaps think them tragically exaggerated. I'm not good at describing emotions in correct psychological terms.

"On the first night of my marriage I was a little awkward and embarrassed. Although I had had one or two flirtations I was never much of a womanizer. In fact I had never had an affair with a woman of my own class. I felt it would make matters easier if I turned out the light. Well, I won't go into any more details. Suddenly Vera began to giggle hysterically. I was a little taken aback and Vera explained why she was laughing. 'You can't think how funny you look,' she said, 'with your hair sticking up like that.' At first I couldn't understand what she meant because, as I have told you, there was no light in the room and it was pitch black.

"Then she went on to tell me that she was able to see in the dark. I didn't believe her at first. I thought she was joking, although it seemed unlike her to joke at such a moment. She soon made me realize that she was speaking the truth. She told me that, ever since she could remember, she had always had the faculty of being able to see things quite clearly in the dark, just as clearly as she could in the daylight. Her aunt, who had brought her up, warned her when she was still quite young never to speak to anyone of this strange gift as, if it were known, it might ruin her chances. And my God, it would have as far as I was concerned! Naturally the discovery gave me a bit of a shock but it wasn't till later that I began to understand how great a shock it had been. The idea seemed to get hold of me and I couldn't help thinking about it all the time. At night the sensation that she could see me in the dark began to prey on my mind, but I was determined not to let her see that this odd advantage she had over me upset me in any way. That was a thing I felt I couldn't possibly allow her to suspect. Neither did I want other people to get to know about it, and I begged her, just as her aunt had done, to keep it to herself. It may seem foolish to you that I shouldn't have told her frankly what I felt about it, but I just couldn't do it. My pride prevented me, I suppose, and if only I could have brought myself to tell her, things might have turned out very differently.

"The nights became a torment to me. I was unable to sleep for fear that she might be awake and looking at me, and I couldn't insist on keeping the light on all night, nor could I suggest sleeping in different rooms. She was so much in love with me that she would have been very much upset if I had. The thing began to get on my nerves. All my life I had never had any difficulty in coping with ordinary experiences. But this was something so utterly out of the ordinary that it fairly knocked me off my perch. Introspection, as you know, was never very much in my line and I had never been accustomed to analyse myself. But this seemed to set me off thinking and the results were disastrous. I felt like the centipede who was asked in what order it used its feet and then couldn't walk any more. It threw everything in my mind into confusion and disorder and cramped my style all round and I began to wonder if other people perhaps had some strange hidden superiority of which I was unaware and, talking to some quite humble individual, I would be suddenly seized with the idea that he too might possess some secret gift, telepathy for instance, and be able to read my thoughts. I began to suspect mysterious powers in all sorts of unlikely people, and feared that, any moment, I might be attacked by unknown forces. I felt as if my soul had been stripped of all its defences.

"I will tell you something that will make you laugh no doubt. In the train when we went through a tunnel I used to make faces at the people in my carriage in case one of them might be able to see in the dark."

"Did you consult a nerve-specialist?" I asked.

"No," Percy answered. "That would have been useless. You see I could never have induced myself to disclose the real cause of the trouble. Besides I always went on hoping that I should get over it and I was determined at all costs to keep up appearances before the world, and before Vera. Especially before Vera. I trusted to my power of will and my pride to pull me through and it is perhaps because there are so few remnants of them left that I am telling you this now.

"I hoped that when I returned to my work at Constantinople and got into a different environment things might improve. But alas! it was not the case. They only got worse.

"We had taken a house near Therapia for the summer. I chose it before I went back to England to be married. It had seemed to me then to be everything one could wish for. A picturesque old Turkish house on the Bosphorus with a charming garden full of cypresses and roses, an ideal place. But my God how I came to loathe it! The rooms and the passages were dark. It was a difficult house to light, and I had come to be afraid of the dark as a child might be. My nerves began to go to pieces. I knew that Vera realized that something was seriously wrong with me. Yet she was so damned tactful that she went on pretending not to notice. I was grateful to her for her tactfulness but at the same time I was humiliated by it. She occasionally suggested that I was working too hard but she knew perfectly well that I wasn't. I don't know what she said to other people. I rather fancy she said nothing.

"My emotional relationship to her was complicated by other considerations. She was as much in love with me as ever, and I couldn't help feeling all the time that I was letting her down. Although she was the source of all the trouble she was unaware of it and I couldn't with any justice blame her. As I had married her and she was so much in love with me I felt that it would be criminal to make her unhappy. The necessity I felt of keeping up my obligations to her under the circumstances made my condition grow worse every day. At last my nerves got into such a state that I was no more use at anything. I could hardly write a consecutive sentence, I couldn't hit a tennis ball and people were beginning to look pityingly at me whenever I appeared anywhere. I couldn't stand it any longer and I chucked the diplomatic service.

"Vera wanted me to return to England but I couldn't face that. I should have liked to have gone away somewhere by myself but I had neither the courage nor the cowardice to detach myself from Vera. It would have been better had I done so.

"We stayed for a time at Aix-les-Bains, where I went through the pretence of doing a cure. But there were too many English people there, people I knew, and the agitation of avoiding them was too much for me. Then we went to other places, in Switzerland and Germany, but we met with the same difficulties there. Vera was all the time wonderfully patient and seemed more in love with me than ever,—and I began to hate her. But up till the very end I don't believe that she ever suspected it. I was perhaps a little irritable at times, but there still remained a strength of kindliness in my nature that kept me up to the mark. It was the only strength that was left in me. Then we came here."

Percy stopped, and when I looked at him I saw a ghastly expression on his face. He had started once more to tremble violently.

I went up to him and laid my hand on his shoulder.

"Don't tell me any more," I said. "There's no point in your upsetting yourself unnecessarily."

"No," he said, "if you don't mind I'll go through with the story to the end. We came here, to this hotel. It was about the same time of the year. It was cold in Vera's bedroom, and when we complained about it they brought in a charcoal brazier just as they did this evening. It is curious, by the way, that they should continue to do it. It just shows what they are like in these old-fashioned hotels. We were warned on no account to leave it in the room over night. I was sleeping in an adjoining room, as we couldn't get a double-bedroom, and Vera must have forgotten to put the thing out in the passage before she went to sleep. I blame myself bitterly for not having seen that she did so, but I was very tired and it was unlike her to forget. Perhaps she didn't take the danger seriously. In the morning they found her dead. I was still asleep in the next room and they came in and woke me up. There were some ghastly formalities to be gone through and I telegraphed to my lawyer to come out. After that I had a really bad breakdown. I can't remember very much about that time. I imagine the hotel tried to hush the thing up as much as possible. I saw an account of it in an English paper, and I noticed they had got the name of the place wrong. Perhaps it was just as well, as it prevented me having trouble with reporters.

"Ever since then I have been wandering about. I don't feel I can stay in any place for any length of time and I keep coming back here. I have often felt tempted to follow Vera. It would be so easy, but somehow I can't bring myself to do it."

"But surely now that the cause of your trouble—I mean now that you can no longer be looked at in the dark, surely that has made a difference?"

"No, it has made no difference. The original cause, as I tried to explain, became mixed up with a lot of other things that still persist, and now there is added the horror of remorse."

"Remorse?" I cried, "what possible reason can you have for remorse? You never let her suspect that your feelings for her had changed in any way—that is, if what you have told me is true——"

Percy sprang to his feet and cried in a quivering voice, "Of course it is true! Everything I have told you is true!"

He spoke in such a way that suspicion was almost forced upon me, and I wondered if, in point of fact, he had indeed told me the whole truth.

"You think that I might have prevented it if I had wanted to?" He went on, his voice rising to a scream. "You believe perhaps——"

"For heaven's sake, Percy," I said.

He seized my wrist.

"Tell me. Did anyone in England ever hint——"

"Of course not. Don't get such ideas into your head."

He collapsed on to the sofa and began to cry. I stood before him in a state of helpless embarrassment. After a while he pulled himself together and stood up. He went over to the fireplace and looked at himself in the mirror. Then he turned and said, in a quiet voice, "Well, whatever people may say or think, nothing can be proved." His words were accompanied by an amazing smile. It was such an unexpected flicker of the old Percy that I burst into hysterical laughter.

"Yes," I said, "you're quite safe. They could never bring a case against you." Having got on to the footing of rather precarious comedy I thought it better to stay there. "So you see, you can quite safely return to England. Come back with me to-morrow."

The smile died and he shook his head.

"No, I can't do that."

"Be reasonable, Percy," I implored him. "You can't go on for ever wandering about the continent. You will end by really going mad. In England you could live somewhere quietly in the country. You needn't see people at first and after a time you will want to see your friends and enjoy seeing them. Your old life will return to you. I am convinced that, however it may appear to you, this odd mental condition you have got yourself into is only a temporary one. But you will certainly never be cured if you go on with the kind of life you're leading now."

After much persuasion I succeeded in convincing him, and he agreed to return to England with me on the following day. When I said good night to him that evening he seemed in almost a cheerful mood. But, next morning, when I went downstairs to pay my bill and order the luggage to be brought down, I was told that he had gone away at an early hour and had left no message and no address.

I felt humiliated, as one does when benevolent plans are disdained without explanation or excuse. The night before, after the extraordinary confession in the Balzac room, I had felt for Percy the pity he so much dreaded, and the reversal of the rôles which, ever since the days of my private school, had continued to rankle in the underground passages of my mind had, I fear, proved rather gratifying to my self-esteem. But even now, Percy had bereft me of my modest triumph. Even now, a ruin of his former grandeur, Percy had won. He had also left me with a fearful doubt, and it continued, as I travelled back alone, to haunt my thoughts.

On my return to England I was taken seriously ill and spent over a month in a nursing-home. During my convalescence Mark Heneage came to see me. I told him of my interview with Percy and of his strange confession.

"Well," I asked him. "What do you think about it?"

"I think there can be no doubt," he answered, "after all she was the only person who ever succeeded in getting the better of him."

Later on—it was the beginning of July, just after the Serajevo murders—I found myself sitting next to Mrs. Pontefract at a luncheon party. I remarked to her that I had seen Percy, but the news failed to interest her. In any case I should certainly not have told her anything further. It was not the kind of story she would have appreciated. She was at the moment—as indeed was everyone else—solely concerned with the international situation. She was convinced that the Serajevo incident was going to lead to a European war.

However the prospect seemed to leave her unmoved. Indeed I got the impression that she almost welcomed the idea.

"It's bound to come sooner or later," she said, "and it's better now, before Germany is fully prepared, than later. We, of course, shall have to do our bit. But it won't be a long war. No modern war can possibly last more than six months. With Russia on our side there can be no doubt about who's going to win. I shall close down Pontefract Hall for the time being and entertain very little. People will expect less of one in wartime. It will be quite an economy."

A few weeks later, on the eve of the catastrophe I heard of Percy's death. He had shot himself in the hotel at Avignon.

THE CAMEL

(1936)

The Camel

Lord Berners

TO

John AND *Penelope Betjeman*

Contents

1

An Early Visitor

S now had fallen during the night and lay heavily on the countryside, on the fields and hedgerows and on the roof and gables of the little Vicarage at Slumbermere.

It was early morning and a faint light was just beginning to show on the eastern horizon.

The Vicarage resembled a Gothic doll's house and, could you have lifted up the roof, you would have seen the Reverend Aloysius Hussey and his wife Antonia asleep, snugly tucked up in their little twin beds.

During the winter months the Vicar and his wife were called every morning at half-past seven, and they breakfasted at eight. The two maids, Bessie and Annie, were supposed to get up an hour before their master and mistress. But, finding by experience, that an hour was ample time in which to heat the water, light the fires, tidy up the rooms and prepare the breakfast, they generally set their alarm clocks for seven.

The Reverend Aloysius was roused abruptly from his slumbers that morning by a loud peal of the front door bell. He sat up in bed, rubbed his eyes and glanced at the luminous dial of his watch. It was a quarter to seven. He wondered vaguely who the early visitor could be. It was certainly much too early for the postman. Possibly it might be a telegram. He rather hoped it was not, as telegrams nearly always meant news of an unwelcome nature. Well, well! there was no use in troubling oneself unnecessarily three-quarters of an hour before the working day began. Bessie or Annie would attend to the door bell and, if it were anything that needed immediate attention, it would be time enough then to get out of bed.

Casting an affectionate glance at Antonia's recumbent form, he lay down again, pulled the bedclothes round him, and was preparing to doze once more when a louder and more persistent peal rang through the house.

This time it woke Antonia.

"Good gracious!" she exclaimed. "Whatever is the matter?"

"That's just what I was wondering," said the Vicar. "That is the second time the front door bell has been rung. I can't imagine why we are being disturbed at this hour. It's not seven yet."

"Oh dear!" sighed the Vicar's wife. "I do hope it isn't anyone dying."

"Nonsense!" said the Vicar rather crossly. "You know perfectly well, my dear Antonia, that nobody in this village is dying, and Lady Bugle and Admiral Sefton-Porter are both in excellent health. Anyhow, I don't understand why those maids of yours aren't attending to the door bell. You must speak to them, Antonia, about the way they lie in bed in the morning."

However it appeared that the maids were at last attending to their duty. The bedroom was situated immediately above the entrance hall, and from below came the sound of hurrying footsteps. The door was unbolted and opened. The Vicar and his wife were then considerably startled at hearing a wild shriek ring out, followed by the sound of the door being violently slammed and bolted again.

"What in Heaven's name!" exclaimed the Vicar.

But Antonia was already at the window. She hastily drew back the blinds and peered out. The reflection from the snowy landscape filled the room with an unusual white light, striking on the ceiling and on the dimity curtains of the beds, casting a deathly pallor on the countenance of the Reverend Aloysius.

Antonia turned back from the window, her usually placid face distraught with bewilderment.

"It's—" she gasped. "It's . . . Oh, Aloysius dear, IT'S A CAMEL!"

"Nonsense!" exclaimed the Vicar, "How could it be a camel at this hour of the morning!"

Antonia realised that her husband's usually acute brain was still clouded by sleep and checked the retort that rose to her lips.

"Well, come and see for yourself, dear," she said.

The Vicar got out of bed and strode to the window. And, sure enough, standing on the snow-covered path in front of the little porch, looking uncouth and enormous in the wintry morning light, was unmistakably a camel.

"Bless my soul!" the Vicar ejaculated.

Unusual occurrences invariably annoyed him. He believed firmly in miracles, and, had he been privileged to witness such a thing as a real miracle, he would have eagerly defended its authenticity. The appearance of a camel at his front door on a winter's morning was definitely not a miracle. It was a highly unusual event, but nevertheless it lay within the bounds of possibility which no real miracle should do. Of course he was well aware that "God moves in a mysterious way his wonders to perform" but, at the same time he felt that it was most unlikely that God would have sent a camel to call upon him at that hour in the morning. No, the occurrence was merely strange and disconcerting, and had, moreover, deprived him of a good half-hour's sleep. He remembered, however, that he was the only man in the house, as well as being a clergyman, and therefore it was his duty to tackle cheerfully, and with clerical efficiency, any situation that might arise, unusual or otherwise.

"Get back into bed, dear," he admonished his wife. "You will catch cold. I myself will deal with the matter."

And, hastily putting on his trousers, socks and boots and a thick woolly dressing gown, he ran downstairs to the front door, brushing aside Bessie and Annie who were still huddled together in a hysterical condition at the foot of the staircase.

Antonia, animated by feminine curiosity as well as by the desire to stand by her husband in an emergency, ventured to disobey his orders. She slipped on a few "things," put on her fur coat and hurried after him.

The Reverend Aloysius opened the front door and was confronted by the camel, who, after regarding him for a while with an air of profound humility, made a step forward as though it would enter the house.

The Vicar was not going to stand any nonsense from a camel.

"SHOO!" he cried, waving it back imperiously.

"Oh, Aloysius dear," cried Antonia, "do be careful. Pray do nothing to infuriate the animal. If it were to run wild in our little garden it might trample on the snowdrops or break the rose bushes."

The camel paid no attention to the Vicar's shooings and remained motionless before the porch. Its eyes had an expression of almost human patience and suffering.

Usually associated with a background of sun-baked sands, palm trees and a torrid sky, the beast looked woefully forlorn in the wintry English landscape. Antonia was moved by a strange feeling of compassion, mingled with distant and romantic reminiscences. Many years ago she had done missionary work in the East and, in the fulfilment of her duties she had been accustomed to ride on the backs of camels. Stowed away somewhere in an attic was an old camel saddle that she had brought back with her as a souvenir. She had often thought of using it for some decorative purpose, but the Vicarage was so small that there had never seemed to be anywhere to put it.

"Poor creature," said Antonia, gazing at the camel tenderly. "It looks so unhappy. I am sure that it is hungry."

"I have no idea," said the Vicar, "what camels eat. But one thing is certain. It can't remain out there indefinitely. There is no doubt that it must have strayed from some circus or travelling menagerie in the neighbourhood and I expect that it will shortly be claimed by someone. Meanwhile it would be as well to shut it up in the barn."

He walked boldly out into the porch. "Come along," he said. "Coop! Coop!" and he attempted to take hold of the camel by the forelock. However the animal ignored the Vicar's endeavours to lead it away and remained immovable as a rock on the garden path. Its air of humility had given place to one of obstinacy.

Now the Vicar was a man of great godliness, but he had one unchristian failing, of which he himself was well aware and therefore he did everything he could to curb it. He was possessed of a very violent temper, and sometimes its violence was apt to overcome his good resolutions.

Antonia was quick to notice the warning flush on her husband's face and she was beset by a sudden fear lest an altercation between her husband and the camel might result in the destruction of her snowdrops or even worse damage to her garden. She thrust herself forward. "Aloysius dear," she said, "let me see if I can do anything with the animal. As you know, dear, I have had some experience of camels."

As soon as Antonia appeared in the doorway, the camel immediately relaxed its attitude of obstinacy. The animal's countenance resumed its former expression of humility. Without any difficulty the Vicar's wife led it through the garden to the stables. She opened the door of the barn and the camel at once walked in and knelt down on the straw.

The Vicar, it must be confessed, was, for the moment, slightly irritated at seeing his wife succeed so easily where he had failed. But the Vicar was a very saintly man, and he knew, from an innate sense of piety, that any form of humiliation to pride ought to be looked upon as a little lesson direct from God. He therefore repressed his feeling of annoyance and sought consolation by saying to himself, "After all, she has had experience of camels."

In spite of her experience, Antonia had completely forgotten (if indeed she ever knew) what camels ate. She tried it with a wisp of hay, a turnip, some Indian corn and a cabbage, but each offering was in turn rejected.

"Well," she remarked, as she closed the barn door, "it can't be really starving. Anyhow the animal won't do any harm in the garden now it is safely shut up, and I can attend to its food later."

"Good gracious!" exclaimed the Vicar, looking up at the church clock, "it's a quarter to eight and neither of us properly dressed. We must have wasted nearly an hour over that silly camel. I hope the maids will have had the sense to delay breakfast."

His spirits rose at the thought of breakfast.

"Dear me!" he said, rubbing his hands, "what would the people think if they were to see us traipsing about in the snow in our négligés! Antonia dear, I trust you haven't caught cold."

"No, dear, thank you, I don't think so. This is a very warm coat and I took the precaution to slip on my . . . "

A hasty bath, a rapid toilet, clothes hurriedly buttoned and hooked and the Vicar and his wife were soon seated at the breakfast table before steaming cups of coffee, hot toast and a heaped up dish of buttered eggs.

They did themselves well at the Vicarage. The house, small as it was and inclined to pokiness, was by no means uncomfortable. The early sun began to shine through the Gothic windows of the little dining-room, brightening the hues of the red and green Turkey carpet and illuminating the Arundel prints that decorated the walls.

Refreshed by his breakfast the Vicar was now in an excellent mood. The camel business had been dealt with, if not accounted for, and the Vicar had no doubt that the animal would soon be claimed. In any case, the incident would supply an excellent subject for conversation the next time he was invited to luncheon by Lady Bugle or Admiral Sefton-Porter. The only thing to be done now was to find out to whom the animal belonged.

"Bessie," he said, to the maid who had just come in to clear away the breakfast, "I see Beaton over there in the churchyard. Just run across and tell him to go to the 'Resplendent Peacock' and inform Mr. Gilpin about this camel that has strayed into the Vicarage. He will probably know if there are any circuses or travelling menageries in the neighbourhood."

Bessie never relished the idea of having to convey any form of communication to the verger Beaton who was painfully hard of hearing and inclined, she thought, to be impertinent. Besides which, she disliked what she termed his "nosiness." In spite of the old man's infirmity there was very little in the matter of local gossip that escaped him. Bessie suspected him of a particular "nosiness" with regard to her own private affairs and whenever he met her he would give her a sly look, nod his head and mutter, with an inscrutable chuckle, "Oi knows what oi knows."

The Vicar liked making use of his verger as a kind of emissary, especially when there was a question of any dealings between the Vicarage and the "Resplendent Peacock," whose landlord Mr. Gilpin, although on very good terms with the Vicar and his wife, was, nevertheless, not a churchgoing man.

The Camel

Having discussed with Antonia the programme of the day's work before him, the Vicar reverted once more to the mysterious affair of the camel.

"I still don't understand," he said, "about the bell. That, to my mind, requires some explanation. I cannot believe that the animal itself can have rung the bell. Granted that it may be a performing camel from some circus, I hardly think that they would have taught it to go about ringing people's door bells. The only other explanation that I can think of is that it may have been something in the nature of a practical joke. Although I must confess that the humour of bringing a camel to the Vicarage at an early hour in the morning and ringing the bell evades me. And, in any case, there is nobody in this village who would go to the expense of procuring a camel for the purpose of playing a practical joke, while such behaviour on the part of either Lady Bugle or Admiral Sefton-Porter is unthinkable."

The Vicar rose from the breakfast table. The moment had come for an important function in the day's routine.

"While I am filling my pipe, dear," he said to his wife, "would you be so good as to go to my study and fetch me a volume of the Encyclopedia Britannica? The volume cab to cam is the one I require. I will endeavour to find out something about the diet of camels."

The Vicar always prided himself on his regularity. "Mens sana in corpore sano" was a motto that came frequently to his lips. Sometimes, in the company of an old College chum or a friendly Ecclesiastic he would paraphrase it "Open bowels and an open mind." He thought that an occasional dash of Rabelaisian humour did not ill become an English country clergyman who was "broad."

Having filled his pipe from the jar of Three Nuns tobacco that stood on the mantelpiece, he proceeded to light it, and placing the volume of the Encyclopedia Britannica cab to cam under his arm he strode down the passage and disappeared through the door at the end of it.

2

The First Adventure

The day passed and nobody came to claim the camel. Beaton had been informed by the landlord of the "Resplendent Peacock" that it was unlikely the animal could have strayed from a travelling circus as it was not the season for such entertainments. The police station was notified and posters were put up in various parts of the village. The Vicar prepared an advertisement to be inserted in the local Press.

There was naturally a good deal of talk in the village, and Bessie and Annie were continually being disturbed by requests on the part of the villagers to be allowed to see the camel. The Vicar gave out that only the more important of the parishioners, such as Miss Justice, the Postmistress, Mr. Gudgeon, the Schoolmaster, and a few others of equal prominence were to be admitted to the barn. He also had the excellent idea of holding out the camel as an incentive to good behaviour among the schoolchildren and he let it be known that any child obtaining good marks for conduct would be privileged to view the camel on Sunday morning after Divine Service, if the beast had not been claimed by then. The announcement had a miraculous effect on the children and Mr. Gudgeon said that never since he had taken on the job of Schoolmaster had he known such exemplary behaviour on the part of his young pupils.

The day after the arrival of the camel, a Saturday, was the day on which Antonia was in the habit of visiting the poorer members of the parish, and she would go round, bestowing on those who stood in need of such things, gifts of woollen clothing, soup, tins of cocoa and other little comforts that brighten the lives of the indigent.

Antonia was accustomed to drive about the countryside in a ramshackle pony cart drawn by Toby, the old pony who had done many years of service at the Vicarage.

Toby was now unfortunately lame, and the Vet. said it was quite out of the question that he should be employed in his present condition. In any case the Vicar's wife, who displayed an almost exaggerated tenderness where animals were concerned, would never have dreamt of driving him out unless he were perfectly sound.

This meant that she would be obliged to perform her errands of mercy on foot and, as old Mrs. Cattermole, to whom she had promised some soup, lived at least four miles away, it was very annoying.

When she complained to her husband he offered her no real consolation.

"We all have our crosses to bear," he remarked. "You and I particularly, dear, should thank God that we have so few."

But all the same it was a great nuisance to have to walk four miles to carry soup to old Mrs. Cattermole.

In order to take her mind off the fatiguing task before her, Antonia paid a visit to the camel.

The Vicar's researches in the Encyclopedia Britannica had not been productive of any very useful information with regard to the diet of camels. He had found it stated that camels had the peculiarity of being able to go for a very long time without water and that they were partial to a leguminous shrub known as camel-thorn which grew in the Arabian Desert. It seemed unlikely that any of it could be obtained in the neighbourhood of Slumbermere, and Antonia was beginning to be worried lest the beast should die of inanition. She contemplated sending a reply paid telegram to the Zoo.

But when she opened the door of the barn she found the camel contentedly munching, and she noticed that the turnip, the hay, the carrot and the various other experimental forms of nourishment she had set down on the straw had disappeared. This, at least, was satisfactory.

The camel looked up as Antonia entered the barn, and it seemed to her as though the animal were regarding her with an expression of almost dog-like affection. It reminded her painfully of the way in which her dear little terrier Jock, now unhappily deceased, used to look at her.

"Poor creature," she murmured. "I really do believe it is getting quite fond of me."

And she patted it gently on the head. The camel closed its eyes and attempted to lick her hand.

At that moment Antonia was struck by a sudden idea, as ingenious as it was strange. "Why," she thought, "should I not try and ride the camel over to old Mrs. Cattermole?" The idea seemed to her so audacious that, for a moment, she felt quite frightened. Nevertheless she clung to it and furthermore began to envisage it as taking a practical shape.

Up in the attic somewhere was the old camel saddle, relic of her early Missionary days when she thought nothing of climbing on to a camel's back and riding for miles through the desert. A spirit of adventure that had lain dormant for many years came over her once again. And, in any case, the beast looked so meek and so affectionate that she was encouraged to think that at least there would be no harm in trying.

She called for Bessie and together they went up to the attic where they found the saddle stowed away in a crate. They unpacked it, dusted it and brought it downstairs.

Antonia found that there was also a halter and a spiked staff, used for guiding the beast.

When her mistress's intention dawned on Bessie she was aghast with amazement and awe. "Lor," she said to Annie afterwards. "You could have blown on me and I'd have fallen down like a ninepin."

"Yes, Bessie," said Antonia, "I certainly intend to try and ride the animal if it is possible. When I was young I used very frequently to ride on camels."

The two women between them managed to fix the saddle fairly securely on to the camel, who seemed to be entering into the spirit of the thing, and rose to its feet as though in order to facilitate operations. When it was harnessed Antonia led it out into the stable yard and, mounting on the gate, she succeeded, with the assistance of a good shove from Bessie, in planting herself firmly on its back.

She walked it several times round the yard and found, to her delight, that it seemed to respond readily to her guidance.

"Now, Bessie," she called to the maid who was standing watching the scene with respectful giggles, "just hand me my basket. And Bessie, I must beg of you not to say anything to the Vicar about this, should he return during my absence."

Antonia was very much averse to publicity of any kind and she feared that, were she to ride through the village on a camel, it might give rise to something bordering on a commotion. She therefore felt that it would be advisable to keep out of sight of the dwelling houses as much as possible. This could be managed by striking through the little wood at the back of the churchyard and keeping to the narrow, unfrequented lanes. By making a slight detour and crossing the further end of Admiral Sefton-Porter's park, she would be enabled to reach old Mrs. Cattermole's cottage unseen.

The camel proved to be a most perfect mount. Antonia had no difficulty whatever in guiding it; the beast responded to the slightest tug of the rein, the lightest tap of the stick. Its manners (to use the jargon of the riding-school) were excellent, and its action extremely comfortable.

Antonia experienced a feeling of exhilaration she had not known for many years. In the first place she was seeing the countryside from an unaccustomed angle. Raised to twice the height of the seat in her pony cart, she had an agreeable sense of dominating her surroundings, while, in the place of the bumping and jolting of iron-rimmed wheels and defective springs, she was being carried forward with a gentle swaying motion. She felt like a bird cleaving the air.

She passed swiftly through the little wood, lowering her head to avoid the overhanging branches, and came out on a path that skirted the hedgerow between two ploughed fields; and then, striking to the left to avoid a group of cottages, she entered Admiral Sefton-Porter's park. She thought it advisable not to pass within view of the house, even at a distance, as the Admiral was known to be in the habit of looking out of his windows with a telescope.

She was a little perplexed as to how she should approach old Mrs. Cattermole's cottage. She feared that if the old lady were to catch sight of her riding up on a camel it might be the death of her; for old Mrs. Cattermole was always complaining of her weak heart. She came to the conclusion that it would be kinder to dismount from the camel somewhere out of sight and then proceed to the cottage on foot. But she wondered if, having once got down from the camel she would be able to get on to it again without the aid of Bessie. Well, she could but try, and, if she found she couldn't, it would mean that she would have to walk the four miles home leading the camel, which would be a great nuisance, but it would be better than frightening the old lady to death.

She stopped the camel by a gate. The animal stood perfectly still and she was able to climb down with ease. She tethered it to the gate post and made her way to the cottage.

The door was opened by Flossie, old Mrs. Cattermole's grandchild.

"Well, Flossie, and how's your Grandmama?" she enquired.

"Pretty middling, thank you, Ma'am," replied the child with a curtsey.

She found the old lady sitting in front of a blazing fire.

"I've brought you some soup, Mrs. Cattermole."

"Oh thank you, Ma'am. I was just saying to Flossie here that it was about time I had another bath. It'll come in handy, Ma'am."

"I said soup, not soap!" Antonia shouted at her. She had forgotten that the old lady was deaf.

"Won't you take a seat, Ma'am."

Antonia sat down in a rickety armchair on the opposite side of the fireplace. The heat was intolerable.

She thought it might be a good thing, in view of further visits under similar circumstances, to tell the old lady about the camel.

"We've just had a very strange visitor at the Vicarage, Mrs. Cattermole. It arrived quite early in the morning the day before yesterday. A camel."

"Bless my soul!" exclaimed Mrs. Cattermole. "You don't say so! Well I *am* surprised! Who'd have thought it? And at your age too, Ma'am, if you'll pardon me for saying so, Ma'am. Well dearie me. Wonders will never cease. And you up and about so soon, Ma'am. Well that's fine. We country folk are better able to manage than them as live in towns I always say. When my daughter was brought to bed of little Flossie here she was up and doing the very next day."

Antonia was horrorstruck by the misunderstanding.

"No! no!" she screamed into the old lady's ear, "I said a camel!"

But it was no good. Mrs. Cattermole having once got the idea into her head seemed determined to stick to it.

Antonia felt her head going round. What with the intense heat in the cottage and the old lady's obstinate imperviousness, she felt it was preferable to leave her under the erroneous impression than to attempt to battle with her any longer. She bade her a hasty farewell and fled from the cottage.

"Goodbye, Ma'am," the old lady called after her. "And thank you kindly, Ma'am. You was always very kind to me. And kindly give the Vicar my congratulations."

When Antonia reached the gate where she had left the camel she found it kneeling down. She then remembered that camels invariably knelt to allow their riders to mount. It had always struck her as a charming trait in camels and she wondered how she had forgotten it. It would have saved her all that trouble in the stable yard. She got on to the animal's back, touched it lightly with her stick and it instantly rose to its feet. The relief she felt at not having to walk home almost compensated her for the annoyance she had suffered at the hands of old Mrs. Cattermole. Indeed she felt so lighthearted that she urged the camel into a trot.

Admiral Sefton-Porter had returned early that afternoon from London. A visit to London always left him in rather an irritable frame of mind. He did not find that hobnobbing with other retired naval and military gentlemen at his club was conducive to his peace of mind. In the country he was able to bully and browbeat his neighbours to his heart's content, but in London he was constantly meeting with people who were able to hold their own, and this always upset him very much.

Although he could hardly be described as a very intelligent man, he had a very active mind, and he took a prominent part in all local activities. His chief aim in life seemed to be to find out what people disliked doing and make them do it, or else to find out what they liked doing and stop them.

He was one of the most talkative members of the Rural District Council as well as the most obstructive. He rigorously opposed innovation in any form. He was also a magistrate, and, on the Bench, he recovered that pleasurable sense of authority that he so much missed, since his retirement from the Navy, in convicting the poorer classes for such offences as riding bicycles without lights, neglecting to take out dog licences and other misdemeanours that are rife in the countryside.

But when he was not thwarted or contradicted, he could be as amiable as anyone could wish, and the general opinion of his equals was that he was a jovial old fellow if a trifle inclined to be peppery at times.

London, as I have said, did not suit him, and, on his return to his country seat, he felt the need of a little gentle exercise to soothe his nerves. He ordered his favourite horse Stalwart to be saddled and brought round to the door, and he set out for a quiet ride round his estate. This he always found to be the best medicine to restore his mental equilibrium.

It was growing dusk when he turned his horse's head towards home. One of the gates he had to go through had been newly set up and he had some difficulty in getting it to open. While he was struggling with it, his horse suddenly began to neigh and then reared up on its hind legs in the most unaccountable manner. The Admiral, taken by surprise, was unseated; his stirrup leather caught on the top of the gate post and for a moment he was suspended head downwards. Then the stirrup leather gave way and the horse galloped off on one side kicking up its heels in the air and behaving as though it were mad, while the Admiral fell heavily to the ground on the other.

Stalwart was, as a rule, a very quiet horse and it was the first time that Admiral Sefton-Porter had known it behave in this extraordinary fashion. The Admiral struggled to his feet and, as he did so, he received another and even greater shock. He saw, in the distance, receding down the lane, the clergyman's wife mounted on a camel. No! It was not possible! He rubbed his eyes and looked again. For a moment he had another distinct and unmistakable vision of this same phenomenon, and then it disappeared round the bend of the road behind some trees.

Stalwart's paroxysm of emotion seemed at last to have subsided and he allowed himself to be recaptured. But the Admiral was sadly shaken both mentally and physically. "Is it possible?" so ran his thoughts during his homeward ride. "Is it possible that I am beginning to 'see things'? I have always led a fairly sober life. But even the most normal people can have hallucinations in their old age so I'm told. I wonder if I ought to see a doctor? There's nothing wrong with my eyesight. I'm sure of that. For a man of my age it's remarkably keen. But something obviously frightened the horse. He has never behaved like that before. He must have seen it too."

When he got home he was aching all over from his fall. He ordered his servant to prepare a mustard bath and decided to have his dinner in bed. He also decided that it was better not to say a word to anyone about the strange apparition he had seen.

3

Tally-Ho!

The Vicar had spoken of crosses. His own particular cross was Mr. Scrimgeour, the organist.

Mr. Scrimgeour was a pale young man with weak knees and the expression of a tired fish. Besides being organist at Slumbermere church he gave music lessons, and was head of the local choral society. He supported an aged mother.

Mr. Scrimgeour was very musical, and knew quite a lot about counter point and harmony and all that sort of thing; but, unfortunately he was a very indifferent executant and his performances on the organ left a great deal to be desired. To make matters worse, he was extremely ambitious and he was continually attempting to play difficult pieces that lay beyond his powers of execution.

A painful example of this excessive ambition had occurred that very

Sunday at morning service. Mr. Scrimgeour had spent some considerable time in practising that cheerful little fugue by Bach (G major in the second book) and, when at last he considered he had got it perfect, he decided to play it as a voluntary.

But alas! public performance was, for him, a very different matter to private rehearsal. When it came to the moment he was very nervous and suffered from stage fright. He lost his head, pulled out the wrong stops and, short as the fugue was, he forgot several bars in the middle of it and was obliged to improvise. To his final discomfiture two hymn books became dislodged and fell down on to the top keys so that an unexpected shrill tremolo was added to the general confusion. The voluntary ended in a riot of nonsense, completely spoiling the effect of the Vicar's entry.

The Vicar was very proud of his entries. He liked to make them as impressive as possible; but how could anyone move impressively to the strains of that extraordinary jig that was being performed on the organ?

When he reached the chancel, the Vicar was quivering with fury and he embarked on the Order for Morning Prayer in a spirit very far removed from the holy calm essential to the conduct of Divine Service.

Owing to his agitation, further and even more serious mishaps befell him during the course of the ceremony. The camel had been very much in his thoughts during the last two days and, as luck would have it, there occurred in one of the lessons that passage in which it is said that it is easier for a camel to go through the eye of a needle than for a rich man to enter into the Kingdom of Heaven. For one brief moment the Vicar contemplated skipping the passage as being of rather too topical an interest as well as being offensive to Lady Bugle who was sitting in the front row of the pews, and whose husband was a very rich man. But of course that was impossible. As he pronounced the word camel, his voice quavered in a rather self-conscious manner, thereby drawing further attention to the allusion.

But there was worse to come. In the prayer for the Clergy and People, his mind still running on camels, he made the most unfortunate slip, saying, "Almighty and Everlasting God who alone workest great marvels; send down upon our Bishops and Curates and all camels committed to their charge," and I regret to say a large proportion of the congregation tittered.

When the service was over and he entered the Vestry, the Vicar was in a towering and most un-Sundaylike rage. The first person he encountered was the offending organist.

"I must confess, Mr. Scrimgeour," he remarked to that unfortunate young man in withering tones, "I failed to appreciate the little Scherzo you favoured us with this morning in lieu of a voluntary."

"But it was by Bach," the wretched young man stammered.

"That is very possible," rejoined the Vicar. "Nevertheless I consider it a most unsuitable piece of music for performance in a church, and I must beg of you never to play it again."

At luncheon alone with Antonia, the Vicar's pent up feelings gave way.

"I feel that some day," he said, "I may be tempted to commit a murder. Indeed I came very near to it this morning in the Vestry. Did you ever hear anything like Scrimgeour's performance on the organ this morning? It was disgraceful! Why should I have to put up with such a thing? That insufferable ass!" he burst out. "That intolerable nincompoop! That . . ." His voice choked with emotion.

"Oh hush, dear!" said Antonia. "Don't say such dreadful things. And on Sunday too."

"If only I could get rid of him," the Vicar went on. "But that, I fear, is impossible under the circumstances. If I were to get him dismissed it would cause a great deal of ill feeling in the village. It would be looked upon as an act of unkindness. And indeed so it would be. It is characteristic of that kind of man that he should have an aged mother to support."

Antonia employed all her soothing wiles to calm her husband's agitation. But the Vicar refused to be soothed.

"Everything," he said, "seems to be going wrong with me to-day. My slip about the camels was most unfortunate. And I was sorry to notice that some of the congregation laughed. They always seem only too ready to catch on to anything of that sort. If I had made a good point in my sermon, I have no doubt it would have passed unperceived. Really there are moments in the life of a clergyman that are distinctly discouraging.

"And," he continued, "as we are on the subject of camels I feel that the time has come to take some definite steps about the one that is now in our barn. We certainly cannot keep the animal here much longer and nobody seems to claim it. I intend to write and offer it to the Zoo."

Antonia was filled with alarm. The escapade of the previous afternoon, of which she had not yet informed the Vicar, had strengthened her desire to keep the camel for good. She had made up her mind that, if anyone did eventually come to claim it, she would offer to buy it. She was even prepared to sacrifice her savings for the purpose.

"Oh Aloysius, dear," she said, "I was thinking that perhaps we might keep it."

"Keep it!" exclaimed the Vicar in a tone of great surprise. "My dear Antonia, that is out of the question. The Vicarage is small enough as it is, and we have sufficient to attend to without the further burden of a camel."

Antonia's eyes began to fill with tears.

"Aloysius dear," she said, "it is not often that I ask a favour of you. But please, please let me keep the camel! I would willingly pay for the expense out of my own pocket. You know, dear, since my darling little Jock died, I have been sadly in need of a pet."

"But my dear Antonia," the Vicar retorted, "if I may say so, a camel is a very different proposition to a small Scotch terrier."

"I promise you, dear Aloysius, I will see to it that the camel will never be any bother to you. On the contrary, we might even find it extremely useful."

She then confessed to her husband the event of the previous afternoon, how she had ridden the camel over to old Mrs. Cattermole, emphasising the complete success of the experiment, but suppressing the misunderstanding that had occurred.

The Vicar was amazed. He hardly knew what to say.

"But really, Antonia dear, you can't go riding about on a camel. What would the people think?"

"Oh, they would soon get accustomed to the idea, they are already far less excited about it than they were at first."

"Yes, dear, but they haven't yet seen you on its back."

"Oh well, it would be just the same. They would stare for the first few days and then they would take it for granted."

"I fear that Lady Bugle might disapprove."

"Oh no, dear, she is the last person to disapprove. She is always saying how much she appreciates originality."

"Well, it would certainly be original," the Vicar remarked grimly.

He got up and paced about the room for a while. At last he turned to Antonia and said, "No dear. I am sorry to disappoint you. But it is quite out of the question. The camel must go."

Antonia's reply was to burst into floods of tears. She hid her face in her hands and murmured, "Cruel! Cruel!"

The Vicar felt that he was placed in a very awkward position. The situation was more emotionally complicated than it would appear at first sight. It had always been a great grief to the Husseys that they had had no children. It seemed so unfair that God, who usually favoured his clergy in this respect (in some instances almost to the point of exaggeration), should have seen fit to withhold these favours in the case of Antonia who would so obviously have made an excellent mother.

Her darling little Jock had proved a solace to her in many ways, although of course a dog could hardly be considered to be a really satisfactory substitute for "little pattering feet." Nevertheless she had loved little Jock dearly and his death had been a great shock to her, and had left her with a poignant sense of bereavement.

As a matter of fact, darling little Jock had been a horrid little dog, and Antonia was the only person who had been blind to his defects. Jock was the type of dog known as a "silent biter." He would steal up behind you and nip you in the calf before you were aware of his presence. Everyone in the village, from the butcher's boy to the postmistress, had hated him, and it was an open secret that Beaton, the Verger, had poisoned him. Antonia however, was unaware of all this. She and the

Vicar were the only two people in the neighbourhood that darling little Jock had not bitten or attempted to bite. To Antonia he had seemed perfect in every way and she had erected a tombstone for him in the Vicarage garden as near as possible to the cemetery and had put an inscription on it: "The Lord gave and the Lord hath taken away."

The Vicar had always very much disapproved of this. He considered that to place a text from the Holy Scriptures on a dog's grave was an act bordering on blasphemy and reminiscent of one of the worst excesses of Lord Byron who buried his dog Boatswain on the site of the High Altar at Newstead Abbey. But poor Antonia had been so prostrated by grief that the Vicar could not find it in his heart to rebuke her; and so the tombstone had remained as it was.

Now there had arisen a similar difficulty about this camel. Antonia had evidently set her heart on keeping it. The Vicar, as he paced up and down the room, was once more assailed by a sense of guilt with respect to their childlessness. The horrid suspicion that perhaps he was to blame for it often weighed upon his mind. Of course Antonia had never reproached him; she was so loyal and devoted a wife that, even had she possessed positive scientific proofs, she would never have dreamt of doing so. The Vicar felt that he owed Antonia every form of consolation that it lay within his power to offer. She had always been an excellent wife and the comfortable income she had inherited from her parents had certainly been of great assistance to him. Perhaps it was rather unworthy of him to object to her keeping a camel if she really wished to. He began to relent. A further paroxysm of sobbing broke down the last barrier of his opposition.

"Well, well," he said, patting his wife's heaving shoulders, "if you really want to keep it, we will see how we get on. Perhaps, after all, it won't be a source of so much trouble as I had imagined. I will postpone my letter to the Zoo."

And so the camel remained for the time being at Slumbermere Vicarage.

A few days passed and Antonia felt a growing desire to go for another ride on the camel, for her own pleasure as well as for practical purposes.

Toby, the pony, was no better, and the Vet. had said that he feared it would never again be fit for service.

When Antonia informed her husband, with a certain apprehension, that she thought of going for a ride on the camel again, she found to her intense relief that he made no objection. He even offered to help her in saddling and harnessing the beast. He was in an excellent humour that day. He had thought of a very good riddle for the Parish Magazine; it had come to him that morning, after breakfast, in the closet.

Q. Why is Sunday unlike any other day?
A. Because it is the Lord's day.

He was delighted with it. These little inspirations always afforded him intense pleasure, and, after all, it was not so easy as one might imagine to think of something bright and original for the Parish Magazine.

So the Vicar was in the best of tempers. He made several jokes during the harnessing of the camel, and when finally he saw Antonia perched on its back he said to her in his most jocular vein, "Really my dear, I can hardly claim to be an authority on the subject, but you seem to me to have an excellent seat on a camel. All the same, dear," he added more seriously, "if I were you, I don't think I should ride through the village."

Antonia thought as he did, and she decided to take the same direction she had taken before, through the little wood beyond the churchyard. She had hardly emerged from it into the open fields on the other side when she was startled by the sudden blast of a horn, accompanied by the distant sound of galloping horses. She saw, through the trees, the flash of a scarlet coat and a pack of hounds moving swiftly over the brow of the hill. She realised that a fox hunt was in progress.

Now Antonia, on account of her great love of animals, was very much averse to blood sports, but she objected far less to foxhunting than to the other forms of harrying wild beasts. Firstly because it gave pleasure to a large number of ladies and gentlemen, some of whom were her personal friends and who were regular in their attendance at Divine Service. And secondly because foxes very frequently made incursions into her hen coops. Only quite recently one of them had carried off a very fine cock with which she was hoping to win a prize at the local poultry show. But when, a few moments later, the hunted fox passed within a couple of yards of her, in an obviously exhausted condition, her heart was smitten with compassion.

"Poor creature," she cried aloud, "I hope it may escape!"

Her words seemed to have a magical effect upon the camel. For it gave a great bound forward that nearly unseated her, and then proceeded in a rapid trot in the direction of the oncoming hounds. It appeared as though it were trying to place itself between the hounds and the fox. The hounds, however, were so intent on their pursuit that they paid little attention to the monster that was attempting to bar their passage and they surged past it, dividing on both sides like a rushing stream meeting a barge. The camel lashed out at them with an unexpected ferocity, severely injuring two of the hounds who lay writhing and whimpering on the ground.

At that moment the Master, Captain Jollyboy, came galloping up; he seemed to be in a fine rage. His usually rubicund countenance was deepened by wrath to a dark purple. He was using the most frightful language. A stream of the foulest expletives flowed from his lips. Antonia had never heard such expressions. He shook his fist and raised his hunting crop with a menacing gesture. The camel turned suddenly and faced its aggressor, whereupon Captain Jollyboy's horse was seized with panic, wheeled round and galloped off in the opposite direction. Captain Jollyboy was powerless to hold it and he was carried for nearly a quarter of a mile before he was able to pull up. The apparition of the camel had a no less disastrous effect on the rest of the hunting field. In every direction horses reared up into the air, unseating their riders; others bucked, kicked up their heels and bolted. The ground was strewn with fallen ladies and gentlemen struggling in the mud. One or two of them were quite badly injured. The hunting field assumed the aspect of a battle field after an unsuccessful cavalry charge.

Poor Antonia was completely dazed by what had happened. It seemed to her like an appalling nightmare. She was saved however from any responsible decision by the camel itself, who appeared to be quite unperturbed by the violence and magnitude of the catastrophe it had caused, and set off gently but firmly in the direction of home, bearing the unresisting Antonia away from the scene of carnage. She was almost in a fainting condition when she reached the Vicarage.

4

The Sable Coat

Antonia explained to the Vicar, as far as she was able, what had happened that afternoon. But her account was so disjointed and confused that he could make very little of it. He thought that his wife seemed slightly delirious and he advised her to go to bed, a suggestion with which she readily complied.

Reports of the camel's disastrous appearance in the hunting field came drifting in from the village, most of them conveyed by Beaton, the Verger. The Vicar was not a little worried. The last thing he wished was to make enemies among the gentry. Like Antonia, he was averse to blood sports, but he felt that it would be most unwise to antagonize the hunting folk.

Next morning he received a letter from Captain Jollyboy couched in terms that were very much the reverse of polite. It was, in fact, a terrible letter. The Vicar did not dare to show it to Antonia. He contented himself with giving her a bowdlerized version, remarking "I could not have believed it possible that anyone, even under the most violent provocation, could have written such a letter to a clergyman."

Antonia had been very much afraid that her calamitous excursion might perhaps induce her husband to reconsider his concession about the camel and that he would insist once more upon its being sent away.

At first he had thought of doing so, but Captain Jollyboy's letter so enraged him that he determined to stand by his wife and the camel. After drafting a number of suitable and dignified replies to the Captain's offensive communication, he tore them all up and decided that, in the end, silence was the best answer.

The effect the incident had upon the neighbourhood varied a good deal according to circumstances. Those who had suffered injuries, either to their own persons or to their horses were naturally resentful. On the other hand a large proportion of the hunting field, consisting of people who preferred to follow the chase on the roads, or at a cautious distance, and were consequently objects of contempt to the more go-ahead members of the hunt, was secretly rather pleased at their discomfiture.

Admiral Sefton-Porter had not been out that day, and when he was told about Antonia and the camel, he was so relieved at finding that he was not, after all, suffering from hallucinations that he was disposed to make light of the matter and even indulged in a little playful banter on the subject with the Vicar when he met him. Whereas Lady Bugle, who was president of the local branch of the Society for Prevention of Cruelty to Animals and strongly disapproved of blood sports, openly professed her delight.

She wrote to the Vicar inviting him and his wife to luncheon, and begged them to bring the camel with them so that she might be enabled to inspect what she playfully alluded to as "the hero of the hour."

The Vicar was always pleased and flattered at being asked to luncheon by Lady Bugle; at the same time he rather dreaded those functions. Lady Bugle, who had failed to ingratiate herself with what she called "the stuck up county families," was obliged to content herself with the company of such artists and intellectuals as her wealth and hospitality was able to attract. She was herself neither artistic nor intellectual but she knew that Art and Intellect had a certain social value. She therefore affected to despise the frivolities of the "Beau monde" in favour of communion with the more respectable members of Bohemia.

Last time the Vicar had lunched at Slumbermere Hall he had encountered what he considered to be a highly objectionable selection of guests, the kind of people he instinctively suspected of immorality and atheism. He had not been able to hold his own at the luncheon table as he was accustomed to do and furthermore he noticed that his utterances were often greeted with thinly veiled contempt.

Thus the Vicar and his wife set out for the Hall, leading the camel, with feelings of not wholly pleasurable anticipation.

When they arrived, they found a groom waiting at the door. The man touched his hat and said that he had orders to take the camel round to the stable where it would be fed. "Her Ladyship," he informed them, "will be pleased to view the camel after luncheon."

Antonia was a little annoyed. "Pray give the camel nothing to eat," she said in a dignified voice, "it has already been given a very good meal at home."

In everything that Lady Bugle did or said Antonia always imagined that she detected an insidious note of patronage and she was inclined to resent it. But, of course, Lady Bugle was by far the wealthiest and most generous of the parishioners and, as the Vicar's wife, it was her duty to put up with a good deal for the sake of the Church.

When they were shown into the drawing-room, the Vicar saw that the assembled company consisted of very much the kind of people he had expected. There was a professor of some obscure science, a Royal Academician who had painted the "Picture of the Year" in last season's Academy; a female composer who had written a Symphony of such incredible length and dullness that it had been immediately hailed by all the leading English musical critics as a masterpiece. There was also a young man who looked like a stock-broker and was really a poet.

Lady Bugle greeted the Husseys with an almost regal condescension.

"I have heard all about your camel," she said, "I consider it too amusing."

Her Ladyship was an imposing looking woman with prominent teeth and a protuberant bust, which gave her the appearance of an upright piano. But, apart from the uprightness of her bust, everything else about her appeared to sag, her flesh, her clothes and her jewels with which she was liberally hung. Her elaborate coiffure, which spiteful people averred to be a wig, was dark brown. A slight moustache ornamented her upper lip and she had a large aquiline nose.

Her husband, Sir Solomon Bugle, had made his money in buttons. The Vicar had once indulged in a joke on the subject. "I hope," he said to Antonia, "that when Sir Solomon comes to church he won't put any of them into the offertory bag."

However Sir Solomon never did go to church and he very rarely visited Slumbermere. He preferred to live in London where, it was rumoured, he found plenty to keep him busy in the shape of a young lady whose acquaintance he had made at the Promenade of the Empire. Lady Bugle, who concealed beneath a majestic exterior a deeply sensitive nature, felt her husband's disaffection very keenly and whenever she had occasion to refer to him she always spoke of him as though he were dead.

"My husband," she would say, "was never partial to the country," "Sir Solomon used to observe," and so forth.

Slumbermere Hall had been purchased some years ago from an impoverished county family and had been done up regardless of expense. A fashionable and expensive decorator had been called in, and the whole place was rampant with good taste.

As they passed through the hall on the way to the dining-room, Lady Bugle drew Antonia's attention to a glass case on a stand which contained a stuffed pug.

"That," she said, "is my dear little Mingo whom I lost a few months ago."

"Did you feel his loss very much?" asked Antonia sympathetically.

"Yes, indeed," replied Lady Bugle. "However, luckily I still have my little Mopsy." She indicated an animated replica of Mingo that was waddling into the dining-room in front of them.

"I always think," she said, "it is wiser never to devote one's affection wholly to one object. I divided my love equally between Mingo and Mopsy, so that when Mingo died I naturally felt his loss less than I should otherwise have done. I believe you also lost your little dog recently, did you not?"

Antonia felt that the subject was too painful for further elaboration, and contented herself with merely replying "Yes, Lady Bugle."

The food at Slumbermere Hall was pretentious rather than nourishing. So, thought the Vicar, was the conversation. However he found himself in agreement with the Royal Academician and the Female Composer in their denunciations of modern art.

"These young fellows," said the R.A., "have no sense of beauty and no respect for tradition."

"That," said Lady Bugle, "is precisely what Sir Solomon always used to say."

"The other day," the R.A. went on, "I had the misfortune to visit an exhibition of modern French pictures. It was disgraceful! How the fellows have the impertinence to exhibit such daubs . . . let alone to paint them! It made my blood boil. Why, if my little girl had produced such things . . ."

"How is your little girl?" enquired Lady Bugle amiably.

"Very well thank you," returned the R.A. a trifle ungraciously. He disliked having his train of ideas interrupted.

The Vicar thought that it was a good moment to enter into the conversation.

"My wife," he said, "has just painted an awfully jolly reredos."

"What on earth is that?" asked the poet.

The Vicar was amazed at such ignorance. He proceeded patiently to explain that a reredos was a painted screen behind the altar.

"Oh," said the poet, "I thought it might be something connected with a lavatory."

The Vicar grew pale with anger and embarrassment. He hoped Antonia had not heard. What a very objectionable young man to be sure! But, before luncheon was over, the Vicar had even stronger reasons to object to him.

Ignoring the Vicar, the poet addressed himself to Lady Bugle and expressed ecstatic admiration of what he had the effrontery to refer to as "her" church.

"Yes," said Lady Bugle, "Slumbermere Church is very nice. Sir Solomon always used to say that it ought to be restored, and that it was much too old-fashioned for modern conditions. Sir Solomon himself never went to church very much I am sorry to say, but he had a strong sense of duty towards the parish."

"Restored!" exclaimed the poet. "Why the whole point of the thing is that it has never been restored."

"Well perhaps you are right," said Lady Bugle. "I myself have rather a leaning towards quaint old picturesque buildings."

Now the "old-fashioned" aspect of Slumbermere Church had always been a source of sorrow to the Vicar and his wife. All the other churches in the neighbourhood had been beautifully restored in the 'seventies or 'eighties, and they considered it most unfortunate that Slumbermere Church alone should have escaped the general rejuvenation.

How agreeable it would have been if, instead of the unsightly box pews and stone floors, Slumbermere Church could have boasted neat symmetrical rows of polished oak and nice red and yellow tesselated pavement. And the windows too were a disgrace. All of them plain glass. There was only one stained glass window in the whole church and that had been put up by the butcher's widow. The main feature in it was a very large lamb, and many people considered it to be a trifle too appropriate.

The Vicar had always hoped that Lady Bugle might perhaps provide a handsome sum towards the renovation of the church and now this wretched poet fellow seemed to be trying to put a spoke in his wheel.

After luncheon at Slumbermere Hall it was customary to visit the orchid houses. At other places in the neighbourhood guests were generally taken round the stables after luncheon, but at Lady Bugle's you were taken round the orchid houses.

Lady Bugle was very proud of the orchids, and well she might be. Year after year they had won prizes at all the horticultural shows. The initiative, however, was due to Sir Solomon. Orchid growing was his only country pursuit, and it was to the orchids alone that Lady Bugle owed her husband's rare visits to Slumbermere. Meanwhile choice specimens of cymbidium or cattleya that were not destined for shows or for the internal decoration of Slumbermere Hall were sent up to London, where they might be seen nightly in some fashionable restaurant or in a box at the theatre adorning the bosom of Sir Solomon's "chère amie."

Visiting the orchid houses took some time, and it was nearly half-past three when they returned to the house. Lady Bugle looked at the clock and said: "Gracious me, I am due at Woxham in a quarter-of-an-hour. I have a very important appointment there. I am afraid," she said, turning to the Husseys, "that I shall not have time to look at your camel to-day. But you must bring it over some other time."

On the way home Antonia said to her husband, "Really Lady Bugle's arrogance is at times most annoying. Fancy making us take the camel all that way and then not looking at it. There are moments when she puts one's patience to a very high test."

"Well, dear," said the Vicar, "next time she asks us we won't take it."

As they were shutting up the camel in the barn, Antonia said, "Did you notice what a very beautiful fur coat Lady Bugle was wearing?"

"It didn't seem to me," the Vicar replied, "that it was any better than your own coat, my dear."

"Good gracious," exclaimed Antonia, "how simple you are, dear. Why, Lady Bugle's coat must have cost at least a thousand pounds."

"A thousand pounds!" said the Vicar. "Well, that is a lot of money. And, if what you say is true, I think it is wicked to spend so much money on a fur coat that, to my inexperienced eye, looks just the same as any other. Think what a thousand pounds would mean to the church. That confounded poet fellow! I could have strangled him when he made those idiotic remarks at luncheon."

"Well, I can assure you," Antonia persisted, "it is a very beautiful coat, and I should be very happy if I had a coat like that."

"My dear Antonia," said the Vicar reprovingly, "you are talking like a vain and frivolous woman."

Antonia was about to make some retort, when she was suddenly struck by the expression on the face of the camel.

"The dear creature," said Antonia, stroking it affectionately. "Sometimes it looks quite human. I am sure it understands every word one says."

"I hope," said the Vicar, "that it didn't understand your foolish rhapsodies about Lady Bugle's coat. I should be ashamed of even an animal hearing such an unworthy manifestation of envy."

Antonia thought her husband was being rather unnecessarily serious. Really, she told herself, even the most intelligent men can show an extraordinary lack of understanding when it is a question of feminine apparel.

Every evening before retiring to rest, it was Lady Bugle's custom to take Mopsy for a little walk. The act known in humbler households as "putting the dog out" was one that Lady Bugle preferred to perform herself, rather than entrust it to the butler or some other menial.

That night, as Lady Bugle paced up and down in front of the house, she had the unpleasant sensation that she was being watched by someone. It was a pitch black night and very still. She could not see little Mopsy but she could hear her scratching on the gravel path. The door which she had left open suddenly swung to, and the only ray of light that emanated from the house was extinguished. She found herself in total darkness, and more than ever she had the feeling that she was being observed.

In spite of her majestic deportment and her awe-inspiring appearance, she was not really a courageous woman. Calling Mopsy, she turned back towards the house. As she passed the shrubbery she distinctly heard the foliage moving, and the sound of heavy breathing. She was terrified, and, at that moment, Mopsy set up a violent barking. Lady Bugle was unable to run, but she hurried with all her might towards the house. There was no doubt now that she was being followed. It was like the worst kind of nightmare. The sound of breathing was close behind her. Just as she reached the doorstep she caught her foot in her dress and fell headlong. She uttered a series of piercing screams and swooned away. Just before she fainted she had an impression of something tugging at her fur coat.

The servants, hearing the screams, came rushing out and found their mistress unconscious on the ground before the door and Mopsy barking furiously. The aggressor, whoever it was, had vanished.

As soon as Lady Bugle came to, her first instinct was to clutch her jewels. Nothing was missing. Then she thought of her fur coat.

"My coat!" she cried. "Where is my coat?"

"You had no coat on, My Lady," the butler said.

"Nonsense!" said Lady Bugle. "I was wearing my coat when I was attacked."

They searched for the coat everywhere, both outside and in the house, but Lady Bugle's coat was nowhere to be found.

"Send at once to the police station," she commanded. "Inform them that I have been assaulted by burglars in front of my own house and that a very valuable fur coat has been stolen."

Within half-an-hour the Superintendent arrived at the Hall and was granted an interview with Lady Bugle. By now she had recovered from her shock and was able to give a fairly clear account of her strange and alarming experience.

"I could see nothing," she said, "it was too dark. But I had the feeling that whoever it was that attacked me was of huge stature. Quite a giant. I remember distinctly noticing that he breathed very heavily and that the sound of his breathing came from above, a couple of feet at least above my head."

"That is a very useful bit of information, My Lady," said the Superintendent, making a note in his little book. "If I may say so, My Lady, you would have made a stunning detective."

"Please don't be flippant," said Her Ladyship haughtily, "I am in no mood at present for flippancy. This is a very serious business."

Next morning there was great excitement in the village over the assault on Lady Bugle and the theft of her fur coat. As is usual in country localities where so little happens that, when anything does, there is an excusable tendency to make the most of it, the rumours attained to a high pitch of fantasy. It was even said that an attempt had been made to abduct Lady Bugle, and old Beaton hinted darkly that Sir Solomon was at the bottom of it all. He came up to the back door of the Vicarage at an early hour for the purpose of making Bessie's flesh creep. Much as she distrusted the Verger, she was not averse to hearing gossip of a general nature.

"Aye, aye," he said to her, "there is summat fishy abroad. They never touched nothing but that there fur coat. I don't say as 'ow Sir Solomon 'ud go as far as murder. But 'e'd like her out of the way. And you mark my words 'e'll get 'er in the end. Oi knows what oi knows."

When Bessie went to open the front door of the Vicarage she was astonished to find a fur coat lying on the doorstep. Her head was so full of Beaton's insinuations about Sir Solomon and his abduction theory that, for a moment, she did not connect it with Lady Bugle and the incidents of the previous night. But the moment Antonia set eyes on it she at once exclaimed, "Why that is Lady Bugle's coat. What is it doing here?"

"I found it on the doorstep, Mum," Bessie explained.

For one brief moment Antonia thought that Lady Bugle had made her a present of it, but her illusions were quickly dispelled when Bessie cried out, "Why, Mum, of course it must be Lady Bugle's coat," and proceeded to tell her about the happenings at Slumbermere Hall.

"Good gracious!" exclaimed Antonia. "Poor Lady Bugle. It must be sent back at once. But how on earth did it come to be found on our doorstep?"

Bessie had no explanations to offer and the coat was packed up and returned forthwith to Lady Bugle.

The whole business was very mysterious. The police were unable to discover a single clue beyond those supplied by Lady Bugle herself. There were no footprints either at the Hall or at the Vicarage, but this was to be accounted for by the fact that there was a hard frost that night and everywhere the ground was like iron. All over the county and further afield the police were searching for the criminal, a man of gigantic stature who breathed heavily, but their investigations proved fruitless and the burglary affair at Lady Bugle's remained an unsolved mystery.

5

———✦✦✦———

An Exhumation

Father Picpus, the Roman Catholic priest, who lived about three miles from Slumbermere, was as much of a bugbear to Antonia as Mr. Scrimgeour, the organist, was to the Vicar. Antonia was a good deal "higher" than her husband; higher, indeed, to the extent of a rood, and of many other things as well. She was in favour of coloured vestments, six lights on the Altar, the changing of the Altar Frontals with the seasons and other symbols of "highness." Consequently she was more hostilely inclined towards Father Picpus than her husband, who was on quite friendly terms with him and would often, to Antonia's intense annoyance, stand up in his defence against her denunciations.

The Vicar knew all about the Church of Rome, and he did not think that it was ever likely to gain very much power in England. He was sorry to see so amiable and cultured a man as Father Picpus struggling misguidedly in the service of a lost cause. Not only a lost cause, as far as England was concerned, but a cause that was damned.

In the course of one of his defensive altercations with Antonia on the subject of Father Picpus, the Vicar said "I like him. He is an excellent man. He is sincere and I have no doubt he means well. It is a thousand pities that such a man should be doomed to Everlasting Damnation."

"If I were really sure of that," said Antonia, "it would ease my mind considerably."

It may seem strange that two habitually charitable people should be animated by such implacable sentiments of enmity, the Vicar towards Mr. Scrimgeour and Antonia towards Father Picpus. But in both cases these hatreds were inspired by the sincerity of their ideals. In Father Picpus Antonia saw an enemy to her faith, while the Vicar considered that Mr. Scrimgeour stood for all the things he most disliked and disapproved of, and, above all, he did not contribute to the efficiency with which the Vicar would have liked the musical side of the Church Service to have been conducted.

The Vicar did not suspect Mr. Scrimgeour of any form of immorality. On the contrary, he seemed to be a chaste young man, and he supported an aged mother. Nevertheless, the Vicar felt that there was something a little unwholesome about him. It certainly could not be said of him that he belonged to the type of man that the Vicar admired, the type of the "nice clean young Englishman." Mr. Scrimgeour was not athletic. He wore open collars and floppy ties. In his spare time he wrote poetry and he talked about artists and authors the Vicar had never heard of. Decidedly he was an æsthete, a decadent, one of the less creditable products of modern education, and he was certainly an anomaly in Slumbermere. But the Vicar might possibly have forgiven him all this, if it had not been for his lamentable performances on the organ.

The Vicar knew very little about music. In fact he did not really care for it at all, except as a traditional accompaniment of Divine Service. He was aware that music was pleasing to God and that there were harps in heaven. However, in spite of his indifference to the secular charms of music, he knew enough about it to realise that the voluntaries, as rendered by Mr. Scrimgeour were not calculated to enhance the impressiveness of his entries and that the hymns and anthems were perpetually going wrong. There was only one good point that the Vicar was obliged to concede in Mr. Scrimgeour's favour. He took a great deal of trouble with the choir-boys.

One morning the Vicar, opening his letters at breakfast, gave an exclamation of surprise and pleasure.

"My dear," he said to Antonia, "what do you think! The Bishop has expressed a desire to take luncheon with us next Wednesday."

"Well," said Antonia, "that will be very nice."

"He seems," the Vicar went on, "to have been very favourably impressed with the luncheon we gave him last year. He writes 'I have memories of a delicious leg of mutton.'"

"Indeed," said Antonia. "Then we will give him a leg of mutton this time. I will go at once and tell the butcher that he must be very careful to reserve us a nice one, as it is for the Bishop. And I think we might invite Lady Bugle to meet him."

"Yes," said the Vicar, "that is a very good idea."

"But I won't say anything to her about the Bishop coming," said Antonia, "so that, if she doesn't accept, she will be very disappointed afterwards when she hears it was to meet the Bishop."

"Do as you like my dear," said the Vicar in a detached voice. He was not going to associate himself with these petty feline amenities.

Antonia went off to interview the butcher. She also wrote to Lady Bugle who accepted the invitation.

The Husseys did not give many luncheon parties, but when they did, it seemed to both the Vicar and his wife that they were very successful. Annie was an excellent cook; the fare was simple, but very good of its kind. The Vicar, though averse to ritual in the church service, liked to see it at the luncheon table. Grace was said both before and after the meal. Bessie carried round the dishes with the pontifical air of a high priestess. But the great moment was the arrival of the joint. It was borne into the room on a large platter, under a silver dish cover, a family heirloom bequeathed to Antonia by her parents. The dish was set down before the Vicar who rose to his feet. After a moment of impressive suspense he would whip off the cover as though he were performing a conjuring trick, and hand it to Bessie. Even the grandest and most blasé of guests never failed to be impressed.

On the morning of the auspicious day upon which the Bishop was coming to luncheon, the Vicar went out into the garden where he found Antonia planting primroses on little Jock's grave. It was the anniversary of his death. The camel stood beside her watching the proceeding with an air of interest. The Vicar saw that Antonia had tears in her eyes. What a sweet, tender-hearted woman she was!

Under the stress of her emotion she was digging rather wildly and scattering the earth in all directions.

"Oh! be careful, my dear," said the Vicar, "or you will be displacing the body of your little dog. I remember he was not buried very deep."

Antonia laid down her trowel.

"My poor little Jock," she said, "it distresses me to think of his poor little body lying there in the cold earth. I often wish that he had been otherwise disposed of. Lady Bugle had her pug stuffed, and very nice it looks too. I wish now that I had thought of having dear little Jock stuffed. The idea never occurred to me. I should feel far happier if he were in a nice glass case somewhere in the house. But alas! now it is too late. Of course," she went on, "I might still dig up his remains and put them in a nice mahogany box. Then I could keep him in the drawing-room, and I shouldn't wake up on cold nights, as I often do, and think of my poor little Jock out here in the freezing soil."

The Vicar was alarmed at the suggestion.

"My dear," he said, "I shouldn't do that. It is better . . . " He was about to say "to let sleeping dogs lie," but he thought it might perhaps sound a trifle heartless, and left the sentence unfinished.

He looked at his watch.

"Antonia dear," he said, "it is growing late, and the Bishop will soon be arriving. Hadn't you better put the camel away and come into the house? I am sure that there are a lot of little things that need attending to."

Antonia sighed and gathered up her gardening basket and her trowel.

"Very well," she said, "I will finish planting the primroses later."

She led the camel to the stables. As she was in the act of closing the barn door, she was struck by an extraordinarily sympathetic expression in the eyes of the beast.

"Ah," she said, "you seem to understand my feelings so well, even though you are but a dumb animal. Had you known my little Jock, I am sure that you would have loved him too."

In inviting Lady Bugle to meet the Bishop, Antonia had made a grave mistake. Indeed, had Antonia mentioned in her letter that the Bishop was coming to luncheon, Lady Bugle would have most certainly refused the invitation. She had no friendly feelings for the Bishop; neither did the Bishop care very much for Lady Bugle. He considered her preten-

tious and vulgar, while Lady Bugle thought that the Bishop was super-
cilious and inclined to be patronising. In fact, on one occasion, it had
come to an actual tiff at a Committee Meeting in Woxham. Lady Bugle
was apt to domineer at Committee Meetings and, when there were no
important members of County Families present, she would "throw her
weight" so ponderously that all opposition was crushed. The Bishop,
however, was not in the least intimidated by Lady Bugle's autocratic
methods, and had openly snubbed her in a way that she could neither
forgive nor forget.

Thus, when they met in the Vicarage drawing-room, their greetings
were anything but cordial. The Vicar and his wife were neither of them
gifted with any great subtlety of discernment where social amenities
were concerned, and they merely attributed the reciprocated coldness
to the reserve peculiar to important people.

As soon as they were seated at the luncheon table, the trouble began.
The Bishop proceeded studiously to ignore Lady Bugle who retaliated
by treating every remark the Bishop made with contemptuous comments. These, however, were not directed openly at the Bishop but delivered either in the form of a soliloquy, or muttered in an audible sotto
voce to the Vicar.

The Husseys, when at last the eccentricity of this conversational
technique began to dawn upon them, were very much perplexed. Antonia thought that perhaps Lady Bugle was feeling indisposed. She was
known to suffer from bilious attacks which made life rather difficult for
people in her immediate vicinity.

The Vicar, realising that something was going wrong, wrestled cou-
rageously with the difficulties of the situation. But the air was filled with
electricity and it seemed as though, at any moment, the storm might
burst. The conversation was tactfully led to a discussion of foreign
travel. That, at least, seemed to be a subject that might prove less con-
troversial than many others, and one that the Bishop enjoyed talking
about. Antonia supplied a few reminiscences of her early missionary
life, and, for a while, Lady Bugle's aggressive policy seemed to have
somewhat abated. The Vicar remarked that it was a long time since he

had been abroad, and went on to expatiate on the discomforts he and Antonia had been obliged to put up with on a trip to Switzerland they had made during their honeymoon.

Then the Bishop took up the theme. "My wife and I," he said, "had a very curious experience in Italy last year."

"Oh Italy!" said Lady Bugle, addressing her remarks to no one in particular, "Nobody goes to Italy nowadays. All the best people are going to Egypt."

The Bishop flushed and raised his eyebrows in an ominous manner. It looked as though at last he were about to deliver himself of a crushing retort and annihilate Lady Bugle.

Luckily at that moment a diversion was provided by the entry of the leg of mutton. Bessie bore in the dish in her most pontifical manner and set it down before the Vicar. The silver dish cover had been newly polished and filled the little dining-room with effulgence. For a moment Antonia caught a glimpse of the Bishop's angry face reflected in it as though in a distorting mirror.

The Vicar rose to his feet and said to the Bishop with a facetious pomposity, "Here, My Lord, is your leg of mutton."

He lifted the cover and, to everyone's amazement, there was disclosed, reposing in a pool of gravy, the skeleton of a small dog.

Antonia realised at once from the mouldering collar that it was the last mortal remains of her darling little Jock and burst into tears. The Vicar gasped and turned to Bessie who stood rooted to the spot, her mouth opening and shutting in a way that reminded one of the spasms of a dying fish.

"What is the meaning of this?" the Vicar enquired.

Bessie's mouth continued to open and shut but no sound came from her lips.

At that moment Annie burst into the room with the missing leg of mutton on a plate. Someone, she declared breathlessly, must have tried to steal it. She had found it on the ground outside the kitchen window.

"I will enquire into this matter afterwards," said the Vicar, handing her the dish with the skeleton, which she hastily removed.

Although Annie assured the Vicar that the leg of mutton had been well wiped, neither the Bishop nor Lady Bugle fancied that it had been much improved by its strange adventure. The Bishop took a very small helping which he left on his plate, while Lady Bugle refused it altogether.

From this point onwards, as you may well imagine, the luncheon party grew more difficult to cope with than ever. Antonia, tearfully excusing herself, rose from the table and hurried out of the room in order to rescue the remains of her beloved pet and put it in a safe place, leaving her husband alone to deal with the situation. He could think of no apology and no explanation to offer.

"It would appear," he said, "that it must have been the skeleton of my wife's little dog, though how it came to appear on the luncheon table I am at a loss to conjecture."

Neither the Bishop nor Lady Bugle seemed inclined to discuss the matter any further. Nor did either of them seem very conversationally disposed, so that the Vicar was obliged to keep up a sort of desperate monologue.

Antonia returned after a while, but she was so upset that her presence did not contribute very much towards relieving the general gloom.

The Bishop left immediately after luncheon, and Lady Bugle left very soon after the Bishop. "Please," she said as she bade them farewell, "never think of asking me again to meet that detestable man."

The Vicar went into the kitchen and held an inquisition. But nothing could be elicited that tended in any way to clear up the mystery. Annie confessed that, after she had covered the leg of mutton with the dish cover, she had left it by the open window in the kitchen waiting for Bessie to take it into the dining-room. She admitted that she had gone for a moment into the scullery while it was there, but both Bessie and Annie were unanimous in their conviction that nobody could have entered the yard and effected the substitution without their noticing it.

"My dear," said the Vicar to Antonia, "we seem to have become the butt of a series of senseless practical jokes. First the camel, then Lady Bugle's coat and now this last indignity. Though what may be the object of this persecution I cannot for the life of me imagine. If it continues I shall most certainly invoke the protection of the police."

"I should not be at all surprised," said Antonia, "if Father Picpus had not something to do with it."

6

—⟨∞∞⟩—

Easter Decorations

The Vicar insisted on Jock's skeleton being replaced in the grave, and Antonia had to abandon her idea of keeping it in the house. As a matter of fact the mysterious disinterment, instead of reviving tender memories, had the effect of weakening them and reconciling Antonia to her loss.

When formerly she thought of her little Jock, she always used to visualize him as an "affectionate wee doggie," with well brushed coat, alert ears and wagging tail, and the sight of his mouldering bones had filled her with horror and repulsion, hastening the curative properties of time.

The urge of her motherly nature and the need for something to love drove her more than ever to transfer her affections to the camel. Every day she grew more devoted to the beast.

Apart from these natural and amiable sentiments, there were others more romantic. As a girl she had always been strangely attracted by the Orient. Her father and mother had selected the Far East for the field of their missionary activities and she had spent a good part of her youth in the East. After the demise of her parents and her marriage to the Reverend Aloysius Hussey, she had settled down in England and had embarked upon a new and very different life. Years of parochial environment had almost, but not quite, obliterated her Eastern memories. She was now perfectly contented with her lot. Devotion to her husband and to her parochial duties occupied her mind to the exclusion of everything else. Nevertheless she was apt, in her idle moments, to indulge in day-dreams, and in these day-dreams the Orient would often figure in a sublimated form.

Although she was, as I have said, perfectly satisfied with the life she was leading, there were nevertheless moments when she took pleasure in picturing to herself an entirely different existence and one that was in the most violent contrast with her own. All women are by nature romantic, but romance, alas! is seldom compatible with respectability, and Antonia was essentially a respectable woman. Thus, whenever her day-dreams carried her too extravagantly into the region of romance, she would check herself with a sense of guilt almost as though she were indulging in some secret vice.

Let me disclose to you the habitual trend of these visionary meanderings, although, in doing so, I feel, I must confess, that I am acting rather like a cad. It is as though I were inviting you to peep at the excellent Vicar's wife through the keyhole of her bathroom door, or surreptitiously lifting her petticoats to enable you to observe a secret blemish.

In these day-dreams, Antonia would picture herself being carried off by some marauding Arab tribe and becoming the darling of a handsome sheikh; or else, captured on the high seas by pirates and sold as a slave, she would end up in the harem of some cruel, voluptuous Pasha. But all the same it was all very nice and respectable; the Sheikh, like the heroes of later popular fiction, was a perfect gentleman, and, while in the harem there might possibly be other wives, Antonia herself was the only legitimate one.

Nevertheless, in spite of these reservations, you will agree that they were rather audacious day-dreams for a clergyman's wife. But you must not think any the worse of her for that. Do we not all need the occasional stimulant of imagining something different from the actual lives we are leading? That is why we read a novel or go to the theatre. Therefore we can all the more readily forgive Antonia her day-dreams, for she very rarely read a novel and never went to the theatre.

Thus, you see, the camel was for her a visible symbol of the Orient. It was a tangible re-evocation of her early memories which now, in her middle-age, were beginning to assume a sentimental aspect. In addition to this, the animal seemed to be genuinely attached to her.

Camels have never had the reputation for being affectionate. On the contrary, even in the most benevolent of natural history books, they are described as arrogant and ego-centric, and it seemed to Antonia that she was being specially privileged in being favoured with such an obvious devotion.

Now that the hunting season was over, Antonia ventured to resume her rides, and the effect on the rural population was very much what she had prophesied. At first she was apt to be followed about by screaming hordes of schoolchildren, but after a while the novelty wore off and they merely greeted her passage with cap-touchings and curtseyings as in the days when she used to drive about in her pony-cart. The very horses in the neighbourhood grew accustomed to the camel, and when she met Admiral Sefton-Porter out riding she was able to stop and converse with him without upsetting Stalwart.

Antonia knew that she ought to go and visit old Mrs. Cattermole in order to try and clear up the misunderstanding about the baby, but she kept putting it off. She dreaded the heat in the cottage and all the shouting the visit would entail. It appeared the old lady still clung to her delusion and the Vicar had come to hear about it.

"I understand," he said to Antonia, "that old Mrs. Cattermole has got it into her head that we have a baby at the Vicarage. Beaton tells me she is making a patchwork coverlet and that she keeps on saying it is for the Vicar's baby. This is most annoying and it tends to bring ridicule upon us. I think, my dear, you had better go and see her as soon as possible and try and make her understand that there has never been any question of a baby at the Vicarage."

So Antonia went. But it was of little use. She brought the camel up to the cottage so that the old lady could see it through the window. Mrs. Cattermole was neither surprised nor impressed. She had read so much in the newspapers about the progress of modern science that a camel seemed far less startling to her than a motor car or electric light. She was much more interested in the baby.

"Well well," she said, "I daresay you know best, Ma'am. I've no doubt he'll take to it when he gets a bit older. But I should have thought, myself, that a nice goat-cart or a pony would have done better for the precious mite."

Antonia was then shown the patchwork quilt. The old lady was obviously taking great pleasure in her labours.

"There ain't much more to do now, Ma'am," she said, "and you'll have it within a month or so. But I don't mind saying as how I'll miss the occupation when it's done. It kind of keeps my spirits up when the days is dull."

So, once again, Antonia had neither the courage nor the heart to disillusion the old lady, and things remained as they were.

Easter was approaching and the time had come for decorating the church with flowers so that, on the event of this important Christian feast, it should be resplendent with God's most graceful handiwork.

Antonia always took great pains with the Easter decorations and the villagers, as well as their more prosperous neighbours, all sent offerings in accordance with their means. Lady Bugle generally sent a lavish assortment of hothouse flowers, but this year, for some reason or other, the contribution from Slumbermere Hall consisted merely of a few bunches of violets, some daffodils and primroses such as might have come from the humblest cottages.

Antonia was very indignant.

"Really!" she exclaimed. "The stingy old thing! It would have been better if she had sent nothing at all. And all those greenhouses full of lovely orchids."

"I fear," said the Vicar, "that Lady Bugle prefers the immediate satisfaction of gaining prizes on earth to the ultimate joy of obtaining rewards in Heaven."

It was true that a Horticultural Show was imminent and Lady Bugle was reserving her orchids for this occasion.

The Vicar added that the church would look just as well decked out in simple country flowers without the aid of Lady Bugle's exotics. It would be more in keeping with the spirit of the thing. However Antonia continued to protest that she considered that Lady Bugle had acted with an unjustifiable meanness.

Antonia had taught the camel to carry a basket in its mouth and she found this very useful when she was gardening. The camel would follow her about, bearing a load of flower pots and plants with a dignity that almost rivalled Bessie's pontifical handling of dishes.

The camel was now being employed in bringing flowers to the door of the church where Antonia, assisted by Mr. Scrimgeour, was engaged in supervising the adornment of the interior. Antonia was expressing her views to the organist about Lady Bugle's meanness with such vehemence that even the camel seemed affected by his mistress's indignation.

Mr. Scrimgeour always assisted Antonia on these occasions and she found him most helpful. He had a decided talent for floral arrangement.

Antonia rather liked Mr. Scrimgeour. Indeed she thought of him almost as a protégé. He entered into her category of people to be sorry for. She was sorry about his aged mother. She was sorry he played so badly on the organ. She was sorry that her husband disliked him so much. In fact he was decidedly an object for compassion. He seemed to Antonia rather a sad young man, and whenever she met him she always did her best to cheer him up. And so when the Vicar came into the church he found them laughing quite merrily. This angered him and he said to Antonia afterwards, "I don't think, my dear, that it is necessary for you to encourage that Scrimgeour."

"Poor Mr. Scrimgeour," replied Antonia with a sigh. "He has so few pleasures. He must lead a melancholy life with that old mother of his. And I really don't know what you mean when you say that I am encouraging him."

"Well, you were joking with him in the church this morning. I do not consider that God's House is a very suitable place for ribald laughter."

"Ribald?" exclaimed Antonia, raising her eyebrows. "That surely is an exaggerated term. We were merely laughing about Lady Bugle."

"Whatever Lady Bugle may have done or not done," said the Vicar with some asperity, "that is no excuse for uncharitable mockery in a church. With regard to Scrimgeour I will say no more. You know my views."

Antonia remained silent. She curbed the retort that rose to her lips and decided to reserve it for the next time she caught her husband hobnobbing with Father Picpus.

On Easter Sunday morning Antonia entered the church at an early hour for a final survey of the decorations. To her amazement she found the steps of the altar strewn with orchids. She beheld, with startled eyes, a thick carpet of cymbidiums, cattleyas and odontoglossums covering the ground in multi-coloured profusion. "An eleventh hour repentance," she told herself, "on the part of Lady Bugle."

She called the Vicar, and they hastily arranged the sprays in vases. Antonia was in favour of placing them on the altar, but the Vicar thought they were a little too exotic and unsuitable, and so they arranged them in prominent positions round the lectern and the pulpit instead.

Lady Bugle did not appear at the Service that morning. The Vicar and his wife thought that this was very strange, as she rarely missed a Sunday and this was Easter Sunday and she had sent those lovely orchids.

The reason for Lady Bugle's absence soon became known, and the circumstances that caused it created no little stir in the village. It appeared that on the previous night someone had broken into the orchid houses and removed some of the rarest and most valuable orchids. But this was by no means all. In order to effect an entry (as the doors were locked) the marauder had smashed a number of panes of glass and, that night, as so often happens in the capricious English springtime, there had been a severe frost, and the cold night air, entering through the broken panes, had worked havoc among the more delicate varieties of cattleya.

Lady Bugle, as you know, was not only very proud of her orchids but she was at that moment hoping to win a number of important prizes at the coming Horticultural Shows. You may therefore easily imagine her rage. It was so violent that it brought on an acute bilious attack. Nor was her condition improved when she learnt that the stolen orchids had figured prominently in the Easter decorations at Slumbermere church. She sent for her secretary and, from her bed, dictated a snorter to the Vicar.

"I do not require an explanation," so the letter ran, "of how my valuable orchids, stolen from my orchid houses, came to form part of the decoration of your church. Neither do I intend to take legal proceedings which I should be fully justified in doing. But you must clearly understand that, for the future, all intercourse between Slumbermere Hall and the Vicarage must cease."

The Vicar was horrified when he heard of the raid on Lady Bugle's orchid houses but he was still more horrified when he received Lady Bugle's letter. He realised that, once again, he had been made the victim of a mysterious practical joke. He was now determined to carry out his intention of invoking the protection of the police. He had a long interview with the Superintendent who promised to instruct the policeman on duty to keep an eye on the Vicarage.

But what upset the Vicar more than anything else was the loss of Lady Bugle's friendship and patronage. He wrote her grovelling letters of apology; (he could not explain, as no explanation seemed possible) but his letters remained unanswered. He begged a personal interview which was refused. And when, one day, Lady Bugle came face to face with the Husseys in the main street of Slumbermere, she cut them.

7

An Invitation to Dinner

Antonia was beginning to be seriously perturbed about her husband. He seemed to be taking the estrangement from Lady Bugle very much to heart and no longer manifested that buoyant cheerfulness with which he was wont to confront the little worries of daily life; he also was beginning to complain of loss of appetite and sleeplessness. She wished that they could have gone away for a little holiday to the sea-side but there was a busy time ahead, and it would be useless to try and prevail on the Vicar to shirk any of his responsibilities. A change of air and scene might have done a world of good, but it was not to be thought of, and the Vicar's temper grew rapidly worse. Domestic bickerings that formerly would have resolved themselves in laughter or immediate reconciliations began to assume more serious proportions and one day at luncheon Antonia had quite an unpleasant scene with her husband on the subject of Father Picpus.

She had perhaps been a little unreasonable in her judgments and the Vicar's defence of his Papist colleague was rather deliberately designed to annoy. The argument ended with the Vicar banging on the table with his fist and saying, "I shall not modify my behaviour to Father Picpus for you, or for anyone else. And I must beg you not to attempt to dictate to me on the subject of my duty towards my neighbour, as I won't stand it!"

Never before had the Vicar spoken to his wife in such an authoritative manner, and Antonia felt deeply hurt. She rose with dignity from the luncheon table, saying as she did so, in a somewhat defiant tone, "I am going into the wood with Mr. Scrimgeour to pick bluebells."

Previous to the altercation Antonia had not had the slightest intention to pick flowers with Mr. Scrimgeour. She had just hit upon the idea as an act of retaliation, but now she was determined to go through with it. She heard the strains of the organ coming from the church and she knew that Mr. Scrimgeour was there practising. The organist accepted her invitation with alacrity. He was flattered by the attention. He was also very fond of flowers.

The Vicar remained seated for a while in the dining-room. That perverse, distorting demon that walks abroad in our brains when we are suffering from nervous depression began its fell work upon the Vicar and let fall a tiny seed of jealousy. Was it possible, he asked himself, that Antonia was really attracted by that confounded organist? He did not believe that any woman could feel anything but repugnance for such a man. And yet women were strange cattle. He certainly did not put it beyond that slimy fellow to make up to another man's wife. It was, in fact, just the sort of thing one might expect from him, and the mere thought of the despised and hated Scrimgeour daring to do such a thing . . . No, it did not bear thinking of!

An enforced distraction in the shape of a Ruri-decanal conference in Woxham came to interrupt his brooding. He went to his room to collect his notes and to fasten on his bicycle clips. Unluckily, as he was wheeling his bicycle out of the porch, he caught a glimpse of Antonia and Mr. Scrimgeour, armed with baskets, disappearing into the wood.

Now if the Vicar had only known, there was not the least likelihood of Mr. Scrimgeour making up to his wife, nor indeed to any other woman. As a matter of fact Mr. Scrimgeour never felt quite at his ease in feminine society. That is no doubt why Antonia thought him sad. However, he felt considerably more at his ease in Antonia's company than he did with many other women he knew, and precisely for the reason that he felt that the Vicar's wife would not be likely to require from him anything beyond a mere respectful subservience.

If Antonia could but have seen Mr. Scrimgeour alone with the choir-boys she would certainly not have thought him sad. After choir-practice, when no one was present, Mr. Scrimgeour became as a choir-boy himself. He would romp with them, enter into their jokes and even allow them to take liberties that were sometimes quite unseemly. His association with the boys was not confined to choir-practice alone. He took a keen interest also in their private lives. He encouraged them to come to him with their confidences and would give them what he considered good advice, and sometimes also an occasional small present.

His favourite chum was a lad called Antony. Antony was a bit of a rascal and caused a good deal of trouble both to his parents and to Mr. Gudgeon the Schoolmaster. But he had a good voice and was not ill looking. He was certainly not the kind of boy who would naturally be impressed or attracted by Mr. Scrimgeour's æsthetic or intellectual qualities. Nevertheless he was intelligent enough to realise the benefits that might accrue to him through the retention of Mr. Scrimgeour's friendship. The thing that had contributed most to win his attachment had been the gift of a football, a possession that had gained for him the admiration and the envy of his comrades. Gratitude has been described as "A recognition of favours past and an expectation of favours to come." Antony's gratitude to Mr. Scrimgeour was of the expectant variety. And so suffered himself with a good grace to be taken for long country rambles, to be told about Art and Literature and to be made to learn the Latin names of flowers.

Thus if only the Vicar could have known, when he saw Mr. Scrimgeour escorting his wife into the wood, how much rather Mr. Scrimgeour would have preferred to have Antony as a companion than Antonia, it would certainly have taken a load off his mind.

After picking the bluebells and dismissing Mr. Scrimgeour, Antonia returned to the house and, finding that her husband had not yet returned, she went out for a ride on the camel. On the way she met with Beaton the Verger, and she stopped to have a chat with him, in the course of which the old man gave her a disquieting piece of news.

It appeared that Admiral Sefton-Porter had invited Father Picpus to dine with him that evening.

Antonia's mind, quickened by suspicion, began to scent the most devilish machinations on the part of her enemy. Obviously, she told herself, Father Picpus had designs on the Admiral who, she feared, was not quite as staunch a Protestant as he ought to have been. These naval gentlemen, in their old age, were apt to grow a little weak-minded, and though prone to bullying and obstinacy in their worldly conduct, they might easily be led astray where religion was concerned. What a triumph for Father Picpus if he were able to boast that he had persuaded one of the principal landowners in the neighbourhood to embrace the errors of Rome! The more she contemplated this possibility the more agitated she became, and whenever Antonia became agitated she had the habit of expressing her thoughts aloud.

"He must not dine with the Admiral to-night!" she cried. "No indeed he must not! But alas! what can be done to prevent it?"

Obsessed by these thoughts, she returned to the Vicarage where she found the Vicar far more agreeably disposed than when she had left him after luncheon. He had very much enjoyed the Ruri-decanal Conference. He had played quite a prominent part in the transactions and had been listened to with attention and respect. In fact he had come away from the Conference with a sense of enhanced personality and in a happy frame of mind that induced him to take a less pessimistic view of Lady Bugle's estrangement and also to wonder whether, after all, he had not been a little rash in his suspicions about Mr. Scrimgeour and Antonia. Indeed he was able to refer to the matter in quite a jocular spirit.

"Well, my dear," he said, "and did you find many bluebells? I've no doubt Scrimgeour will compose a symphony about your little expedition. I only pray that he may not attempt to play it as a voluntary."

Antonia was overjoyed by her husband's apparent change of heart and his return to his normal self. She thought it wiser not to broach a subject that might provoke a renewal of acrimonious discussion, and she kept silent on the subject of the Admiral's invitation to Father Picpus.

Meanwhile Father Picpus was setting out on his way to dine with the Admiral. He bicycled into Slumbermere and, after leaving his bicycle at the "Resplendent Peacock," he proceeded to take the path through the wood which was the shortest way from the village to the Admiral's house. It was growing dark when he entered the wood and, as he reached the gate that led to the Admiral's park, he saw a huge form looming in front of him. It was the camel.

"Dear me," he said to himself. "The creature has evidently got loose. I wonder if I ought to go back and inform the Husseys. But I'm afraid that if I were to do so it would most certainly make me late for dinner and I understand that the Admiral is a great stickler for punctuality."

And so he hastened onwards. But as he approached nearer to the camel he saw that it was looking at him very strangely. Its eyes were glaring, and it seemed to him as though it were foaming slightly at the mouth. "Good gracious!" he thought. "It looks to me as if the animal had gone mad."

The camel made a threatening advance in his direction and Father Picpus took refuge behind a bush. But the camel continued to follow him. Father Picpus retreated still further into the wood. The camel was slightly impeded by the close-growing saplings which, however, Father Picpus realised, would afford but meagre protection if the animal really meant business. There was an ominous cracking of the branches and, spurred by terror, Father Picpus did a thing he had not done since the days of his boyhood. He climbed a tree.

Panting with fear and with the unwonted exertion, he swung himself desperately on to an overhanging bough which, luckily, proved to be just out of the monster's reach. Baulked of its prey, the camel remained under the tree glaring up at the unfortunate priest and from time to time baring its teeth at him in the most ferocious manner. And there it remained.

Dusk deepened into night and the moon rose on the strange spectacle of a Roman Catholic priest in a torn and dishevelled soutane, imprisoned in a tree like one of the damned souls in Dante's Inferno, while the camel, a fearsome sentinel, kept guard below.

At intervals Father Picpus shouted for help, but nobody came to his rescue. Nor was there any sound except the occasional cry of a nightbird and the distant chimes of Slumbermere Church marking the weary hours.

At last, when midnight had struck, the camel gave up its hostile vigil and moved away in the direction of the village.

Father Picpus remained in the tree for a good half-hour after the camel's departure. Only when he had satisfied himself that the beast had really gone, did he venture to clamber down from his perch and hurry out of the wood in the opposite direction, glancing fearfully over his shoulder lest the camel should take it into its head to return. He made his way to Admiral Sefton-Porter's house, but when he reached it he realised from the complete silence and darkness reigning there that its occupants must have gone to bed. He thought it inadvisable, under the circumstances, to waken the Admiral and make his apologies with such a strange, improbable tale. Nor did he venture to return to Slumbermere to get his bicycle lest he should encounter the camel who might still be wandering about in the wood. He was thus obliged to make a detour of more than six miles before he reached his home.

8

The Poems

Admiral Sefton-Porter was very much annoyed with Father Picpus. He had waited nearly three-quarters of an hour for him and the dinner had not been improved by the delay. The Admiral had got the idea into his head that all Roman Catholic priests were gourmets, and he had taken a great deal of trouble over the menu. He had also invited one or two Roman Catholic neighbours to meet him, people whom he would never have thought of inviting had it not been for the fact that they were co-religionists and therefore likely to be more congenial to the guest of honour than some of the Admiral's Protestant friends. And so, when the guest of honour failed to materialise, the Admiral found himself faced with a spoiled dinner and a party of guests in whom he was not particularly interested. Nor did the letter of apology he received, with its highly improbable excuse, tend to make him think any more kindly of Father Picpus.

Antonia's fears of a possible conversion of Admiral Sefton-Porter to Roman Catholicism were quite unfounded. The Admiral would never have dreamt of deserting, in his old age, the faith in which he had been brought up. He would as lief have got himself naturalised a Frenchman. But, as a landowner and a magistrate, he thought it would be a good thing to let it be seen that he viewed local religious problems with tolerance and impartiality. It is true that Father Picpus's suavity of manner sometimes struck the Admiral as being slightly "foreign" but on the other hand Father Picpus had one quality that, in the Admiral's eyes, overrode every other possible defect. He never contradicted.

After a good night's rest, Father Picpus, on thinking over his adventure with the camel, felt rather ashamed of it; he feared that it might place him in a ridiculous light. In his letter to the Admiral he begged him not to mention the matter to anyone. However, the Admiral (as soon as he recovered his good humour) was unable to resist making a good story out of it, and reports of the camel's nocturnal assault on Father Picpus were not long in reaching the Vicarage.

Antonia, when she heard of it, hotly denied the possibility of such a thing and said, "I have always known that Father Picpus was untruthful. I now have every reason to believe that he drinks."

The mollifying effect of the Ruri-decanal Conference had soon worn off and the Vicar relapsed once more into a state of nervous dejection. His irritability increased and so did his obsession of an amorous intrigue between his wife and Mr. Scrimgeour. He was continually on the look out for signs to confirm his suspicions and, when people are in this frame of mind, they generally succeed in finding them.

Antonia, though painfully aware that by some process unknown to herself she had become a source of annoyance to her husband, was completely ignorant of its principal cause. She was so far removed from having any sentiments towards Mr. Scrimgeour other than those prompted by her generous and motherly nature that it never entered into her head to think that her relationship to the organist could be interpreted as anything other than innocent. However she was often exasperated by the unreasonable asperity of the Vicar's remarks and, reacting subconsciously to a feminine instinct, she would occasionally indulge in a laudatory appreciation of Mr. Scrimgeour, with the deliberate intention of "getting back" on her husband. Even the most exemplary types of womanhood, when provoked, find it difficult to resist the temptation to tease.

Thus she came to regard Mr. Scrimgeour as a weapon with which to retaliate upon her husband, thinking of him merely as an object of the Vicar's dislike and not at all as a suspected lover.

If the Vicar had only been sensible enough to give voice to his suspicions instead of brooding over them in silence, things might have turned out very differently and a tragedy would have been averted. But the Vicar, though candid and outspoken in most things, was both proud and prudish where there was any question of sex, and he feared that if he were to accuse Antonia openly of inconstancy it would lower his dignity and emphasise an unseemly situation. Tormented as he was by his present state of doubt and anxiety, he dreaded bringing matters to a head. Supposing, for instance, Antonia were to admit her guilty passion and ask for liberation.

The object of the Vicar's jealous suspicions was sitting at his desk by the open window looking affectionately at a little album which bore the inscription "Poems by Herbert Scrimgeour."

Mr. Scrimgeour was fond of expressing his moods, his reactions to nature or to people in lyrical effusions. It is a trite reflection that poets are often apt to feel more inspired in the spring than at other seasons of the year, and this particular spring, what with the fine weather, the crop of spring flowers which this year had been more profuse than usual, and the companionship of Antony, Mr. Scrimgeour had felt himself literally bubbling with inspiration.

He had composed quite a number of short poems, the best of which he had copied out into an album in his neat, punctilious handwriting, and they looked so nice that he wondered whether it might not be possible to get them published. Lady Bugle knew a lot of literary people. He would ask her to help him. How wonderful it would be to see them in print, to go into a bookshop and see "Poems by Herbert Scrimgeour" reposing on the counter! And then there would be criticisms in the newspapers. That would be wonderful too! But of course some of the criticisms might be unkind. He would not like that. He had a very sensitive nature and would be easily wounded by unkindness especially if it were to appear in print. (Mr. Scrimgeour was not sufficiently conversant with the ways of the literary world to know that, owing to the unfortunate affair of Keats, no modern critic ever dares to be too unkind about poetry.) However he decided he would take the risk for the sake of the prestige that the mere fact of having a book published would give him in the village. Even the Vicar would not fail to be impressed.

Now it happened that nearly all the poems he had selected as worthy of publication were dedicated to his choir-boy friend Antony, and the name Antony perpetually recurred throughout the verses. As some of the poems were of a slightly erotic nature, he had considered it advisable to change the name Antony to Antonia, following the example of other Platonist poets who have lacked the courage of their convictions. It had never occurred to him that Antonia was the name of the Vicar's wife, and this is not so improbable as it might seem. The Vicar invariably referred to Antonia as "my wife" and in public he always addressed her as "my dear" while Antonia, except in letters addressed to intimate friends was in the habit of signing herself "A. Hussey."

Had Antonia been privileged to see the poems their titles and their contents would certainly have startled her.

"To Antonia bathing."

"To Antonia singing in the dusk."

"To Antonia in the apple tree."

"To Antonia birds nesting."

And there was one that was particularly audacious, beginning with the lines, "When first I held thee in my arms, Antonia, and pressed my lips to thine."

While engaged in these pleasant thoughts of publication and literary fame, Mr. Scrimgeour looked out of the window and saw the Vicar's wife approaching on the camel. She was coming to pay his mother a visit. Mr. Scrimgeour did not wish to be involved, as he had made an appointment with Antony to go birds nesting in the woods. He waited until Antonia had gone round to the front of the house and then stole out through the back door.

Mr. Scrimgeour's mother was sitting on the little lawn in front of her house enjoying the morning sun. Antonia had brought her a basketful of plants for her garden.

Mrs. Scrimgeour was believed to be immensely old, indeed almost the oldest inhabitant of Slumbermere. Her son, however, was only thirty; so it seemed unlikely that she could really be much more than seventy. Nevertheless the legend of her great age was accepted by nearly everyone in the neighbourhood, and people were very kind to her, although there were some who thought she had a tendency to trade on it and to employ it as a device for attracting sympathy.

Antonia was very sorry for Mrs. Scrimgeour for being so old, and did what she could to try and cheer the old lady's remaining years with little gifts.

Mrs. Scrimgeour thanked Antonia profusely for the plants.

"Albert will plant them out," she said, "when he has time. He is for ever writing poetry nowadays and seldom seems to have any time to spare for me."

"Writing poetry?" said Antonia. "How very nice. I am quite devoted to poetry."

"Well, Mrs. Hussey, I can't say what sort of stuff it is. He never shows it to me. Personally I don't approve of him wasting his time in that way."

"Wasting his time, Mrs. Scrimgeour? Oh you mustn't say that. Perhaps he has a real gift for it. One never knows."

"I very much doubt it," said Mrs. Scrimgeour. "All I can say is that it makes him neglect his poor old mother. I sometimes call for him when he's in there writing poetry and he pretends not to hear."

"Well I'm sure that's very naughty of him, Mrs. Scrimgeour. But the artistic temperament you know."

"I know I'm only a poor old woman," said Mrs. Scrimgeour, "and I ought to have been in my grave a long time ago."

"Oh don't say that, Mrs. Scrimgeour. You are looking wonderfully well; and I'm sure it is very nice to be able to write poetry even though your son may not be a second Lord Tennyson. I must say I should like very much to see the poems he writes and I hope some day he will show them to me."

As Antonia was coming out of the gate, the Vicar happened to be passing down the lane near the house. He saw the camel's head appearing above the hedge and he hastily hid himself behind a bush. He was afraid that if his wife were to see him in the neighbourhood of the Scrimgeour's house she might suspect him of prying on her. In ordinary circumstances the Vicar would have been loth to indulge in any form of dissimulation, but jealousy, alas! is apt to play strange pranks on the working of our brains. He was convinced that Antonia's visit to Mrs. Scrimgeour had merely been a subterfuge to enable her to arrange an assignation with her son, and he did not wish to be discovered in a position that might bring matters to a head.

Antonia returned to the Vicarage, little knowing that her husband was following behind her, a prey to evil thoughts. When she got home she turned the camel loose into the orchard and left it to its own devices while she went on foot into the village to do some shopping.

A few hours later Mrs. Scrimgeour, who was still sitting in front of her house enjoying the fine weather, was startled by the sudden appearance of her son in the doorway. He seemed to be in a great state of agitation.

"Mother," he cried. "Someone has taken my poems!"

"Well, deary," said Mrs. Scrimgeour. "I'm sure I don't know who would want to take them."

"Well somebody HAS taken them! I left them lying on my table near the window and now they're gone."

Mrs. Scrimgeour could offer no explanation, nor did the matter seem to interest her very much.

"You've probably put them away somewhere and forgotten," was her only suggestion.

Mr. Scrimgeour searched high and low, ransacked every drawer and cupboard for the poems, but they were nowhere to be found.

He returned to question his mother.

"Are you sure, mother," he asked, "that nobody has been in my room while I was out?"

"Yes, quite sure," Mrs. Scrimgeour replied.

"Did you see anybody in the garden?"

Mrs. Scrimgeour shook her head.

"Nobody at all?" her son insisted.

"Well there was Mrs. Hussey's camel. It came again after she had left. I saw it wandering about at the back. I was just going to get up and drive it away when it went of its own accord."

"I hardly think," said Mr. Scrimgeour sarcastically, "that Mrs. Hussey's camel can have taken my poems."

9

—⟨ϕϕϕ⟩—

The Green-Eyed Monster

In view of other strange things that have happened in the course of this narrative the reader will no doubt have guessed already what had become of the poems, and will therefore not be surprised to learn that the Vicar, on going into his wife's room in her absence noticed a small album lying on her writing table. The inscription, "Poems by Herbert Scrimgeour," caused him to pounce on them and carry them off to his study. As he scanned the titles his heart began to palpitate violently and a mist swam before his eyes. "To Antonia bathing!" So it had come to this! He began to read, and with each poem his agitation increased. When at last he reached the lines, "When first I held thee in my arms, Antonia" he beat with his fists on the desk, leapt to his feet and began to pace furiously up and down the room.

Here at last was definite proof. There could be no doubt now in the Vicar's mind that the organist was in love with his wife. The only thing that remained to be discovered was the extent to which she had responded to the wretched man's advances. The fact that from the very beginning she had always stood up for the organist, and that latterly she had professed to be even more favourably disposed towards him was in itself ominously suspicious. Yet if her sentiments for him were really serious would she have acknowledged openly that she liked him? Would she not have attempted to conceal her meetings with him? Hitherto he had always been struck by the simple candour of Antonia's nature. She had always seemed to him to be incapable of practising deceit. But then a horrible fact suddenly confronted him, a fact that seemed to provide incontrovertible evidence of her guilt. That dreadful poem "When first I held thee in my arms." Would Scrimgeour have dared to send such a poem to her unless his advances had met with her acquiescence? No, there was no doubt of it. She was guilty . . . guilty!

Through the open window he saw his erring wife in the orchard. She was sitting with the camel under the shade of an apple tree in flower. The scene was replete with charm and innocence. But, instead of soothing the Vicar's troubled spirit, it only roused him to greater fury.

"An actress!" he cried, wringing his hands. "That is what she is! A consummate actress!"

He rang the bell for Bessie.

"Bessie," he said, "I want my bed moved into the empty room at the end of the passage. I will sleep there to-night."

"Yes Sir," said Bessie, and allowed no trace of emotion of any kind to appear on her face.

"Aha!" said the Vicar to himself, when Bessie had left the room. "That is a move that will perhaps bring her to her senses."

And he rubbed his hands together in grim satisfaction.

The Vicar locked up the poems in a drawer of his writing desk. He would say nothing about them. Antonia would miss them and she would not dare to make any enquiries, unless of course she had left them there intentionally for him to see. But that he did not think likely. She had merely been careless. And when she was unable to find them, she would wonder if it had been he who had taken them, if he had at last discovered her guilty secret. But he would continue to keep silence. He would torture her by suspense, until at last the wretched woman's barrier of assumed innocence would break down and she would confess.

But Antonia had, of course, not seen the poems. She had not been inside the house since her return from the village. When at last she came in and went upstairs to her bedroom and found that her husband's bed had been removed, that the twin beds were now separated from one another by the length of a corridor, she felt very perplexed and unhappy.

What did it all mean, she wondered? And suddenly a fearful thought entered her brain. Could her husband be going out of his mind? Clergymen had sometimes been known to go mad. His behaviour during the last weeks had become so strange that she could account for it in no other way.

But what ought she to do about it? To whom could she go for advice? She felt she could hardly trust the local doctor who was both incompetent and a gossip. She might perhaps have consulted Lady Bugle, who was a woman of the world, had it not been for their unfortunate estrangement. She felt alone and miserable.

She decided to pass over the incident of the beds in silence. She would not refer to it. She knew that people suffering from mental derangement ought to be humoured. She would be very sweet and patient, and always return a soft answer. She remembered having once been told that it was part of the education of Japanese women always to smile no matter what happened. Well, she would be like a Japanese woman and would continue to smile in the face of adversity.

But the Vicar did not give her much opportunity either to smile or return a soft answer, for he maintained a morose silence during the evening meal.

At last Antonia could bear it no longer and made a desperate effort to coax him out of his taciturnity.

"Aloysius dear," she said. "Don't you think it would be a good thing if you went for a little holiday? You are looking so terribly overworked. I would willingly stay here and look after things and I'm sure we could get in a curate to take over your duties for the time being."

"Ah," said the Vicar, looking at her sternly. "So you would like to send me away and remain alone at the Vicarage? I've no doubt that would suit your book very well."

Antonia went over to her husband and put her hand on his shoulder.

"Aloysius dear," she said, her eyes filling with tears. "I beg of you tell me what is the matter. Tell your Antonia, dear."

But the Vicar pushed her roughly away from him and cried out in a terrible, accusing voice, "If your conscience does not tell you, Antonia, I certainly shall not do so."

That night Antonia, alone in her bedroom, after she had put out the light, lay awake for a long while sobbing bitterly.

10

—◦◦◦—

The Revolver

The Vicar, also, passed a troubled night, and he only fell asleep as dawn was beginning to break. When he awoke a few hours later and saw the sunlight glittering on the fresh green foliage outside his window and heard the birds singing, he felt a momentary respite from his unhappiness. But it was all too brief; once more the cloud descended on him and plunged him in a fog of misery. He remembered those dreadful poems locked away in the drawer of his writing table and he was seized with rage and despair.

Several times during the morning he crept into his study, unlocked the drawer and re-read the poems. Each time he did so it was as though he were tearing open a wound in his tortured heart. It is a strange yet common feature of jealousy that those who are suffering from it take a painful, self-tormenting pleasure in recurring to the incidents of their disease.

On one occasion the drawer stuck and he was obliged to pull it out with some violence. A couple of heavy objects shot forward from the back of the drawer. It was a revolver and a small box of cartridges he had purchased some time ago when there had been a number of burglaries in the neighbourhood. Happily he had never been obliged to make use of it. The burglary scare died down and he had entirely forgotten the existence of the revolver. He remembered that, at the time, Antonia had very strongly objected to his buying it. He even remembered her actual words, "We are God's children," she had said, "And we should trust in His protection alone."

"Well," he said to himself bitterly. "God has not seen fit to protect me from the greatest misery a man can be made to suffer."

He looked out of the window and saw Antonia walking in the garden with her flower basket on her arm. Her calm and dignified bearing filled him with fury. It maddened him to see her hiding her sinful secret under an exterior of well-simulated innocence. Why, he asked himself, should she go about her daily duties, apparently unmoved by the stirrings of a guilty conscience while he was undergoing the tortures of Hell? He would put up with it no longer! He was no Job to sit down meekly under such sore affliction. Antonia must be punished! Yes, she must be made to suffer for her wickedness. He would get the organist dismissed. But then he reflected that the man would probably remain on in the village and things would be no better. However there were other ways of punishing her. He would send the camel away. That would be an ingenious revenge. As he thought of it, he realised that, for some time past, he had begun to cherish a growing antipathy to the beast and that, in the depths of his understanding, he had begun to suspect that the camel was, in some mysterious way, connected with the various disasters that had overtaken him in the course of the last few months, all the weird, unaccountable happenings that had culminated in Antonia's inconstancy and Lady Bugle's displeasure. Ever since the camel had come to the Vicarage things had begun to go wrong. Certainly the camel must go. And he sat down to write a letter to the Zoo.

Bessie came to say that luncheon was ready. However troubled might be the state of domestic affairs in the Vicarage, meals went on as usual. The Vicar pulled himself together. To-day he would adopt different tactics. Instead of keeping silent he would indulge in icily polite conversation with his wife. He had written his letter to the Zoo, and the knowledge that she was soon going to be made unhappy by the removal of her pet gave him strength.

As he sat opposite to her at the luncheon table he marvelled at her not showing any sign of being perturbed by the loss of the poems. Perhaps inwardly she was harassed by anxiety; yet outwardly there was no trace of it. She merely looked a little sad; that was all; and she greeted all his remarks with a smile that was certainly rather forced. The woman had more control over her emotions than he had ever given her credit for. Towards the end of the meal he thought he would see whether he could perhaps disturb her serenity, and he said to her, in deliberately measured tones, "Have you seen anything of your friend Scrimgeour lately?"

Antonia replied, with an equal detachment, "Why no, I have not seen him for several days. But how curious that you should enquire. I had promised to go and pick flowers with him in the wood this very afternoon. But I have so much to do that I don't suppose I shall be able to go."

The Vicar had difficulty in containing himself. He left the room hurriedly and shut himself in his study where he paced up and down in a frenzy.

"The comedian!" he cried. "The hypocrite! The whited sepulchre!"

As a climax to his agony he saw, through the window, Mr. Scrimgeour, basket in hand, walking in the direction of the wood.

At the sight of the hated rival going complacently to his rendezvous, something seemed to burst in his brain. He opened the drawer of his writing table, took out his revolver and, slipping a couple of cartridges into his pocket, he dashed out of the house.

11

The Village Fête

The disappearance of Mr. Scrimgeour was the one topic of conversation in the Village. He had not returned to his home for three days, and his mother's house was besieged by inquisitive and sympathetic visitors. The old lady was pleased and flattered by all the attention she was receiving, but externally she presented a tragic picture of maternal anxiety.

"Yes, Mrs. Hussey," she said to Antonia, "I'm sure I've always tried to do the proper thing by him and it's cruel of him to have gone off and left his poor old mother all alone."

"Oh don't cry," Antonia begged her. "I'm sure you have a great many very good friends in the village and you know that we shall all stand by you. No doubt he will come back very soon. I daresay he has only gone away on a walking tour to collect material for his poems or to look for some rare flowers. But of course he ought to have told you he was going. That was very naughty of him."

Beaton the Verger had a curious and sinister theory to account for Mr. Scrimgeour's disappearance. He insinuated that the father of the choir-boy, Antony, had been making trouble about the organist's friendship with his son, that he had been trying to blackmail Mr. Scrimgeour and that this was the reason for his flight from Slumbermere. Very few people in the village were sufficiently sophisticated to appreciate the Verger's theory. However the rumour that there was something fishy about Mr. Scrimgeour's sudden departure, having once been started, began to spread, and soon the impression grew that he was fleeing from justice. One of the rumours most in vogue was that he had gone off with the church funds. And, curiously enough, while Antonia hotly protested against this allegation the Vicar did not deny it.

However the interest in Mr. Scrimgeour's disappearance was soon eclipsed by the imminence of an important local event. The annual Slumbermere Fête was to take place in a couple of days and the preparations for it were already beginning to encumber the village green. Tents and booths were being erected and the course for the Gymkhana and the Boys' Sports was being prepared.

The Vicarage garden adjoined the village green on one side, and Antonia was continually popping out with offers of help and useful suggestions. She always enjoyed the Slumbermere Fête, and this year it came as a welcome diversion to distract her mind from her husband's strange behaviour.

In the last two days it had become stranger than ever and Antonia began to notice that he was developing a curious furtiveness in his movements and that there was an odd hunted look in his eyes. She was now quite certain that he was going out of his mind, and she determined that, on the first possible opportunity, she would go into Woxham and consult a specialist.

On the morning of the Fête, Antonia came out of the Vicarage and found two men standing on the doorstep. She asked what they wanted and was told that they had been sent by the Zoo to collect a camel. She was very indignant and was about to send them away, when the Vicar appeared from the garden. Ignoring Antonia, he told the men to come with him, and walked off in the direction of the barn. Antonia followed them at a distance. It was too dreadful of her husband sending away her camel like this without even so much as an explanation. She was of course very sorry for him because she knew that, in his present state, he could not help himself; but when it came to sending away her beloved camel, it was too much! And, for a moment, she felt that she almost hated him.

When they reached the barn the Vicar went and opened the door, but the barn was empty. The camel was not there. They looked in the orchard. They looked everywhere, but the camel was not to be found. The men suggested looking in the wood, but the Vicar said hastily, "No, it is not likely to be there." He then turned to Antonia.

"Where have you hidden the camel?" he asked angrily.

"I have not hidden it, Aloysius," she replied. "I had no idea that you were intending to send it away."

The men from the Zoo were very annoyed at having come all that distance for nothing, and one of them muttered sulkily, "I don't believe there ever was no camel."

The Vicar was apologetic.

"It will come back sooner or later, I've no doubt," he assured them, "and then I will send it to the Zoo at my own expense."

The men went away, more or less pacified, after being given a drink of beer.

The Fête was already beginning and Antonia had no further opportunity of speaking to her husband. But she had made up her mind to go into Woxham that very evening as soon as the Fête was over.

On returning to the house to change her dress, she found a note lying on the hall table. It was from Lady Bugle. She opened it with some trepidation, wondering what further trouble was in store for her. To her intense surprise and joy, it turned out to be a letter of reconciliation. "Let us bury the hatchet," Lady Bugle wrote. "My nature is such that I am unable to continue bearing rancour for very long. Let us therefore let bygones be bygones and resume once more our friendly relations. I am coming to the Fête this afternoon," she added. "And I am bringing with me a little present that I hope will be a proof of my goodwill towards you and your husband."

Antonia was overjoyed and, for a moment, things seemed much brighter. The recovery of Lady Bugle's friendship and patronage, the cessation of hostilities between Slumbermere Hall and the Vicarage, could not fail to have a salutary effect upon the Vicar. The quarrel with Lady Bugle, Antonia had no doubt, had been the beginning of all the trouble, and now that this unexpected reconciliation had come, all would be well again. Her first instinct was to go and find her husband and tell him about it. But no, she would let it come to him as a surprise. A sudden shock, she felt, would be more likely to effect a miraculous cure.

She felt quite light-hearted as she went upstairs to put on her best frock, and she hummed to herself gaily as she made her way through the garden to join the jollifications of the Fête. She did not see her husband anywhere and, had she done so, she would in any case have avoided him until the arrival of Lady Bugle.

Admiral Sefton-Porter had undertaken to manage the Boys' Sports this year in the place of Mr. Scrimgeour, who, although he himself was not at all athletic, had hitherto always proved very efficient in organising this particular department of the Fête.

Antonia watched anxiously for the arrival of Lady Bugle, and when at last she caught sight of her black and yellow barouche driving up, she ran forward eagerly to welcome her.

Lady Bugle stepped out of her carriage and advanced towards Antonia with her usual dignity. When they met, she embraced Antonia, a thing that she had never done before. Then she handed her a bulky envelope.

"A little present for you, my dear," she said. "And I hope you may find it useful for your church."

The envelope contained two hundred pounds in notes. Antonia was overcome with joy and gratitude. Her emotion was so great that she felt very near to crying. She emboldened herself to embrace Lady Bugle again and Lady Bugle also seemed quite affected.

The Boys' Hundred Yards Race was just about to begin, and the competitors were already lined up for the start. At that moment Admiral Sefton-Porter emerged from a tent carrying a gun.

"Good gracious!" exclaimed Lady Bugle. "Whatever are you going to do with that gun?"

"I'm going to shoot you, Lady Bugle," replied the Admiral gaily, and then, remembering that she had no sense of humour, he hastily added, "It's for starting the races," and hurried on.

"Dear me!" said Lady Bugle. "How very nasty. I detest the noise of firearms."

"So do I," said Antonia. "I can't think why the Admiral should want to use a gun for starting the races. Mr. Scrimgeour always used to call out, 'Ready, steady, go!' It was so much nicer."

"By the way," said Lady Bugle, "has anything been heard of Mr. Scrimgeour?"

"No," replied Antonia, "I can't think where he can have got to. Oh dear!" she exclaimed, as the Admiral raised his gun. "How I wish poor Mr. Scrimgeour were here now!"

As she spoke, there was a movement among the trees on the edge of the wood, the branches parted and the camel appeared. It was carrying a heavy burden in its mouth. The interest of the spectators was concentrated on the race, and nobody noticed it until it had approached quite close to the fringe of the crowd. Then, all of a sudden, there arose murmurs of amazement and horror, for the burden that the camel was carrying was seen to be a human body; it looked as though it had been freshly disinterred and fragments of earth were still clinging to its clothes.

The murmurs died down to an awestruck silence, and the camel continued to advance, the people drawing back on both sides with fear and disgust. It went up to Antonia and dropped its gruesome burden at her feet. It was the corpse of the missing organist.

The Vicar, who had been standing in the background, came rushing forward, elbowing his way through the crowd. As soon as his eyes fell on Mr. Scrimgeour's body lying on the ground in ghastly inertness, he threw up his hands and uttered a cry so terrible that it echoed for many days in the ears of all who heard it. Then, turning tail abruptly, he fled across the green, his coat-tails flapping in the wind.

A great confusion followed; those on the outskirts of the crowd pushed forward to see what had happened, while those nearest the corpse backed away from it in horror.

The Vicar reached his house and, a few minutes later, there came the sound of a gun shot from within. Bessie appeared shrieking in the doorway. "Help! Help!" she cried. "He's gone and shot himself!"

Lady Bugle screamed, and there was a general rush in the direction of the Vicarage. The entire crowd that had been assembled on the village green, and even Lady Bugle herself, joined in the mad stampede, but she got no further than the garden gate where she fainted away unnoticed.

Only Antonia remained alone with the camel. She felt utterly dazed and incapable of any movement. The whole of her world seemed to have fallen about her ears. The one thing that retained any reality for her was the camel. It came nearer to her and knelt down before her. Automatically she got on to its back. The camel rose to its feet and walked slowly away.

Two policemen arrived at the Vicarage and were vainly endeavouring to keep back the excited throng that was pressing round the doorway, trampling down the garden and trying to peer through the windows.

Antonia and the camel disappeared into the distance and nobody saw them go.

MR. PIDGER

(1939)

Mr. Pidger

Lord Berners

TO

Phyllis de Janzé

The canine characters in this story are purely imaginary

and no reference is intended to any living dog.

1

The scene, a railway compartment. Its occupants a married couple. The husband aged about thirty, the wife somewhat younger. Both of elegant and fashionable appearance. The man was good-looking and serious, the woman pretty and frivolous. The faces of these two agreeable people became faintly clouded with irritation as the following dialogue ensued.

"Whatever you may say, Millicent, I still think that it is most unwise to have brought him."

"Nonsense, Walter, and please don't go on about it."

When the Denhams addressed one another by their Christian names —it was generally "dear" or "darling"—it meant that the time had come to bring discussion to a close.

Walter, disregarding the warning signal, continued.

"It is more than unwise. It is positively dangerous."

"Really, Walter, you exaggerate."

"You can't have forgotten what happened in the case of Charles and Emily," Walter went on. "They ruined their chances for ever, and you surely don't wish our prospects to be ruined now for exactly the same reason."

"That was very different," Millicent retorted. "Charles and Emily are boring and vulgar, and Charles is mad as well. Uncle Wilfred was simply longing for an excuse to get rid of them. He practically admitted it."

"I don't agree with you. Charles and Emily are just ordinary people like ourselves. But even if we were paragons of perfection, relationship with Uncle Wilfred is always precarious, and it would be fatal in any way to annoy him."

"Well," said Millicent, her indignation rising. "If you're going to compare me with that stupid dowdy Emily——"

"I'm making no comparisons. In dealing with an eccentric old man like Uncle Wilfred, one can't be too careful, and I repeat that I think it would have been better to leave him behind."

"Leave him behind!" exclaimed Millicent. "My child, my precious one, my little angel of light, my little pearl without price. May Mummy kiss you?" she inquired, as she leant over a basket containing a diminutive Pomeranian dog, the subject of the altercation.

"Mr. Pidger," for that was his name, was a bright-eyed fox-hued little creature with pointed, cocked-up ears, and a tiny inquisitive snout. "A sweet, attractive little dog," people used to say of him, until he drove them crazy with his barking, or tore their clothes.

Regarded as a pet, Mr. Pidger had many faults. His energy was boundless. He was never for a moment still. He was always jumping up or jumping down, wanting to go out of a room or come into it, dancing on his hind legs or leaping into the air, in his unrestrained joie-de-vivre. A fretful midge, he was the centre of his own agitated universe. He was determined never to stop drawing attention to himself and, if he remained for a moment unobserved, he would start scratching the carpet or tugging at your clothes.

The agitation of his soul was also vocally expressed by a high pitched incisive bark that seemed to lacerate your brain, so that after a time you felt it must be beginning to look like a pianola-roll or a nutmeg grater. His presence was destructive to any kind of concentration, indeed to any thought at all. He would often bark for hours on end and would rush yapping from one end of the house to the other, determined that everyone should hear him. He was as disturbing to household peace as a modern dictator to that of Europe.

Although he was perfectly house-trained, he contrived sometimes, out of sheer devilry, to convey the impression that he was not, especially in other people's houses. He would go up to a curtain or a table leg and sniff at it, disappear behind a sofa or squat on the floor in a highly equivocal manner.

No one could accuse him of a lack of courage. In his diminutive way he was as fierce as a tiger, as brave as a lion, and he would bite people and fly at larger dogs without provocation. His bite, as Millicent so frequently pointed out, was comparatively painless. It was just his fun, she used to say, and she seemed surprised that it did not increase your affection for him.

In love as in hatred, Mr. Pidger was equally unrestrained, and the ostentatious manner in which he demonstrated his attachments was highly embarrassing. Nor were these demonstrations confined to the canine species alone and shy visitors would often be considerably disconcerted by his attentions.

In spite of all these shortcomings, for Millicent Mr. Pidger was the embodiment of all canine and human perfections, and to the well-being of this tiny speck of fur she devoted her life, and, as far as lay within her power, the lives of others.

2

Millicent Denham was an attractive young woman. She belonged to the type that is described in society papers as "piquante" and by more sophisticated connoisseurs of feminine charm as "jolie laide." She was small and delicately built. Her hair, between auburn and gold, was exquisitely dressed and her clothes were always in faultless taste. She had a tiny uptilted nose and her dark grey eyes, though a trifle on the small side, were bright and intelligent looking. Indeed she appeared more intelligent than she really was. Her voice had amusing intonations, and when she said foolish things, as she very often did, she gave you the impression that she said them on purpose.

Walter and Millicent had been married for over four years and they were still devoted to one another.

Walter Denham was a barrister. He was tall, and rather ascetic looking. His features, slightly pinched, were regular, and his hair was greying on the temples. He was serious, amiable and humourless. Apart from a disposition to temporize, there was, in his personality, little indication of his profession.

The ménage was a singularly happy one. A system of reciprocal toleration had become well established. Millicent's natural gaiety of heart lit up the sombre background of Walter's earnestness which, in its turn, gave Millicent the comforting sensation that, if need there was for seriousness, Walter possessed enough of it for both of them. They were sufficiently well-off not to have to bother unduly about material things and Walter had a wealthy uncle of whom he had very solid expectations and whom they were now on their way to visit.

Mr. Wilfred Davenant, the wealthy uncle, was considered to be slightly eccentric, but more on account of some of his personal views than in the manner of his living. He proclaimed a violent hatred for politicians and dogs. His rudeness to the local member, whenever he met him, was the talk of the county, and he was continually sending to Cabinet Ministers telegrams that were so obscenely abusive that they had to be suppressed. But while he admitted that it would be difficult to dispense with politicians, he said that for the existence of dogs there was no necessity whatever. His loathing for them amounted almost to insanity. Visitors who brought them to his house were treated in such a way that they were not likely to forget it, and so many dogs had been destroyed on his estate that, among dog-lovers, he had come to be looked upon as an ogre.

It was owing to Mr. Davenant's morbid hatred for the canine race that the Denhams were now in the fortunate position of being his heirs, a position previously enjoyed by Charles and Emily Tompkinson.

Emily was Mr. Davenant's niece. Her mother had been Mr. Davenant's favourite sister. With his other sister, Walter Denham's mother, he had quarrelled. For this reason he had decided to leave his country house and his fortune to the Tompkinsons. But Emily Tompkinson had been incredibly foolish. She was an incredibly foolish woman. On one of her visits to her uncle, regardless of his idiosyncrasy, she had smuggled her chow, Peter, into the house. She failed perhaps to realize the full extent of the danger to which she was exposing herself and her hopes of heritage. Or possibly, like so many owners of dogs, she imagined that hers was different to those of other people and that her Peter was so full of charm that he would soften the old gentleman's heart.

One day Peter, escaping from her room, went and lay in the passage outside Mr. Davenant's study. Mr. Davenant stumbled over him in the dark, flew into one of his violent rages and Charles and Emily Tompkinson were forthwith banished from his patronage and his will.

The Denhams were summoned and approved of. Now they reigned in the Tompkinsons' stead and this was their third visit since their rise to favour.

Apart from these phobias and a few of the crankinesses to which elderly bachelors are prone, Mr. Davenant was a fairly normal cultured old gentleman. He collected pictures and books and was a great lover of beauty in all its forms, whether it manifested itself in nature, art, the human form or in food and drink. He was an eighteenth-century epicure, a type which in spite of all the difficulties imposed by the advance of civilization still, here and there, continues to persist.

3

Lawnton court, Mr. Davenant's country house, on the borders of Wiltshire and Berkshire, stood in undulating wooded parkland on the edge of a small lake. It was a very lovely house of red brick and stone built in the period of transition between William and Mary and Queen Anne. No very violent excesses of taste, either good or bad, had ever come to ruffle its serenity. One or two of the rooms, it is true, were distinctly Victorian in character, but Mr. Davenant had done nothing to change them. He did not feel that for his spiritual well-being absolute purity of style was necessary. He was not averse to an occasional incongruity as long as it was genuine and not unpleasing to the eye, and he turned a deaf ear to decorators who suggested setting the matter to rights.

His library was curious and individual rather than comprehensive, and some of his books had to be kept under lock and key. The pictures he collected were chiefly those of English landscape artists of the late eighteenth and early nineteenth century, Turner, Constable, Wilson, Bonington, and Cotman. He also possessed a number of French prints among which there were some that caused visitors to start and pass on hastily, returning later on for a closer surreptitious examination.

Mr. Davenant took rather a selfish view of humanity and his duties towards it. He did not believe in the Perfectibility of Man and in any case it was not likely to occur within his lifetime, so what was the good of bothering about it. During his long life he had done his best to ignore the follies and wickednesses of the human race. To be enabled to do so, he said, was one of the chief advantages of being rich.

He admitted that he had done very little good in the world. At the same time he professed to have done very little harm. He likened himself to the people in Dante's *Inferno* who had "lived without praise or blame." On the other hand, he said, he had very much enjoyed "the pleasant air" and was continuing to enjoy it at his advanced age, in spite of the lameness and the heart attacks to which he was subject.

He was well pleased with his new legatees and considered them a considerable improvement on Charles and Emily for whom he had never very much cared. The more intimately he had come to know the Tompkinsons the more he had grown to suspect that they were unworthy of being entrusted with a beautiful house, a valuable collection of pictures and a library of rare books. Charles was too modern in his tastes—he would probably sell the pictures and the books and fill the house with abstract monstrosities and chromium-plated furniture—while Emily had no taste at all.

Mr. Davenant had cause to regret that his fondness for his sister should have saddled him with Emily as it became more and more apparent how little of the mother's charm had been inherited by the daughter, and the dog episode had been, as Millicent's intuition had told her, the last straw.

Up till then he had seen nothing of the Denhams. His quarrel with Walter's mother had estranged him from everything connected with her. But when the necessity arose for appointing another heir, he felt he might as well let bygones be bygones and at any rate see what they were like.

He had invited them to Lawnton and was favourably impressed by them at the outset. He was attracted by Millicent's gay frivolity and her pretty clothes, and although he was a little dismayed at times by Walter's earnestness, he felt that, with regard to the more serious aspects of art, literature, and interior decoration, his tastes were sound. The Tompkinsons had perhaps displayed a more enthusiastic admiration for his possessions, but Mr. Davenant had guessed that this was actuated by a desire to ingratiate themselves rather than by sincerity of conviction.

Millicent, responding to Mr. Davenant's appreciation of her charms, had already grown quite fond of the old gentleman and declared that, if it were not for his hatred for dogs, she would really adore him. Although of course she would never dare suggest such a thing, she wished that he could be psychoanalysed, for she was sure that this strange antipathy was the result of some childish experience. Mr. Davenant himself attributed it to the observations and experiences of later years.

He had once been asked, in the days before his views had become as widely known as they were at present, to open a local dog show. He had taken advantage of the occasion to express them.

"Dogs," he said, "are rapidly becoming the curse of England, the scourge of this green and pleasant land. In no other country, except possibly in Ancient Egypt and Ethiopia, has dog worship attained to such a pitch of folly. The Israelites, a hard-headed practical race, knew what to think about dogs. When they left Egypt they spoiled the Egyptians of their jewels of gold and silver, leaving them, as the last and greatest plague, their dogs. In the East these creatures are tolerated as scavengers. The function is a suitable one, but unnecessary in this country.

"Why are these loathsome beasts known as the friends of man? It is because they flatter his foolish self-esteem in a way that no other animals do. Their subservience gives the weakest character a sense of domination. However, they often end by dominating their owners. They fawn their way into the affections of their masters and mistresses and corrupt their minds, so that children and domestic duties are neglected for their sakes. Their disgusting habits and the attention that is paid them destroy the amenities of life. Rats and grey squirrels are looked upon as vermin. The havoc they cause is only material while in the case of dogs it is both material and spiritual."

The speech, when it came to be understood by the country audience, caused something of a sensation.

4

When the Denhams arrived at Lawnton station, Mr. Pidger was stowed away in his basket for the transport from train to car.

Mr. Davenant's car was of antiquated design and as they got into it, Millicent said, "I wish to goodness Uncle Wilfred would get a new car. It makes me feel quite ashamed to be met by this antediluvian relic."

The elderly chauffeur gave her a reproachful look and Walter was pained. He had often occasion to be embarrassed by Millicent's indiscretions but, even after four years of them, he was still so much in love with her that he always forgave her and very rarely commented on them. The indiscretion had to be a very bad one indeed, such as the present repetition of Emily's folly, for Walter to indulge in such expostulations as those recorded at the opening of this tale and which were now, as they drove away, continued.

"I should like to know how you propose to prevent Uncle Wilfred from finding out."

"Oh really, Walter darling, do stop nagging. It will be perfectly simple. I shall keep him in my room."

"But he'll have to go out sometimes."

"Of course he will. I'll take him out in the morning and whenever Uncle Wilfred is resting. As Uncle Wilfred never gets up till lunch time and rests a good deal in the afternoon, he'll get as much outing as he can possibly want."

"What about his barking?"

"The walls are thick, all the bedrooms have double doors and, with his bad foot, Uncle Wilfred is never likely to go upstairs."

"Well I can only hope that you'll be able to manage the thing successfully. Pray God there may be no disaster. But I still wish that you had left him behind. The risk is out of all proportion."

"Oh listen to him, the wicked man," said Millicent, lifting Mr. Pidger out of his basket. "He doesn't know what love is. But Mr. Pidger knows, doesn't he, the little Sweetie-Pie? He wouldn't leave his Mummy behind, would he? Pipsy-Wopsy," she went on, dancing Mr. Pidger on her knees, "Pootsy-Wootsy, the weeny weeny ickle Sugar-Poppums. Mummy's in love with you. Kiss your little incestuous mummy." She held Mr. Pidger up to her face. "Now don't lick all the powder off Mummy's nose."

There were moments when Walter felt vague stirrings of jealousy but he repressed them. He was a reasonable man and it would really be too ridiculous to be jealous of a dog, especially of one that he had given Millicent himself. He was pleased that it had brought so much joy into her life and he was quite fond of the little beast.

Although Millicent was at all times inclined to interrupt normal conversation with outbursts of dog nonsense, it was only when her attention was distracted from matters of utmost gravity that Walter began to feel uneasy.

He looked out of the window and consoled himself with the contemplation of the flitting landscape while Millicent, waving her forefinger like a pendulum, kept up a refrain of "Wigger wogger wigger wogger wigger wogger," until Mr. Pidger exploded in a frenzy of barking which was kept up until they arrived at the front door when Millicent hurriedly restored him to his basket.

5

W hen Grimbly, the butler, announced that Mr. Davenant was resting and was looking forward to seeing his guests at tea-time Walter heaved a sigh of relief; the initial danger attending the smuggling in of Mr. Pidger was removed.

"I will go straight to my room," Millicent said. "Which one is it?"

"The same as you had last time, Madam."

Millicent ran upstairs with Mr. Pidger in his basket concealed under her fur wrap. She sent for Ellen, the head housemaid and took her into her confidence.

Ellen was sympathetic. She was fond of dogs and, below stairs, she sometimes ventured to deplore their absence from Lawnton Court. It was arranged that whenever Millicent left her room she should lock the door and give the key to Ellen who promised to look in from time to time and tend to Mr. Pidger's wants and keep him company.

Walter walked out on to the terrace and stood for a while gazing at the view. It was late spring, and the fresh green of the park was spangled with buttercups and dandelions. The lake glittered in the sun and the gently sloping woodlands and the outlines of the distant hills beyond them were shrouded in a bluish haze. Walter felt a great happiness descend upon him. He turned and looked up at the house bathed in sunlight, its façade of rosy brick and stone half covered on one side by a huge magnolia. It was already his spiritual home, and one day it would be his home in fact.

He caught sight of Millicent at her window and was, all of a sudden, assailed by a pang of uneasiness. He walked quickly into the house and went up to her room, where he found her settling Mr. Pidger in a comfortable armchair. "There," she was saying to him, "My little angel-face, in a minute Ellen will bring you your tiny tea. Tiny tea, tiny tea," she repeated by way of encouragement.

"Darling," said Walter, "I really feel a little anxious about his being here. Couldn't we possibly keep him somewhere else—in the gardener's cottage, or anywhere that isn't actually in the house? There must be lots of places in the neighbourhood where you could go and see him whenever you wanted to. It would be much safer and I should feel more easy in my mind about him."

"What an idea, Walter. He's perfectly happy here and I've arranged everything with Ellen."

"I've no doubt he's perfectly happy. But the question is whether we shall be perfectly happy if he's discovered."

"Oh how you go on, Walter. How can you suggest such a thing? You couldn't sleep away from Mummy, could you, sweetheart?" she inquired of Mr. Pidger who replied by faintly wagging his tail. "There, you see. He says he couldn't possibly. And he is very angry with you for suggesting such a thing. Aren't you darling? Please forgive him, he's only a silly man."

Walter gave up the struggle.

"We'd better go down to tea," he said. "Uncle Wilfred will be waiting for us."

Ellen came in with a saucer of milk and a piece of cake. "Forgive him and forget about it, Bright-eyes," Millicent implored Mr. Pidger, "and here's the tiny tea for the tiny Tiddlums." She handed the key to Ellen and, bestowing a final kiss on Mr. Pidger, she followed Walter downstairs.

Mr. Davenant was sitting at the tea table in the library, a pleasant room opening on to the garden. He was about to rise and greet them when Millicent ran forward and kissed him. "Oh don't get up, Uncle Wilfred," she cried.

Walter wondered how Uncle Wilfred would have felt had he known on what, a few minutes before, a similar kiss had been bestowed.

Mr. Davenant was in one of his most amiable moods. He had had a very satisfactory day. He had received that morning an interesting consignment of books from London, and he had been sent on approval a small oil painting by Constable which so enchanted him that he had decided to buy it. And at luncheon that day he had indulged in one of his favourite amusements, teasing the clergyman.

Poor Mr. Evans was invited once a month to Lawnton, and as Mr. Davenant was the patron of his living he felt himself obliged to accept. But on these occasions Mr. Evans seldom enjoyed himself.

The particular form of teasing Mr. Davenant employed was to pretend that although he was pining to "get religion," he was unable to do so until certain theological problems were cleared up. These were always of so difficult and complicated a nature that poor Mr. Evans was unable to give his patron the assurance he required. At first the clergyman had been very much distressed and feared that he might be considered unworthy of his cloth. But, after a while, as Mr. Davenant continued to submit conundrums that became, each time, more intricate and more difficult to answer, it began to dawn on Mr. Evans that possibly his patron might not be in earnest, but he could not, of course, give vent to his suspicions. He was also given books of subtle infidelity to read, upon which his tormentor would catechize him the next time he came to luncheon, so that at last the unlucky man began to fear that, if it continued much longer, his own faith might be undermined.

Mr. Davenant had occasionally employed similar methods with Charles Tompkinson, showing him modern abstract pictures and asking him what they meant and which was the right way up. In all probability he would soon start on Walter, whose earnestness marked him for a suitable victim.

That afternoon, however, there was no thought of teasing. Mr. Davenant seemed anxious only to please.

"My dear," he said to Millicent. "You seem to grow prettier every day and your clothes are exquisite. They bring a breath of Paris into this prim old house. I doubt, Walter, whether I dare show you the little masterpiece I have bought to-day. It has been so sadly eclipsed by our charming Millicent."

However he showed it to Walter all the same. He also showed him the books that had been sent him. While they were examining them together, Millicent slipped away and ran upstairs to her room.

"Here," said Mr. Davenant, "is an edition of Gibbon with Beckford's disapproving comments on the margins. This is a rare edition of the first English translation of the *Decameron*. And this little volume will appeal to you. It is a masterpiece of platitude, the *Table talk of Dr. Parr.* And here is another little book I shall not let you see. It was described in the catalogue as 'very curious and disgusting.'"

While Mr. Davenant was replacing the volumes on the shelves Walter glanced round the room at the tawny mellow bindings of the books in the high cases; he looked through the open windows at the garden and the landscape glowing in the soft evening light and inhaled the scent of wallflowers mingled with the distinctive aroma of old books. What contentment, what peace of mind would have been his, had it not been for that little time bomb upstairs that might at any moment explode.

6

M^r. Davenant had taken a good deal of trouble with the ordering of the dinner. He knew that the Denhams appreciated good food, and he was grateful to them for providing him with an excuse to demand special efforts from his chef. When he dined alone or entertained country neighbours his appetite was less inspired than in the company of connoisseurs and, as he enjoyed the happy digestive condition, that is sometimes vouchsafed to the aged, known as presbypepsia, he was able to eat whatever he liked with impunity.

"It is odd to think," said Mr. Davenant, "that, up till fairly recently, food, in many English households, was held to be as improper a subject for discussion as religion and sex, and just as religion and sex were considered to be the province of the clergy and the police, food was left almost entirely to the mercy of cooks. Since the ban has been lifted there has been a noticeable improvement in English cooking. I remember the days when one had to go to Paris to eat."

"I'm afraid you might find the food less good there now," said Walter. "It has been ruined by the English and the Americans. But you can still get good cooking in the provinces."

"Well you'd better make the best of these good things while they last," said Mr. Davenant.

"Oh Uncle Wilfred," cried Millicent. "How ominous you sound. Do you really think there's going to be a war?"

"I'm afraid so, my dear."

"But all the astrologers say there won't be."

"The folly of our politicians, my dear Millicent, is such that it will defeat even the stars in their courses. For my part I must be thankful that I am nearly eighty, and that my life lies behind me. A pleasant life it has been and I can afford to look forward complacently to the deluge. I have no wish to outlive my period, which has already been protracted beyond expectation."

"Please, Uncle Wilfred," Millicent beseeched him, "don't be so depressing."

"I am sorry, my dear. I often grow melancholy in the evening. I trust I may be wrong and that you and Walter will live to enjoy these things for many years."

After dinner Mr. Davenant and Walter discussed painting and architecture. After listening for a while, Millicent grew bored with the conversation and her thoughts wandered to her bedroom. She was longing to rejoin Mr. Pidger and, while the two men discoursed on Gainsborough and Gibbs, she amused herself by inventing little phrases for Mr. Pidger's benefit. "Boolah Woolah piggy wiggy wog wog," she murmured to herself and looked forward to trying it on him as soon as she got upstairs.

7

—◦◦◦—

Next morning, profiting by Mr. Davenant's late rising, Millicent took Mr. Pidger out in his basket. There was a small stairway at the end of the passage that led directly down into the garden, and, as soon as she was hidden from the house by one of the high yew hedges, she let him out. She sat down on a stone bench and watched him scratching in the flower beds. It was a real pleasure to see how much he enjoyed it. When he seemed to have had enough of it, Millicent took him back into the house and spent the rest of the morning playing with him in her room. The depredations in the flower beds caused some consternation among the gardeners and one of the underlings was severely reprimanded for having left a wire gate open and let in the rabbits.

At luncheon Mr. Davenant suggested that Walter and Millicent should go out that afternoon in his car and do some sight-seeing. There were one or two interesting houses in the neighbourhood that Walter was very anxious to see.

"I am sorry I cannot accompany you myself," Mr. Davenant said. "I go out very rarely in the car and I feel a little tired to-day. Also I am expecting my agent, who is coming to go through the estate accounts with me. I fear it may be a rather painful interview."

When the time came to start, Walter went into Millicent's room and found her on her knees scrubbing the Aubusson carpet with a nail brush. Mr. Pidger stood beside her looking at her complacently.

"There," she said. "It hardly shows now."

"What has happened?" Walter asked.

"I'm afraid the poor sweetheart is a little out of sorts. Ellen must have given him something that disagreed with him. She couldn't think what it could have been. I was quite annoyed with her."

"Are you ready, dear? The car is waiting."

"Ready?" Millicent exclaimed. "You surely don't expect me to leave him when he's not feeling well."

"He looks all right now."

"How unobservant you are, Walter darling. Just look how sad his little eyes are. It may be that he's feeling his captivity. He has never been deprived of his liberty like this before, has he, the little prisoner of Chillon, little Monte Cristo?"

"Perhaps we could take him with us," Walter suggested. "But no," he hastily added. "That would be dangerous. He might start barking on the way down. Couldn't you get Ellen to look after him?"

"No, darling. It is her afternoon out. And, anyhow, I wouldn't dream of leaving him with Ellen when he is feeling unhappy. In such moments he wants his Mummy and his Mummy only."

A new idea struck her.

"I wonder if perhaps he is upset by the atmosphere of hostility in this house. It's quite possible. He has an uncanny sense of atmosphere. It's almost clairvoyant. Do you think he can be clairvoyant, Walter?"

"I really don't know, dear. If you think he is, then probably he is. So I shall have to go by myself?"

"I'm afraid so, darling."

"I was so much looking forward to seeing these places with you."

"But, Walter dearest, I shouldn't be able to enjoy myself. I should be thinking all the time of my little sad eyes."

So Walter went sightseeing alone.

8

—⟨⟩—

A s Walter was passing through the hall on his return he heard Mr.
Davenant's voice raised in anger behind the closed door of his
study. He was alarmed and rushed up to Millicent's room.

"Is everything all right?" he asked nervously.

"Yes dear, thank you, he's much better now. Quite his little self again.
Isn't he, little Piccaninny?"

Mr. Pidger testified to the truth of her statement by a series of short
sharp barks. Walter hurried to the double doors and closed them.

"I heard Uncle Wilfred shouting in his study as I passed and I was
afraid that perhaps he had found out about Mr. Pidger."

All that evening Mr. Davenant was in a very bad temper. Walter
gathered that it was connected in some way with the estate accounts.
Conversation at dinner was far from being as agreeable as it had been
on the previous evening. However, later on, Mr. Davenant seemed a little conscience stricken and apologized for his ill humour.

"I am not feeling very well this evening," he explained. "It's my old
heart trouble, I suspect. It always comes on when I have been annoyed.
And one is bound very often to be annoyed. However much one may
seek to take refuge from humanity, there is no hour of the day or night
when one is not liable to have thrust upon one some form of wickedness
or folly."

Just before going to bed Mr. Davenant glanced at an evening paper
and threw it down in disgust.

"Gas masks for dogs!" he cried. "My God, what a country!" He
turned to Millicent. "I hope, my dear, that you are not given to har-
bouring these pestilential beasts?"

Walter gave her a significant look.

"You mean, Uncle Wilfred, have I got a dog? No, certainly not."

"I am glad to hear it, my dear. Well, good night, both of you." Supported by Grimbly, he limped off to bed.

"Oh, Walter," Millicent gasped as they went upstairs. "Wasn't it dreadful my having to tell that lie?"

"I am very glad you did, darling."

"Yes, but whatever will Mr. Pidger think of me?"

"You needn't tell him," said Walter, entering into the spirit of the thing.

"Oh, but he's sure to know. He always knows everything. He's psychic. Oh my darling angel," she cried, as she flung herself down on her knees and buried her face in Mr. Pidger's fur. "Forgive your poor little cowardly mummy. Forgive the wretched woman. She ought to be crucified upside down like St. Peter."

"Really, darling," said Walter smiling indulgently. "You sometimes go a little too far in your similes."

9

Next morning, when Millicent took Mr. Pidger out into the garden, he seemed quite to have forgiven her and licked her face in the most conciliatory manner. She found a nice bed of forget-me-nots for him to scratch in and thought how prettily the pale blue of the flowers set off his russet colouring.

Walter also had a happy morning inspecting the house inside and out, and making mental notes on any alterations that might be made when he came into possession. He found very little that needed to be changed. He considered, for a time, whether or not to remove the magnolia from the western façade and decided he would content himself with lopping one or two of its branches that hid some of the architectural details.

Mr. Davenant had had a restless night and was still in a very bad temper.

"Really," Millicent said to Walter after luncheon. "Uncle Wilfred's moods are insufferable. He's as capricious as an elderly prima donna, charming one moment and beastly the next. I'm beginning to wonder if the game is worth the candle."

Walter thought that it very decidedly was.

"We must be patient, darling. I have every reason to believe that Uncle Wilfred is not long for this earth. These violent rages he gets into are undoubtedly very bad for his heart and both his heart and his tempers seem to be growing worse. He may pop off one day quite suddenly."

"Poor Uncle Wilfred," said Millicent. "You really make me feel quite sorry for him."

It was a lovely day and Walter suggested walking round the lake. Millicent thought of taking Mr. Pidger, but she saw that he was asleep in his basket and decided not to disturb him.

"Poor little man," she said. "He has had a busy morning."

She called for Ellen who promised to look in from time to time and see that he was all right.

They set off along a path that skirted the lake and led to a little temple standing on a wooded mound. They sat for a time on the bank watching the water fowl splashing, chasing one another and swimming round in circles. Collecting rare duck and geese was another of Mr. Davenant's hobbies and the lake was covered with aquatic birds of every shape and colour; mandarins, carolinas, pintails, widgeons, teal; geese of every nationality, Canadian, Siberian, Chinese, Egyptian.

Walter contemplated this scene of animated peace, the reflections of the overhanging trees and the pink façade of the house quivering in the water, and thought that the possession of such a heritage would enable him to preserve his equanimity for the rest of his days. All anxiety that such things might founder in the imminent collapse of civilization vanished into the pale blue sky and was broken up like the rippling shadows on the lake. He saw himself an amiable old man, like Uncle Wilfred without his tantrums, happily interested in his house, his books, his pictures, his gardens and his waterfowl, fading gently away in his appropriate setting.

"Oh dear," said Millicent. "I forgot to lock the door and give the key to Ellen. However, I expect Uncle Wilfred will be resting and, in any case, he is hardly likely to go upstairs. All the same, it might be better perhaps to be getting back."

10

U ncle Wilfred was not resting. He was at the moment visiting his orchid houses. His inner calm had not yet returned to him and he thought that the process might be accelerated by the contemplation of exotic flowers. Often, after one of his outbreaks of ill humour, his conscience was a little uneasy. He was sorry he had not made himself more agreeable to his nephew and niece at luncheon.

A huge mauve and yellow cattleya caught his eye and he directed the head gardener who was accompanying him to cut it.

The man protested.

"It's one of the finest specimens we've ever had, sir. I was thinking of sending it up to the Horticultural——"

"Do as I tell you," said Mr. Davenant.

Reluctantly the flower was cut and handed to its owner who intended to present it to his niece as a peace offering.

"Grimbly," Mr. Davenant said to the butler as he entered the house, "I am going upstairs to Mrs. Denham's room."

Climbing the stairs was a laborious process and the old gentleman was obliged to rest on a settee for a few minutes before going further.

Supported by Grimbly he made his way down the passage and tapped on Millicent's door.

There was no reply, and he tapped again. There came a sound of furious yapping from within.

"What the devil is that?" exclaimed Mr. Davenant and he opened the door.

Too soon he knew. Like a little whirlwind Mr. Pidger came rushing towards him and bit him in the ankle. Mr. Davenant uttered a yell and fell back in Grimbly's arms. The orchid dropped on the floor and Mr. Pidger pounced on it, tearing it to shreds.

11

W hen Walter and Millicent returned to the house, Grimbly met them in the hall with a solemn face in which there flickered a tiny glint of satisfaction.

"I regret to inform you, Madam," he said to Millicent, "that there has been an accident. Mr. Davenant has been bitten by your little dog and is now extremely unwell. Before retiring to bed he expressed the wish that you and Mr. Denham should leave the house immediately. The car has been ordered and I have ventured to give instructions for your luggage to be packed. You will be in plenty of time to catch the four-thirty. It is a good train and it has a restaurant car."

"Good gracious," Millicent exclaimed. "I hope he's all right. Where is he now? Tell me at once."

"I have told you, Madam. He has retired to his bedroom."

"No no," Millicent cried. "I meant Mr. Pidger—my dog. Where is he?"

"As far as I know, Madam, he is still in your room."

Millicent dashed up the stairs, while Walter, recovering from the immobility and speechlessness to which the news had struck him, prepared himself to tackle the situation.

"Please tell me," he asked Grimbly, "exactly what has happened."

Grimbly told him in a manner that was worthy of a messenger in a Greek Tragedy.

"Do you think I could see him?" Walter asked.

"No, sir, I fear not. If you will pardon me for saying so I consider that it would be highly unwise for you to attempt to see Mr. Davenant in his present mood."

Walter appreciated the wisdom of Grimbly's advice. He did not feel that an interview with his Uncle, under the circumstances, could be anything but unsatisfactory. He also noticed the undercurrent of *Schadenfreude* in the butler's unctuous tones and thought that it would be ignominious to persist.

"Very well," he said. "I will wait in the library until the car comes round. Will you inform me when it does?"

The butler bowed gravely and retired.

Walter went and sat in the library in a mood of deep dejection. After a while the optimistic side of his nature began to assert itself. It would be a mistake of course, as the journalists say, to underestimate the gravity of the situation. However, all hope was not lost. Uncle Wilfred, after one of his violent rages, often had a change of heart and when his anger died down it was possible he might forgive. Walter knew that his Uncle appreciated his taste and he had once told him that there was no other person to whom he felt he could so confidently entrust his possessions. Mr. Davenant would certainly not reinstate Charles and Emily and that, at least, was some slight consolation.

Millicent came in carrying Mr. Pidger in his basket. She was far from contrite.

"I hope we are leaving soon," she said. "I can't stand another minute of this horrible house. I can't say I'm sorry that this should have happened. It has at least cleared up the position, and the ridiculous deceit that I've been obliged to practise for the last two days was beginning to tell on my nerves. I am sorry about Ellen though. She had grown so fond of him and when I said good-bye to her just now she was in tears."

Millicent lifted the lid of the basket.

"Don't be restless, little Twinky Winky. You'll soon be back in your nice home. And I think it was horrible of Uncle Wilfred," she went on, "to go messing about in my room like that. It just shows the kind of man he is. It serves him right. Mr. Pidger knows how to deal with people who come nosing around, doesn't he, my little brave one, my little Cœur de Lion, my little St. George. Did he bite the nasty old dragon?"

The car was announced and the Denhams drove away, Walter in despair and Millicent in a state of righteous indignation.

She sat with Mr. Pidger on her knee silently brooding over her grievance. When they got into the train she burst out afresh.

"It serves him right for taking up that ridiculous attitude about dogs. How can anyone expect people to come to their houses nowadays if they aren't allowed to bring their dogs? It's positively mediæval."

Walter made no response and she glanced at his gloomy face.

"Oh, Walter darling, I'm sorry if you feel badly about it. But after all, what does it matter? It isn't as if we were frightfully poor and in need of money. We have always been very happy as we were and, anyhow, it isn't a very nice idea to think of our sitting waiting for an old man to die."

"I think we could have been very happy at Lawnton."

"I don't think I could ever be happy there now, after all I've been through these last two days. I could never be happy in a place where my little Popsikins has been hated, and I don't fancy he could ever be either. You know, darling, I'm sure it's an unlucky house. It has an unpleasant atmosphere, and even if Uncle Wilfred were to beg me on his knees to go back there I should hesitate about doing so. Yes, I'm positive it's an unlucky house, and that's what made my little one ill yesterday. Let's go to the restaurant car and have some tea. I feel I need it, and so, I've no doubt, does Mr. Pidger. Come along Popsy Boo, Tiny Tea! Tiny Tea!"

12

Walter sat at his writing table composing a letter to Mr. Davenant.

"Dear Uncle Wilfred," he wrote, "I am grieved beyond words by the unfortunate incident that took place yesterday. I hope that you will not think that I in any way countenanced Millicent's behaviour in introducing her dog into your house. I had no idea that she proposed to bring it. Had I known of her intention I should of course have forbidden it. She kept the dog concealed from me during the journey and it was only on arriving at Lawnton Court that I became aware of its presence. I implored her at once to send it out of the house. I did my best to persuade her but she refused. I fear that, in spite of all I said to her, she failed to realize the great antipathy you have for dogs. It is an antipathy that I also share, and if it were not for my devotion to Millicent I should not put up with her possessing one. I ought to have taken up a stronger line from the very beginning, but you know what women are, and I very foolishly acquiesced."

At this point Millicent burst into the room, her face beaming with enthusiasm. Walter hastily hid the letter under the blotting paper.

"Walter darling," she cried excitedly. "It has just arrived. It is too lovely. You must come and look at it."

"What has just arrived?"

"Why his portrait of course. Surely you haven't forgotten that it was being sent to-day?"

Millicent had seen in the Royal Academy that year a picture called "A Tragedy in Bow-wowland," by Miss Lucy Kimpton-Potts, and she realized at once that she had found an artist worthy to portray Mr. Pidger's transcendant charm. Although Millicent knew very little about art, her judgment in this case was sound, for Miss Kimpton-Potts is universally admitted to possess greater insight into canine psychology than any other of her contemporaries.

The artist had done Mr. Pidger proud. Reposing on a crimson velvet cushion with quite a modernistic background of flowers and drapery, he fixed you with his bright little eyes. The extraordinary thing was, as Millicent so justly pointed out, that wherever you went in the room, his eyes seemed to follow you.

Having duly admired the portrait, Walter returned to the composition of his letter.

"Millicent has a light and childlike nature. Now that she has come to realize the extent of her transgression, it has upset her so much that it has made her quite ill. She is at present in bed and the doctor has forbidden her any form of exertion. As soon as she recovers, she will of course write to you and beg your forgiveness. She is devoted to you, Uncle Wilfred, and if only you could see your way to writing her a few lines or letting her know that you have forgiven her, it would, I am sure, hasten her recovery.

"I am sending you an interesting edition of the *Satirae* of Petronius. I do not believe that you possess a copy of it in your library."

It was such a letter as Adam might have written to the Deity after the Tree of Knowledge episode, and Mr. Davenant was as little affected by it as the Deity had been by Adam's more concise apology. The letter remained unanswered and the Petronius was not returned.

13

As soon as Mr. Davenant had sufficiently recovered from the shock to be able to sit up and write, he set about drawing up a new will. According to its terms Lawnton Court and the surrounding estate was to be an asylum for decaying connoisseurs and bibliophils. There was an elaborate scheme for their selection, and the institution was liberally endowed. The rest of his fortune, apart from one or two annuities to servants, was left to the National Art Collection Fund.

Mr. Davenant had sufficient knowledge of legal technicalities to enable him to dispense with the assistance of a lawyer. As a matter of fact one of Mr. Davenant's eccentricities—if indeed it can be called an eccentricity—was a profound mistrust of lawyers, and when he made a will he not only did so without consulting his solicitor but kept it hidden away in a secret place, disclosed in a sealed letter to the executors to be opened by them after his death. This time the procedure was more than ever necessary, as Walter was a barrister, and Mr. Davenant's suspicious nature led him to suspect that he might succeed in corrupting his own lawyer (they were all hand in glove) and attempt to tamper with the provisions of the will, especially as they were of rather an unusual nature.

The agent and the clergyman were summoned to witness the will and, when it had been signed and witnessed, it was placed in a small flat tin box, after which it disappeared from the eyes of man.

A month later Mr. Davenant died. He had omitted to leave any indication as to where the last will had been hidden and had neglected to destroy the former one, which was found in a drawer of his writing table. The most thorough and extensive search was made for the missing will but it could not be found. Finally the opinion was given that Mr. Davenant had changed his mind and destroyed it, and the former will appointing Walter heir to Lawnton Court and the rest of his possessions was declared valid.

14

Walter was informed by his lawyer of the circumstances of the inheritance and his joy was at first a little darkened by the prospect of this sword of Damocles in the shape of the undiscovered will hanging over his head. However, he was encouraged by the account of the very minute search that had been made for it and, fortified by legal opinion, he ended by persuading himself that Mr. Davenant had relented, in spite of the fact that he had never given him the least sign of forgiveness. However, it was characteristic of the old gentleman that he should, as a punishment, have kept him in a state of uncertainty.

The idea of the missing will appealed to Millicent's romantic imagination.

"When we get possession of the place," she said, "I will devote my mornings to hunting for it, and Mr. Pidger will help me. You know, darling, I'm coming more and more to believe that he's psychic. When I hide things he finds them in the most extraordinary way. If that horrid old will exists I'm quite sure he'll be able to unearth it and then we can destroy it ourselves. And as a reward he shall have a little bit of it for himself to chew. He won't ask anything more than that."

The anticipation of the serious uses to which Mr. Pidger's clairvoyant powers could be put seemed to give Millicent almost as much pleasure as the possession of Lawnton Court did to Walter.

Millicent was also at the moment very much interested in a little practical joke she had perpetrated. She had made Mr. Pidger a member of the Sunday Observance League. When pamphlets and circulars arrived for "Mr. Pidger" she amused herself by reading out to him any extracts that she considered applicable. She hoped that one day he might be invited to speak at a meeting—she would suggest it herself—and what fun it would be when, instead of some crusty old puritan such as the audience might be expecting, a sweet little dog appeared on the stage. It would create quite a sensation and bring the silly old League into ridicule. The incident would be written about in the papers and Mr. Pidger would become a popular national figure.

15

A few days later, Walter, Millicent and Mr. Pidger set out early one morning for Lawnton.

"There won't be any trouble about him this time," said Millicent.

"Not unless he sees Uncle Wilfred's ghost," suggested Walter playfully. "I'm afraid that with his psychic powers he probably will."

"Oh he's not afraid of ghosts. Are you my little Popsy-Woo? He'll drive them all away. Especially Uncle Wilfred's ghost. It would be awful to have that hanging round."

As the house came into view at the end of the long avenue of lime trees, Walter was overcome with emotion. This thing of beauty that he had believed to be lost to him for ever, that he had almost succeeded in banishing from his mind, had been miraculously restored to him. The dream that had been shattered had returned as a reality. The place was now his own.

He ran eagerly into the house and stood for a moment in the hall, admiring with an owner's eyes, its elegant design and admirable decoration. He then walked rapidly and rapturously through the rooms. In the library he paused again, sniffing voluptuously its distinctive aroma of books and flowers. He noticed the Petronius he had sent his Uncle lying on one of the tables and it dawned upon him why it had not been returned. The old gentleman had thought it unnecessary to do so, as eventually it was going to become once more the property of the sender.

Millicent went out through the window that opened on to the garden and deposited Mr. Pidger in a flower bed.

Walter remembered that he had made an appointment with Mr. Price, the agent, and returned to the hall where he found him waiting. Mr. Price had brought various maps and plans relating to the estate and the two men went into the library to examine them.

"It's an odd thing about that will," the agent said, "I witnessed it myself. But we made so thorough a search for it that I am convinced that Mr. Davenant must have destroyed it."

It was a little tactless perhaps, but Walter was reassured by the Agent's confidence.

"Tell me," Walter said, "did Mr. Davenant, after making the second will, ever say anything to you that might lead you to think that he had changed his mind?"

"Never to me, sir. After you left Lawnton that time, as far as I know, he never mentioned your name to anyone. As a matter of fact he became very queer towards the end and it was difficult to discuss any serious business with him."

At that moment there arose a clamour in the garden outside. The head gardener had appeared on the scene and, seeing Mr. Pidger busily engaged in scratching up one of the flower beds outside the library window, had admonished him rather roughly.

"Get out, you little varmint. Stop it. Shoo." He picked up a stone and flung it at the dog. Millicent flew into a rage.

"How dare you speak like that to my little dog?" she screamed. "This is my property now. How dare you interfere with him? Go away and leave him alone. Go on, Sweetie Pie," she exhorted Mr. Pidger. "Scratch away as much as you like and pay no attention to that horrid man."

Mr. Pidger needed no incitement and continued his excavations, scattering earth and flowers into the air.

Millicent burst angrily into the library.

"That gardener has been most insulting," she cried. "Walter, I insist upon your dismissing him at once."

"That will be unnecessary, Madam," said Mr. Price. "He has already given notice."

Walter introduced Mr. Price to Millicent, but she was so annoyed by the behaviour of the gardener and the frustration of her revenge on him that she hardly nodded to the agent who was a little disconcerted by her manner. She sat down on the arm of Walter's chair and looked peevishly over his shoulder at the maps and plans spread out on the table.

A few minutes later the head gardener came in through the window, followed by Mr. Pidger who was jumping up at him and barking furiously. He held in his hands a flat tin box.

"I think, sir," he said as he handed it to the agent, "this must be the missing will."

Mr. Price opened the box and took out of it several folded sheets of grey paper tied together with a green ribbon.

"By jove," he exclaimed, "so it is."

16

They drove to the station in silence. Walter was too dazed and miserable to speak. When they got into the train and Millicent began quite unconcernedly to caress Mr. Pidger and talk to him in her customary dog language, Walter's misery turned to rage. He was professionally self-controlled and very rarely expressed his anger in any other form than a kind of legally flavoured sarcasm.

"Well, Millicent," he said, "I can't congratulate you on your Mr. Pidger's psychic gifts."

"I am sorry, Walter," Millicent replied, "but you really can't blame the poor little Sweetie. It's a dog's nature to scratch the earth. He can't possibly have known that he was going to do you any harm. You must admit that." She was suddenly struck by an idea. "Oh, Walter, you know I always had a feeling that Lawnton was an unlucky place. I believe that if we had lived there something frightful might have happened to us. I felt quite depressed when I got back there and I had an odd feeling that I should never be happy in that house. And in any case if there is going to be a war we certainly don't want to be saddled with a place like that. I believe he really is psychic and that he wanted to preserve us from some great danger and that is why he acted as he did. He was determined to save us. Perhaps we have every reason to be grateful to him."

Walter felt his anger rising to a further pitch of exasperation, but he again controlled himself and made no answer. Millicent was irritated by his silence and his glum expression.

"Oh Walter," she cried. "For Heaven's sake stop looking like a funeral. I know you're angry with my poor little Pettikins. Try and be more like Sir Isaac Newton. When his little dog set fire to his papers all he said was 'Diamond, Diamond, you little know what harm you have done,' and they were important scientific papers that were going to be of some use to the world, while this is only a silly house and an unlucky one into the bargain. Of course it would have been nice to have had all the money that went with it. But after all, money isn't everything and we've got quite enough of our own. How can you be so money-grubbing, Walter? I've always said that women are less materially minded than men. Try and take it in a more philosophical spirit. Oh look at him wagging his little taily! We don't care, do we? We're philosophers, aren't we? Little psychic philosopher dog. Little Mr. Plato. Little Mr. Schopenhauer. Kiss Mummy. Pidgy Widgy Wodgy——"

Walter snatched Mr. Pidger from her arms and hurled him out of the window.

For a moment Millicent sat bewildered and motionless as if unable to grasp what had happened. Then she rushed screaming to the communication cord and pulled it. She turned on Walter and, in blind fury, struck him and scratched his face.

The train slowed down and stopped abruptly, so that Millicent and Walter fell together on the seat. She pushed him from her violently, wrenched open the door and scrambled out. Walter struggled to his feet and stood irresolutely, his brain benumbed, only dimly conscious that some unusual catastrophe had occurred. When his mind grew clear again he saw the guard standing before him and the corridor crowded with excited passengers.

"My wife's dog," he exclaimed, "has fallen out of the window."

The words sounded inadequate and he felt slightly ridiculous.

"How long can you hold the train?" he asked the guard.

"Not more than about five minutes, sir."

Walter thrust a pound note into the man's hand. "Well hold it as long as you can," he said and, jumping down on to the track he started off in search of Millicent. He saw her in the distance huddled on the ground and ran towards her. She was sitting motionless, bent over the pitiable little corpse. As Walter approached, calling her name, Millicent rose to her feet and, carrying the lifeless little body in her arms, walked swiftly past him to the train without looking at him. Walter followed her and, as he glanced up at the long line of gaping faces at the windows, he felt humiliated and ashamed.

When he got back into the train, he found Millicent directing the removal of her belongings to another compartment. She had wrapped up Mr. Pidger in her fur coat and was receiving the condolences of two old ladies. The corridor was still blocked with inquisitive passengers. In such circumstances it was impossible for him to speak to her.

The train started off again and Walter remained alone in his compartment. He tried to review the situation dispassionately, but it was difficult. Although he felt that there had been ample justification for his action, that he had been goaded into losing control over himself, he was haunted by the vision of that pathetic little figure on the railway line, bent in despair over a tiny bundle of fur.

He walked down the corridor and found that there were several people in the compartment Millicent had chosen. She had probably chosen it for that very reason. In any case, even if she had been alone, Walter thought, it would have been unwise to approach her at the moment and he decided to wait until they met again at the flat.

But when he got back to the flat she was not there. He heard that she had gone to a hotel.

17

Walter telephoned to her, wrote to her and tried to see her, but she refused either to see him or listen to a message. He was told that she was trying to get a divorce. Millicent, in her innocent way, thought that this would be quite a simple matter and that she would easily be able to obtain a divorce on grounds of cruelty, especially as all her friends had expressed their sympathy in so marked a manner. Walter found that he was being very much censured and that he had become almost an object of execration. He was amazed at the injustice of the world. Surely no one in their senses, he thought, could possibly set a dog on the same level as one of the most beautiful country houses in England.

Walter and Millicent had both lost the thing they loved, and both of them thought their loss the greater of the two, but though Walter was obsessed by a sense of guilt, Millicent's conscience was perfectly clear.

Then the war broke out. Walter in a spirit of pig-headed penance, enlisted in the army as a private soldier and died the following year of pneumonia. Millicent has another dog of which she has grown quite fond but she never ceases to mourn Mr. Pidger.

At the beginning of the war, Lawnton Court was converted into a hospital. After most of the panelling and wood carving had been removed and a great deal of money spent on structural alterations the house was declared unsuitable, and abandoned. It was then taken over by a girls' school who set fire to it. Little remains to-day of Lawnton Court beyond its blackened walls.

COUNT OMEGA

(1941)

Count Omega

Lord Berners

TO

Rosamond Lehmann

1

In a modestly furnished bed-sitting room on a third floor a young man, dishevelled and of frantic appearance, was pacing up and down in a state of great agitation. He was unable to pace very far in any direction for the room was encumbered with a great many things; an upright piano, a divan, a bust of Beethoven on a pedestal, a number of musical instruments, some with cases, some without, a table heaped with books and bulky scores, and a writing desk littered with music paper.

The young man, as you may have guessed, was a musician. His name was Emanuel Smith. He was twenty-three years of age, fair haired and of slender build. Not ill-looking on the whole, though his present state of agitation made his face appear lined and furrowed beyond his years.

Contrary to the popular belief, the composition of music is not necessarily attended by violent manifestations of unrest. Like poetry, it is emotion remembered in tranquillity, and is usually recorded in a more or less orderly manner. The young man's turbulent gestures, although not denoting the throes of composition, were nevertheless directly concerned with music.

For four years Emanuel had studied at the National Academy of Music and had left it with the assurance that in the way of technique, he had nothing further to learn. He had already produced several academic compositions of a very high order, but he had allowed none of these to be presented to the public. He was determined to burst upon the world with something really sensational and entirely new.

He thought that the actual state of music was far from satisfactory. The atmosphere of the concert room, he considered, had become like that of a museum and the works of even the greatest composers only called forth the same kind of emotions as those aroused by museum pieces. Serious music had ceased to be vital. People were moved by it, sensually or intellectually, and then returned to their ordinary state of mind. Music was no longer an essential and enduring part of the human soul. It had become a mere temporary drug of which the effects soon wore off. In this insensitive and blasé world, absolute music was inadequate. Something more was needed to enhance its message, to galvanise its votaries into new life.

Other people seemed to have had the same idea, and various devices had been tried: colour symphonies, the introduction of strange noises into the orchestra, the flooding of the concert-hall with vaporised benzedrine. Emanuel had assisted at the performance of a symphony by a young American composer towards the end of which a rapidly revolving aeroplane propellor had been turned on to the audience. The violent rush of air had caused the occupants of the first rows of the stalls hurriedly to vacate their seats and the resulting confusion had rendered the experiment a complete fiasco.

These devices had failed, Emanuel thought, because they were not in themselves sufficiently musical. Instead of intensifying the effect, they had merely acted as distractions even more trivial than the addition to music of dramatic action and dance. Emanuel had a profound contempt for opera and ballet. For him they were frivolous entertainment and mongrel art. He only acknowledged music that could stand upon its own.

During the months that had elapsed after his leaving the Academy, Emanuel had written nothing, and had spent his days in deep and concentrated thought, searching for the magical addition, the transcendental device that would impart to his music a vivifying force and electrify the musical world. For this he sought long and feverishly. At last one day, in despair, feeling the creative urge come over him, he had started to compose. He hoped that by blindly setting out on an adventure he might perhaps meet with illumination on the way.

The working out of the composition was now all but complete. It was in the form of a symphony in one movement. With logical persuasiveness and vigorous flow it led onwards to a gigantic climax. Emanuel was pleased with what he had done. There was no doubt that the listeners would be carried upward by the sheer force of the music; upward, right out of themselves—but to what?

That evening Emanuel had a presentiment that he was very near to discovery, that the solution was almost within reach and might at any moment be revealed to him in a blinding light. But it was still lurking obstinately in clouds of darkness and the supreme effort to dispel them was nerve-racking in its intensity. Hence all this frantic pacing, the dishevelled hair and the distraught features.

Outside a storm was raging. The wind shook the casement and roared down the chimney. Nature seemed to be in as great a turmoil as Emanuel himself.

Even when it was quiescent, he had no exaggerated fondness for the open air, although he enjoyed it as an occasional relaxation. He could only think and work in an enclosed space. Now he suddenly felt a wild desire to rush out into the night, to mingle with the storm. The impulse drove him madly down the stairs. In his headlong descent he nearly capsized his landlady and her daughter who were returning from the cinema.

"Good gracious!" she exclaimed as Emanuel pushed past her. "He looks as if he'd got the horrors."

A curious and interesting woman the landlady, and like many landladies, a "character," but we cannot allow her to detain us at present. We must continue to follow Emanuel in his tumultuous course.

Outside, the streets were almost deserted. Isolated taxis seemed to be hurrying to shelter from the storm. The trees shook and quivered. Jagged clouds fled across the sky and the moon itself looked as if it were struggling with the wind. Emanuel rushed on distractedly, without purpose or direction, battered by the gale. For how long and how far he knew not. Time and space had become as chaotic as the sky above him. At last, breathless and panting, he found himself in a square where the wind seemed all at once to have dropped, or it may have been that the tall houses were a barrier to the blast. The square seemed a haven in the storm, and all was silence and shadows. Emanuel could not remember having seen the place before or, if he had, night and his emotion gave it an unfamiliar air.

One of the houses, much larger than the others, attracted his attention. It was a queer-looking building, standing back some distance from the road in a garden, and the entrance to it was flanked by huge stone gate posts surmounted by rather malicious-looking sphinxes.

The moon had disappeared behind a cloud but there was sufficient light to enable Emanuel to see that the architecture was peculiar, and unlike that of the other houses in the square. A bewildering medley of styles, it was more curious than beautiful, and the prevalence of Gothic and oriental motives gave it the appearance both of a cathedral and a mosque. The massive archway of the door, sculptured with grotesque demons and monsters, was reminiscent of the kind of thing one sees in a Luna Park.

As Emanuel approached to examine it more closely, the door was suddenly flung open and he was dazzled by a blaze of light. His natural reaction would have been to beat a hasty retreat, but everything that night seemed so strange and incongruous that he walked into the house with the assurance of someone in a dream.

He found himself in a large hall sumptuously furnished in the same Gothic-oriental style. Although the place was lit by many chandeliers and candelabra, the illumination was misty and unreal, and created the impression that at any moment the scene might change or fade away altogether.

A party was in progress and, before he realised what he was doing, he found himself in the midst of a throng of people. Many of the guests, who stood about in groups, looked as peculiar as the house itself and some of them seemed to be wearing fancy dress. But there was no element of Bohemianism about the party. It was obviously a very grand gathering and everyone had an air of importance and respectability. A distinguished-looking middle-aged man detached himself from the crowd and advanced upon Emanuel with outstretched hand.

"I must apologise," said Emanuel, "for this intrusion, and I trust you will allow me to withdraw without comment. I am afraid I am here by mistake."

"Surely no mistake," said the gentleman with a very amiable smile. His voice and manner were faintly ecclesiastical. He had the air of a fashionable bishop.

"I mean," Emanuel explained, "that I have not been invited."

"You are welcome nevertheless. I should not say that to everyone. There are many who would be distinctly unwelcome. With you it is different. I noticed at once that you were a higher mathematician and that you were in search of something."

"I am a composer," said Emanuel, "and it is indeed true that I am in search of something."

"Better still." The man smiled again. "I hope that you will find what you are looking for. I will not be indiscreet enough to enquire what it is. Here, I have no doubt, you will at least find something, if it is only a new way of envisaging life. Let me introduce you to someone. Are you at all interested in reincarnations?"

"I really don't know," replied Emanuel, "I have never met any."

"So much the better. It will be a new experience for you. There are several famous reincarnations here to-night. That lady," he pointed out an extremely ugly, over-vivacious little woman in spectacles, "is the re-incarnation of Cleopatra. She has the soul of Cleopatra but unfortunately not her body. Or would you prefer Joan of Arc?"

Emanuel jumped at any alternative.

"Thank you very much. I should like to meet Joan of Arc."

"Will you kindly give me your name and address?" said the man. "It will be a pleasure to put you on our list for future invitations."

Emanuel gave his name and address which was written down in a small pocket-book. He was then led up to a handsome matter-of-fact looking woman with grey hair, very smartly dressed in black, with a large scarlet flower on her shoulder.

"This is Mr. Smith, the famous composer."

"Not famous yet," said Emanuel bashfully.

The lady scrutinised him for a few moments and then motioned him to sit down beside her.

"I must now leave you, I fear," said the man with another amiable smile. "My duties on these occasions are manifold. Madame D'Arc will entertain you or you will entertain Madame d'Arc, as the case may be." And, with a low bow, he disappeared into the crowd.

"What an agreeable man our host seems to be," Emanuel remarked.

"Good gracious!" exclaimed the lady. "That is not the host. He is merely the social secretary."

"Oh dear," said Emanuel. "He seemed to have some authority. I hope it is all right. You see, I was not invited to this party. I am here by accident."

"What sort of accident?" Madame d'Arc enquired.

"I can't exactly explain. I found myself in front of an open door and walked in without knowing where I was going."

"That is the way we enter into life," said Madame d'Arc.

"I daresay," Emanuel replied, "but it doesn't make my position here any more satisfactory. It doesn't dispel the sensation of being an interloper."

"All people who are worth anything are interlopers," said Madame d'Arc, "and, by persuasion or force, they must make the world accept them. In my last incarnation I failed, and, in the end, the world got the better of me. But I'm not complaining. The same thing happened to Socrates, to Caesar, to Napoleon."

"But you can hardly consider yourself to have been a failure," Emanuel protested. "Are you doing better in your present incarnation?"

"On the whole, yes," replied Madame d'Arc. "As you may know, I am the head of an important dressmaking concern. I impose my fashions on a vast clientèle. My clothes are famous all over the world. My career up till now has been extremely successful. I started life as a humble seamstress without a bean to my name and now I should hardly like to tell you the amount of my super-tax. At an early age I felt that it was my mission to rescue the fashions of my country from foreign domination. I was born plain Mary Jones, but as soon as I became aware of my former incarnation I took the name of Jeanne d'Arc and, paradoxically enough, the assumption of a foreign name has been a great help to me in my profession."

"Forgive me for asking foolish questions," said Emanuel, "I know so little about the matter. How does one find out about a previous incarnation?"

"The conviction grows," replied Madame d'Arc. "Certain memories come back. The first time I read the story of Joan I felt as though I were reading my own autobiography. I visited Domremy and found the place familiar. At Rheims in the cathedral I distinctly saw the Dauphin, and at Rouen a fire broke out in my hotel." Madame d'Arc shuddered. "I have always had the greatest horror of being burnt alive. That in itself, I should say, was conclusive proof."

"And your voices?" asked Emanuel. "Have you still your voices?"

"In my present incarnation I have my visions," replied Madame d'Arc. "They design dresses for me."

Although Emanuel was very interested in what Madame d'Arc was telling him, he had been obsessed all the time by a more immediate curiosity.

"Pardon me," he said at last, "for changing the conversation. I hope that we may return to it later. But at the moment I feel that it is imperative for me to know something about the circumstances in which I find myself. I haven't the least idea how I got here, where I am, or who is giving this party."

"I can't tell you how you got here," said Madame d'Arc, "but Count Omega is your host."

"I'm afraid I have never heard of him," said Emanuel.

"How extraordinary!" exclaimed Madame d'Arc, examining him again as if he were a curious specimen.

"I am a composer," Emanuel explained. "I live for my art and don't go about very much in society."

"I should have thought," said Madame d'Arc, "that even a hermit would have heard of Count Omega, the most famous mystery man of our age and also one of the most wealthy. He is reputed to be the richest man in existence. His enormous fortune, like so many great achievements, originated in a very simple idea carried out with determination and thoroughness. He bought up all the cemeteries, mortuaries, morgues and crematoriums all over the world. He realised that people have got to be buried. That is all."

"How macabre," said Emanuel. "Would you mind pointing him out to me?"

"He is not likely to be present. He never appears at his own parties.

Indeed, he very rarely appears at all, anywhere. But he is no doubt somewhere in the building. He looks at his guests through peepholes in the walls." Emanuel started. "Yes, I know. A lot of people object to this habit and won't come to his parties. I, personally, am not in the least afraid of being watched. God is watching us all the time. So why anyone should mind being spied upon by a mere mortal I can't imagine."

"I find the idea a little alarming," said Emanuel, "especially as I'm not properly dressed for a party."

"You are properly dressed for a composer," said Madame d'Arc. "It would be absurd as well as deceitful if you had come dressed as a soldier or a clergyman."

"Please tell me more about Count Omega," Emanuel continued. "He seems to be an odd character."

"I haven't the least idea whether he is odd or not. I have never seen him. He keeps well out of the public eye, and in that he shows sense. The public is very unreasonable. It is always wanting to see its favourites and if it sees too much of them it either loses interest in them or expects too much of them. Great financiers, however, are among the few celebrities that the world is interested in without wishing to see, and I think that the Count's secrecy is perhaps a little overdone. If you are too mysterious you are liable to get a bad reputation. And the Count's reputation is distinctly sinister. I have heard him described as the embodiment of evil. Heaven knows why. I must say that in my business dealings with him I have always found him very satisfactory. I dress his so-called adopted daughter, the famous Gloria. I suppose you have never heard of her either?"

"No," replied Emanuel, "I'm afraid I haven't. Is she here to-night?"

"She may perhaps appear. At these parties she is sometimes allowed to perform."

"Perform?" Emanuel asked. "What sort of performance?"

"She is a musician. As you are a composer you will naturally be interested."

"I am not interested in female executive artists," said Emanuel. "They are either conceited or unmusical and often both. I suppose she is a prima donna."

"Well, yes. In a sort of a way, though she has none of a prima donna's nonsense. She is a nice, simple girl. I am very fond of her, though she is by no means easy to dress. You see, she is over life size, and it requires the greatest care and ingenuity to prevent her looking like a strong woman in a circus. However, the sartorial problem appeals to me, and it is one that I have solved, I think, successfully. You will see. If not to-night, then perhaps some other time."

"She sounds appalling," said Emanuel. At the same time he felt vaguely fascinated.

"Well, perhaps there is something about her that is rather appalling," said Madame d'Arc, "and if she were wrongly dressed, she might even appear ridiculous. The Count, I am told, is very pleased with the clothes I design for her. But there's no denying that she has great beauty. All the men, and many of the women, are crazy about her. The Count is very jealous and never allows her out of his sight, or out of the sight of one of his trusted menials. Even when she comes to me to try on her clothes she is always accompanied by a eunuch just like a Sultana out of a Seraglio."

"I am astounded," said Emanuel, "that any woman of the present day should put up with such treatment."

"Women of the present day put up with worse things than that," retorted Madame d'Arc. "In some ways Gloria is much to be envied. The Count allows her everything she can possibly desire. She is a primitive creature. Her desires, I should say, are limited and she owes everything to the Count. Heaven only knows what her origin was or where and in what circumstances he discovered her. She doesn't seem to know herself."

"Does she love the Count?" asked Emanuel.

"I really couldn't say," replied Madame d'Arc, "I have no idea what their relationship may be. She strikes me as being rather sexless and my psychological insight, so useful in my profession, tells me that she is one of the most valued objects of the Count's collection of artistic treasures, and nothing more. His collection is said to be one of the finest in the world, although I have never met anyone who has seen it."

"The Count appears to be a very negative individual," remarked

Emanuel. "One never sees him. One knows nothing about him and yet you say he is very well known."

"We know nothing about God," said Madame d'Arc, "and yet He is very well known."

"That is true," replied Emanuel, "but one requires something more from a human being."

"It's no use requiring anything more from the Count, because you won't get it. We must be grateful at least for these parties. I always find them very enjoyable. I hope that you are enjoying yourself."

"I enjoy talking to you," said Emanuel. "You are so full of information. I don't know what I should have done if the secretary hadn't introduced me to you. I am not acquainted with a soul in the place. I should probably have left."

"You couldn't do that," said Madame d'Arc. "No one is supposed to leave before the party is over."

"Good heavens!" exclaimed Emanuel. "I have never heard of such tyranny."

"As a rule nobody wishes to leave. You see, these parties have a singular attraction. Everyone who comes here is supposed to find something they are looking for."

"Is it true?" cried Emanuel eagerly. "Do they really find it?"

"Each time I have been here," said Madame d'Arc, "I have enjoyed myself, and that is something. This evening I have found an agreeable companion. In fact I have taken quite a fancy to you and I don't as a rule care for young men. I hope you will often come and see me. I am at home any day after five o'clock, except Sunday, which is the day I reserve for prayer, meditation and massage."

Emanuel was flattered, but charming as he had found Madame d'Arc, she was far from being the culmination of his own particular desires. But what she had said to him about the nature of Count Omega's parties stirred him deeply. To find what he was looking for! His adventure seemed to be taking on a significance that filled him with hope.

At his unresponsiveness to her amiability Madame d'Arc stared at him again, and Emanuel felt guilty of discourtesy.

"Madame d'Arc," he cried, "I like you very much, and I shall be delighted to come and see you. It is very kind of you to ask me. But how can I explain? What you told me just now has a particular interest for me. What I am looking for, however, has nothing to do with human relationships. It is something theoretical, an aesthetic quest."

"My dear boy," said Madame d'Arc, laying her hand on his knee, "I fear you have misunderstood me. I am a business woman and far above all foolish sentimentality. I have never been moved by carnal passion. My only passion is for designing clothes, running my establishment successfully and imposing on the world 'les dernières modes.' When I have time, I enjoy helping my friends. If you will tell me your trouble, for I can see that you are troubled, I may perhaps be of some assistance to you."

"Alas!" cried Emanuel. "It is impossible to explain, and I doubt if anyone can help me. What I am seeking I must find by myself without external aid."

"Nonsense," said Madame d'Arc. "Nothing can be found without the aid of God. Let us go into the supper room. I feel I could do with a bite."

As Emanuel followed her, he understood at least one of the qualities that had made her a successful business woman. She elbowed her way through the crowded supper room without appearing unduly to push and, although several people were making at the same time for two vacant places, she secured them neatly with no appearance of effort.

"I rather pride myself on my crowd technique," she said. "It's very simple really. It merely consists in knowing where you want to go, making a straight line for it and ignoring competition. Most crowds are irresolute and make way for anyone with determination as long as it is not too apparent. Above all you must never let people see you push."

* * *

The suppers that Count Omega provided for his guests were in keeping with his fabulous wealth. Never, except on cinema screens, had Emanuel seen so lavish a display, so opulent a profusion of crystal, silver and rare porcelain, such bouquets of exotic flowers, such pyramids of fruit. Each dish that was handed round was a masterpiece of elegance and it seemed almost barbarous to eat it. Emanuel wished that he were more able to do justice to the delicious fare but his appetite was cramped by bewilderment and self-consciousness. Madame d'Arc, he noticed, was not suffering from any such inhibitions either as regards herself or anyone else, and she kept on filling up his glass with champagne. He was unaccustomed to strong drink and became slightly intoxicated.

"Tell me, Madame d'Arc," he asked, waving his hand comprehensively, "all these people, are they reincarnations?"

"We are all reincarnations," Madame d'Arc replied gravely, "but it is not given to all to recollect, probably because many former existences were not worth remembering. One meets of course with a good many frauds. Some women are so conceited. I know at least six of them who insist that they were Mary Queen of Scots, whereas they were probably obscure members of her household, or perhaps had merely seen her. Would you believe it, one of my mannequins actually thought she had been Joan of Arc. I said to her, 'There's no room in this establishment for two Joans of Arc' and I sacked her."

The vivacious spectacled lady who was Cleopatra was sitting at the same table. "Take those figs away," Emanuel heard her say, "they give me the creeps."

"You know," said Madame d'Arc, turning to Emanuel, "I have just the same feeling about fire. I never have open fires in my house. Only central heating."

At that moment a gong sounded and the social secretary appeared in the doorway. "Ladies and gentlemen," he shouted, "I am happy to be able to announce to you that Madam Gloria has consented to appear to-night. Will you please take your seats in the concert room."

"Come along," said Madame d'Arc.

Emanuel followed her into an enormous circular room filled with gilt chairs. It was decorated in the same style as the rest of the house and the ceiling was lofty and domed. The stage was small in proportion to the room and was hung with deep blue velvet curtains framed in a massive border of blue and gold mosaics. The air was heavy with incense.

Again Madame d'Arc applied her crowd technique. Knowing that people show a hesitation in occupying the front seats, she made a bee line for them and secured places in the second row.

When all the guests were seated, the lights were lowered and a single beam of opalescent light was directed on the stage. The chattering stopped abruptly and there was complete silence.

Emanuel did not expect very much from the artistic activities of a rich man's mistress and, from what Madame d'Arc had told him, he feared that the performance might even prove slightly embarrassing. However, when he glanced at the audience, he was struck by the look of eager excitement on every face. He noticed that on Madame d'Arc's face also there was the same tense expression. There was something so strange about the atmosphere of suspense that Emanuel became infected by it. He was assailed by a curious feeling of nervous exaltation. It was as though a crucial moment in his life were approaching. A few minutes elapsed. The suspense was growing almost unbearable, and Emanuel's heart began to beat with violence.

At last, swiftly and silently, the curtains were drawn back. On the stage was standing the most gigantic woman Emanuel had ever seen. She was dressed in glittering cloth of gold and her golden hair was crowned with a high, spiked tiara. She seemed to radiate a metallic glow. She was very young and she certainly had great beauty. But it was the beauty of a giantess, of an over life-size statue of some pagan goddess. It was true, what Madame d'Arc had said, that there was something appalling about her but there was also something that was siren-like and alluring. In her hands she held a shining golden instrument. When Emanuel's eyes had grown accustomed to the brightness he saw it was a trombone.

She bowed rather stiffly and greeted the audience with a childish and almost apologetic smile. There was a wild outburst of applause and she bowed again.

Then she raised the instrument to her lips and sounded a single note. Emanuel could not tell what note it was. It seemed to belong to no earthly scale. Starting softly at first, almost imperceptibly, it gradually swelled in volume. Louder and louder it grew until the air seemed to quiver with its vibration. As the sound continued to grow in intensity Emanuel felt as though it were penetrating into the innermost core of his being. On the performer's classic features there appeared no trace of effort. Only, as the volume of the note increased, the golden light that emanated from her person seemed to increase also. It was impossible, Emanuel thought, that the sound could grow any louder. It was now almost painful, yet at the same time it brought excitement and pleasure. He gripped his seat. He felt as though the audience, the house, nay, the universe itself, were about to disintegrate. Like this would be the last trump and such a one the archangel who sounded it.

Then gradually the sound began to diminish and, as imperceptibly as it had begun, faded away into silence. Madam Gloria bowed and smiled. The curtains fell together and hid her from view.

"What did you think of her clothes?" Madame d'Arc asked excitedly. "The effect was good I think. It was a little risky and might have looked vulgar. I confess that, before the curtain went up, I had a moment of anxiety."

An argument started in the row behind.

"It was B flat."

"Nonsense it was B natural."

"I bet you twenty pounds it was B flat."

"Done. But you've lost. I know it was B natural."

Emanuel heard nothing of what was being said around him. His mind was filled by one thought only. He had found the miracle he had been looking for, the great climax he required.

The curtains drew aside once more. Madam Gloria advanced to the edge of the stage and an elderly gentleman handed her a bouquet of orchids.

"That is Mr. Robinson," Madame d'Arc explained, "the reincarnation of Dr. Burney. Quite a parvenu."

Emanuel turned to her eagerly.

"Madame d'Arc," he cried, "you said just now that you would help me if I needed it. You know Madam Gloria. Will you introduce me to her?"

Madame d'Arc looked at him with some concern.

"My poor boy," she said, "it would be useless. It might be dangerous even."

"No, no," Emanuel hastened to assure her. "My intentions are not what you suspect. You must believe in the purity of my motives. There's no time to explain. I will tell you later. I must speak to her at once. Please, Madame d'Arc!"

"Very well," said Madame d'Arc, with an air of resignation, "I'll do what I can. Come with me."

Madam Gloria had gone into the supper room and was standing near a buffet. She towered over the crowd like a golden colossus and was eating an ice with an expression of great beatitude. The throng of people who were trying to get near to her was so large that Madame d'Arc's technique was taxed to the utmost. Their progress was slow and difficult. For a moment Emanuel was separated from his guide and, in his efforts to rejoin her, he trod heavily on a foot whose owner uttered a piercing yelp. Madam Gloria turned towards the commotion and her eyes met those of Emanuel. Her eyes flashed upon him like azure searchlights. Could it be that they expressed a certain interest? That they expressed something, there could be no doubt. No woman, as far as he could remember, had ever looked at him quite in that way before. Whatever might have been the meaning of that penetrating glance, it filled Emanuel with the most violent emotion. He reacted as if to an electric shock; his body thrilled and his knees began to quiver.

At that moment a small door opened in the panelling behind the buffet and a hand protruded. Its apparition was so horrible that Emanuel remained transfixed with fear. He had never realised that a hand by itself could be expressive of so much evil. It was a hand that might have belonged to Abdul Hamid or to Alexander Borgia, but it had at the same time the inhuman quality of a claw of some loathsome prehistoric monster. The apparition seemed to have a magnetic effect on Gloria. She started and turned as though she had been touched. The hand beckoned. She set down her ice hurriedly and disappeared through the door.

"Too late!" exclaimed Madame d'Arc.

Emanuel remained rooted to the spot. He was stunned by this last incident in an evening of surprises. But out of the chaos of his thoughts two definite facts emerged. He had found what he had been seeking and he was in love.

The Social Secretary approached him.

"I hope you have enjoyed yourself," he said, "and that you will come again. I think," he continued, addressing Madame d'Arc, "we may consider that the party is over. You will pardon me for not escorting you to the door. I have many things to attend to."

"Let me give you a lift in my car," said Madame d'Arc to Emanuel.

"That will be kind of you," he replied. "I haven't the least idea where I am, and I might have some difficulty in finding my way home."

"You are perhaps nearer than you think," said Madame d'Arc cryptically.

They had not long to wait before a linkman at the door called out her name, and a very smart coupé appeared, driven by an equally smart chauffeur.

"Now tell me what it is all about," said Madame d'Arc as they drove away.

"I fear the whole matter may appear to you very foolish and un-important. But it is everything to me. The performance we assisted at to-night is exactly what I have been looking for as the finale of a sym-phony I have composed. Together with my music it will be the most astounding thing the world has ever known."

"I don't suppose for a moment," said Madame d'Arc, "that the Count would allow her to perform in a concert hall."

"But if I could get her interested? I might succeed in that, you know. I have great hopes. She looked sympathetic, I thought."

"One has always to reckon with the Count, and he is difficult of ap-proach. However, I will do what I can. Come and see me in a week's time and perhaps I may have some news for you. My address you will find in the telephone book under Madame Jeanne d'Arc. Look it out under D. I am always at home after five, any day except Sunday."

"Oh, Madame d'Arc," cried Emanuel ecstatically. "You are an angel."

The car stopped.

"This is your house I think," said Madame d'Arc. "Good night. A bientôt."

It was nearly three o'clock, and Emanuel's habitual bedtime was half-past ten. On reaching his room he undressed hastily and jumped into bed. Although his brain was in a whirl he was so exhausted that he soon fell into a deep and dreamless slumber.

2

—⟨◦⟩—

Emanuel was awakened next morning by a tapping on his door. The landlady put in her head.

"It's nearly ten o'clock," she announced. "I was getting worried. You looked in such a state coming down the stairs last night I was afraid you'd had bad news."

"I'm quite all right thank you, Mrs. Darwin," Emanuel reassured her. "I came home unusually late and I fear I have overslept myself."

"Well, I'm glad it was nothing serious," she said, as she drew up the blind. "I'll tell Milly to get your breakfast."

Emanuel sat up in his bed and looked out of the window. The sky had been swept clean by the storm. The morning was bright and cloudless and the room was flooded with sunshine. In the clear light of day the memories that came crowding chaotically into his brain seemed fantastic and unreal. Yet among them there shone a golden vision that was brighter and more real than even the sunlight itself. For a while he contemplated it in ecstasy. But alas, like all secular ecstasy it did not endure, and all too soon the radiance of the vision was dulled by considerations of bleak reality. The glittering chimaera had materialised, but it still eluded his grasp. The difficulties of capture were yet to be overcome.

However, he had great hopes of Madame d'Arc. She seemed to be the type of woman who, if once she gave her mind to it, would succeed in getting anything she wanted. A week, she had said. It seemed a long time to wait.

Emanuel had an independent spirit. He did not wholly relish the idea of being beholden to anyone, especially to a woman. In matters artistic and amorous he felt it his duty to work out his own salvation. Some sort of action on his own behalf was imperative, and he disliked the idea of just sitting at home waiting for things to happen through the mediation of a kind lady.

As soon as he had finished his breakfast he went out to look for the mysterious house, the scene of last night's adventure. He cursed himself for not having ascertained the address. But even if he found it, what did he propose to do? He would never have the courage to ring the bell and ask for Gloria. He could only hang about in the hopes of a chance encounter. And even that, as Madame d'Arc had warned him, might be inadvisable and even dangerous. However, he was obsessed too strongly by the necessity for action and he spent the whole morning wandering about in futile search. Beyond increasing his knowledge of the town and gaining information that would be useful for a taxi-driver, his peregrinations were without profit. Occasionally he came upon a square that for a moment raised his hopes, but there were no signs of the house. It remained as undiscoverable as if it were non-existent. It might have been whisked away like the palace of Aladdin.

At last, in despair, he went home and looked out Madame d'Arc's address in the telephone book. He would go and take a peep at her house. It was the next best thing and the sight of it would reassure him. But no, he reflected, that also was unwise. If he were to meet her coming out, or if she were to see him out of the window—not that she seemed the sort of person who would look out of a window—but if she did—no, he thought, it would never do. His premature appearance, after having been told to wait for a week, might seem to her suspicious and might make her disinclined to help him. He would have to be patient until the week was up. Yet what was he to do in the meantime? It was useless to continue his search and he dreaded the thought of sitting idly at home, for he was in a state of mind that rendered work impossible.

He took up his composition and read it through. This restored to a certain extent his calm. The work, as far as it went, was perfect, and he felt no doubts about the effect it would create with the addition of its sensational finale.

He had not yet thought of a title, and he racked his brains to think of something suitable. "The First Symphony" was not sufficiently descriptive. "The World Symphony" struck too mundane a note. "A Symphony of the Universe" was good, but it sounded perhaps a little too bombastic. He gave up trying. No doubt when the matter was settled, an appropriate title would come spontaneously.

Wondering desperately how he could employ his time, he thought of his fiancée. For he had a fiancée. Her name was Evangeline Brown and she lived in the country. Emanuel had lost both parents at an early age, and Evangeline's father, who was a distant relation, had been appointed his guardian.

Emanuel thought of a solution of his immediate difficulties. He would go and stay with Evangeline and her family until the week was up. The country air, the tranquillity of the surroundings and placid conversation would act as balm to his troubled soul.

He sent a telegram, packed his bag and took the earliest train.

The Brown family lived in a pleasant villa in a remote, but not too remote, part of the country. The surrounding landscape was picturesque in an ordered way and suggestive of the period in which romanticism had calmed down into peace and prosperity. It had no wildness or imprevu. It was thoroughly respectable and had the suave charm of a water colour by Birket Foster. The house stood on the banks of a river whose gentle current reflected the lives of the occupants.

Mr. Brown was a retired clergyman and an invalid. Mrs. Brown was an amiable and cultured housewife who spent her spare time, of which she had a good deal, in reading the works of English authoresses. She was a great authority on Mrs. Gaskell, Jane Austen and George Eliot. Her ideals were those of Cranford. She disapproved of the modern trend of civilisation and, as far as she was able, ignored it. Even the telephone she regarded as an obnoxious innovation.

Evangeline was a very intellectual young woman. She was devoting herself to the study of philosophy and was regarded by some of her friends as something of a blue stocking. There was nothing very striking about her appearance except her hair which was a rather vivid red. When she removed her pince-nez and was not immersed in thought she was really quite pretty.

She had a brother whose name was James. He was about thirty and was a mental specialist. He believed that nearly every mental illness was due to sex-disturbance or inappropriate occupation. He had a genius for diagnosis and a single interview was sufficient to enable him to decide on the proper form of curative activity to be prescribed. In his practice he was very successful and had already made a name for himself. He had cured a well-known banker who suffered from persecution mania by inducing him to take up horticulture, and a neurotic member of the royal family by recommending a course of saxophone lessons.

In this tranquil and edifying milieu Emanuel hoped to find relief from the impatience of temporarily thwarted ambition.

The afternoon of Emanuel's arrival was warm and sunny. Spring was at its height and the countryside had all the optimistic exuberance of youth. The fresh foliage of the trees and hedgerows, the profusion of blossom, the fleecy clouds in the light blue sky and the triumphant shrillness of the larks, singing away like an enthusiastic village choir, seemed to be proffering to Emanuel messages of goodwill and encouragement.

There was, however, a sombre patch in all this vernal joy. It appeared for a moment in the background of Emanuel's thoughts. But he turned away from it hastily. He refused to consider it. He cut it dead. The sombre patch was his relationship to Evangeline. He had been definitely engaged to her for over a year. They had been brought up together, and ever since their childhood the idea of their eventual union had been contemplated. Emanuel had grown accustomed to it and had ended by taking it for granted. He was very fond of Evangeline but his feelings for her were mental rather than physical. He looked upon her as a perfect soul-companion. Although her intellect was superior in many ways to his, she was vastly inferior in all that concerned art and the creative faculties. Her philosophical instincts inclined her to prize the unknown and, as she was unmusical, her admiration for Emanuel was unbounded. Emanuel respected her erudition and the clarity of her mind and, as a left-wing aesthete, he liked the colour of her hair. The marriage would be one of sublimated convenience.

But that afternoon Evangeline was not, as she should have been, the centre upon which all this spring-tide elation focused. A golden vision and a trombone note had come between Emanuel and his betrothed. They dulled the crystalline clarity of her mind. They eclipsed the effulgence of her hair.

When Emanuel arrived at the house he was told that Evangeline was out of doors. He found her sitting on the banks of the river, deep in meditation. She was wearing a flowered muslin dress and she looked like a combination of Botticelli's Flora and a school mistress.

If only, he thought, as he observed her profile, she hadn't such a very long nose. Curiously enough it was the first time this defect had struck him unfavourably.

"What are you thinking about, Evangeline?" he called to her.

She was absorbed in thought.

"Evangeline," he repeated, "what are you thinking about?"

She looked up and smiled.

"Oh, Emanuel," she said, "how pleased I am to see you. I was thinking about Time. I was trying to solve the problem of whether Time flows past us, or we flow past Time. Are we a point on the river bank, I was asking myself, or do we flow past the banks with the stream?"

"And what conclusion have you come to?"

"I have come to none. It was perhaps a mistake to allow myself to be inspired by a pictorial image taken from nature, and it is difficult to concentrate in the open air. The larks distract one so."

"Let us abandon speculation for a while," suggested Emanuel, "and give ourselves over to the idle contemplation of the landscape. Let us be distracted by the larks."

He sat down on the grass beside her.

"You look pale," Evangeline said. "I fear you have been working too hard."

"I have been working hard," replied Emanuel. "And I have completed my symphony—or practically completed it."

A tender look came into Evangeline's eyes.

"Oh, Emanuel," she cried. "How I wish I were more worthy of your genius. It's not for want of trying. During the last months I have studied harmony and counterpoint. I have read all Professor Tovey's analyses and the biographies of the great composers. But alas! although I know by heart the rules of fugal structure and sonata-form, the essential significance of music remains for me as a fountain sealed."

"No matter," said Emanuel, patting her cheek. "At least we shall never quarrel about music and, as I am equally unresponsive to philosophy, we shall not quarrel about that either. The situation is ideal. Let us go for a walk."

"Certainly," said Evangeline. "Where shall we go?"

"I should like to see the Castle again. It is a long time since I have been there. It's not too far, is it?"

"No," said Evangeline. "We have plenty of time."

The Castle—as it was called in the neighbourhood—was a sham mediaeval stronghold built in the early nineteenth century by an enthusiast of the Gothic revival. The building was a wild conglomeration of towers, turrets, cloisters and winding stairways. There was a drawbridge, a keep, a banqueting hall, a Lady's Bower, a dungeon and a profusion of stained glass. From the interior all light had been carefully excluded. It was built of russet coloured stone and in spite of a somewhat gingerbread appearance it contrived nevertheless to create a grim and gloomy impression conformable to the popular idea of the Middle Ages.

It had been for many years unoccupied and was beginning to fall into disrepair. As it lay outside the beaten track of trains and buses, it was seldom visited by tourists. In its immediate neighbourhood the country suddenly ceased to be prim, and grew more romantic, in a creditable attempt to achieve the terrible and the sublime. It looked as if the architect of the Castle had transported a suitable environment from some other part of the country. The river narrowed and formed a gorge and the Castle stood on a sandstone cliff overhanging the water, and on one side there was a deep ravine. It was approached by a winding road through a wood of battered fir trees and gnarled oaks.

Emanuel had always been attracted by the place. It appealed to him more than it did to Evangeline whose taste was guided by the principles of Pure Reason.

As they made their way across the fields, Emanuel was beset by a feeling of uneasiness. Hitherto he had enjoyed and admired Evangeline's earnestness. That afternoon, for the first time, he found it slightly irritating. They had been walking rather fast and Evangeline was out of breath. He caught himself taking a guilty pleasure in the fact that it stopped her talking.

As they approached the Castle, Emanuel's impressionable mind reacted to the atmosphere of the place. It looked grimmer and more deserted than ever and, although its aspect was completely different, there was something about it that made him think of the mysterious house in the square.

The gate leading into the courtyard was closed.

"I never remember it being shut before," said Evangeline. "One could always walk straight in."

They rang the bell and waited for several minutes, but nobody came. They rang again. This time, in a distant part of the building, they heard a furious barking of dogs.

"How strange," said Emanuel. "There never used to be dogs here."

"There's nothing strange about it," remarked Evangeline. "If the custodian is out it is very annoying, and we shall have had our journey for nothing."

"We might try to get in from another side," Emanuel suggested.

They took a narrow path skirting the castle walls and came to the foot of a tower that jutted out over the ravine. Just above their heads were three windows that were open.

"I could get through one of those windows," said Emanuel, "if you would help me up, and I could unbar the gate from the inside."

As he spoke there appeared in each window the head of an enormous dog. In the shadow of the overhanging trees and framed in the dark background of the room beyond, the apparition was sinister and menacing. The dogs seemed to belong to some abnormally large breed of mastiff. They remained there, immobile and silent, glaring at the intruders, their bloodshot eyes full of hatred and ferocity.

Emanuel started back and Evangeline gave a scream.

"Good gracious," she said. "Those were the dogs we heard barking."

"Obviously," replied Emanuel, "and I don't propose to tackle them."

He was annoyed at having been so startled, but he did not feel like assuming the role of St. George or Perseus just for the sake of getting into the castle.

They turned and hurried away down the path, a little shaken by their experience.

"Shall we try ringing again?" Evangeline suggested. "It seems a pity to have come all this way for nothing."

"For God's sake no," said Emanuel. "We had better come back another day."

As they were descending the road through the oaks and fir trees Emanuel heard a sound that made him pause and caused his heart to beat.

Evangeline turned.

"What is it, Emanuel?" she asked. "Are you feeling ill?"

"That sound," whispered Emanuel. "Do you hear it?"

"What sound? I heard nothing."

"Someone playing a trombone. Don't you hear it?"

Evangeline listened.

"No. I hear absolutely nothing."

"It has stopped now. But it seems impossible you didn't hear it."

"You know, Emanuel, that I have no ear for music."

"That has nothing to do with it," said Emanuel angrily. "At one moment it was quite loud. You aren't getting deaf, are you?"

"Not that I know of. I can hear father snoring at night quite distinctly although his bedroom is far from mine."

They continued on their way in silence. A new fear was beginning to take shape in Emanuel's mind. Could it be that he was growing mentally unbalanced? Had the trombone note existed only in his disordered imagination? Several musicians had ended their lives in madness. He thought of Schumann, of Smetana, and he recalled with horror that Smetana had been haunted by a persistent note that obsessed and distracted him during the last years of his life. He had reproduced it in one of his compositions; an enharmonic on the violin sounding high above the other instruments like the long drawn out cry of a ghostly bat. To be haunted by a trombone note was an even more terrifying proposition.

And then he began to wonder if the whole adventure of the previous evening had been purely imaginary, the result of overwork and his feverish searching. The party, the reincarnations, and the beckoning hand had all of them the characteristics of a delirious dream. But Madame d'Arc must at least be real as he had found her address in the telephone directory. The solid evidence of the telephone book reassured him. But he would make doubly sure by looking it out again.

Evangeline noticed Emanuel's sombre distraction but refrained from interrupting. She thought he was engaged in elaborating some musical theme.

* * *

At dinner that evening Emanuel seemed to have regained his spirits and did his best to make himself agreeable. He affected a great interest in old Mr. Brown's account of a diocesan conference in which he had once taken part and he listened with respectful attention to Mrs. Brown's detailed exposition of the plot of Mrs. Gaskell's "North and South" and went so far as to promise to read George Eliot's "Romola" which she strongly recommended. He also took part in a discussion between Evangeline and her brother James on the relative merits of metaphysics and psychology. Afterwards, the conversation degenerated into small talk. Evangeline referred to the unsuccessful visit to the castle.

"Now let me see," said Mrs. Brown. "What did I hear about the Castle? Oh yes, it has been bought, I heard, by a millionaire."

Emanuel nearly jumped out of his seat and with a great effort controlled himself.

"It seemed quite deserted," said Evangeline, "except for three very large dogs that looked at us out of the windows. And on the way back Emanuel said he had heard somebody playing a trumpet."

Emanuel changed the conversation abruptly and for the rest of the evening although he strove to appear bright and cheerful, it escaped neither Evangeline's tender scrutiny nor the acute professional eye of James that he was suffering from some latent trouble. And when Emanuel had retired to rest Evangeline called her brother into her bedroom for a consultation.

"I am worried about Emanuel," she said to him. "He is so unlike his usual self. He seems preoccupied and irritable, and I believe him to be suffering from aural delusions. Perhaps it is only that he has been working too hard at his music." ·

"There is no doubt," said James, "that even the most suitable occupations may be overdone. But I do not believe that to be the correct explanation."

"I wish I knew what was wrong with him," Evangeline continued. "I wonder if, in some way, his ethical basis has been shaken. That is liable to happen to those who rely on feeling and intuition rather than on reason."

"In my opinion," James pronounced, "his symptoms point to a physical and not a spiritual disturbance. I believe it to be far more probable that he is suffering from sex-starvation. Why on earth you two don't get married I can't imagine."

"Emanuel won't hear of getting married until he has made a name for himself."

"That may take some time, and if it is, as I suspect, a case of sex-starvation, something ought to be done about it at once."

"You are surely not suggesting——," exclaimed Evangeline, in a horror-struck voice.

"No, no," her brother assured her. "Nothing of the sort." And he hurriedly left the room.

3

Emanuel was one of the lucky people to whom joy cometh in the morning and, when he woke up in his pleasant bedroom and saw the sunlight coming through the chintz curtains, giving promise of warmth and fair weather, his spirits rose. Everything that had seemed, last night, dark and menacing was now tinged with brilliant colours and his soul was filled with hope. It was nice to be in the country, to feel the fresh air in the room, to hear the twittering birds. A few more days and he would no doubt hear from the capable dressmaker that an interview with Madam Gloria had been arranged. All was for the best in the best of possible worlds. He would get Evangeline to tell him about Leibnitz and the philosophy of optimism.

When, after breakfast, he sat alone with his fiancée in the garden, she seemed unwilling to discuss philosophy. She was pensive, Emanuel noticed, and appeared to have on her mind some subject that she hesitated to broach.

"Emanuel," she said to him at last, "you still love me, don't you?"

"Why of course," he replied. "What ever can have made you think I didn't?"

"Then why, oh why, can't we get married? This endless procrastination seems so unnecessary. What does it matter that you are not yet famous? You will be soon enough. Of that I have no doubt. Have you no faith in yourself? And, in any case, I would marry you whether you were famous or not."

Emanuel was dismayed by this sudden insistence. It was the last thing he had foreseen. He came to the rapid conclusion that the best way to treat such a contingency was to meet it with a promise.

"Very well," he said, "but it can't take place at once I fear. In two months' time, a month perhaps. I have great hopes that my symphony will bring me instant fame. But its performance depends on certain matters that I shall have to deal with. In a month's time I trust that everything will be settled. Does that satisfy you?"

Evangeline raised her face to be kissed and once more Emanuel thought it was a pity that her nose was so long.

"Thank you, Emanuel," she said. "You have made me very happy, and I am sure it is for the best."

"And now," said Emanuel, "do you mind if I leave you alone for a bit? I must do some work. I feel the moment is propitious. I feel inspired."

What Emanuel really felt was a sudden and violent desire to re-visit the Castle, but he wished to re-visit it alone. He knew that, with regard to his work, Evangeline was tactful, and when he expressed a desire for solitude she always respected it. However, he did not want her to know where he was going. Brandishing a piece of music paper he set off across the fields in an opposite direction to that in which the Castle lay and, as soon as he was out of sight, he changed his course.

By the time he was half-way to his destination he had forgotten all about Evangeline and the marriage. His mind was full of day dreams. Strange how moods can transfigure circumstances! He was sure now that Gloria was there. Mrs. Brown had said that a millionaire had bought the place and who else could it be but the mysterious Count? He felt no longer any fear of this graveyard profiteer. No doubt his sinister reputation had been greatly exaggerated and he was perhaps just a lonely shy old man, like Silas Marner, and Gloria was his Eppie.

Emanuel decided he would ring the bell and ask to see the Count, who would receive him politely. One was always received politely in the country. He would propose his scheme and if the Count demurred he would go to the piano—there would of course be a piano, a magnificent Steinway—and play him the symphony. The Count, an art lover and a man of great discernment, would at once realise that it was a work of genius. He would be overcome with emotion and enthusiasm and would offer to finance the concert. Then he would send for Gloria and Emanuel would see her, and speak to her.

The Castle looked as deserted as ever and the door of the gatehouse was still closed. Emanuel tugged at the bell and its peal echoed through the castle walls. Again there was silence. Emanuel rang several times but always with the same result. He felt a slight misgiving. Perhaps they had gone. But it seemed unlikely that the place could have been left completely deserted.

He made his way along the path that led to the open windows. This time, instead of the dogs, a man was standing there looking at him. He recognised the social secretary. Emanuel approached and waved his hand to him.

The secretary stared at him coldly.

"You are no doubt unaware," he said, "that you are trespassing."

"Don't you recognise me?" Emanuel cried. "I am Emanuel Smith. I came to the party the other night. You were so very kind to me."

"I have not the least idea," said the man, "to what party you may be referring. I can only repeat that you are trespassing. This house is now private property and is closed to visitors. It is decidedly closed to visitors."

"Oh, but this is absurd," Emanuel persisted. "I want to see the Count. I have an important proposition to make to him."

The man's face assumed a momentary expression of alarm. Then he leant out of the window.

"If you do not go away at once," he hissed, "I shall adopt drastic measures to hasten your departure."

The man disappeared from the window, and a few minutes later Emanuel heard an ominous sound of barking. He took to his heels and fled away down the hill, through the wood and never stopped until he had gained the open fields beyond.

He was bewildered and terrified. The logical consistency of his experiences broke down and gave place to a crazy conflict between the real and the unreal. Was it possible that the insolent hostile figure in the window was the same as the amiable person who had welcomed him at the party? All his doubts and fears returned to him and once more he began to wonder if he had been suffering from hallucinations. Was he, in fact, going mad? However, in all these fantastic happenings, one character at least had the elements of stability and common sense. Madame d'Arc. She was in the telephone book. She was the one rock to which he could cling amidst the rising tide of nightmare insanity. He must return to the town at once. The blithe indifference of nature and the placid company of the Browns would only accentuate the tumult of his soul, and the proximity of the Castle might prove too dangerous an attraction for his moth-like flutterings.

On getting back to the house he sought out Evangeline.

"Much as I enjoy being here," he said to her, "I'm afraid I must leave to-day. I find I am unable to work in the country. I never could, you know. I am very sorry, but I am sure you will understand."

Evangeline said that she too was very sorry but that she quite understood.

She accompanied him to the station. Although Emanuel made a valiant effort to master his emotions and appear normal and affectionate, Evangeline was left with a sense of uneasiness. She consulted once more her brother.

"I am convinced," she said, "that there is something seriously wrong with Emanuel. I took your advice and spoke to him about our marriage. He has agreed that it shall take place in a month's time. But, although he seemed pleased with the idea, I fear that the prospect has not removed the disturbance from which he appears to be suffering. I believe it to be far more fundamental than the sex-starvation you suggested, and I am now more convinced than ever that something has occurred that has severely shaken the foundations of his ethical system."

"Sex-starvation cannot be cured by mere prospects, my dear Evangeline," said James, with an indulgent smile, "and every student of psychology knows that the ethical system is founded on sex."

"It is founded on reason," said Evangeline.

James was not persuaded, but he acknowledged the superiority of his sister's dialectical skill and knew that in an argument of this kind he was likely to be worsted.

"You may be right, my dear," he said, "but I am sure that if he would consent to place himself in my hands I should, by one method or another, succeed in curing him."

4

When Emanuel returned to his lodgings and was passing the door of his landlady's sitting room, she rushed out in a state of unusual excitement, holding a letter in her hand.

"Oh, Mr. Smith," she cried, "this has just come for you. I was to give it you at once. My goodness, you do have grand friends."

Obviously Emanuel had risen considerably in her estimation.

The letter was from Madame d'Arc and the notepaper was headed with two little engraved views, one of Domremy, the other of Madame d'Arc's dressmaking establishment. The contents were brief but they threw Emanuel into an ecstasy of delight.

"Have arranged meeting with G.," he read. "Come and see me to-morrow at 4.30. Jeanne."

He wondered if she had brought the letter herself. It seemed unlikely, and enquiries proved that it had been Madame d'Arc's smart chauffeur who had so impressed Mrs. Darwin.

Emanuel suddenly noticed that the letter bore yesterday's date, and that to-morrow meant to-day. He looked at his watch. It was already four o'clock.

"Good heavens!" he cried. "I must hurry. Will you ask Milly to call me a taxi, Mrs. Darwin?"

He ran upstairs to tidy himself up and change into his best suit. He jumped into the waiting taxi and got to Madame d'Arc's a few minutes after the half hour.

The facade of Madame d'Arc's establishment had a discreet and al-most modest appearance and gave no indication of the opulent ele-gance within. A commissionaire led him down a corridor into a small room that looked like an office. Madame d'Arc was sitting at a writing table.

"Well," she said, "you can't say I'm not a quick worker. Everything is arranged for your interview. Gloria will be here in a few minutes. With regard to the eunuch Achmed, I have evolved a plan of campaign——"

"Oh, Madame d'Arc," cried Emanuel, "however can I thank you——"

She put up her hand.

"Defer your gratitude until after the interview. We can only hope for the best. Meanwhile wait in here."

She took him into an adjoining room. It was larger than the office and was very luxuriously furnished in Louis Quinze style. At the same time there was an air of comfortable intimacy that is so often lacking in French eighteenth century apartments. In one corner of the room was a tea-table covered with the most tempting-looking cakes and sweets.

"Wait here," said Madame d'Arc, "and I will bring Gloria to you. I expect her at any moment. Only you must waste no time. I am not quite sure how my plan for dealing with Achmed will answer. In this life we must never put too much trust in probabilities. Oh, by the way," she added, "be sure and see that she has plenty to eat."

She hurried out of the room. Emanuel noticed that Madame d'Arc's manner was no longer that of the pleasant society woman he had known at the party. She now resembled a military commander intent on some point of strategy. Her voice was abrupt and authoritative.

Emanuel examined the room. The walls were hung with the most exquisite Beauvais tapestry with designs by Boucher. He had hardly time to look at them more closely when the door opened and Madame d'Arc appeared with Gloria. High as the doorway was, she was obliged to stoop to enter. She was dressed in flowing draperies of brilliant blue covered with exotic embroideries and on her head there was a sort of helmet composed of long, brightly coloured feathers. She looked like an Aztec warrior.

"This is Mr. Smith," said Madame d'Arc. "He will explain to you the nature of his request. I will return presently."

Gloria's face lit up with a smile of recognition.

"Why," she said, "you are the man I saw at the party."

Emanuel made a superhuman effort to control his nerves and to get his voice into working order. He felt like some puny mortal addressing a goddess.

"Madam Gloria," he stammered, "forgive me if I seem presumptuous. But I must tell you that your performance on the trombone is the most wonderful, the most miraculous, the most———"

Gloria giggled shyly and looked a little embarrassed.

"Oh nonsense," she said. "That's nothing."

Her manner reassured him. She was certainly, as Madame d'Arc had said, a simple creature. In her movements she was almost gawky, but it was a gawkiness that was divine. Had she been more sophisticated, more graceful, she would have lost a great part of her charm. Her ingenuousness was like the bloom on a peach.

Emanuel plunged into an exposition of his musical ideas. He used every artifice of eloquence and persuasion. But although Gloria seemed to be listening to him with interest and continued to smile at him encouragingly, he noticed that her eyes were continually straying to the tea table. He remembered Madame d'Arc's injunctions.

"Oh," he said. "How stupid of me. Won't you have something to eat?"

"Thank you," said Gloria eagerly. "I should like one of those marrons glacés."

He handed her the plate. She took it from him and placed it on her lap. Emanuel was slightly disconcerted by the avid way in which she stuffed the marrons into her mouth. In a very short time the plate was empty.

"Now," she said, "I should like some of those pink sugar cakes." Noting a look of surprise on Emanuel's face she felt that perhaps an explanation was necessary.

"You see," she said, "He never lets me eat sweets. He's afraid of my getting fat. And I do love them so. It's only at Madame d'Arc's that I ever get them, and then only when Achmed isn't looking."

And this was the woman, Emanuel thought, of whom Madame d'Arc had said that the Count allowed her everything she wished for. In his eyes she assumed the additional attraction of a martyr, a maiden to be rescued.

When the pink cakes were finished and Gloria was half-way through a plate of éclairs, Emanuel thought it was time to return to the main theme of the interview.

"Will you consent," he entreated, "to perform in my symphony? For God's sake say yes, Madam Gloria. The whole fate of my musical career depends on it. I implore you."

Gloria smiled.

"Well, of course," she replied. "I should simply love to. But everything is very difficult and complicated. He might allow me to do it. But one never knows. It all depends on his mood. He might say 'Yes' one day and 'No' another. One can never tell. Perhaps if I could persuade him that it was a good joke———"

"A good joke!" Emanuel nearly screamed. "What on earth do you mean?"

"He is very fond of practical jokes," Gloria replied. "They are the only thing he is really interested in."

"But this is serious," Emanuel exclaimed indignantly. "It can have nothing to do with a practical joke. I don't understand what you mean. This is an artistic venture of the highest importance. It will be the most serious thing that has happened for many years, the most epoch-making event in the world of music."

Gloria saw from Emanuel's earnestness that she had made a faux pas.

"Of course," she said, "I know. I didn't mean that. But he is a very strange man. He doesn't see things quite as other people do. You must leave it to me. I will do everything I can to persuade him, because I should simply love to play in your symphony. It is very kind of you to have asked me. And oh," she looked rather frightened, "it is very important that he shouldn't know that I've seen you. I must pretend that the idea came from Madame d'Arc."

Emanuel was overcome from joy.

"Thank you, Madam Gloria. This is all too wonderful. My brain is in a whirl. You perhaps don't realise what this means to me."

He became speechless with emotion, and for a few minutes they sat in silence. Gloria continued to smile at him. There was something about her smile that was so disturbing, so inviting that Emanuel lost all control. He flung himself upon her and clasped her in a wild embrace. The plate of éclairs flew into the air and its contents were scattered over the carpet.

"Oh, mind my hat," cried Gloria, but she made no attempt to repulse him. On the contrary she threw her arms round his neck and clasped him more closely to her. How long they remained in this attitude Emanuel knew not. All measurement of time was annihilated in an ecstasy of bliss.

Suddenly he felt her body grow limp.

"I feel faint," she murmured.

Emanuel sprang up.

"I don't know what's come over me. I feel so queer. I've never felt like it before."

"Shall I get you something?" Emanuel asked anxiously. "Some brandy? I wonder if there is any." He looked round the room.

"No," said Gloria, "I feel better now. But I should like another cake."

At that moment Madame d'Arc reentered the room. She uttered an exclamation of surprise on seeing the dishevelled condition of its occupants and the floor all littered with éclairs.

"Oh good gracious, your hat!" she exclaimed. She rushed at Gloria and began smoothing out the feathers.

"That's better. What on earth have you been doing? But you must hurry, Gloria. We can't hold Achmed any longer. Duty seems to have got the better of his sensuality. However, Rosalie has been wonderful. I shall certainly promote her. Come along."

She hurried Gloria out of the room without giving Emanuel time to say good-bye. As she left, Gloria kissed her hand to him.

After a short time Madame d'Arc came back.

"Well," she said, doing a sort of egg-dance among the éclairs, "your interview seems to have been a lively one. And what about the purity of your motives? My goodness, I was quite taken in by all that nonsense you told me. Why couldn't you have been frank with me? I'm no prude, you know, even though I've never cared for that sort of thing myself."

"Madame d'Arc," he stammered. "Believe me. It wasn't entirely my fault——"

"That's what Adam said," retorted Madame d'Arc, with an ironical smile. "Really, you men are all alike. No moral courage."

Emanuel hung his head like an admonished schoolboy.

"I really must apologise."

"There's nothing to apologise about. I don't mind your having hoodwinked me so thoroughly. I don't resent a lover's subterfuge. If it had been a business matter, that would have been very different. I suppose it was all nonsense about that concert?"

"No indeed. It is perfectly serious, the most serious thing of all. And she has consented. She said she would simply love to do it. It's only a question of getting round the Count, and she thinks she'll be able to manage that too."

"Well, I suppose it's as good a way of sealing a contract as any other."

"Oh, Madame d'Arc," cried Emanuel, ignoring the allusion, "it's all too wonderful. How can I ever repay you for what you have done for me?"

"The success of your interview is sufficient reward for me," replied Madame d'Arc. "I take no small pleasure in the fact that I too have achieved my object. It was due to my ingenuity and foresight that you were enabled to have your interview at all, and I really don't care what use you made of it as long as you got what you wanted."

"You still don't believe me," Emanuel persisted. "I promise you that what happened—well, it just happened. I can't explain how."

"You never seem to be able to explain anything," said Madame d'Arc. "You couldn't explain how you came to a party uninvited and now you can't explain how you came to take advantage of an innocent girl in my drawing room."

"I am an artist," said Emanuel, "and artists should never explain. If they do, it means that something is wrong with their art."

"Well, I am a business woman," replied Madame d'Arc. "I am always ready to explain, and there's nothing wrong with my business. Would you like me to explain how I dealt with the eunuch Achmed? It was by no means easy. He has the soul of a watchdog, and is terrified of the Count. Fear, with him, takes the place of devotion and he knows what would happen to him if he were to fail in his duties. He is not allowed into the room where Gloria is trying on, but he sits outside watching the door. Eunuchs, however, in spite of their disabilities, are not wholly unsusceptible to feminine charm. I had noticed him looking at one of my mannequins, a very attractive girl, and I set her to work on him. It entailed of course no risk. It was merely a matter of—let us call it—fascination."

She rang a bell. It was answered by a smartly dressed woman in black.

"Send Rosalie to me."

Rosalie was also very smartly dressed in black and she was extremely pretty. Confronted with her dark hair, fresh complexion and eyes that flashed alluringly, Emanuel thought that a man would have to have even more disabilities than a eunuch to resist her voluptuous charms.

"I am very pleased with you, Rosalie," said Madame d'Arc. "I intend to raise your salary."

Emanuel felt as if he were assisting at a promotion on the battle field.

Rosalie's protestations of gratitude were interrupted by the entrance of the commissionaire with a letter.

Madame d'Arc opened it and gave an exclamation of pleasure.

"It is from the Palace," she said. "The Queen Mother has at last decided to make use of my services. This is a great moment. A moment I have long been awaiting. Hurrah!" she cried, her eyes lighting up with loyal devotion. "You can go, Rosalie."

With a smile that also included Emanuel the exultant girl left the room.

"God helps those who help others," said Madame d'Arc, turning to Emanuel. "Divine justice often seems strange and unreasonable to our finite minds, and it is often deferred. But in this instance its logic and promptness are evident. For many years the intrigues of my enemies have prevailed, but at last I have triumphed over them. I have no doubt that this is my reward for helping you. It may also be a sign that your enterprise is pleasing to God—I mean your musical enterprise, of course. And now I must ask you to leave me. I have great work before me."

Emanuel's heart sank.

"Madame d'Arc," he implored, "you won't desert me. This means, I fear, that you will no longer have time to help me. I depend upon you more than ever now. Gloria said it would be dangerous for me to appear as the originator of the proposed concert and that the idea must be supposed to have come from you. I trust to you to deal with the Count. If you withdraw your aid the whole scheme will be ruined."

"Of course I shall continue to help you," Madame d'Arc assured him. "When once I take up a cause I never rest until victory is won. You can trust to me. As for the Palace, it is an end that I have always had in view and the designs are ready. It is only a question of a few hours to put the matter in order. But I must get to work at once. I will keep in touch with you and let you know how things proceed. All will be well. You can rest assured. I never fail my friends."

As Emanuel took his leave, she patted his head and an almost tender look came into her eyes.

"My little Dauphin," she murmured.

5

E manuel went on his way rejoicing. Madame d'Arc's determination and Gloria's persuasion would, between them, assuredly prevail. In one direction at all events his hopes had met with fulfilment beyond his wildest dreams. He basked in the erotic memories of that strange encounter. His star was in the ascendant. The world was paradise and, on its threshhold, stood the censor of his thoughts excluding with a flaming sword all that came to disturb it. Evangeline, a pale wraith, was banished to the unconscious.

After two days a letter came from Madame d'Arc. "I have good news for you," it ran. "Come at 4.30."

Emanuel set out long before the appointed hour and in order to occupy the time, he took a circuitous route. As it often happens that when we are no longer looking for a thing, we find it, Emanuel came upon the mysterious house. There was no doubt about it this time. As he passed through the sphinx gates he saw that a scaffolding had been erected and that the house was being demolished. How strange, he thought. The Count was certainly a man of caprices. But it seemed a pity. The house, in its peculiarity, was unique and worthy of being catalogued as a national monument.

Madame d'Arc received him in her office.

"The news is excellent," she said. "The Secretary came to see me this morning to tell me that the Count is delighted with the idea. He has promised to finance the concert and talks of buying the Arena which, as you may know, is the largest theatre in the town. So large in fact that, up till now, it has always been a failure. I expect he will get it cheap. In a few minutes I am expecting Gloria, but to-day, I am afraid we may have some trouble with Achmed. Rosalie has been detained at the Palace. (I saw the Queen Mother yesterday. She was most gracious.) I am going to try Diana but she is not as attractive as Rosalie, nor is she so clever. I intend to hide you in the room where Gloria tries on her clothes so that, even if Diana fails, you will at least have a few minutes conversation with her. But you must speak in undertones and confine yourself to serious business. Let there be no nonsense this time. The walls are far from being soundproof and the last thing I should wish would be for this establishment to get an evil reputation."

She thrust into his hands a flat cardboard box tied up with narrow ribbon and emblazoned with a figure of Joan of Arc in gilt relief.

"To give you a professional air," she explained, "in case you are observed."

He followed her down a passage into a small cubicle furnished with grey panelling and long mirrors. There were two gilt chairs and a circular Louis Seize table on which there was a tray of friandises.

"Wait here," she said, "and no nonsense please."

After about a quarter of an hour Gloria appeared. She was wearing a dress of imprimé silk covered with flowers and leaves of every hue, and on her shining hair there was a very high crown of artificial flowers and butterflies. She put out her hand to ward off the possibility of a too enthusiastic greeting.

"We must keep very quiet," she whispered, "and we may not have much time."

She pounced on a meringue.

"Everything is all right," she said between mouthfuls. "He is very pleased. In fact he was quite enthusiastic. He talks of buying the Arena and Madame d'Arc is going to make me a lovely dress for the concert. Of course I never mentioned that I had seen you and he thinks that the idea came from Madame d'Arc. He has a high opinion of her and is always very pleased with the dresses she designs for me."

"Perhaps I could go and see him?" Emanuel suggested.

The proposal seemed to fill Gloria with alarm.

"Oh no. That is quite impossible. Everything will be arranged by the Secretary."

"But you?" said Emanuel. "When can I see you? I mean when can we have a proper meeting. These hole and corner interviews are so unsatisfactory."

"It would be very nice if we could," said Gloria. "Perhaps Madame d'Arc will be able to arrange something later on. At present we are going to the country for a few days. He has bought a castle."

"I know the castle," cried Emanuel excitedly. "It is within a few miles of a house I often visit. I know the place quite well. Perhaps we could meet there."

"No, no." Gloria seemed terrified. "That is out of the question. You don't realise how difficult everything is. You must never attempt to see me or to communicate with me. It would be dangerous. It might be fatal. Promise me you will do nothing rash."

Emanuel took her hands in his.

"Gloria," he whispered, "our last meeting encouraged me to believe that I had made an impression on you."

"I think you have," she replied, "but I have no experience. I never see any men. Sweets and men are the two things he simply won't allow. If he were to find out that I had seen you alone, you would be in danger of your life. He is a terrible man and there is nothing he would stop at. So for God's sake be careful. It is lucky he is so pleased about the concert. I somehow thought he might be. I knew the idea would appeal to his sense of humour."

Madame d'Arc opened the door.

"I'm afraid your time is up," she said. "Diana has not been very successful. You must come, Gloria."

"Oh, dear," said Gloria, casting a reluctant look at the tray, "I haven't had any of those lovely things."

She quickly emptied a dish of fondants into her bag, smiled at Emanuel and hurried out of the room.

What on earth, Emanuel wondered, had Gloria meant when she spoke of the Count's sense of humour? That was the second time she had mentioned it. Did the Count think that music was funny? Emanuel thought of compositions by some of his contemporaries that resembled bad jokes and he often found grand opera mirth-provoking but, if the Count imagined there was going to be anything funny about his symphony he would be disappointed.

Madame d'Arc reappeared.

"I am sorry your interview to-day was so short," she said. "Poor Diana is very upset about her failure. Of course, poor child, she hasn't Rosalie's experience. Let me give you some tea."

"Perhaps you can tell me," Emanuel said to her as they entered her private room, "what Gloria meant when she said that the idea of the concert might appeal to the Count's sense of humour?"

"I haven't the least idea," Madame d'Arc replied. "She is a silly girl and she often talks nonsense. I believe it is true that the Count is given to practical joking. He has never tried anything of that sort on me. I imagine his practical jokes are generally practised on the stock exchange and he is said to have been responsible for one or two minor wars."

"And there is another thing that puzzled me," Emanuel continued.

"I passed just now the house where the party took place and saw that it was being pulled down."

"Yes," said Madame d'Arc. "I heard that it had been sold for an enormous sum to a hotel syndicate. It was probably done to annoy the Society for the Preservation of Peculiar Houses. There have been out-cries of protest in the 'Architectural Gazette.' "

"Another of the Count's practical jokes, I suppose," Emanuel re-marked. "Oh, by the way, Gloria said I couldn't possibly see him. Why not?"

"Why do you want to see him?"

"Well I shall have to see him sooner or later, to arrange about the concert."

"All that will be attended to by the Secretary. You can reckon on everything being to your satisfaction."

"But does nobody ever see him?"

"I really can't answer any more questions," said Madame d'Arc. "What did you think of Gloria's dress? I am rather pleased with it. That flowery hat was a little daring for her type. Perhaps you have noticed that I always make her appear even taller than she really is. That is one of the secrets of successful dressing. A physical peculiarity that can't be concealed must be exaggerated. It is a fact that few people seem to real-ise. When Mrs. Thompson, the reincarnation of Cleopatra, came to me I said to her 'You are monstrously ugly. There is nothing to be done about it except to accentuate it. Your clothes must emphasise your ugli-ness.' She has cut me ever since. It is the same with our characters. In-stead of trying to change our defects we must turn them into assets."

As he was leaving, Emanuel admired the tapestries.

"Yes," said Madame d'Arc, "they are very fine. A recent acquisition. I'm afraid I paid a rather large price for them. However, they are worth it. It is lucky that Beauvais can boast of other things than bishops."

6

———

The following morning Emanuel received a telegram from James to say that Evangeline had been taken seriously ill. This sudden popping up of his fiancée in pathetic guise out of his subconscious aroused qualms of remorse and drove for the moment all thoughts of the concert from his mind. Three hours later he was at her bedside.

It was a form of nervous breakdown, James told him. It had come on quite suddenly and had alarmed him. She was better now, he said, although her temperature was still high and her pulse was racing.

When he went into her bedroom Emanuel was moved by the virginal purity of her appearance as she lay back on her pillows and in perspective her nose seemed less long.

"How kind of you to come," she said, and pressed his hand.

"Dearest Evangeline," Emanuel cried, as he knelt down by her bedside, "this is very distressing."

She closed her eyes.

"I think we had better leave her for the moment," said James. "I have given her a sleeping draught. She is really much better to-day," he continued, as they left the room. "I know you are very busy, but it is a good thing that you have come. There is no doubt that your presence will be beneficial."

"What do you think can have caused it?" Emanuel asked.

"Such illnesses are often brought on by repressions or disturbances of the sexual impulses. From her demeanour and her interests we have been led to believe that Evangeline is wholly spiritual. But there are certain indications—have you noticed for instance, that she bites her nails?"

Emanuel had noticed it, but being unacquainted with Freudian theories he had failed to understand its significance.

"However," James continued, "I am not seriously worried by Evangeline's condition. The remedy is as obvious as it is simple. As soon as

215

you and she are married you will find that there will be no further trouble. I am glad to hear that you have at last decided to take the matter in hand."

"We are to be married in a month's time," Emanuel said. "I don't know what can have occurred to make her doubt my sincerity. She must surely understand that the preparations for my concert occupy my thoughts and keep me away from here. If she is not interested in my musical career then I shall begin to doubt her affection for me."

"She is devoted to you," James replied, "and she is most certainly interested in your musical career. But, in spite of her belief in the supremacy of reason, like many of her sex, she is apt at times to be unreasonable."

"Then," said Emanuel, "as you are a mental specialist, it seems to be a matter for you to deal with."

"I will naturally do everything I can," James assured him, "but you must also help."

"I will, I will," cried Emanuel desperately.

* * *

Mrs. Brown that evening was in a proselytising literary mood.

"Well," she asked Emanuel, "have you read 'Romola' yet?"

"No, I'm afraid I haven't," he replied. "I have had very little time for reading."

"Oh," said Mrs. Brown, "then Thomas will read some of it aloud to us. That will be very nice. Thomas, my dear," she shouted to her husband who was getting a little deaf, "we want you to read aloud to us from 'Romola'."

She took the book from a shelf and handed it to him.

Mr. Brown enjoyed reading aloud and although many of his faculties were beginning to fail, his clergyman's voice remained intact. James excused himself on the grounds that he had work to do. Emanuel suggested that he ought to go and sit with Evangeline but Mrs. Brown said she was aSleep. And so, for nearly two hours, he was obliged to listen to Mr. Brown's monotonous clerical intonations. It was a ghastly evening. Emanuel was exhausted but when at last he got to bed, sleep refused to come to him.

Emanuel, as we know, had a happy faculty of laying aside unwelcome thoughts, but that night, in the agitation of insomnia, the prospect of his marriage with Evangeline thrust itself upon him in its dreary reality and filled him with dismay. He could not go through with it, he told himself. He did not really love Evangeline. If only he had taken the trouble to analyse his feelings for her sooner; but now it was too late.

Emanuel, in spite of his artistic temperament, had a thoroughly nice nature. He was grieved for Evangeline's sake, and racked by pangs of compunction. If he were to break off the engagement, he knew it would break her heart. He was overwhelmed by a sense of guilt. All the same he could never marry her, that was certain. It would be unfair to both of them. But what was he to do? At moments it seemed to him that the only way out was suicide. At last, after many hours of tormented imaginings he fell into an uneasy slumber.

When he awoke next morning, though unrefreshed, he felt a little less gloomily disposed. There might be a way out after all. Perhaps Madame d'Arc would think of something. However, for the time being, he must continue to do his duty. Duty must always be done even though it be a duty of hypocrisy.

And so the first thing he did was to visit Evangeline. He found her sitting up in bed drinking beef tea. She was obviously much better. His presence would be no longer necessary and he would be able to leave that afternoon. The thought restored his equanimity and for the moment he felt almost cheerful.

He sat down by her bedside.

"I am glad to find you so much better," he said.

"Oh, Emanuel," exclaimed Evangeline taking his hand in hers, "I am so ashamed. I hardly know how to excuse myself, bringing you down here when you have so much to do. But it was James's idea, not mine. I should have never dreamt of disturbing you—and all on account of a silly dream."

"A dream?"

"Yes, an idiotic nightmare, so foolish that I hardly like to speak of it, terrible as it seemed to me at the time."

"Won't you tell me what it was?"

"I had really rather not. You will think me so childish and impressionable."

"It is quite usual to be upset by a nightmare. There's nothing to be ashamed about. Please tell me what it was."

"Well," said Evangeline, "if you insist. But really it is too silly. I dreamt that I was in a large open space in a city. It was filled with people and they all looked strange and hostile. In the middle there was a great golden statue. I approached it and at its base I saw a man clinging to it and kissing its feet. When I got nearer I saw that it was you. People were laughing, and I hated to see you making yourself ridiculous. Because, you know, it really did look rather absurd. I called out your name but you paid no attention. Then I pulled your coat and you turned and looked at me, and this is where the dream became a nightmare. Your face was full of anger and hatred. It was not the face of the kind sweet Emanuel I know. It was that of a horrible, malignant stranger, yet all the time I knew it was you. Still I persisted and tugged at your coat tails. 'Go away,' you cried, 'I never want to see you again.' And you used a dreadful expression. Then you tried to kick me in the face and I woke."

Emanuel listened to the dream with growing alarm. If Evangeline were going to develop a talent for clairvoyance, it would add to his already considerable difficulties.

"It was a silly dream, wasn't it?" Evangeline went on, "and, now I come to think of it, I am sure it was the lobster mayonnaise we had for dinner. Mother is very fond of it but it never seems to suit me."

"You must avoid lobster mayonnaise in future if it upsets you like this. But really, what a dream!"

He got up from his chair.

"I will go into the garden and get you some flowers," he said.

"Oh, thank you, Emanuel. How kind you are. How considerate."

She was a nice girl, Emanuel thought, and how pleasant their relationship could be if it were not for the question of marriage.

Outside in the garden, other thoughts took possession of his way-
ward mind and the flowers that he intended to gather for Evangeline
became, in his imagination, patterns on silken draperies and wove
themselves into a chaplet crowning the head of a tall golden figure. He
knew how dangerous it might be for him to approach the castle. But he
felt himself drawn to it as fatally as the fishermen of the Rhine were
lured to the rock where Lorelei sat combing her golden hair.

An ingenious idea came to him. He thought of a cupboard in the
house containing articles of make-up which had formerly been used in
charades and amateur theatricals. He rushed into the house. Yes, they
were still there. He selected a false beard and a pair of black spectacles.
He put them on and looked at himself in the glass. The disguise was
certainly effective. Stuffing the beard and the spectacles into his pocket,
he crept stealthily out of doors and made his way across the fields.
When he reached the edge of the little wood, he put them on again and
an eccentric-looking professor might be seen climbing the road that led
to the castle.

He had evolved no plan of campaign and resolved to trust to luck.
When he reached the castle gates he found them open. He walked cautiously into the courtyard. The place as before, seemed completely deserted. Then he remembered the dogs and for a moment his heart failed
him. But siren-lurings imbue their victims with a reckless audacity. He
would no doubt find some way of dealing with them.

The entrance door was also open. He passed through it and found
himself in the banqueting hall. He stood still and listened. There was
not a sound of anyone stirring. He continued his exploration. Ahead of
him was a wide corridor that led to a winding stair. He thought it would
be wiser at first to confine his investigations to the ground floor and entered a small, dark passage leading to the Lady's Bower. "Ye Ladye's
Bowere" in Gothic letters over the entrance was evocative. How wonderful, he thought, if he were to open the door and find—— In the
pitch darkness he struck against a heavy object suspended in his path.
It swayed away from him and back again. In warding it off he came
in contact with a stiff and clammy hand. He started back in horror.
With trembling fingers he struck a match and the flickering flame lit

up a ghastly mis-shapen face. The match fell from his fingers and went out, but he had time to see that the corpse was wearing a fez and was hanging from a beam. Without further ado he fled down the passage, out through the courtyard, down the hill, across the fields. When he reached the Browns' house he came face to face with James who was coming out. James looked at him with some amazement.

"What on earth is the matter?" he enquired. "And why are you wearing that extraordinary beard?"

Emanuel realised that in the agitation of his flight he had forgotten to remove his disguise. To find a plausible explanation was beyond his powers of invention and he stood there speechless and panting.

Luckily James relied on his talent for diagnosis and preferred to trust to intuition rather than to cross-examination. He merely said, "I beg you not to let Evangeline see you like that. She might have a relapse," and passed on.

"Poor boy," he said to himself. "He is in a far more serious condition than Evangeline. If only he would place himself in my hands. Reserve and obstinacy, those are the worst enemies of the medical profession."

The experience of bumping into a hanging corpse in a dark passage, though not entirely out of place in its surroundings and in keeping with the Gothic imaginations of Horace Walpole and Mrs. Radcliffe, was not one that could be viewed academically. The eunuch's fate, horrible as it was, disturbed Emanuel less than fears for his own. It seemed obvious to him that the Count had become aware of Achmed's lapse of vigilance and, if he had discovered so much, had he not discovered everything? In which case Emanuel also would stand in danger of his life. In such circumstances one sought the protection of the police. But would they believe him? Might they not say to him in the words of Blake, "Are such things done on Albion's shores?" And any investigations into the Count's nefarious dealings might involve Gloria. Also it would be difficult to explain why the Count might be supposed to have murderous designs on him. It would be wiser perhaps to leave the discovery of the hanging corpse to others. Then Emanuel remembered Gloria's references to the Count's sense of humour. Perhaps the thing had been a practical joke and a waxwork figure had been hung there to frighten possible intruders. That would explain the doors being open and the place apparently deserted. However rich and evil the Count might be, it was highly improbable that he would leave a real body hanging in a country house he had just bought. He would hardly wish to invite such incriminating publicity. Of course it was a practical joke. Emanuel felt considerably relieved. He bade Evangeline an affectionate farewell and returned to the town in a cheerful mood.

*   *   *

However, when he got back to his lodgings he was once more thrown into an agony of terror. Mrs. Darwin came into his room and closed the door. "There has been a queer-looking man watching the house," she announced. "He has been there all the morning. I wondered if I ought to call the police, but I thought it might be a writ." She looked out of the window. "He has gone now. Well, that's odd. If it had been a writ, he would have come after you."

"I have no debts," said Emanuel in a trembling voice. "I think that perhaps we had better call the police. No, no," he added, on second thoughts. "Leave it to me. I will deal with the matter."

He rang up Madame d'Arc and asked for an immediate interview. She would certainly know if anything catastrophic had occurred. And if advice were needed she would be the best person to give it. Mrs. Darwin was an imaginative woman and perhaps the watcher had only been a casual loiterer.

He found Madame d'Arc in her usual state of serenity.

"Everything is going very well," she said. "The Count has now definitely bought the Arena, and the Secretary has asked me to arrange an appointment with you to meet the musical director. The Secretary is, as you know, a very agreeable person and you will find him, in matters of business, easy to deal with. And to-morrow you will be able to have a talk with Gloria, a longer one this time, I hope, as Rosalie will be available."

Madame d'Arc's comfortable words disposed of all Emanuel's fears. How unnecessary appeared to him now all his terrors and perplexities.

"How is it, Madame d'Arc," he asked, "that you always give me such a sense of security, that you inspire me with courage?"

"My dear boy," said Madame d'Arc, "the experiences of this and my former life—well, one doesn't have them for nothing. They have given me enough courage and assurance for there to be some left over to give to others. There is only one thing in the world that I am afraid of and that is fire. I mention it because a fire broke out here only yesterday. It was traced to an electric iron and, I am thankful to say, quickly suppressed. My fear, I believe, is justified, for whatever our reincarnation may be, our material destiny is the same, and my end, when it comes, will be by fire. But I intend to put it off as long as possible. I have made special arrangements with the fire brigade. I shall expect you tomorrow at the usual hour."

* * *

Emanuel was met on his doorstep by the landlady.

"That man has come again," she said. "He swore he hadn't brought a writ so I let him in. He seemed to be a gentleman but you never can tell. I hope I've done right."

Emanuel's first impulse was to take flight, but afterwards he reflected that it would be better to face whatever was coming to him and get it over now. He took a heavy stick from the stand in the hall and, creeping up the stairs, he opened the door of his room cautiously and peeped in.

A man was seated at his writing table poring over his manuscript; a queer little man with a beard and black spectacles. He looked as if he were wearing the disguise in which Emanuel had visited the castle. The resemblance was so striking that for a moment Emanuel thought that this fantastic double must be an accusation.

"A very remarkable work," said the stranger, looking up, "very remarkable indeed."

"Who are you?" asked Emanuel in quavering tones.

"I am Count Omega's musical director," the man replied. "I am favourably impressed with your work, young man, and I am not easy to please. Praise from Professor Grumbelius is praise indeed. A quotation, yes?"

"You are Professor Grumbelius?" exclaimed Emanuel. He had often heard of this celebrated Central European figure, the editor of the great musical encyclopaedia, the man whose musical erudition was world famous. The Count had certainly done himself proud in the way of musical directors.

"I had already made enquiries about you at the Academy," said the Professor, "and what they told me there has been amply justified by further investigation—and more, Mr. Smith. I congratulate you. This is not the first time I have read your manuscript," he continued. "The Count, before undertaking to produce your work, instructed me to make investigations. I must confess to having trespassed on your privacy and I took advantage of an occasion when the house was empty——"

"But why?" cried Emanuel. "I would have shown it to you any time you cared to ask."

"The Count's methods are not those of other men," the Professor answered. "If your work had proved unsatisfactory you would have been disappointed and the Count is averse to discouraging the young."

The Count, after all, thought Emanuel, must have some elements of kindness in his nature. Owing to his faith in himself, it had never struck Emanuel as curious that the Count had taken up the idea of producing his work merely on Madame d'Arc's recommendation. The Count had a high opinion of her as a dressmaker but there was no reason for trusting to her musical judgment. It was unlikely, now he came to think of it, that the Count would have bought a cemetery or a crematorium without first sending somebody to prospect.

"I have already noted the composition of your orchestra," continued the Professor, "and if you will entrust your manuscript to me I will superintend the copying of the parts. You can safely leave everything to me. I have written an article on your symphony which will appear in a few days in the 'Musical Digest.' Any other publicity, which in these times is unfortunately necessary, will be dealt with by other hands. You have nothing to worry about. Any enterprise undertaken by the Count will, you may rest assured, be crowned with success. You are indeed fortunate to have found such a patron. To-morrow at eleven o'clock you will come to the Arena where you will meet the Secretary, myself and others concerned. By the way," he added, "I have already drawn up the programme of the rest of the concert. It will be composed of the works of the great composers but I have purposely selected the most trivial and tedious so that they may serve as a foil to your own composition. Good-bye. Auf Wiedersehen."

The Professor tucked Emanuel's symphony into a portfolio and left with it under his arm.

Emanuel threw himself into his armchair with a great sense of relief. Although the affair of the hanging body still remained unsolved he decided not to worry about it. There was no doubt that the Count moved in a mysterious way. However, he thought, it would be more sensible, as in one's relations with a more important personage, to accept his methods without attempting to explain them.

7

At eleven o'clock next morning Emanuel went to the Arena. He was shown into the auditorium. The place was being entirely redecorated, and he stood for a moment amazed by the sight that met his eyes. The inside of the gigantic theatre was being made to look like the interior of a Byzantine church. The walls already glittered with sham mosaic designs in vivid blues, greens and purples on a gold background. On either side of the orchestra platform enormous golden archangels with folded wings were being erected. It was not, however, exactly the setting that Emanuel would have desired for the first performance of his symphony.

The Secretary, all smiles, advanced to meet him. Emanuel thought of the man who had scowled at him and threatened him from the window of the castle, but it was no use worrying about problems of identity, nor was it the moment to do so.

"I am glad to see you," said the Secretary. His manner was less ecclesiastical than it had been at the party. "I hope you approve of what we are doing to improve the appearance of the place. We are making use of the decorations of a house that is being demolished. We are also perfecting the acoustics. They were not satisfactory and the matter is being adjusted by the Director of the Institute for Acoustical Research. The lighting will be done by Lux Perpetua and Co. and Madam Gloria's dress will of course be designed by Madame d'Arc. We are employing only the best people. Now will you kindly step this way? The press photographers are waiting to take some shots of you."

Emanuel was made to pose in front of one of the archangels while a bevy of little men photographed him from every angle.

"Now," said the Secretary, "I should like you to have a few words with our publicity agent. Mr. Macaw!" he called to a rotund, Semitic-looking person with a pronounced squint. His oblique vision had been a great help to him in his journalistic career.

"Well, Mr. Smith," said the publicity agent, speaking with a strong but not quite convincing American accent, "I'd like to get a few particulars of your private life."

"My symphony——" began Emanuel.

"We're not handling the musical side," said Mr. Macaw. "We don't consider that news. What we want is snappy personal stuff. Married?"

"No," said Emanuel.

"Pity. Musician's wives are often good news value. Engaged?"

"As a matter of fact I am. But I'd rather you didn't mention that. The situation is a little difficult."

"Well, I daresay we can make a story out of that. Any hobbies?"

"None," replied Emanuel. "I live entirely for my art."

"We're not handling the art side," repeated Mr. Macaw. "Art isn't news. Ever been co-respondent in a divorce case?"

"Certainly not," replied Emanuel indignantly.

"Pity," said Mr. Macaw. "That would have been good publicity. Well, Mr. Smith, you haven't given me much to go on but you can trust me to make something out of it."

Emanuel was somewhat disconcerted by his first introduction to the world of advertisement and hailed with relief the approach of Professor Grumbelius.

"I forgot to ask you," he said to Emanuel, "what title you propose to give to your work."

"Good gracious," exclaimed Emanuel, "I haven't decided yet. I really don't know."

"You must make up your mind," said the Professor a little crossly. "We want to get on with the programmes and my article is appearing in to-morrow's 'Musical Digest.'"

Emanuel looked round him wildly, and his eyes fell on the golden archangels.

"The Last Trump," he replied.

"Too sensational for a serious work," remarked the Professor. "Can you think of nothing better?"

"It expresses the meaning of my music," Emanuel persisted.

"Meaning?" retorted the Professor scornfully. "What an old-fashioned idea. What has meaning got to do with music? We are no longer in the days of Richard Strauss."

"I don't of course rely on meaning," Emanuel said. "But if my music means anything it is a call to the human race, a great awakening."

"You are optimistic, my young friend. But never mind. Your music is competent to stand up on its own and the addition of a silly title will do it no harm. If you insist on 'The Last Trump' you shall have it. Now to more serious things. I have engaged the finest orchestra in the country. What an orchestra!"

The Professor kissed his hand to the air in a way that seemed oddly coquettish for one so important and unemotional.

"The only trouble I am having is in collecting the trombone players."

"But there are only four in my orchestra," said Emanuel with some surprise. "It is surely not difficult to find four trombone players."

The Professor gave him a curious glance. Then he smiled and patted Emanuel on the shoulder.

"It will be all right," he said. "You needn't worry." And, as he took leave of Emanuel he gave him an unmistakable wink.

What a strange man, Emanuel thought. But then everybody and everything connected with the Count was strange. How utterly alien was this fantastic new world into which he had been swept to the peaceful, orderly atmosphere of the Academy, to the world of serious artistic endeavour. He thought of the publicity agent and shuddered. He felt like a scholar involved in a gangster racket. Nevertheless, he reflected, all these people seemed to be working in their different ways for the success of his symphony and he must be thankful, however much he was humiliated and mystified.

* * *

At four-thirty Emanuel rang the bell of Madame d'Arc's establishment and was ushered into her private room. As she greeted him Emanuel noticed there was a look of annoyance on her face.

"To-day is no good I fear," she said. "I am sorry to have to disappoint you. It appears that Achmed has been sacked, and Gloria has arrived in the company of an elderly female of grim and repellent aspect."

"Good God!" Emanuel cried. "Then the Count has discovered——"

"No," Madame d'Arc reassured him. "That is what I feared at first. But on making enquiries I learnt that it was because Gloria was found in possession of a box of Turkish Delight. The Count has forbidden her to eat anything containing sugar and when his orders are disobeyed he is ruthless. I am very much put out at being suddenly confronted by a new problem of strategy. Everything was going so well. Now of course Rosalie will be useless. My psychological insight tells me that this du-

enna is not susceptible to feminine charms. She is not that kind of
woman. Nor do I imagine that Charles the lift-boy would be of any use
either, although he has been very successful with some of the elderly
members of my clientèle. The woman insists on sitting in the room
while Gloria is trying on. However, I have evolved a new plan of campaign. I refuse to believe that any woman, however debased, is impervious to the lure of clothes. My plan will succeed. Of that I am convinced.
In matters of finance I admit the Count's superiority, but in strategy he
is no match for little Jeanne."

* * *

On returning home Emanuel found a letter from Evangeline.

"I am now quite recovered," she wrote. "I have resumed my studies
with renewed enthusiasm and am starting to tackle seriously the problem of Causality. Father has had a slight attack of lumbago. Mamma
ironed him last night with a hot iron and to-day he is much better.
James is away on an important case. We hear that the castle is being
pulled down. Personally I don't mind very much as I never appreciated
it, but I am sorry for your sake as I know you enjoyed going there.
Everyone in the neighbourhood is up in arms, even people who had
never taken the trouble to go and see it, and the President of the Society
for the Preservation of Peculiar Houses has written a very strong letter
to the 'Architectural Gazette.' A lunatic asylum is to be built on the site.
I should have thought reconstruction was unnecessary as the house
would have been an ideal one for mad people. Mamma is very upset at
the idea of having a lunatic asylum so close to the house. We have decided not to tell father as he has always had such a horror of lunatics."

So the Count was at his tricks again. What, Emanuel wondered,
what was the motive of all this destruction? Was it, as Madame d'Arc
had suggested, to annoy? Was it a dislike for peculiarity? That seemed
very improbable. The motives of the Count's actions were as unfath-
omable as the problems of Causality.

Emanuel was, however, more concerned with his own affairs. Disappointment often indicates to us barometrically the degree of our desires, and the frustration of his meeting with Gloria brought home to

him the intensity of his passion. His Muse, even, was dwarfed by the colossal figure of his adored one. An hour of music, what was that to an hour with Gloria? He reviewed in retrospect all that had happened since that first look she had given him while he was struggling in the crowd. He had perhaps been too complacent and had taken his good fortune too much for granted. He had been guilty of ingratitude to divine providence. This contretemps had come as a punishment, as a reminder. But Madame d'Arc was his divine providence. She was his guardian angel and to her he owed his thanks. To her he had not been sufficiently grateful. To-morrow he would pay her a visit and prove to her that he was visiting a friend rather than a guardian angel and an arranger of lovers' assignations.

8

———⟨0⟩⟨0⟩⟨0⟩———

Next morning Mrs. Darwin burst into Emanuel's room with a bundle of newspapers.

"My goodness," she cried, "just look at this. Headlines on the front page. Even the 'People's Popular.' Well, I never! Who'd have thought it? I'm sending Milly out to get some more."

Emanuel snatched the papers. Mr. Macaw had certainly done his job efficiently. "Count Omega spots a winner." "Millionaire discovers Genius." "From Garret to Palace of Fame." "Young Composer's Love Romance." The last headline was disquieting and Emanuel began to read the paragraph with some trepidation.

"Good God!" he cried.

Mrs. Darwin who was standing over him with an expression of motherly pride was disconcerted. "Well I never," she exclaimed. "You've got your name all over the papers and you aren't satisfied."

"They have said a lot of things that aren't true," said Emanuel in a voice of despair. "It's too awful."

"Well, well," Mrs. Darwin comforted him. "What does that matter, as long as you're talked about and it isn't a murder or anything nasty."

"It's damned awkward," said Emanuel.

The love romance that had been evolved by Mr. Macaw's fertile invention seemed to have been based on that of Romeo and Juliet. Stubborn parents. Family feud. Secret meetings. Lovers kept apart. The article ended with the words "Love will find a way." But the worst of it was that Mr. Macaw had succeeded in discovering his fiancée's identity. There was even a description of Evangeline. "Pale, interesting, dazzling auburn hair, studious and devoted to good works."

Although the Browns never read the popular newspapers and might for a time remain unaware of this publicity, it would soon enough be brought to their notice by kindly neighbours.

"There's a lot of nonsense about Miss Brown," Emanuel said.

"Well, I'm sure she won't mind," Mrs. Darwin assured him. "No girl minds being in the newspapers. My goodness, if Milly——"

"Miss Brown is very different to Milly—I beg your pardon, Mrs. Darwin, I'm not saying anything against Milly. But Miss Brown, I fear, will be very much upset by this publicity."

"You bet she won't," said Mrs. Darwin. "You can take it from me. Don't you worry."

People were always exhorting him not to worry, Emanuel thought, but here was cause enough for worry. What would Gloria think of him when she learnt that he was engaged to a pale young girl in the country? He would swear to her of course that the story was a lie but he resented having to lie himself. The odious Mr. Macaw had placed him in an awkward situation. Any pleasure that the newspapers might have brought to him that morning was marred by this unfortunate paragraph. Nor, when he came to read them, was he very much elated by the contents of the other articles. It was not the sort of publicity he desired and might prejudice him in the eyes of the more serious musical public. He thought of Professor Grumbelius. His article, at least, would be more satisfactory.

"Mrs. Darwin," he called to his landlady as she was leaving the room, "will you please ask Milly to get me the 'Musical Digest'?"

"'The Medical Digest?'" she said. "I don't suppose there will be anything about you in the medical papers."

"The 'Musical Digest,' I said."

When Milly brought the magazine, he searched eagerly for the article. Here it was. "'A new symphony,' by Ludwig Wolfgang Grumbelius, Professor at the University of Notenburg, Editor of the 'Encyclopaedia of Music,' etc., etc." Emanuel felt belittled at the outset by sheer weight of nomenclature. However, the article, though in places a little difficult to understand, seemed on the whole to be favourable.

"Concentric unity of structure is obtained by contrasting the fluid contrapuntal evolution of subsidiary linear fragments with the insistent building up, in a manner both cumulative and dynamic in effect, of other linear formulae treated periphrastically, derived from closely wrought logical distortions of characteristic aspects of the original theme.

"The lines are alternately sinuous and explosive with a strange quality of precariousness, technically incarnated in a tendency to extend atonality to the utmost limits and with a latency which finds an almost metaphysical manifestation in the subtlety of his idiom.

"Mr. Smith has made an important contribution to the complex problem of symphonic form and there is in his work no contrapuntal ingenuity that is not sanctioned by an intense dithyrambic experience, no development of linear formulae that are not also incarnations of inner emotional coherence."

It was nice to have one's music described in such impressive language. All the same Emanuel was left with the impression that the Professor had come better out of the article than he had himself.

On re-reading some of the paragraphs in the popular press, he realised that, here too, he had played a subsidiary role. In most of them he seemed to have been a mere excuse for social panegyrics on the subject of Gloria and the Count. And he was amazed by the ingenuity with which practically all mention of music had been excluded. It was hardly touched upon except in relation to Gloria's performance. "The clou will of course be Madam Gloria's trombone solo." "Madam Gloria is entirely self taught and her performance will be a revelation to those who have not yet been privileged to hear her." "Madam Gloria, who has been studying for several years with Professor Grumbelius, the Musical Wizard." "Madam Gloria's exquisite performances on the tuba have long delighted the musical élite," and so on.

In comparison, Emanuel appeared a pallid, unsensational figure. It is true he had not supplied Mr. Macaw with the snappy personal stuff he had asked for. Perhaps if he had told him that he always stood on his head before composing, that he sought inspiration in coffee flavoured with cayenne pepper, that he attributed his genius to Yogi exercises— that was the sort of thing the public wanted to hear. That was news. He began to understand.

However, he did not resent playing second fiddle to Gloria. Her triumph would be his.

*   *   *

He was summoned again to the Arena. In the auditorium he found Professor Grumbelius and Madame d'Arc. Above the orchestra platform, workmen were constructing a bower of golden clouds.

"That is where Gloria will appear," Madame d'Arc explained to him, "and I have to take into account every angle from which she will be seen, as well as the general composition of the picture. Too high!" she called in her authoritative dressmaker's voice to a workman who was fixing a cloud. "Drop two feet and move one and a half to the left."

Again she reminded Emanuel of a military commander.

Professor Grumbelius advanced with an armful of scores.

"I have made out the programme," he announced. "I told you that I intended to select some of the less happy inspirations of the great composers to set off your own. I propose starting with Beethoven's 'Weihe des Hauses' and following with the Brahms Serenade, Opus 16, without violins. It is a tedious work. These will be taken by our chef d'orchestre. You will of course conduct your own symphony. The rehearsals will start to-morrow. Everything is taking a satisfactory course. Placing the trombones will be the only difficulty."

Emanuel was puzzled.

"I don't understand your difficulty. There are only four of them and they will occupy their usual position in the orchestra. You mean perhaps that Madam Gloria's platform is too high and that those clouds may deaden the sonority?"

"There is no cause for apprehension," the professor assured him. "It will be arranged, and everything will be, as you say, O.K." The Professor winked.

It was really very odd, Emanuel thought, the Professor's habit of winking. But he refrained from asking for an explanation lest it might be a nervous twitch.

Madame d'Arc was now directing the lighting with a highly technical vocabulary. "Amber flood," she called to the operator. "No. Kill that. Try the Semiloff blue." She beckoned to Emanuel. "I want a word with you," she said, leading him into a corner. "To-morrow afternoon I can promise you a nice long time with Gloria. The Duenna has proved a far easier proposition than I had expected. That grim and forbidding exterior conceals the soul of a debutante and I had no trouble in arousing an enthusiasm for clothes that amounts almost to a frenzy. To-morrow afternoon when she accompanies Gloria I have arranged for her to try on a confection I have designed for her to wear at the concert. I will be able, I hope, to spin out her fitting for over an hour. Now don't make a noise." Emanuel was about to burst out into a paean of tumultuous gratitude. "To-morrow then. I must return to the lighting."

Emanuel left the theatre the happiest man in the world. He almost feared the envy of the Gods and wondered if, like Polycrates, he ought to throw his piano, or at any rate the bust of Beethoven, out of the window as a sacrifice.

9

———✿✿✿———

While waiting for Gloria in Madame d'Arc's private room, Emanuel endeavoured to estimate the spiritual and sensual proportions of his love. It is unusual for lovers thus to dissect their emotions. Nor, if they are very much in love, is it of any use.

Emanuel would have preferred to believe in a preponderance of the spiritual, but facts hardly seemed to point that way. What, after all, did he know of Gloria's soul? Her conversation had done little to reveal it. Was it merely an expensive box of chocolates? The box might even be empty. Well, other men of genius had loved beautiful fools, and imagination could provide spiritual garments more wonderful even than those designed by Madame d'Arc. When the door opened and Gloria appeared, Emanuel knew that only one thing mattered, and that it mattered little in what way he loved.

She was dressed in black and wore a high black head-dress a little reminiscent of that of an Armenian priest. Yet, with its slight absurdity, it seemed to enhance more than ever her radiant loveliness.

"Oh, Gloria," Emanuel murmured. "How marvellous to think we have a whole hour before us, although, alas, it is far too little. Would that it were eternity!" He clasped her by both hands and together they sank on to the sofa. It was better thus. When they were both standing up Emanuel's head was on a level with Gloria's breast.

"Gloria darling," he went on, mindful of the unfortunate paragraph. "That nonsense in the paper about my being engaged. It's quite untrue."

"I never read the papers," she said.

"Oh, thank God!" Emanuel cried. "But if anyone tells you, you'll know it is a lie."

Gloria looked wistfully at the tea-table and Emanuel was about to offer her something. "No, not to-day, thank you," she said. "He found out about it. It was terrible." She closed her eyes. "I don't like to think of it. Poor Achmed was sent away and they say he has committed suicide. He was such a devoted servant. I also found that I had been putting on weight and I've made up my mind not to touch another sweet until after the concert. Oh, perhaps I'll just have one; something very small. A preserved apricot."

"I'm afraid the Count is cruel to you," said Emanuel, as she munched the apricot. She appeared to him once more as the persecuted maiden, a heroine of romantic literature.

"Oh, no," replied Gloria. "He is really very kind to me and he is quite right about the sweets. It would be awful if I got fat. He is only terrible when anyone annoys him or gets in his way. As a rule he's great fun and he makes me laugh a lot."

"That reminds me," said Emanuel. "What did you mean when you said the Count might consider the concert a good practical joke? It has been puzzling me ever since."

"Did I say that?" asked Gloria, looking a little scared. "Well, he is very fond of practical jokes."

"I don't see what it has got to do with my music."

"It has nothing to do with your music. Don't be a silly boy." She leant forward and kissed his upturned face. In the transports that followed Emanuel forgot to pursue the matter further.

When the situation had lapsed once more into quiescence and Gloria had had another preserved apricot, Emanuel said to her, "What is the note you play on the trombone, Gloria? I gather it is somewhere in the neighbourhood of the middle C."

"The middle C?" Gloria looked bewildered.

"Yes. What is the exact note you play? I ought to have asked you before. I took it for granted that it was the middle C. If it isn't I may have to make some slight adjustment in my score, although the passage leading to it is atonal."

Gloria looked even more bewildered.

"Eternal?" she repeated. "I really don't know what note it is."

"You don't know?" Emanuel gasped.

Gloria giggled and looked rather sheepish. Then she put her hand in his.

"You know, Emanuel, I can't play the trombone at all."

Emanuel sprang to his feet. "What?" he almost screamed.

"Yes," Gloria went on. "My performance is a fake. Fifty trombone players are concealed behind the walls and play through amplifiers. That's why it sounds so loud. I oughtn't perhaps to have told you. He said I wasn't to."

Emanuel wrung his hands, tore his hair. He went through all the gestures of desperation. "Good God!" he cried. "This is the ruin of all my hopes, the shattering of my dreams. Now I understand what you mean. A practical joke indeed, and the joke is on me!"

Gloria was surprised by Emanuel's outburst. "But really, Emanuel, I don't know why you're making all this fuss. The effect will be the same, even better, as we're going to have a hundred trombones this time, a hundred and fifty if we can get them."

Emanuel stamped up and down the room. Then he turned and faced her.

"You must understand, Gloria, I am a serious composer. I will never consent to prostitute my art———"

"Don't be ridiculous," said Gloria, "and don't use such improper language. As long as the effect is the same I don't see that it matters."

"Were I to lend myself to a vulgar deception of this kind it would ruin my musical career for ever. I don't propose to make my debut with a silly practical joke."

"It isn't a silly practical joke. It's a very good one," Gloria protested. "He was very pleased with it. He says the musical public is the silliest of all publics and the most easily fooled, and that they will lap up anything as long as it's well advertised and makes a lot of noise."

"That may be true," Emanuel retorted, "but it is not my mission to fool the public. On the contrary———"

"Nobody in the audience will suspect," Gloria interrupted him. "You didn't yourself."

"They'll soon find out."

"Not if he doesn't mean them to. He's very good at keeping things dark. He says practical jokes are better when people don't find out."

"It's no good going on about the aesthetics of practical joking, Gloria. I have made up my mind. I shall have nothing to do with it. I shall withdraw my symphony."

Gloria assumed an air of pathos.

"You are very unkind," she said. "I was so looking forward to the concert and Madame d'Arc has designed the most lovely dress."

"Nothing will alter my decision."

Gloria began to cry. She buried her face in her hands and her gigantic frame shook in mountainous convulsions. To Emanuel the spectacle of Gloria in tears was stupefying. It was as though he were confronted by some great upheaval of nature. He flung himself upon his knees before her. "Gloria, Gloria," he entreated. "Don't cry, my darling." He felt like a diminutive beaver trying to dam Niagara.

At that moment Madame d'Arc appeared in the doorway. "Good gracious!" she cried. "Whatever is the matter now?"

"Oh, Madame d'Arc," Gloria sobbed, "Emanuel is being so cruel. I told him about the trombones and now he wants to back out."

"Trombones?" said Madame d'Arc. "I don't understand. But there's no time for explanation. You must come now, Gloria. The Duenna has finished her fitting. Emanuel will tell me all about it. Dear me, your face! We must repair the ravages before she sees it." And she hastily dabbed at Gloria's cheeks with her handkerchief.

"Persuade him, Madame d'Arc, persuade him," Gloria cried, as she was hustled out of the room.

When Madame d'Arc returned, Emanuel told her the whole story. "So you see," he concluded, "I can't possibly go through with it."

"I don't see at all," said Madame d'Arc. "Your attitude, both as an artist and a lover, is ridiculous and your arguments are unreasonable. To say nothing of your ingratitude to me after all I have done for you."

"I am very grateful to you," Emanuel protested, "and I love Gloria. But neither of you seem to understand the soul of an artist. How can you expect me to lend myself to so monstrous a deception? Sincerity in art——"

"Don't speak to me about sincerity in art," Madame d'Arc interrupted him. "I know enough about art not to be taken in by any twaddle about sincerity. It sounds as if you had been reading Tolstoy. Art is based on deception. Surely you must know that. It is precisely in his capacity for deceiving that an artist is great. The function of art is to create illusions. It seems odd that I should have to teach you the first principles of aesthetics."

"I don't agree with you," said Emanuel. "Even if what you say were true, this particular deception is inartistic."

"Inartistic!" Madame d'Arc repeated scornfully. "You discovered the effect you wanted. What does it matter how the effect is obtained? Do you suppose that if I found I could get a better effect with cotton wool than with ermine I should hesitate to use it?"

"You wouldn't charge the same price for it."

"That is precisely what I should do. I might even charge more, for the ingenious idea."

"I consider it immoral."

Madame d'Arc threw up her hands. "Good God!" she cried. "Are you a clergyman? No, a clergyman would have more sense. And you are selfish as well as foolish. Do you imagine that Gloria and my clothes have no part in your effect? I suppose you hadn't thought of that? Have you thought of anything at all except your silly ideas of sincerity? Even the most elevated ideals must have in their composition a grain of common sense. This concert will establish your reputation as a composer. You will have the musical world at your feet. Is fame nothing to you?"

"Not if it is based on deceit."

Madame d'Arc decided to adopt other tactics.

"Do you suppose," she went on, "that the Count, after taking all this trouble, having bought the Arena, having spent all this money—although of course to him it is a mere flea bite—do you suppose he will pay any attention to your idiotic scruples? He will merely find another composer to take your place, and from what I know of the Count it will be your most hated rival, if you have one. You may flatter yourself that the music will be less good, but your substitute will reap the benefit of your idea and publicity will do the rest. Do you like the prospect?"

Emanuel didn't like it at all. He was dumbfounded. The possibility had not occurred to him. The thought of some other composer—and he could think of several—stepping into his shoes and snatching from him the fame, the glory that was now within his reach, was too much for him and he capitulated.

"Very well, Madame d'Arc," he said. "I will go through with it, for Gloria's sake—and for yours," he added hastily. "But you must understand——"

"I don't want to understand anything," Madame d'Arc cut him short, "except that you've regained your senses. You have been behaving like a prima donna. And you made poor Gloria cry. I hope you are ashamed of yourself."

"I am ashamed," said Emanuel, "of having recanted."

"I did that myself once," Madame d'Arc mused. "I admit it didn't help very much, but the circumstances were different."

10

Emanuel had given way, but in his conscience there was no easy acquiescence. All that night a battle raged between the two sides of his nature. There was civil war in his soul. He reproached himself with having been a coward, a weakling. A true artist would have stuck to his guns. Was it worth while, he pondered, for the sake of immediate success to risk his reputation as a serious musician? Sooner or later the imposture was sure to be discovered. How would it be possible to bind a hundred and fifty trombone players to secrecy?

It might be true, as Madame d'Arc had said, that it mattered little how an effect was produced. Yet the main point of this one was that the trombone note should appear to be sounded by the lips of this splendid, divine creature. What would have been his impression if he had known that she was a mere dummy figure and that fifty concealed men were playing through amplifiers? Would not the public, if the fraud were discovered, feel the same resentment as he himself had felt when Gloria confessed to him the truth? He had forgiven her because he loved her. But after treating them to such an imposture, would he ever be forgiven by the public? If only he could be sure that the deception would never be found out! That would perhaps make things easier for his conscience.

He thought of Gloria's tears, of Madame d'Arc's persuasiveness. With a true artist, should such things prevail? No, his artistic sincerity must come before everything. How strange that neither of these women had seemed to appreciate his feelings. After many hours of mental struggle his higher nature won.

On the following day the first rehearsal was to take place. He dreaded having to face the members of the orchestra with the announcement that he was withdrawing his symphony. It was cruel also to think of another taking his place. That whoever did so would not be a man of much artistic integrity, was a reflection that did little to console him.

* * *

Emanuel went early to the Arena next morning. The orchestra had not yet arrived. He found instead Professor Grumbelius who met him with a beaming countenance.

"It is very good," he said. "Now we have no trombone players at all."

"No trombone players?" exclaimed Emanuel.

"Yes, my young friend, they will not be necessary."

"But I don't understand," Emanuel stammered. "Are you proposing to do away with the finale?"

It was extraordinary, he thought, the way in which things were done without consulting him. Another point that justified his decision.

"No, no," said the Professor. "You will have your finale. It is natural you do not understand. The Director of Acoustics, ah, he is a clever man. He has made a little invention." The Professor kissed his hand in the air. "Come with me," he said, "I will show you."

He led Emanuel up on to the stage. In a corner of the wings, hidden behind a curtain, there stood what appeared to be a large radio set with switches, glass bulbs and coils of wire. Connected with it were a set of tubes that looked like organ pipes.

"Now listen," said the Professor and turned one of the knobs. After a slight whirring noise a trombone note was heard. It began gradually to swell and was so exactly like the sound Emanuel had heard in the Count's house that he was amazed. In the same way it filled the whole theatre as it increased in volume, and it seemed to come from the platform of clouds where Gloria was to appear. The Professor turned it off before it became unbearably loud.

"What do you think of that?" he asked. "Now you see why no players are needed. The crescendo is regulated automatically. It has saved us a lot of trouble."

Emanuel had not forgotten the intention with which he had come to the Arena that morning, but now he felt he might have to reconsider his decision. This invention of the Director of Acoustics had made a good deal of difference, and the fact that the trombone note could be produced by a machine seemed to remove the more sordid aspects of the deception. It was no longer necessary for him to visualise a hundred and fifty little men concealed in the walls counterfeiting the sound that was supposed to emanate from those divine lips. The impersonal element saved the illusion from vulgarity and Gloria could now be envisaged as a symbol of the gigantic wave of sound.

There was far less danger now of the deception being discovered. The secret would remain in the possession of a handful of people whereas not even the Count, he felt, could have checked the indiscretions of a hundred and fifty trombone players. That consideration, also, made a good deal of difference.

Madame d'Arc appeared in the stalls accompanied by Rosalie.

"Come up, Madame d'Arc," said the Professor. "Let me show you our little toy. We will let you into the secret." He turned it on again.

"It is wonderful," said Madame d'Arc. "Explain to me how it works."

When she had mastered the details of its construction as far as the Professor was able to explain them, she turned to Emanuel. "Gloria is trying on her dress upstairs," she said. "I should like you to see it. Come with me."

As they were climbing the stairs Madame d'Arc whispered to Emanuel, "The Duenna will be there. I shall have to introduce you to Gloria as if it were the first time you were meeting her."

Gloria's dressing room was on a level with the platform on which she had to appear and was separated from it by a vestibule which had a large French window looking on to the street below.

"Wait here," said Madame d'Arc.

Emanuel went to the window and looked out. He was surprised at the elevation. He had forgotten that the theatre was so immense. The people in the street were dwarfed to pigmy size, and, as he stood and looked at them, the last remnants of his scruples vanished. The artist, as Madame d'Arc had said, was justified in deceiving the public, if the deception was worth while. It was the effect that mattered and not the method of its production. He would include the maxim in his theory of artistic sincerity. His conscience was now quite clear and, looking down from the window he was filled with a sense of exhilaration. He felt that he dominated the world.

Madame d'Arc called to him and Gloria came out of her room. Her dress was of some silver tissue edged with blue. "My patroness's colours," Madame d'Arc explained to him. On her shoulder were gigantic blue and silver wings and on her head a halo of silver rays. Behind her loomed the dour figure of the Duenna.

Madame d'Arc presented him formally and, as he shook hands with Gloria, she gave him a wink. With his frank, impulsive nature, Emanuel had little aptitude for dissimulation. Keeping one eye on the Duenna, he expressed in halting phrases his appreciation of Gloria's dress. He felt he was making a fool of himself.

The strain of the situation was relieved by a message from Professor Grumbelius that the orchestra was assembled and waiting. Bowing stiffly to Gloria, Emanuel hurried down the stairs.

The orchestra was magnificent. All that Emanuel had hoped for in respect to the sonority of his orchestration was more than fulfilled, even at the first reading. The symphony was rehearsed without the finale and when all the musicians had left, Emanuel and the Professor tried out the duration of the trombone note. They came to the conclusion that three minutes was about as much as anyone could bear. Emanuel decided that, instead of dying away, the sound should continue to increase and when it attained its maximum, the work should end with a single crashing chord on the whole orchestra and a roll on the drums. In order to time this exactly it would be necessary to fix an electric clock on the conductor's desk.

Madame d'Arc was anxious to see the effect of the costume in its setting and, when Gloria stepped out from among the golden clouds with her wings and her halo, Emanuel felt that her appearance alone would ensure success. The golden archangels below sank into vulgar insignificance. If the angel who sounded the last trump, he thought, were half so glamorously splendid, then it would indeed be something to look forward to.

All Emanuel's enthusiasm and joy returned to him. He thanked God that he had not been obliged to take the course his artistic conscience had at first dictated to him.

He was once more radiantly happy. Yet, he was troubled at times by a certain uneasiness. Things seemed to be going too well with him. He felt as if he were being swept along in a triumphal chariot and the chariot was driven by a strange sinister figure.

Why was all this being done for him? He felt like a puppet, a marionette whose strings were being worked by invisible hands. His movements had ceased to be his own. Whither was the chariot taking him? To what destination was he being whirled? He thought of the Count's evil reputation, his fondness for practical joking. Perhaps the triumphal path led to an abyss? Emanuel had already had one practical joke played on him and perhaps it was not the last. Was he destined to be the victim of some fearful satanic sacrifice?

For a moment he wondered if the Count knew about his meetings with Gloria. Was she possibly a decoy? But that was nonsense, and anyhow he would love her, even in the role of Delilah. All men of genius, he reflected, were assailed at times by doubts and hesitations. He must not allow himself to give way to them. Whatever happened, Madame d'Arc would be there to rescue him. Under her aegis he felt safe. The consideration restored his confidence.

Increasing intensity of advertisement had lashed the public into a state of frenzied excitement. The house was sold out and the Queen Mother had announced her intention of being present.

Emanuel had been sent a number of tickets to be distributed to his friends. Three he sent to Evangeline and he gave two to Mrs. Darwin and Milly. The rest he sent to former fellow-students at the Academy, particularly to those he thought might be most unpleasantly affected by his success. Acting on Madame d'Arc's advice, he had ordered an evening suit at one of the smartest tailors in the town, and, trying it on in front of his mirror, he was not dissatisfied with the result.

He spent most of the day before the concert wandering about the town with his head in the clouds. Despite the monotony of the proceeding he stopped before every poster he saw, and each time he read his name it gave him a renewed thrill of delight. Sometimes a crowd was gathered before one of the posters and he thought how little the people knew who was in their midst. He was obliged to exercise the utmost self-control to prevent himself from proclaiming his identity.

Evangeline wrote, "Thank you very much for the tickets. James and I are looking forward very much to the concert. I am returning one of the tickets as Mamma fears she will be unable to go. Father has not been very well lately and Mamma thinks it would be unwise to leave him. There are extraordinary stories about the castle. They say that, before the people left, one of the servants hung himself. But it has been hushed up and nothing more has been heard about it. Mamma is sending you 'Romola.' She thinks it would make a wonderful opera."

Emanuel was slightly irritated by the letter. Apart from the information about Achmed, he thought it was inadequate to the occasion.

Tickets were sent back by one or two of the ex-students with some rather flimsy excuse for not being able to attend the concert. But these slight causes of annoyance were to some extent compensated for by the joyful anticipation of Mrs. Darwin and Milly.

11

——◦◦◦——

On the day of the concert Emanuel worked himself into a feverish frenzy and spent his time fussing about in the Arena. His excessive zeal ended by exasperating everybody and, as the hour for the performance drew near, he was firmly requested to absent himself and not reappear until his presence was needed.

He went outside and stood on the theatre steps near the entrance. He felt himself once more a mere cipher in his own glory.

It was the close of a fine summer day and the sky was still bright. Sunlight shone into the portico and lit up the faces of the people. Made up for artificial light most of the women resembled garish waxworks and the men in their evening dress had an unnatural, self-conscious air like guests at a foreign wedding.

Crowds, especially when struggling to get somewhere, never give a very flattering impression of humanity, and every face seemed to bear the stamp of folly or unpleasantness. Presumably most of them were cultured people, many of them ornaments of society, members of the élite. And these were the people, Emanuel reflected, on whose verdict the life of a work of art depended. Immortal fame seemed hardly worth striving for. Better to live for a few years obscurely in the heart of a friend than for ever in the memories of such people as these. The type, he feared, would persist until the final cataclysm came to sweep away humanity itself and all the fruits of human endeavour. He felt a sudden desire to fly from the town and bury himself far off in the country.

His melancholy thoughts were interrupted by the arrival of Madame d'Arc. Her dress was composed of some metallic material that resembled armour plating. He watched her cleaving the crowd like a battleship. Here at least was a friend it was worth while to please and the sight of her cheered him.

She saw him and beckoned. "I have a seat for you next to mine," she said to him as, after some difficulty, he reached her side. "On such occasions it is well to be near a friend. The places are close to the orchestra so that you can pop up easily when the time comes."

"Thank you, Madame d'Arc, you think of everything. I fancied you would be going with some of your smart friends."

"You are the smartest friend I have here to-night," Madame d'Arc replied, laying her hand on his arm.

He followed her into the auditorium, which was already nearly full. Seen in a more advantageous lighting the people Emanuel had observed in the portico seemed transformed. Beauty and distinction had come once more to earth. Complexions bloomed, jewels glittered discreetly, clothes looked natural and elegant and nearly everyone appeared interesting, attractive or well-bred. It was a brilliant audience.

"Madame d'Arc," Emanuel asked, "do you think that everything depends on lighting?"

"Of course it does," she replied. "That is a thing that every dressmaker, every art dealer knows. I should never wish a client of mine to wear in the daytime a dress that was meant for the evening. A picture, a tapestry hung in the wrong lighting loses half its beauty. The same principles can be applied by analogy to all the other branches of art, to music, to literature and to life itself. Everything must be seen in its proper light. Even politics."

"And religion?"

"Religion must be seen in the light of God," Madame d'Arc replied absently, as she scanned the audience through her opera glass.

"There is the famous first-nighter, Mr. Muffin."

She pointed out a benign-looking little man with a portentous nose. He was standing up with his back to the stage, smiling and waving to all the important people in the boxes. For twenty years he had never missed a first night. He was popular with theatrical managers and members of the dramatic profession because of his indiscriminate appreciation.

Near him, scowling and morose, sat Mr. Crab, whose musical criticism often spelt death, or at any rate delay, to rising genius. He was unable to read a score and was now stone deaf, so that his criticism had to be evolved from his inner consciousness.

Emanuel heard his name mentioned in the row behind him. He turned and observed a little woman in an auburn wig. Her eyes looked as if they saw everything and took in nothing.

"That is Mrs. Purdonium," Madame d'Arc informed him. "She has my models copied and claims my acquaintance, but I don't know her."

Mrs. Purdonium was speaking ecstatically of "Emanuel" and "Gloria." Emanuel was surprised to hear her say that she knew him intimately.

"The intimacy she claims," said Madame d'Arc, "is generally fictitious. However, the woman has the courage of her imagination," she added, as she heard Mrs. Purdonium referring to "the dear Count."

"She moved heaven and earth to get an invitation to his parties," Madame d'Arc commented grimly, "but she never succeeded. I know it for a fact."

There was a stir of excitement and a hush. The Queen Mother had taken her seat in the Royal Box.

"Examine carefully her clothes," Madame d'Arc whispered. "She little suspects that I have used her as part of a dramatic scheme."

The Queen Mother was wearing a long black robe. Here and there, touches of an intense gleaming blue lit up the sombre austerity of her dress and made it glow like the sky of a tropical night. Contrary to the custom expected of royalty she wore no jewels. Only on her high coiffure there was a tiara of onyx and turquoise.

"An admirable Queen of the Night," thought Emanuel.

"Her costume," Madame d'Arc explained, "is a question to which Gloria's is the answer. The contrast of their costumes will strike even the most unobservant and will provoke discussion. It is excellent advertisement. Later on, in the interval, I will draw your attention to the dress I have designed for the Duenna. A macabre caprice."

The first two items on the programme were the Beethoven Overture and the Brahms Serenade. The latter was punctuated by fragments of conversation from Mrs. Purdonium in which the names "Gloria" and "Emanuel" and the "dear Count" occurred frequently. "Franck is always delightful," she declared when it was over. "I mean Brahms," she corrected herself, glancing at the programme.

When the applause died down and the Queen Mother had retired into the depths of her box, the audience began to troop out into the foyer.

"Come with me," said Madame d'Arc to Emanuel. "Let me show you the beau monde. It will distract you from your anxiety."

Emanuel noticed that the two seats reserved for James and Evangeline were empty. He would no doubt find them in the foyer. Here, however, there was so much to observe that he soon forgot about them altogether.

Mr. Muffin was poking his nose ingratiatingly into the face of one of the ladies-in-waiting who had escaped from the royal box to relax at the buffet.

Madame d'Arc pointed out to him other social celebrities. Lady Cynthia Cow, the eternal debutante, romping in a corner with two lady-like young men. Mr. Bray, the Cabinet Minister, whose abdominal protuberance had not been reduced by the exercise of constantly jumping from one party to another. Mrs. Harridan the American hostess, whose prodigious memory enabled her to place a dinner party correctly without having recourse to the peerage. The Mirabel sisters, nature poetesses and leaders of a modern coterie, wearing thick tweed trousers and coats of masculine cut, outrageously decolletés. Signora Tamburini, the diminutive prima donna, her temperamental rotundities tightly confined in a sheath of purple velvet.

"Look," cried Madame d'Arc. "There is the Duenna."

Her costume, as Madame d'Arc had said, was indeed a macabre caprice. Subtly, without actual definition, it suggested skeletons, tombstones and all the emblems of death. It gave her the appearance of a prison wardress lately arisen from the grave. A terrifying apparition that created a sensation in the crowd. On her face was a look of grim satisfaction with the consternation she was causing.

Prince Campo Santo, a diplomat suspected of necrophily, enquired eagerly of Mrs. Purdonium "Who is she? Do you know her?" Mrs. Purdonium, loth to admit her ignorance, moved away.

Madame d'Arc overhearing, turned to Emanuel. "There," she said. "You see what clothes can do."

A bell rang in the foyer. Emanuel rushed down to the artist's room where he found Professor Grumbelius.

"Is everything all right?" he enquired.

"Everything is all right," the Professor assured him. "Be calm, my young friend. There is no cause to worry. Everything is O.K."

"And Madame Gloria? Have you seen her?"

"I have not seen her," the Professor replied. "But you can take it for granted that she, too, is O.K."

12

————

When the audience had regained their seats, the lights were lowered and in the darkened auditorium only the orchestra desks and the conductor's stand remained illuminated. The royal box was suffused with a faint bluish glow.

Emanuel appeared and bowed. He was greeted with an outburst of applause. He was quite calm now. All anxiety had left him. He felt triumphant and sure of victory.

"He is very young," observed the Queen Mother.

Two ladies-in-waiting agreed enthusiastically. "Yes, ma'am. Very young, very young indeed."

"Hush!" somebody hissed. What presumption to hush the royal box!

Mrs. Purdonium's chattering died away. Mr. Muffin assumed the air of ecstasy with which he always listened to music. Even the most frigidly intellectual were moved by the strange, mysterious opening. More effectively than the prelude to the Rhinegold it suggested the moving of deep waters, a stirring in the primeval depths, and created an atmosphere of suspense and expectation that promised the emergence of something more stimulating than three foolish Rhinemaidens. Mr. Bray, finding nothing to beat time to, sat in rigid perplexity.

Out of this flowing chaos, there arose the fragments of a theme and, as the movement proceeded, these kaleidoscopic fragments came together and formed a definite pattern.

"Dynamic," whispered Mrs. Purdonium. Her musical vocabulary was extensive if not always accurate.

Anyone unacquainted with Mr. Crab's habitual expression might have imagined that he was judging unfavourably the development of Emanuel's linear formulae. However, owing to certain considerations, he had made up his mind to like the work. It was only that his features were incapable of expressing appreciation.

Lady Cynthia Cow, scenting a new attraction, kept her opera glasses fixed on Emanuel's form swaying above the orchestra. Mrs. Purdonium was arranging a luncheon party for him. The increasing vitality of the music drove from Prince Campo Santo's mind all thoughts of the Duenna.

The gigantic audience sat spell-bound. Not a cough was heard, no programme rustled. It was not easy music nor was it at all melodious, yet such was the compelling power of its logical persuasiveness that, like God and his creation, they saw that it was good.

Slowly and surely the climax approached. After a long upward procession of the whole orchestra the great moment arrived. The bower of clouds was suddenly lit up by a beam of light and Gloria appeared.

There was a murmur in the audience. There were one or two attempts at applause but they were quickly suppressed. Gloria raised the trombone to her lips and the note began in gradual crescendo.

Emanuel stood with raised baton, his eyes fixed on the electric clock on his desk. All his attention was needed to bring in the final chord at exactly the right moment. He longed to look round and see how the audience were taking it.

The note swelled out and when it attained its maximum, the great building seemed to quiver with its vibrations. Mr. Muffin crumpled in his stall and held his hands to his ears. Mrs. Purdonium closed her eyes and gripped her neighbour's knee. Only two members of the vast audience remained unmoved. Mr. Crab, in the immunity of his deafness, and the Queen Mother, bolt upright in her box, her noble features displaying no emotion.

The three minutes had passed and the sound showed no signs of abating. Emanuel looked towards the wings in desperation. It would be impossible now to time the final chord; the end would be bungled and the effect ruined. Another minute passed and it still went on. The sound had ceased to be exciting and had become monotonous, exasperating.

Professor Grumbelius appeared from behind the curtain beckoning wildly. Emanuel could sense a growing restiveness in the audience. The Director of Acoustics hurried on to the stage and went behind the curtain.

"It is impossible," Mrs. Purdonium shouted to her neighbour, "that anyone could hold a note as long as that." Through the din Emanuel could hear cries from the gallery.

At last Gloria put down the trombone from her lips. The trombone note continued relentlessly. There was an uproar in the theatre. The Queen Mother rose with dignity and withdrew.

Emanuel, after clinging for a while to the desk like the captain of a foundering ship, turned and faced the audience. Some, he saw, were laughing, but most of them seemed infuriated. An angry old gentleman in the front row of the stalls shook his fist at him and someone threw an opera glass.

Madame d'Arc ran up on to the stage. "I will stop it," she cried. Emanuel jumped down from the stand and followed her into the wings. Professor Grumbelius and the Director of Acoustics were still tugging at the knobs and switches. Madame d'Arc thrust them aside, seized a coil of wire and tore it away from the machine.

A great tongue of blue flame shot out and quivered for a moment over her metallic dress. She fell to the ground. The noise ceased abruptly, but so, also, did Madame d'Arc.

Two firemen ran forward and lifted her lifeless body.

"Stand back!" someone shouted at Emanuel as he tried to approach.

"Is she dead?" he asked, dazed by the swiftness and horror of the accident.

"Dead as a door nail," was the reply.

He gave a great cry and rushed up the stairs to Gloria's dressing room. He felt that at all costs he must see her and break to her the fearful news before she heard it from anyone else.

He found her in the vestibule. She seemed quite calm and was smoking a cigarette. She looked at his distraught face and giggled.

"Wasn't it awful?" she said.

"Gloria!" Emanuel cried. "Madame d'Arc is dead."

"What?" she asked incredulously.

"Yes. She managed to stop the noise but in doing so she was electrocuted. I saw it happen. It was terrible."

He sank on to a chair and hid his face in his hands.

"Oh, dear," said Gloria. "How dreadful. And who on earth will make my clothes for me now?"

Emanuel was thinking desperately of his own situation.

"I wish that I too were dead," he went on. "My musical career is over. How can I ever lift my head again? What is there left for me to do?"

"Really Emanuel," Gloria protested. "I don't see why you should make a fuss. It was much worse for me. It made me look such a fool."

"But don't you understand?" cried Emanuel. "Do you suppose that after this anyone will ever take my music seriously? I have been made ridiculous. I am disgraced for ever. I am finished."

"Nonsense," said Gloria. "And besides, music isn't everything. If you feel like that about it, you can go into a bank or take up politics."

"Go into a bank? Take up politics?" Emanuel screamed. "Are you out of your senses?"

"Please don't shout like that, and you must really go away. He's coming to my room to fetch me. He may be there already and it would be dreadful if he found me here talking to you."

She moved towards the door.

"Gloria, don't go," Emanuel entreated. "I must see you again as soon as possible. But how are we to manage it now that Madame d'Arc is gone?"

"I don't know, I'm sure," Gloria answered. "And anyhow I'm leaving in a few days. He's taking me to America."

"To America?"

"Yes. Isn't it nice? I'm looking forward to it no end."

"But, Gloria," Emanuel pleaded. "You can't abandon me like this. You're all I have to live for now."

"Don't be absurd," Gloria laid her hand on the door knob. "And for God's sake go!"

At that moment a voice called out her name, a voice that was more horrible even than the beckoning hand. Emanuel started back in alarm. Gloria put out her tongue at him and hurried into the room. From behind the closed door came the sound of raucous laughter.

Emanuel felt as if he were suffocating. He gasped for breath and staggered towards the window. He looked down at the people leaving the theatre, and thought of the last time he had stood there, surveying the scene with a sense of domination. Now he knew that each figure scurrying along the streets was bearing abroad the tale of his disgrace, the tale of a man who had set up to be a serious composer and was nothing but a feeble practical joker. However favourably his music might have been judged by some, for ever now it would be connected with a ridiculous hoax.

Where could he hide himself from the derision of the world? To whom could he go for consolation? Madame d'Arc dead, Gloria indifferent. He shuddered at the thought of facing Evangeline and her family. Their kindly sympathy would be harder to bear even than the world's laughter and Gloria's heartlessness. Every door was closed to him. There was only one escape.

*   *   *

James and Evangeline had missed their train. They came by a later one and were over two hours late. When they got to the Arena people were coming out. An excited crowd had collected in front of the theatre. Two policemen emerged bearing away a struggling dishevelled woman.

"Modern music," said James, "often provokes a riot. I remember the first night of the Sacre du Printemps."

"Oh dear," said Evangeline, "I hope Emanuel hasn't been hurt."

They pushed their way into the auditorium. Here there were further signs of disorder. Angry men and women were shouting and gesticulating. A rowdy band of youths was being rounded up by the police. On the stage a few members of the orchestra remained. A woman harpist looked sympathetic, and Evangeline enquired of her where Emanuel was to be found.

"He was here a minute or two ago," she said. "He seemed very much upset by the accident."

"Accident," Evangeline cried. "What accident?"

"A lady was electrocuted."

"Electrocuted? But Mr. Smith—where is he? Oh, tell me, please!" A fireman was helpful.

"He went this way, Miss."

He showed her to the stairs that led up to the vestibule. Evangeline reached it in time to see Emanuel standing before the open window. She called to him.

Then she saw him leap forward into the darkness.

13

E manuel fell on an awning below and lay there suspended, stunned but not dead.

Evangeline and James arrived on the spot in time to prevent him being taken to a hospital. Evangeline was wonderful. In spite of the mental agony she had been through she kept her head, and James, as usual, was full of common sense. After satisfying himself that, beyond concussion, Emanuel had sustained no serious injury, he had him taken to his lodgings where he and Evangeline spent the night.

Mrs. Darwin and Milly were in a twitter. The happenings at the theatre and Emanuel's accident provided them with more "news" than they were able to digest.

When Emanuel recovered consciousness, his brain was for a time clouded by nightmarish memories. But when he saw Evangeline sitting by his bedside, James standing at the window, Mrs. Darwin bringing in a tray; when, in convalescent mood, he contemplated the familiar objects of his room, the piano, the bust of Beethoven, his writing table, he was glad to be alive. The sunshine cheered him. So did the extracts from the newspapers read out to him by Evangeline.

On the whole public opinion was kind to him. His music was favourably reviewed by Mr. Crab, and by several other critics who had been squared beforehand. By many Emanuel was regarded as a victim, and the Count was censured for having involved the Queen Mother in one of his practical jokes.

In the afternoon Emanuel left with James and Evangeline for the country. As he sat that evening with his fiancée by the river watching the swallows skimming over the water and the cows grazing placidly in the fields, a great peace descended upon his soul. All the strange adventures of the last weeks faded away like the happenings of a ghastly dream and with them a great many pretensions and illusions.

He thanked God once more for his escape. How silly it would be to be dead on this pleasant evening. His life was only just beginning.

The symphony of course would have to be re-christened. He would call it "The New Life" or something of the sort.

He observed Evangeline. In the evening light she was really quite pretty.

His passion for Gloria had evaporated. The scales had fallen from his eyes. He saw her plainly now. She was nothing but a great frivolous cow.

He was relieved to think that Count Omega had betaken himself and his mysterious activities to America. But the memory of Madame d'Arc filled him with sadness. How kind she had been to him, though perhaps her influence in his life had not been a very wholesome one. Later on, after reading the biography of Joan of Arc in the "Encyclopaedia Britannica," he began to have doubts about her reincarnation. Evangeline assured him that, anyhow, reincarnation was nonsense.

Emanuel married Evangeline. Her brochure on Kant's Critique of Pure Reason was well received in philosophical circles, and Emanuel's symphony, when it was performed again with a different ending, had a great, if not sensational, success.

THE ROMANCE OF A NOSE

(1941)

The Romance

OF A

Nose

Lord Berners

1

In my opinion it can hardly grow any longer," said Theodotos, Master of Rhetoric, as he walked out through the palace gates with the Professor of Deportment.

"Yes," replied the Professor, "and it is indeed a great misfortune for the young Princess, for what does it avail to possess such grace of movement, such elegance of gesture, when coupled with so monstrous a disfigurement? Had you but seen, this morning, her Ascent of the Throne, it was admirable! And her Greeting to the Ambassadors, it was exquisite! But alas, that nose! It seemed to transform the exercise into a parody, and it needed all my powers of dissociation to judge the movements apart from the unfortunate impression of the nose. The performance of the little Princess Arsinoe, though far less perfect, was more pleasant to behold."

Theodotos smiled.

"One can foresee the kind of nicknames the ribald citizens of Alexandria will invent for her when she comes to the throne. And according to the latest reports of His Majesty's health," he added, "I fancy that moment is not far distant."

"The Alexandrians are merciless in their ridicule," the Professor agreed, "and especially where their rulers are concerned. Poor little Princess! One remembers her beauty as a child. Who could ever have thought she would have developed such a proboscis? I fear it is weighing on her mind. She seems to have lost a good deal of her boisterous vivacity."

"Perhaps that's as well," said Theodotos, recalling some of the practical jokes the little princess had played in the past.

"Were the citizens of Alexandria more serious people," the Professor went on, "they might perhaps respect her wit and her intellectual qualifications—"

"She's a clever girl," Theodotos conceded. "She has a natural gift of speech and an incredible facility for foreign tongues. Owing to my tuition she is now able to orate fluently in the languages of the Medes, the Hebrews, the Syrians and the Troglodytes. Her eloquence is perfect."

"And so are her gestures," said the Professor. "That is also important. However perfect the diction, it is of no account unless it is accompanied by correctness of gesture."

"The two things go together," said Theodotos, rather crossly. "Imperfection of speech cannot be redeemed by gesture, be it ever so elegant and apposite."

"Perfection of both," replied the Professor, not wishing to embark on a discussion with one he knew to be his superior in dialectical skill, "will, I fear, never redeem that unlucky organ, and it grieves me to think that the poor Princess should be so distressed by it. The waiting-ladies tell me that she frequently withdraws to her room to weep."

The two men bowed to one another ceremoniously and parted.

As Theodotus made his way through the palace gardens his mind was filled with ambitious schemes in which, strangely enough, the princess's nose was no inconsiderable feature. It was an excellent thing, he considered, that she should have become a prey to melancholy moods and a sense of inferiority. As a child she had been far too wilful and obstreperous. Her impertinent caprices had often aroused in him an apprehension that, later on, she might prove altogether too much of a handful.

The King, during the last few years, had given himself over entirely to a life of pleasure, and had left the affairs of state to be managed by the Eunuch Potheinos, a man who had been brought up in the best traditions of palace intrigue. Theodotos himself, while teaching rhetoric and philosophy to the royal children, had managed at the same time to acquire a certain popularity among the proletariat of Alexandria. He was on the best of terms with Potheinos and, together with the Commander in Chief, Achillas, these two men formed a kind of triumvirate, a reflection of the mighty Triumvirate across the sea. Only in Alexandria there was less quarrelling. How lucky it was that there should be these perpetual rivalries among the Roman leaders! It was the only thing that, up till now, had saved Egypt from being devoured by her powerful and hungry neighbour. The King, in one of his lucid intervals, had made a will leaving the Kingdom to his two eldest children, the Princess and her brother, a boy of ten. They were to marry, according to the custom, and rule conjointly.

The little prince had never shown any signs of character beyond the mischievous propensities common to children of his age. He would be easy to manage.

But the Princess was a very different proposition. She was headstrong, ambitious and far too intelligent. She had no great affection for Theodotos, and Potheinos she loathed. At the age of twelve she had composed a bawdy poem about the Eunuch's physical deficiencies and had had it circulated in the town. She had, during a banquet, pinned a stinking fish inside his cloak and once, when he was addressing a public meeting, she had thrown into the air a powder that caused him to sneeze violently and had spoilt the effect of his oratory.

On another occasion she had gained access to the Eunuch's chamber and had substituted for the depilatory ointment he was in the habit of using another of so caustic a nature that it had caused him great pain and had incapacitated him from attending to his business for several days. These and many other tricks she played on him; the dislike she felt for him was heartily reciprocated.

Yes, Theodotos thought, the Princess's nose was providential, a godsend. What the Professor of Deportment had said of the Alexandrians was very true. They were a ribald, irreverent folk and they delighted to ridicule their rulers. In Alexandria lampoons and caricatures were the deadliest of political weapons.

2

The Princess had sent away her waiting women and sat alone in her chamber, deep into the night, reading the *Rape of Helen*. It was a story that had always profoundly moved her. Helen of Troy was, for her, a very real person, in spite of the fact that Theodotos had said that she never existed. But then Theodotos was a sceptic. He questioned the Divinity of Kings, and even the existence of the Gods themselves. He was scornful of human love and said it was a disease that only led to trouble. It was quite natural that he should disbelieve in Helen of Troy. The young Princess saw no reason herself for not believing in things that gave her pleasure and she was fond at times of indulging in moods of girlish sentimentality.

She was nearly seventeen. In many ways she had remained a child, and she clung to many of childhood's superstitions. At the same time she was, in other respects, thoroughly sophisticated. She had always rather deliberately lived in a world of romantic make-believe. In the world of reality, however, she was bent on playing a conspicuous part. She was ambitious to figure in it as a great romantic heroine whom historians would record and of whom poets would write as they had written of Helen of Troy.

But now alas, this great misfortune had come upon her and her dreams of emulating Helen had been shattered.

As a child she had possessed great beauty, and her mother and her nurses had often had occasion to reprove her for her vanity. Her features, apart from this lamentable appendage, still retained their former grace. Nothing in her face had very much altered except the nose which, in elongating itself out of all proportion, had completely ruined everything.

When at first it had begun to grow, it had caused her little concern. But later, when its length became so exaggerated that her younger brothers and her sister Arsinoe began to tease her about it, she was seized with panic and despair.

Why, she wondered, had the Gods visited her with this singular affliction? Was it to punish her for some unknown fault? Was it a piece of spite on the part of Khnoum, the Moulder of the Human Form, because she preferred the Gods of Greece? Yet she had never failed to sacrifice to the Gods of both countries, and she had always set aside most delicious morsels for the sacred cats. But still her nose had gone on growing, and she feared to look at herself in the mirror.

Then there occurred an incident that brought a climax to her despair. A handsome Roman officer had come to the Palace, a cavalry commander in the army of Gabinius. As he had helped to reinstate her father on his throne, the children had been instructed to treat him with every courtesy. As far as the young Princess was concerned the exhortation was quite unnecessary, for she thought him the most attractive young man she had ever seen, the ideal of manly strength and comeliness, the embodiment of the Gods and heroes she most admired, Heracles, Apollo, Theseus.

He was also polite and amiable. He brought to her father a gift of Falernian wine and had listened with patience to his performance on the flute. He had danced her younger brother on his knee and had amused the elder with stories of his campaigns. He had patted her sister Arsinoe on the head and kissed her. But when she herself had stepped forward to greet him with a witty speech, he took one glance at her nose and then hastily looked away. He made amends for it afterwards by engaging her in conversation, but it was obvious that he did not find her attractive.

From that day she realised that she must give up all hope of conquering the hearts of men.

Yet, she reflected, there were other ways of dominating them than by beauty alone, and she determined to cultivate her mind. She applied herself diligently to every form of learning. She studied philosophy, geography, history, medicine, astronomy, architecture and languages. She took lessons in rhetoric and in deportment, for she could at least attain perfection in eloquence and grace of movement, and she paid great attention to the modulation of her voice.

Instead of the simple Grecian fillet she had been accustomed to wear she now adopted the elaborate headdress of Egyptian royalty, hoping thus to minimise the prominence of her nose. Yet she knew that the device though possibly effective when she appeared in public, would be of no avail in the intimate contact of love.

She had enquired of the Court Physician whether there was anything that could be done. The old man knew of no remedy and took refuge in compliments. He pointed to a picture of the Ibis-headed Thoth, drawing her attention to the resemblance. It was a proof, he told her, of her divine descent. The feature had been bestowed on her as a signal mark of favour by the Gods.

To the young girl's vanity his words brought little consolation.

As she sat alone in her chamber, the lofty windows open to the night, her heart was full of sorrow. She looked out into the garden, at the full moon mirrored in the lotus-pool, at the outlines of the palms and cypresses black against the silver sky and beyond them, towering into the air, the great lighthouse of white marble with its beacon that outshone the moon.

The gentle night-breeze bore into the room the heavy scent of the waxen flowers that glowed like lanterns on the glossy leaved tree lately imported from the East.*

It was a night for lovers. But she, alas, would never wander in a moonlit garden on such a night with a handsome Roman cavalry officer. Such joys would never be hers. Her place would be in the Council Chamber or in the Museum, discoursing with philosophers and politicians. It was unwise to have read of Helen on such a night. It brought back all the dreams she had resolved to set aside for ever. She must really pull herself together and no more give way to vain and foolish thoughts unworthy of a future stateswoman.

*See Professor Nöldeke. "The importation of the Magnolia into Ptolemaic Egypt."

Heaving a deep sigh she thrust the papyrus into the flame of the lamp and watched it burn to ashes on the mosaic floor.

"What is it Sister? A spell? An incantation?"

She turned and saw a small figure in the doorway; a boy with unprepossessing, rodent-like features.

"Get out, you little rat!" the Princess cried angrily, picking up a small ornament of lapis lazuli to throw at him.

"Sister," the boy complained, "I can't get to sleep."

"Well, what of it?"

"Father is making such a row with his flute that it keeps me awake."

"Well, what do you expect me to do about it? You don't propose that I should go and ask him to stop?"

"I thought you might perhaps have some suggestion."

"I suggest that you find somewhere else to sleep where you won't hear it. The palace is large enough."

"There is nowhere in the Men's Quarters where one can get away from it. He's walking up and down the passages practising a new piece. And he's drunk too. The squeaks and wails are simply ghastly. This seems to be the only place in the palace where one can't hear it. Can I come and sleep here?"

"No, you most certainly can't. Get out."

She threatened him with the lapis ornament.

The boy walked sulkily out of the room. A few seconds later he crept back and put in his head at the door.

"Nosey!" he shouted and scampered away down the passage.

The Princess hurled the missile at him. In her fury the aim was misdirected and a crystal goblet, standing on a table near the door was shattered. It was one of the gifts that the young Roman commander had left when he departed. She gathered up the fragments sadly and emptied them into a casket and then, throwing herself face downwards on a pile of cushions, she burst into a flood of tears.

3

After a series of recoveries and relapses the King was at last really dying. It was remarkable, the Chief Physician said, that, after a life spent in an almost uninterrupted state of intoxication, His Majesty should have lasted as long as he had. He attributed it to his own particular treatment to which, it must be avowed, His Majesty had never paid the slightest attention.

If, as he lay on his deathbed, the King's fading mind recalled memories of his past life, he can have found in them but little cause for satisfaction. A mean, ignoble figure, he was hedged by no divinity, and his reign, from beginning to end, had been nothing but a series of futilities and humiliations.

Of doubtful birth, he had been accepted by the Alexandrians as a *pis aller* after a double murder had put an end to the legitimate dynasty. Perpetually menaced by the shadow of Rome he had spent his time and money in bribing the Romans. Constant fears of dethronement disturbed the life of ease and pleasure he might otherwise have led as the ruler of the richest city in the world with all the wealth of Egypt at his disposal. All he asked for was to be left alone to booze and play his flute, for these two things he at least took seriously. After a while his debaucheries, his extravagance, his political incompetence were too much even for the Alexandrians and they drove him out, putting his eldest daughter Berenice in his place. He fled to Rome where Pompey and Cæsar, stimulated by handsome bribes, befriended him. It was thought to be an excellent occasion for annexing Egypt, but political squabbles and the rivalries of the Roman leaders for a time delayed the project. However, as a preliminary measure, an army commanded by Gabinius and Mark Antony was sent to put him back on his throne, and the King had the satisfaction of having Berenice strangled. "That will teach her," he remarked, "the sanctity of filial duty." He would have further edified his subjects by a wholesale massacre, had he not been dissuaded by Mark Antony.

He recovered his throne, but he soon found that life thereafter was not to be all beer and skittles. He owed money right and left to the Romans and was obliged to make his principal creditor Chancellor of the Exchequer so that he might get his money back from the Alexandrians. Gabinius left behind him a garrison composed chiefly of rough, outlandish Gauls and Germans who were inclined to make a nuisance of themselves in the streets. But the worst of all was that the attention of Rome was now more than ever fixed on Egypt and the shadow of the great Republic became a deadlier menace than before.

Domestic life in the Palace was distracted by the antics of four motherless children, and the King had neither the inclination nor the ability to attend to their education. He continued in an increasing degree to seek consolation in an artificial paradise of drink and music. His flute playing was the only thing in which he excelled. But it was jeered at by his subjects. Neither was it appreciated by his youthful family and, once, when he had been about to perform in public (which he was fond of doing) the young princess had stopped his flute with wax and smeared the mouthpiece with bitter aloes.

If the King had failed to gain the esteem of his contemporaries and the affection of his children he was determined at least to cut a noble figure in the eyes of posterity, and he caused to be inscribed on a pylon at Philæ a glorified portrait of himself triumphing over his enemies.

4

In the Royal Bedchamber the Eunuch Potheinos, Theodotos, Achillas, the four children, the Court Physicians and a number of courtiers and attendants were gathered together waiting for the King to die. But he was a long time about it, and the children were beginning to grow restless. When they were together for any length of time they inevitably began to quarrel.

"I wish he'd hurry up," said the rat-faced boy, "I want to be King."

The Princess turned on him angrily.

"You won't be King at all if you don't behave yourself."

"And who's to prevent me? Papa said I was to be King and when you're my wife you'll have to obey me."

"Your wife indeed! You'd better get that idea out of your ugly little head."

"Well I'm sure I don't want you. But if Papa says I'm to marry you I suppose I'll have to go through with it."

"You can suppose anything you like. When I'm Queen I'll have you put away and nobody will miss you."

"You can't do that. Potheinos won't let you."

"Nonsense. I'd have you chopped up in little pieces now and given to the crocodiles, if I didn't think it would make the poor things sick."

The boy could think of no suitable repartee and resorted to personalities. "Anyhow I haven't got a face like an ibis," he cried. "Nosey!"

"Shut up!" the Princess screamed, and gave him a formidable whack on the head with her fly whisk. "And you shut up, too," she shouted at Arsinoe who was grinning maliciously.

Both the children retorted with cries of "Nosey! Nosey!"

The dying King moved his head slightly and Potheinos turned towards the noisy group.

"Children, children," he besought, "pray refrain from disturbing the last moments of your exalted father."

The youngest child, feeling that he was being left out of things set up a howl which was almost immediately drowned by the loud wailing of the attendants. The King was dead.

"Hurrah!" cried the rat-faced boy, "I'm King! I'm King!" and he started to dance about the room. His elder sister caught hold of him and boxed his ears. He retaliated by pulling her hair. Theodotos ran forward and tried to separate them. And so, in the atmosphere of turmoil and confusion in which he had spent his life, Ptolemy Neos Dionysos gave up the ghost.

5

Potheinos was extremely annoyed, and his sallow face was puffed with anger. He had just had another very unsatisfactory interview with the young Queen.

"It is difficult to know how to deal with her," he complained to Theodotos. "She is as obstinate as a mule and her skill in argument is supplemented by violence and insult. The things she has said to me in the course of the last few days I shall neither forgive nor forget, and she simply won't hear of marrying her brother. She says he is too young."

"Well, I don't hold with child marriages myself," said Theodotos, "but one mustn't allow private morality to interfere with politics."

"You are right, Theodotos, and who in this country ever does? She wants to reign alone during her brother's minority."

"The prejudice against female rule is strong," said Theodotos. "Possibly it might be wise to let her rule alone for a while and see what happens."

"Yes. I thought of that. But it would be dangerous for me to relinquish the power I hold. I can't afford to disappear from the scene even for a few months. Were I to efface myself there is the probability of her causing me to disappear for ever. Indeed it is more than a probability. It is a certainty."

"She would hardly dare."

"Oh, wouldn't she? She is afraid of nothing, curse her. But after all she is a woman and, although a clever one, she has little practical experience of politics and she has many of womanhood's defects. That, it seems to me, suggests the angle from which we must attack."

"She has one particularly vulnerable defect," said Theodotos, "and one of which she is more painfully conscious than are at present the amiable people of Alexandria. We must lose no time in drawing their attention to it. You have no doubt appreciated the cleverness of her costume each time she has appeared in public. The exaggerated headdress she has adopted tends to minimise the effect of her deformity. By most people she is only seen from afar, and my observation specialists inform me that, on the whole, she has made a favourable impression."

"All the more reason," said Potheinos, "for destroying it as soon as possible. That is a task I leave to you, my dear Theodotos. Let us thank the Gods for the Alexandrian sense of humour."

The Queen, on her side, had found the interviews with Potheinos rather stimulating. They had afforded her the opportunity of letting him hear a few home truths, and she never lost an opportunity of referring to his inadequacies in a manner that he found peculiarly offensive. He had tried for some time to keep up the fiction that the term "Eunuch" was merely an official designation, but both circumstances and his appearance proved that it was more than that.

In ordinary intercourse, however, he was more than able to hold his own and every interview had ended in a complete deadlock.

Apollodoros, the only man of the Queen's entourage she felt that she could trust and whose opinions she respected, had advised her to compromise and share the Government with Potheinos. She was beginning herself to wonder if the task of governing alone might not prove too difficult and dangerous. It was certainly wiser not to be too ambitious at first, and there was no doubt that the Alexandrians did not like being ruled over by women. They certainly never took much trouble to prevent their Queens from being assassinated. She thought of Berenice.

Finally, after long deliberation, she decided to take Apollodoros's advice and sent for him.

Apollodoros was a Sicilian. He had been attached to her father's household in the capacity, it was rumoured, of a minion. But she thought none the worse of him for that. Many famous men had started their careers in that way. Once, when her sister Arsinoe had referred to him as "a nasty pansy" she had slapped her face and said "Have you never heard of Julius Cæsar and the King of Bithynia?" But Arsinoe was an ignorant child. She had never heard of Julius Cæsar and the King of Bithynia.

Apollodoros had got over all that sort of thing now, if indeed he had ever had any genuine taste for it, and although his manner was a trifle effeminate (he paid an almost abnormal attention to his clothes) in other respects he was particularly virile.

Some years ago he had initiated the young Queen into the mysteries of sex. She had regarded his instruction in a purely academical light and so had Apollodoros himself. He had always conducted himself as a respectful, devoted servant and although at times he was apt to be a little familiar in his manner he never attempted to presume. The Queen was very fond of him. She was impressed by his learning, amused by his wit, and he was an excellent mimic.

"Greetings to Your Divine Majesty, Daughter of Isis, Royal Egypt," said Apollodorus as he entered the room bowing low in imitation of the Court Physician, "And how are we to-day?"

"We are very well, thank you. But our affairs are in a bit of a jam. However I've made up my mind at last and I thought you might like to hear what I have decided."

"Speak, O Queen. Your servant's ears are as the fertile land of Egypt drinking in the waters of the Nile."

"Oh, stop that nonsense. Please be serious. There are important matters to discuss. Old Flabbyface proposes to set up a Regency, with himself of course as Regent, and he says he'll very kindly let me be a member of the Council along with Theodotos and that numskull Achillas. If that old drawing-room cat thinks I'm going to accept favours from him he's very much mistaken. By Serapis, how I hate eunuchs. I know that most women dote on them. I suppose it's because I'm what they call 'whole-hearted.' "

"He's certainly a nasty piece of work," said Apollodorus, arranging his hair with his forefinger.

"Don't do that," exclaimed the Queen in whom the thought of eunuchs had aroused a flash of irritation. "You know what they say in Rome about men who fiddle with their hair."

"We aren't in Rome."

"We soon shall be if we don't look out—parading the streets in a Roman Triumph. That's why it is essential that there should be some sort of order here. We must leave political bickering and petty rivalry to the

Romans, and trust to its continuing. As you know I'm not over fond of Potheinos, but we mustn't let personal feelings enter into politics unless we are strong enough to indulge them. At present my position is a little rocky. And that is why I've decided to share the government with him—at any rate for the present."

"And what about your dear little brother? Are you going to marry him?"

"I may perhaps do so later on, in order to prevent his getting into the hands of some other woman. He doesn't count anyway. My present policy is to establish a funk. I pinch him and kick his bottom whenever I see him."

"Isn't that a little unwise?"

"It may be unwise, but it's very enjoyable. Even a Queen must be allowed a few pleasures occasionally. The whole lot of them are only waiting for a chance to put me away. Even Arsinoe, who takes very little interest in politics, is studying poisons I hear. As for that little rat, he hasn't the guts even to kill a fellow rat. Much as I resent having to do it, I think my idea of compromising with Potheinos is sound."

"Well, it's what I have been saying all along."

"Nonsense. It is entirely my own idea."

Apollodoros knew that it was wiser not to dispute the matter. He bowed low and kissed the tips of her fingers.

"The Queen," he said, "is always right."

After Apollodoros had left, the Queen sent for Potheinos.

"Listen you old humbug," she said, as the Eunuch came shambling into the room and greeted her with his insidious smile. "The people are beginning to grow restive and if we don't come to some agreement soon there'll be a riot. We shall have the Romans in and then we shall all be in the soup—now don't start arguing. It's cards on the table this time and I'm dealing."

"Well," said Potheinos, "since you put it that way, I should like to hear what Your Majesty has to propose."

"What I have to propose is very simple. We split the Government.

You take the Ministry of the Interior and I take Foreign Affairs. It's a very handsome offer as it gives you control of the exchequer."

"Well," said Potheinos, massaging his chin, "this requires thinking about."

"Of course it does," the Queen retorted, "I've thought about it and there it is. You can take it or leave it."

"On the whole," said Potheinos, "I am in favour of your proposal. But before giving Your Majesty a definite answer I must of course consult my colleagues."

"Nonsense. Consulting your colleagues merely means giving them your orders. And I'll trouble you not to assume any airs of patronage with me. Please remember I am Queen, daughter of the Gods, rightful heir to the throne. And as for you—well, you know what you are—"

"Very well, O Queen," said Potheinos hurriedly, wishing to avoid further elaboration of the subject. "We will do our best to fall in with Your Majesty's desires. But for the sake of appearance I must call a consultation. As for your Majesty being the rightful heir to the throne, it must not be forgotten that Your Majesty's brother—"

"Don't imagine that you can frighten me with that little poop. He's nothing. He doesn't exist. I advise you to leave him out of your calculations. You can go now, and call your consultation. Call anything you like. But if I don't get a favourable answer by this evening I shall know how to act."

Potheinos bowed and retired. He was still hesitating whether or not to comply with the Queen's wishes, and her last threat alarmed him. She was quite capable of staging a *coup d'état* and he too thought it undesirable that there should be, at the actual moment, any kind of disturbance of which the Romans might take advantage.

The Queen was certainly not an easy person to deal with. She was unlike any other woman he had ever known, and he found her profoundly disconcerting. Potheinos had a tortuous, evasive mind and her directness disturbed him. Her strategy was so different from his own. Her frankness always made him suspect that she had something up her sleeve of which he was unaware.

At present, perhaps, it would be wiser to humour her, to ingratiate himself even. But this was no easy task. He knew that she hated and despised him. Perhaps the latter sentiment was one of which he might take advantage. He would play upon her contempt. He would admit her superiority of judgment and seek her counsel. It would not be necessary to follow it of course, but her self-esteem would be flattered and she would be less on her guard against an enemy she considered inferior. Her very cleverness could become a weapon to be used against her. He would inveigle her into parading it on every possible occasion. Clever women were not popular in Alexandria.

The most effective weapon of all, however, was in the hands of Theodotos. Potheinos rubbed his chin and smiled. In spite of his defeat he felt quite optimistic.

6

Accompanied by Apollodoros, the Queen would often wander at night through the meaner quarters of the town. This she did partly for her amusement and partly to gain information, for she trusted more to the acuteness of her own observation to that of her spies.

Although Apollodoros enjoyed these expeditions, they always caused him a certain amount of anxiety, especially when the Queen's love of amusement got the better of her prudence.

Just outside the walls, near the Grove of Nemesis, there was a little settlement called Eleusis. Here there were restaurants and fun-fairs, but the fun was so noisy and the folk who frequented the place so disreputable that it was avoided by the more respectable citizens of Alexandria.

There was a game to be found here that the Queen particularly enjoyed. It was a kind of disk-shy in which the Aunt Sally was represented by the head of a Roman Lictor. On one occasion the Queen took part so energetically in this entertainment that her veil slipped and her too recognizable feature was exposed. Luckily it was unnoticed by the crowd and Apollodoros hurried her away.

The incident had given him a bit of a shock, and he implored the Queen not to go there again. But she had taken such a fancy to the place that a few weeks later she insisted on returning. This time it was she who got a shock. The Roman lictor had been replaced by a woman's head with the royal diadem and an unmistakable nose.

Her first impulse had been to have the owner of the booth arrested, the fun-fair closed, to despatch the Palace Guards to massacre and destroy. With difficulty she controlled her rage.

"Come," she said to Apollodoros, "let us get away from here."

As she passed through the side streets on the way back to the Palace, she saw chalked on a wall a caricature of herself and a poem full of obscene allusions. And further down the street there was another and yet another.

"Apollodoros," she gasped, clutching him by the wrist, "for the first time in my life I am alarmed. My enemies have found a weapon against which I have no defence."

In spite of the intimacy that existed between herself and Apollodoros, the Queen had never seen fit to allude to the feature that caused her so much heart-burning. Had she consulted him instead of the Court Physician she would have done well. For he actually knew of a remedy. But he had hesitated to suggest it, for he knew that women were apt to resent any reference to a physical defect, however kindly meant. Now that the Queen had broached the subject herself, he felt emboldened to speak.

"I have a friend," he told her, "a doctor who for many years has been practising a branch of medicine known as Plastic Surgery."

"What is this plastic surgery?" asked the Queen. "Why have I not been told of it? The physicians I have discoursed with have never mentioned it to me. But that is not surprising. The physicians of Alexandria are permanently behind the times."

"It is an art that is condemned both by the doctors and the priests, and that is why the science has remained unknown. This moulder of living faces met with such opposition in the city that he retired to Thebes, where he conducts his experiments in solitude and secrecy."

"Thebes? That is a long way off. I will summon him to Alexandria."

"I fear, Your Majesty, he might be unwilling to venture here. He has many enemies."

"Write to him at once and tell him he has got to come, that it is the Queen's command and that he shall have the Queen's protection."

After many days Apollodoros received the doctor's reply. He refused to budge. He said that, although he was greatly honoured by the command, he could not undertake to perform so important an operation away from his own clinic and in an atmosphere of hostility.

At first the Queen was furious.

"What," she cried, "he dares defy me. Tell him that if he doesn't come at once I'll send an escort for him. No," she added, her anger dying swiftly, "on second thoughts I think it would be rather fun to go to Thebes. I've always wanted to see the town and it would be nice to do a little sight-seeing on the way. I'm ashamed to think I've never seen any of all those wonderful things Herodotus describes. But this face-moulder, do you really think he'll be able to——"

"I know he will. I have seen examples of his work and that was some years ago. Since then, he tells me he has much improved his technique."

"Apollodoros," cried the Queen flinging her arms round his neck and kissing him, "you are wonderful. You always know everything. If only I had consulted you before. I wish that we could set out to-morrow, but the situation at present is a bit tricky and does not permit me to absent myself."

Bibulus, the new Governor of Syria, about to embark on a Parthian campaign, had sent his two sons to Alexandria to recall the troops left there by Gabinius.

The soldiers of the garrison refused to stir. They had little desire to fight the Parthians and still less to leave Alexandria. Romans, Gauls and Germans alike were enjoying life in the gay city and many of them had settled down and married. They found the society of Alexandrian ladies particularly agreeable. Those that were married and those that were not were equally unwilling to leave their homes and their brothels.

The Roman garrison commander, himself as loth to leave the town as anyone else, told the sons of Bibulus that it was a hopeless quest, and recommended them to return to Syria. Being foolish, arrogant youths, instead of taking his advice, they started a lot of heroic stuff, which, had they known a little more, they might have realised would not go down in Alexandria. They upbraided the legions for their cowardice and altogether un-Roman behaviour. Their harangue left unmoved the Roman and German soldiers, but it was too much for the Gauls. Their native susceptibility was wounded and without further ado they set on the two young men and murdered them. The commander's comment was that they had asked for it.

The Queen who had been, for some time, veering towards a policy of appeasement with regard to Rome, saw in the incident a chance to ingratiate herself. She had the murderers arrested and sent in chains to the bereaved Bibulus. It was an unfortunate move. It infuriated the garrison, and Bibulus snubbed her for her pains. He adopted a pompous line and sent the murderers back to her with a curt message that the right of inflicting punishment in such cases belonged to the Romans alone and that she would do well to mind her own business.

When he heard of it Potheinos was delighted. He came into the Propaganda Department beaming and rubbing his hands.

"A few more blunders like this, my dear Theodotos," he said, "and the game is ours. And how is your little campaign progressing?"

"It is going ahead. What do you think of this?"

He showed the eunuch a mathematical problem. "How long would it take a fly travelling on foot at the rate of three and a half minutes per yard to proceed from one end to the other of a nose measuring six and a half inches?"

"Very good," said Potheinos, "I suppose it will be quite clear to whom the nose belongs?"

"Quite clear," replied Theodotos. "By this time every child will guess. One must be careful of course not to give her any pretext for legitimate suppression. In the case of things not set down on papyrus one can, of course, be more outspoken. Here, for instance, are some jokes that I am having circulated in the salons of Alexandria."

"I don't think they're very funny," remarked Potheinos, as he scanned them—but then he never did care very much for that kind of joke. "I should concentrate at present on attacking her pro-Roman policy. I understand that she is contemplating sending military assistance to Pompey. If she were to supply him with ships and money, as I believe she proposes to do, it will be an easy matter to stir up the people against her and we can get her driven out of the city."

"Or even—"

"No," said the cautious Potheinos, "it is a little too soon for that."

When the growing accusations of pro-Roman sympathies were brought to the Queen's ears, she protested violently.

"I'm not pro-Roman," she said, "I am pro-Egyptian and I'm looking ahead. These foolish people have no foresight. They see no further than their noses."

It was an unfortunate simile and Theodotos was quick to seize upon it.

"If the Queen," he said, "can see further than her nose, she must indeed be far sighted."

The final struggle between Pompey and Cæsar was approaching. The Queen, like nearly everyone else, was backing Pompey. Apart from being likely to win, he had been a friend of the family and he had had her father to stay with him in Rome. He had also a very attractive son who was at that moment in Alexandria. His father had sent him to commandeer the famous garrison troops. This time, they were quite willing to go, and the men who had refused to take part in a doubtful campaign against the Parthians under Bibulus felt that it was a very different mat-

ter to fight under the greatest general of the age against the famous
Cæsar himself.

The young Queen made herself very agreeable to the handsome
Gnæus Pompey. Potheinos and his friends pretended to be scandalized
at the way she was carrying on with him. If she had been pro-Roman
by policy, they said, she was now definitely pro-Roman by sentiment.

The banquets with which she entertained the young man were more
magnificent than anything he had ever seen in Rome. She showed him
all the sights of Alexandria both picturesque and curious. She took him
fishing on the lake. Her vivacious jokes and her saucy repartee kept him
in continual roars of laughter. She certainly knew how to amuse a fellow and give him a good time, Gnæus thought. But what a pity she had
that nose, poor girl. He wondered if she minded very much.

When he left, the Queen loaded him with gifts, and, in addition to
five hundred soldiers of the garrison, made him a present of fifty ships.
The Alexandrians on beholding most of the Egyptian fleet sailing off to
the Adriatic, laden with corn and gold, were in no mood to excuse their
young Queen's partiality for a handsome face and a pair of well turned
legs. An angry crowd besieged the palace, crying "Down with appeasement," "Pro-Roman strumpet" and worse things still. And, as the
Queen was carried in her litter, that afternoon, down Canopus Street,
a band of youths shouted "Nosey" at her and made rude noises.

"It is intolerable," the Queen remarked to her ladies-in-waiting,
"where-ever I go I get an impression of cross faces."

In the cool of the evening she went up on to the roof of the palace to
escape the turmoil and anger below. She sat there for a while watching
the last rays of the sun dying on the marble lighthouse and the waters of
the Mediterranean turning to a deeper blue. A ship with sails outspread
moved slowly across the harbour and disappeared from view.

She thought of the pleasant young Roman who had sailed away that
morning. Her thoughts went further back to another young Roman.
Where was he now, she wondered? With Pompey? With Cæsar? And always, in the background of her thoughts, loomed the strange physician
of Thebes, the moulder of living faces. Ever since her conversation with

Apollodoros she had never ceased to think of him and she would sit before her mirror covering her nose with her forefinger. When it was hidden she saw that she was beautiful. Her eyes, her mouth, her chin, the shape of her face, all were perfect. But could this man really do all that Apollodoros had promised? The priests had said it was an evil thing to change the face. The doctors had said that it was impossible. However, Apollodoros was reliable. When he promised anything he always delivered the goods.

She wondered if the operation was very painful and, in spite of her great desire to have it performed as soon as possible, she dreaded the thought of it.

Her meditations were interrupted by the sound of hesitating footsteps creeping up behind her and she turned abruptly, fearing an aggression.

It was her brother.

"Dear me," she exclaimed, "rats on the roof. How very disagreeable. Is there no place where we may be free from these nasty creatures? Shoo. Be off." She waved her fan at him.

The little King removed himself out of striking range and held his ground.

"Sister," he said, "you're going to be deposed."

"What? This rat can speak? How curious."

"Yes," the boy went on, "you're going to be deposed and I'm to reign alone. The terms of Papa's will haven't been carried out and it's going to be declared null and void. Potheinos says so."

"I'll make you null and void if you don't clear out."

She jumped to her feet and made a grab at him. He dodged her and fled away down the staircase.

"All right," she shouted after him, "I'll deal with you later."

As she was returning to her apartments, she was approached by one of her spies.

"Your Majesty," the man whispered to her, "the position I fear is grave. The Palace Guards and most of the attendants have been suborned. They are no longer to be trusted."

"Thank you for your information," said the Queen as she detached a bracelet and handed it to him. It was customary to tip purveyors of bad news.

She sent for Apollodoros.

"Pack your bags," she said to him, "we leave to-night for Thebes."

7

Doctor Serapion was an Egyptian. His name was Sakhebu-Kaka but, on entering the Alexandrian School of Medicine, he had assumed the name of Serapion for the sake of its euphony and its associations.

He was a man of means. He had no need to earn his living, and had taken up the study of medicine in its special branch of anatomy purely for the love of it.

Since the great days of Herophilus and Erasistratus the art of medicine in Alexandria had sadly declined. Disinterested research after knowledge for its own sake had given place to self-seeking professionalism, and Doctor Serapion had been looked upon by his colleagues as an interloping amateur.

The science of anatomy, once the pride of the Alexandrian School, was now despised and considered the province of the embalmer. At present, drugs were all the rage. The fashion had been introduced by Mithridates, King of Pontus, who was anxious to popularise the produce of his country, and, under the accumulation of quack prescriptions, panaceas, "Mithridatics" and cosmetics, the art of medicine was well nigh suffocated.

Doctor Serapion had made no attempt to conceal his scorn for the new craze. "Alexandria," he used to say, "has become a hot-bed of druggery," and he was wont to refer to his fellow doctors as "a lot of bloody druggers."

The attitude he had taken up, and the superiority of his intelligence, did not increase his popularity in medical circles, and when he embarked on plastic surgery, there was a great outcry. His colleagues attempted to stir up the enmity of the priests and accused him of sacrilege and insult to the God Khnoum, the Moulder of the Human Form. Had the ancient religion been taken more seriously by the Alexandrians, things might have gone badly with the ingenious doctor.

It was his great love for beauty, especially as represented in the human face, that had primarily directed his mind to this particular form of surgery. The sight of misshapen noses, coarse lips, receding or too prominent chins distressed him, and he resolved to devote his life to correcting nature.

His first experiments had not been at all successful, but as they had been carried out on slaves, it was of no very great consequence. He acquired, later on, a greater proficiency, but his enemies saw to it that he found few clients among the upper-class Alexandrians. They intensified their campaign of denigration, and many of those who, dissatisfied with their faces, might have applied to him for remedy, were dissuaded from undergoing an operation that was proclaimed experimental, dangerous and sinful.

Finally an unlucky attempt to relieve an influential Alexandrian matron of her triple chin led to Doctor Serapion's expulsion from the Schools of Medicine, whereupon he decided to leave the city and retire to his native Thebes.

Here he converted a derelict palace into a clinic and dwelling-place combined, and laid out many acres of gardens, vineyards and palm groves, for he had also a great love for horticulture and husbandry. Amid the fallen grandeur of the ancient city he continued, undisturbed, to pursue his labours in the cause of beauty.

In his art he had at last acquired consummate craftsmanship, and his house was filled with handsome, regular-featured slave girls who acted as his assistants or ministered to his pleasures.

When he received a message from his friend Apollodorus that the Queen of Egypt was anxious to take advantage of his skill, he was much elated by the prospect of so exalted a patroness. Yet he hesitated to expose himself once more to the turmoil and the vexations of the great city, especially as he had heard that the Queen's position at that moment was far from secure. He was therefore much gratified when a second message came, informing him that the Queen was already on her way.

He began at once to prepare a reception that should be worthy of the royal lady. A suite of apartments was hastily redecorated and filled with the choicest specimens of his artistic collection. The valley was scoured for rare game and fish. The pastry cooks were set to work devising new and exquisite sweetmeats and, in the laboratories, fragrant perfumes were distilled.

8

The Queen explained to Apollodoros, as they entered the royal barge that she had thought it advisable under the circumstances to "travel light."

She had brought with her only sixty heavy trunks of ebony and electrum containing wearing apparel, carpets, books, musical instruments and jewelry, and a hundred lighter valises of wicker-work packed with odds and ends. She also took with her a number of statues, pictures and a mosaic floor. She was accompanied by most of the palace attendants who had remained faithful to her. They numbered some three hundred.

The Queen herself was heavily disguised, and was travelling under the name of Mrs. Memphis. She was so pleased with the idea of being a fugitive Queen that she kept up the fiction even after she discovered that she was not being pursued.

Travelling was a new experience for her and Apollodoros had some difficulty in checking her insatiable passion for sightseeing. She would often insist on going miles out of the way in order to see something mentioned by Herodotus or Manetho, and even the discovery that it was non-existent or untrue failed to damp her ardour. Her enquiries ranged from politics and commerce to botany, natural history and local sexual practices, and many of her questions Apollodoros was hard put to it to answer.

She asked him if he thought Helen of Troy had really stayed at Thonis, as Homer had said, and what could have been the "goodly drugs" Queen Polydamna gave her, and whether at Mendes the he-goats still had intercourse with women. She enquired if the nitre beds of Gynæcopolis were as productive as ever and if Osiris had really been buried at Sais.

She admired the great Sphinx, but the pyramids she thought vulgar, ostentatious and lacking in Grecian elegance and was much more interested in the treasures they were said to contain, and she wondered if the curiously formed stone chips lying at their base might not be the petrified food of the workmen.

She was anxious to know why the crocodile was made such a fuss of at Arsinoe while at Tentyra it was held in particular dishonour and considered the most hateful of all animals, and whether it was true that ichneumons, arming themselves with breastplates of mud, seized the asp by its tail, dragged it down to the river and drowned it, and whether they really jumped into crocodiles' mouths, ate their way through their entrails and came out the other end. She said she would like to possess an ichneumon and try it on Potheinos.

She asked searching questions of the custom officers at Hermopolis, and at Panopolis she inspected the linen-works. At Abydos she descended into the vaulted galleries of the great well and she had been with difficulty dissuaded from travelling hundreds of miles inland to have her fortune told at the Oracle of Ammon. She said that the great

Alexander had been very pleased with what they had told him there and she herself was in need of a little encouragement. Apollodoros put his foot down, said there really wasn't time and she must resign herself to going there later on.

At every stopping-place the Queen bought objects that caught her fancy, jewelry, pottery, furniture, fabrics, curious birds and animals, so that many extra barges had to be chartered for their conveyance. Her energy was boundless, her mind so enquiring, her love of sightseeing so relentless that, by the time they reached Thebes, Apollodoros was quite exhausted.

9

They arrived in the early morning just before sunrise. The Queen awakening from her slumbers—she always slept on deck under a tent of fine transparent net—was entranced with her first vision of the ancient capital.

She lifted the gauze veils of the tent and called for Apollodoros.

"Come," she cried, "we are in time to hear the great statue Memnon singing to greet the dawn."

Apollodoros was perturbed by the idea of setting off sightseeing so early in the morning.

"Let us sit and listen to it here," he suggested. "The view is very beautiful. Let us not disturb our first impressions by rushing about. The outline of the temples seen from the river at sunrise is the eighth wonder of the world. Let us enjoy it in tranquillity."

"Oh, what are those birds?" cried the Queen, as a flock of rose-coloured water fowl settled on the bank. "What are they called?"

"They are a kind of goose, I think."

"Nonsense, goose yourself! Iras," she called to one of her attendants, "bring me the manual of natural history."

Apollodoros knew that the birds were a variety of ibis, but had refrained from saying so out of delicatesse. He wondered, as she scanned the papyrus, whether she would appreciate his tactfulness or be annoyed by it.

"I can't find them," she said and threw down the scroll. "That little temple over there must be the one built by Osirei and dedicated to Amun. It is quite pretty, but its construction is wanting in rhythm. To what do you attribute the Egyptian distaste for symmetry?"

The sky grew brighter and the sun rose, lighting up with a golden glow the distant pylons and the palm groves on the further bank.

"Silence!" the Queen cried angrily to the chattering waiting maids. "All of you listen."

They listened but no sound was heard except the lowing of oxen and the cries of the water fowl.

Apollodoros had omitted to mention the fact that the musical colossus was at least two miles from the river bank.

"How very disappointing," the Queen exclaimed, "I was so looking forward to hearing the statue sing. Another illusion gone, I fear. I shall end by not believing anything. Theodotos always used to say we should believe nothing of what we're told and only half of what we see."

Doctor Serapion had been informed of the Queen's arrival and appeared on the quay with a sumptuous litter and a crowd of attendants and slaves. He advanced and prostrated himself before her as she stepped out of the barge. "Welcome, oh Queen," he said, "to the city of Zeus, the city of a hundred gates, blessed be the return of Egypt's glory to its ancient abode."

The Queen drew Apollodoros aside. "Tell him," she said, "to cut out that ceremonial stuff except in front of the servants. When I'm with intelligent men I prefer to speak with them as an equal."

The procession started off, preceded by dancing girls and musicians, while Nubian slaves burnt incense and scattered blossoms on the path.

When they reached the house, a steward came forward and presented to each of the Queen's ladies a lotus flower and a vase of perfumed ointment. It was an old Egyptian custom and it made them giggle.

The Queen was much pleased with her apartments and she complimented the doctor on his taste. He was astonished to find how much she knew about Egyptian furniture, for he had always imagined that the Ptolemies only cared for things that were Greek.

After she had bathed and perfumed herself and had done the physical exercises she was accustomed to perform every morning she partook of some light refreshment and then sent for Doctor Serapion so that he might explain to her the economy of the household and take her to visit the gardens and the vineyards.

"Would you believe it," she said to him, "I have hardly any knowledge of how a country estate is run. Although I have made an extensive study of most of the arts and sciences, in such matters as horticulture and husbandry I am woefully ignorant."

Doctor Serapion was very proud of his estate and he seldom had the opportunity to display it even to personages of minor importance.

The gardens were entered through a monumental gateway of stuccoed brick ornamented with hieroglyphics. As he ordered the massive doors of cedar wood and bronze to be thrown open to admit his royal guest, the Doctor felt very happy indeed.

The gardens were laid out according to the ancient Theban design and were divided by low walls of stone into several plots of unequal size and connected with one another by rustic gates of brightly painted wood. Four large oblong pools with stone borders, decorated with great bunches of lotus, were placed symmetrically amidst shady groves of fruit trees and palms. Beyond them a belt of carobs and acacias protected the garden from the sandy winds of the desert.

The Queen exclaimed with pleasure as she came upon a carpet of yellow, pink and purple flowers.

"Ah, Your Majesty," Doctor Serapion apologized, "had you but seen the garden a month ago. Then it really was a sight."

He pointed out to her a palm tree of unusual size.

"That," he told her, "is very rare. I might almost say it is a unique specimen. It is the tree that is said to have been brought by the father of Nakhtmin from the land of Akiti. The poets compare it to Thoth, the God of Wisdom, on account of its marvellous properties. The sweet liquor its fruit gives forth may be likened to the honeyed flow of knowledge."

"I should like to taste it," said the Queen.

"Alas, Your Majesty, it is not the season."

As they passed under the trellised vines, the Queen observed some slaves working a primitive and rather ineffectual water-hoist.

"I am sure," she remarked, "that I could devise a better method of irrigation."

"Certainly," the doctor agreed, "the contraption is a little out of date. But it is difficult in these parts to induce the people to abandon the things they are accustomed to."

"It is perhaps unwise," said the Queen, "to enforce innovations on those who feel no need for them."

At the end of the vineyard was a vast reservoir flanked with avenues of sycamore trees and on its surface there floated a gaily painted boat.

"Are there fish in it?" asked the Queen.

"Indeed there are, Your Majesty. It is the best stocked piece of water in the neighbourhood."

"That is good," the Queen cried, clapping her hands with joy. "I'm simply crazy about fishing. I rather fancy myself with the angle, but I'm not skilled at spearing fish. They say it's a man's sport; however I never let such considerations deter me. You will teach me how to spear fish."

On the edge of the water, half hidden in a clump of persea trees, was a small pavilion. The Queen pointed to it.

"Let us sit there awhile, for I wish to speak to you of business."

She sent away her attendants and remained alone with the doctor. As they approached the pavilion a flock of curious birds flew out with a great twittering and settled at their feet.

"I will ask you their names another time," said the Queen. "At present there are matters of more immediate importance to discuss. I want to know all about this operation. Will it be very painful? I'm not in the least a coward, you know, but I can't stand being hurt."

"Your Majesty need have no anxiety whatever," the doctor assured her. "In these last years I have perfected a certain vapour which brings oblivion to those who inhale it. Your Majesty will pass into a deep slumber and when Your Majesty awakens, it will all be over."

"What is the vapour made of?"

"It is composed of Scythian hemp, mandragora and several other ingredients that are secret."

"You will tell me them later. Shall I have nice dreams? O, dear, that reminds me. I stupidly left the dream interpreter behind. It is most annoying, as I've been having the most extraordinary dreams lately. I have dreamt of flying through the air and crocodiles. What do you think it means? But we'll speak of that another time. Are you sure this vapour is quite safe? And that the pain won't wake me up? Or supposing I never wake up at all? You will pardon my asking. Experience of the Alexandrian physicians has left me with a great mistrust of medicine."

"To whom do you say it, Your Majesty! No, no. It is perfectly safe. I have employed it a hundred times. It never fails."

"Very well then. Let us get it over as soon as possible. I should like it done to-morrow."

"Whenever Your Majesty commands."

10

What do you think of her?" Apollodoros asked the Doctor that evening, when the Queen had retired to her apartments.

"Delightful! Charming!" replied the doctor. "Most gracious. Such wit and learning and so natural too. Such easy manners. But, my goodness, she does ask a lot of questions!"

"You're telling me!" said Apollodoros. "And, unlike most people who ask questions, she listens to the answers. Her thirst for knowledge is insatiable."

"She certainly has character," the doctor added. "She seems to know exactly what she wants."

When the question had arisen of what shaped nose the Queen desired, Doctor Serapion had paraded before her some twenty or thirty slave girls to enable her to decide. But he discovered that she had already decided the matter for herself.

She had brought with her a bust* of a Syrian woman which she invited the doctor to examine.

"You will notice," she said, "that the features resemble mine. The eyes, mouth and chin are identical." She pointed to the nose. "That is exactly what I want. It is not too short, as, are many of the noses you have shown me, and it is slightly curved, a nose such as I am told the Romans admire. Can you reproduce this faithfully?"

"If Your Majesty will pardon me—" Doctor Serapion passed his finger respectfully along her nose, pinched it and moved it gently from side to side. "There will be no difficulty at all, Your Majesty. It is merely a question of removing cartilage. I shall not have to touch the bone at all. I shall take the most exact measurements and Your Majesty may be sure that the result will be exactly as Your Majesty desires."

Had she been dealing with a jeweller or a dressmaker the Queen would have resorted to threats in order to ensure perfection of workmanship, but Doctor Serapion appeared to her to be a man of almost magical power and she was a little overawed.

She smiled at him and said, "Well, I expect you to do your best."

Doctor Serapion bowed and said, "Of that Your Majesty may rest assured."

When the time came, the Queen entered the operating chamber with great fortitude. She smiled as she saw Doctor Serapion and his atten-

---

*The bust is now in the British Museum.

dants awaiting her, dressed in long robes of fine linen, and a row of musicians in the background. It reminded her of a religious ceremony.

She was invited to extend herself on a high padded couch of basalt and the doctor brought forward the appliance for generating the narcotic vapour. It had a flexible tube that terminated in a small cup.

"Now," said the doctor, "if Your Majesty will kindly inhale through the nostrils and relax."

He took her wrist and counted the pulsations with his pocket waterclock. The musicians began to play a soft, drowsy air and, in a few minutes, the Queen fell into a deep slumber.

When she woke again she believed for a while that she was dead and that her spirit had passed out of her body into another world. Then a dull pain and the sight of Doctor Serapion's face, smiling as he bent over her, recalled her to earth. She put her hand to her nose and found it swathed in bandages.

"Bring me a mirror," she murmured.

"Your Majesty must have patience," the Doctor urged.

The Queen felt too sick and faint to move. She moaned and closed her eyes.

After a little while she felt better and tried to sit up.

"How has it gone?" she asked.

"It has gone wonderfully well," Doctor Serapion assured her, "Your Majesty will be delighted. Would that Your Majesty could see the results immediately, but the scars will take many days to heal. Your Majesty must be patient."

"Well," said the Queen, "I can have patience as well as anyone else. But the one thing I cannot do is to waste my time. Send for Apollodoros that he may read to me Aristotle's Treatise of Physiognomy."

11

The Queen lay in her bedchamber, a long cool room opening on to a colonnaded court in the centre of which was a lotus pool and a pomegranate tree covered with scarlet blossom. Two slave girls stood on either side of the couch with ostrich feather fans, and at the further end of the room a group of waiting women sat, playing draughts or working at embroidery.

The pain in her nose had almost gone. It required a good deal of strength of mind not to remove the splints and bandages and take a peep. It was dreadul to think that the results of the operation could not be seen for so many days. But she was wisely following the counsels of the doctor who had urged her to wait until the scars were healed and the nose could be revealed to her in all its beauty. She had even had all the mirrors removed lest, while the bandages were being changed, she might succumb to temptation.

"The exercise of restraint," she said, "is no doubt beneficial to the character—but oh, how boring!" And she would refer jokingly to The Unveiling of the Nose. "On that day," she told the doctor, "we must sacrifice to Khnoum the Moulder to propitiate him lest he become jealous of your art."

At first Doctor Serapion had done everything he could think of to alleviate the Queen's impatience and make the time pass quickly. But he noticed that she soon grew weary of the musicians, dancers and buffoons he had engaged to distract her, although out of politeness she pretended that she enjoyed them. At last she confessed to him frankly that she would rather converse with him on such subjects as medicine, philosophy or literature than watch the antics of jugglers and acrobats. He was beginning to understand that her tastes were not those of most of the royal personages he had heard about and that she was more intent on improving her mind than on being diverted. He recounted to her his medical experiences in Alexandria. When he spoke of the degeneracy of the Alexandrian School of Medicine he found a ready listener and they laughed together over the remedies employed by some of the Alexandrian doctors.

"Papa," she told him, "was once recommended a cure for night-blindness that consisted of crocodile's dung, hyena's gall and the liver of a he-goat eaten on an empty stomach during the period of the full moon. Poor Papa's stomach I don't suppose was ever empty and his night-blindness was due to very simple causes. There was no need for so elaborate a remedy. Papa was very credulous. He believed in magic and incantations."

"One laughs nowadays at such absurdities," said Doctor Serapion. "Nevertheless physicians are often justified in calling superstition to their aid. It is often possible to enhance the effects of certain remedies by means of amulets, magic spells and such like nonsense."

"That is true," said the Queen, "I am superstitious myself when it suits me."

Doctor Serapion was a man of varied interests. He had an extensive knowledge of Greek literature and philosophy, and he possessed a fine collection of books. The Queen discovered among them one or two that bore the stamp of the Alexandrian Library and laughingly taxed him with the theft. "It's of no consequence," she assured him, "I have frequently taken out books myself and kept them. The Librarians have grown so careless that they are never missed. And anyhow the Alexandrians don't deserve to have a library at all. If things go on as they are going now I doubt if, in a few generations, any of them will be able even to read. And when one thinks of what Alexandria was! However I don't despair of making it once more the foremost city in the world. You wait till I have suppressed Potheinos and his crew."

She took up a scroll of Homer. "Tell me," she enquired, "do you think the Odyssey was written by a woman?"

Doctor Serapion confessed that the idea had not occurred to him.

"I'm sure it was," the Queen persisted. "I once asked Theodotos if he thought so and he said 'No, certainly not,' and when I asked why not he said 'because no woman is capable of writing a line of decent poetry' (rude wasn't it?) and so I said 'What about Sappho?' and he said 'Oh,

Sappho's different.' Now tell me, Doctor Serapion, to what extent do you think her work was influenced by—"

"I have no idea at all," said the doctor. "Such speculations are not very much in my line. My great namesake, the Empiric, wrote a treatise on sexual aberrations."

"Oh, where is it?" the Queen asked eagerly, "I should like to read it."

"It is unfortunately lost." The doctor sighed. "It was stolen from my collection by a priest."

12

O ccasionally the queen had fits of childish impatience and her threats to tear off the bandages filled the poor doctor with consternation. But reason always prevailed and with great resolution she filled every minute of the day with some engrossing occupation to distract her mind and make the time pass quickly.

During the heat of the day the Queen sat in her apartments with her ladies, surrounded by piles of fabrics of every hue and texture, designing clothes. She herself directed the cutters and seamstresses and tried out effects on mannequins. Her two favourite ladies-in-waiting, Iras and Charmion, were highly skilled in the art of attire, but neither of them could rival the Queen in taste and imagination.

The fashions of the Ptolemaic court were Greek and it was only on state occasions that Egyptian ceremonial dress was worn. The Queen had always preferred the simplicity of Grecian costume that set off in natural folds the beauty of the human form. But now she was attracted by the idea of combining it with Egyptian motifs. She composed ornaments of artificial flowers, the making of which was a local speciality, and she was particularly pleased with a flexible collar she had designed of gold and coloured glass in the traditional shape of a hawk with out-spread wings. For walking in the garden she invented a wide brimmed hat of plaited straw with golden fringes.

In the evening, accompanied by Apollodoros and the doctor, she would go out fishing in the little lake beyond the vineyards. She was an expert angler and caught many fish. Each time she caught one she grew so excited that she nearly overturned the boat.

"The Ptolemies of Pharos and Canopus have always been great fishermen," she told the doctor, and she recounted to him a joke she had played on her father. She had bidden a slave dive into the water and attach to his hook a salted fish. The King had been so intoxicated at the time that he had failed to notice, and had boasted of his catch.

"As a matter of fact," the Queen explained, "it's one of our family jokes—quite an old one you know—which made it all the funnier that Papa should have been taken in by it."

"A merry joke, indeed," the doctor said. He was beginning to feel a great affection for the young Queen. She was so high spirited, so simple and unaffected in her manners, yet at the same time so erudite, so grown up in her worldly wisdom. He was amazed by her general knowledge and her skill in speaking foreign languages. Among his attendants there were many Syrians, Hebrews and Ethiopians and she would converse fluently with them in their native tongues.

Apollodoros said that she did it to show off; to which the doctor replied that, whatever her reasons might be, her talents were remarkable and that she was a truly original Queen.

Although Apollodoros and the doctor urged her to confine her activities to the limits of the estate she insisted on visiting the temples. She was torn between the importance of concealing her identity and the desire to appear to the priests in an authoritative role. However, reason again prevailed and she wore a veil that, concealing the bandages, only allowed her eyes to show. Doctor Serapion explained to the priests that his niece was suffering from antrum trouble.

The doctor was a little shocked by her lack of appreciation of Egyptian architecture. She pronounced it heavy and pretentious and only approved of the Ptolemaic restorations. "Lacking in Grecian elegance," was a phrase she frequently employed. However, she admired the ceilings, with their golden stars on azure ground, the flying vultures symbolically protecting the path of kings and the astronomical designs. Although she was indifferent to the grandeur of the temples, she delighted in the minor arts of Egypt, the furniture, the jewelry, the coloured faience and the carved ornaments of ivory and wood.

Of Thebes itself she was loud in her praise. She declared it was her spiritual home. She was sure, she told the doctor, that in its present state of desolation it was a far more delightful place to live in than when it had been a great and busy metropolis. "Rus in urbe," she said, "that is my ideal."

Doctor Serapion very much enjoyed acting as cicerone to the Queen. But he found that it was a whole-time job, so lively an interest did she take in everything. Even the poultry farm and the larders did not escape her investigation, and she made a special study of the incubating ovens and the testing of eggs, as well as the various methods of preserving ducks and quails in salt.

She visited the herb gardens, the spice stores and the perfumery, and enquired into the manufacture of scents and ointments. She also plied the doctor with questions about poisons and reproached him with his lack of interest in toxicology.

"That is a branch of medicine," said the doctor, "that I prefer to leave to your physicians of Alexandria."

The Queen laughed.

"It is one," she said, "that must not be despised. Everyone, especially a ruler, should have at hand the means of commanding easy death, both for himself and for others. At present I'm perfectly happy and have no intention of quitting this earth, but nobody can tell if it may not become one day expedient to do so swiftly and without pain."

13

At the end of three weeks Doctor Serapion said that the scars were sufficiently healed and that the Unveiling of the Nose might now take place. The Queen had a full-length mirror brought into her room and sent everyone away, even Charmion, Iras and Apollodoros. Then, turning her back to the mirror, she let the doctor remove the bandages. "Now you go too," she said, "I want to enjoy it quite alone. Good gracious, how my heart is beating."

As soon as the doctor had left the room she hastily threw off her clothes and turned to confront her reflection in the mirror.

She gave a cry of delight. She looked at herself long and intently, moving her head from side to side. After she had done this for several minutes she took up a small hand mirror and examined her profile.

Then she called to the two women and the two men to return. They found her naked, turning cart wheels round the room. She flung herself upon the doctor and kissed him on both cheeks. She kissed Apollodoros, Iras and Charmion. "We must have a banquet," she cried, "a royal banquet to celebrate the beginning of my new life."

Apollodoros stared at the Queen in amazement. Now that her nose had been reduced to normal proportions, the face was one which he felt might well launch a thousand ships—and a good deal more. Although not a face of classic beauty, it was one that, he knew, could melt the hearts of men. And how clever she had been to choose that type of nose. She had the same instinct about noses as she had about clothes. She had known exactly what was right.

That evening Doctor Serapion received disturbing news. The Governor of Thebes, Kallimachos, sent word that he heard the doctor was entertaining a very important guest and that he desired to come and pay his respects.

On the face of it the proposal sounded harmless enough. But the doctor had private intelligence that the Governor had received orders from Alexandria to trace the Queen and bring her back. The doctor had always feared that it would be difficult to conceal her identity for very long, especially after that rash visit to the temples. The priests no doubt had not been taken in by the fiction of his niece, and the Queen never seemed able to do anything very quietly.

Doctor Serapion consulted Apollodoros and together they sought the Queen whom they found playing diabolo with her ladies.

"Why these grave faces?" she enquired.

The doctor informed her of the Governor's message and the danger that threatened her.

"We must be on the move again," said Apollodoros wearily.

"Nonsense," said the Queen, "I won't hear of it. I am enjoying myself here and I'm sure the doctor doesn't want me to leave, do you doctor?"

Doctor Serapion hesitated.

"Well, Your Majesty—"

"Now you're going to say something disagreeable. I've always noticed that when men are preparing to be disagreeable to women they always assume a pompous air. So you want me to go, my dear doctor?"

"No, indeed, Your Majesty."

"Then you don't want me to go. That's just as well, as I have made up my mind to stay. Remember that I am the Queen of Egypt, daughter of the Gods and such a person does not run away from a silly old governor. I have heard of this man Kallimachos. Papa used to say of him that he was the perfect type of civil servant. Such men are easily impressed. I said that we should have a banquet to celebrate the day. Very well, we'll include him in the banquet. Invite him to-morrow, doctor, and give orders for the preparations. And, Apollodoros, have the cases of Falernian wine unpacked. We'll make him roaring drunk."

"Your Majesty," exclaimed Doctor Serapion, "he is a very serious man. He has but little appreciation of drollery."

"We shall see," the Queen replied.

She turned to Apollodoros and struck an attitude. "I'm invincible," she said. As she smiled at him, Apollodoros knew that what she said was true.

*

The Queen busied herself with the preparations for the feast. All night long the slaves were at work, decking the house with garlands, hanging it with tapestries and embroideries and spreading on the floors rare carpets of exquisite design. The Queen brought out from her treasure chests her finest chalices of gold and silver and disposed them on the tables filled with flowers and fruit.

"We'll show him something," she said. She bade Doctor Serapion invite the priests. "Provided one doesn't give them pork or beans," she remarked, "there's nothing the priests enjoy so much as a good blow out."

Doctor Serapion was not at all happy in his mind. "I fear," he complained, "that this banquet may create an exaggerated impression of my wealth and may cause my taxes to be raised."

"Have no fear," the Queen assured him, "you will see that by the end of the day the Governor will be eating out of my hand."

She inspired Apollodoros with a little of her confidence, but the doctor who knew Kallimachos was far from being convinced. Luckily the Governor was favourably disposed towards him, as he had once cured his son of a strange malady which had baffled other doctors and Kallimachos was devoted to his son. At the same time he was a man of great integrity and earnestness and would not be likely to be turned from his purpose by material considerations. Still less was he susceptible to the charms of women.

The Queen asked many questions about the Governor's character, his habits, tastes and the disposition of his mind. "He sounds a little difficult," she said, "but men of his kind are often easier to deal with than one might imagine."

14

Kallimachos, the Governor of the Thebaid, was an elderly man. His grim, earnest expression bore out the Doctor's description of him as a man who had little appreciation of drollery. However he was well liked in Thebes, for he had laboured to relieve the misfortunes of that city, and to preserve its privileges. He had also done much to secure the proper observation of the religious rites in the temples and was popular with the priests. He was a man of learning, too, and had written commentaries on Plato and Aristotle. Trivial matters amused him not and he very rarely smiled.

He greeted Doctor Serapion with a sombre mien. It grieved him to think that the man who had earned his gratitude by curing his son should have laid himself open to official reprimand, and possibly even worse, by sheltering the fugitive queen. He was touched by the efforts the doctor seemed to have made to accord him a noble reception and he did not immediately announce the nature of his mission.

When Doctor Serapion led him into the banqueting hall he was a little taken aback. It was not at all the atmosphere in which he expected to carry out his orders.

Across the courtyard a slow procession advanced. First came slaves scattering flowers and swinging censers of burning perfume: then the Queen's stewards clad in gorgeous ceremonial gowns, Iras and Charmion magnificent and glittering with jewels. Apollodoros followed, bearing the wand of state and looking very handsome in his robes; after him came Nubian slaves leading leopards on golden chains, with collars studded with precious stones; a bevy of dancing girls and slaves waving fans of ostrich plumes. Finally the Queen appeared. She was wearing a simple silken tailor-made of Grecian cut with a single golden fillet in her hair. She looked a child and she looked divine.

Kallimachos gasped. He turned to Doctor Serapion, "But surely that's not the Queen?" he asked. Doctor Serapion nodded.

The Queen advanced to meet him smiling, and motioned him to the banqueting table. As she took her place beside him she turned to Doctor Serapion and whispered, "I feel like Heracles about to tackle the Nemean lion."

The Governor was never very much at his ease with women. His wife, now deceased, had been a homely soul, chaste and pious, and he was inclined to believe that all other women were vile.

"Papa often spoke to me of you," the Queen said to him. "He had a very high opinion of your worth. Whatever people may say of poor Papa's failings, he had at least one merit. He always knew a good man when he saw one."

"Your Majesty is most kind," the Governor replied gravely. He was determined not to allow himself to be imposed upon by flattery.

"I have heard so much of all that you have done to improve the condition of the country, of how you alleviated the sufferings of the people in the time of famine. And I so much appreciate your attitude about the temple services. Please don't think that I share my brother's indifference in religious matters."

"No, no," said the Governor, waving aside the cup-bearer, "no wine."

"Oh, but you must," the Queen cried, "it's Falernian, the very best."

"I drink no wine," the Governor replied, "it doesn't agree with me."

"Oh, but please. You must just taste it. And anyhow it isn't wine. It's nectar. You will surely not refuse the nectar of the Gods."

"Well, just a drop," the Governor conceded. "It is certainly excellent," he said as he tasted it.

The Queen made a sign to the cup-bearer to fill his goblet.

"And now tell me about your son," the Queen went on. "He is in Ptolemais, I hear. I have had the most favourable reports of him. You know, I was intending to give him an important post in Alexandria, only I was unfortunately frustrated. Potheinos and his friends, like all ambitious weaklings, are terrified of excellence in others. I'm afraid if they retain their power it may go badly with your son. But have no fear, he may always rely on my protection. Oh, you must have some of that fish. You will offend me if you refuse. I cooked it myself."

It was a lie, but it surprised and impressed Kallimachos.

"Your Majesty concerns herself with the arts of the kitchen?" he exclaimed.

"Oh, dear," said the Queen, "I'm afraid you're shocked. You consider it an un-royal occupation? But it is not so. If you read Homer you will find that many Queens have occupied themselves with menial tasks."

"Well, in any case, the fish is excellent," said Kallimachos unbending slightly.

The air was heavy with incense and the scent of flowers, and the Governor's cup was continually refilled. He was so engrossed by the Queen's learned conversation, her subtle flattery that eluded his wariness, her charm that vanquished his rigid defences, that he failed to notice how often he raised it to his lips.

The Queen had prepared a little surprise. Thousands of large flies had been caught and enclosed in papyrus boxes, each one having a tiny streamer of brightly coloured silk attached to it.

She beckoned to her steward. "You may release the flies," she whispered.

Like miniature birds of paradise they filled the air with swirling colour as they flew out into the courtyard and settled on the trees.

"A pretty invention," said Kallimachos. More than ever he felt that this was not the atmosphere in which to carry out his orders.

When the banquet was over, he took Doctor Serapion aside. The doctor noticed with some surprise that he was a little unsteady on his legs.

"I am bewitched," said the venerable Kallimachos, " 'tis Circe come again." And he slapped the doctor on the back—a most unusual gesture.

Meanwhile the Queen held audience with the priests. To each one she said a pleasant phrase. She professed great interest in the temples and the religious rites. She deplored the hostility to the religion of Egypt manifested by her enemies and explained that it had been largely on account of her concern with religious matters that she had been driven out of Alexandria.

She beckoned to Doctor Serapion, who by this time was himself a little tipsy.

"Tell me," she asked, "has the Governor's wife much influence over him?"

"Most decidedly not, I should say."

"Really, why?"

"Because for the last fifteen years she has been dead."

The Queen struck at him playfully with her fan.

"This is not the time for pleasantry. Pray be serious. Tell the Governor that I would speak with him alone. Beg him to join me in the pavilion by the lake."

As Kallimachos walked through the gardens towards the pavilion, his heart was heavy. He could no longer delay informing the Queen of his instructions. Yet inclination struggled with duty. As he approached the pavilion and saw the Queen, in all her innocence, awaiting him, he took a grave decision. Instead of arresting her, he would give her an opportunity to escape. After all Alexandria was a long way off and the priests, he knew, would not betray him.

She made room for him on the marble bench.

"Please sit down," she said, "I am happy to have this occasion of speaking with you alone. I have evolved important plans in the execution of which I am about to appeal to you for assistance. You are not perhaps fully aware of the circumstances that have driven me from Alexandria, and I have no doubt that my enemies have caused lying reports to be circulated. According to the terms of my father's will my brother and I were to have ruled conjointly. But my brother is but a child and undeveloped in his mind. He is a mere tool in the hands of Potheinos. Such weakness Potheinos also hoped to find in me. But he is disappointed. For although I too am young, I am neither inexperienced nor weak. Mindful of my sacred duties, I have made a careful study of the art of politics and, whereas for Potheinos and his friends politics are synonymous with intrigue, for me they have a more lofty significance. The Good, the Beautiful, the True, those are my ideals. I have studied Plato and Aristotle, while Potheinos has studied nothing but his own interests. Justice, uprightness and wisdom, to him these things are hateful. That is why they have put your son on the black list. Oh, dear, I oughtn't to have told you that. But have no fear. I am no weakling and I am determined to see that right and justice prevail. But to do so I need an army. And this is where you can help me. I will ask you to advise me as to the best and quickest methods of obtaining soldiers. I have plenty of money and that, I believe, is the keystone of recruitment."

Kallimachos listened to the Queen's speech with growing amazement and admiration. There was no longer any doubt in his mind. The principles of government, domestic interest and personal inclination, all these things indicated to him which cause he should espouse.

"Your Majesty," he said, "I am at your command."

"It's all right," the Queen assured Doctor Serapion and Apollodoros who were awaiting her anxiously in the palace. "I've got him taped. I just fed him up with a lot of high-falutin' stuff, and he simply lapped it up. He's the most gullible old bird I've ever seen. All the same he's rather a pet. He has promised to help me get together an army."

"An army!" exclaimed Apollodoros.

"Why, of course. A Queen must have an army. And I have arranged with the High Priest to have myself proclaimed a Goddess to-morrow in the temple of Amun. And girls," she called to Charmion and Iras, "you had better start designing your uniforms. I have already got an idea for mine."

15

The formation of the Queen's army went on apace, and there was a great stir in Thebes and in all the valley. Recruiting agents were sent out far and wide, into Libya, Arabia, Ethiopia and Syria. The pay offered was so high that many young Egyptians who would in ordinary circumstances have fled into the mountains to avoid conscription came eagerly to join up and, further afield, the recruiting offices were besieged by men of every type, tribesmen, bandits, fugitive slaves and Roman deserters.

Apollodoros, at first, was inclined to be a little sceptical about the Queen's new military ardour, but he soon discovered that it was no laughing matter. The Queen was determined to figure as a martial leader, and when he suggested that more might be effected by a woman's allurements than by force of arms she replied, "You seem to forget the nature of the man I have to deal with. It is by force alone that I can regain my kingdom."

The High Priest of Amun, with whom the Queen was now on the best of terms, had brought her books on strategy. They were a little out of date, but she read them carefully. "There are certain factors of warfare," she said, "that never alter, and much can still be learnt from the ancients."

Regiments of cavalry were equipped from the breeding stables for which the district was renowned and the Governor presented the Queen with a magnificent charger which she named Bucephalus the Second. Every day she would ride out to practice military exercises and she had herself instructed in the manipulation of a chariot. For her own use she had a very beautiful one constructed of acacia wood and leather, tastefully decorated with gold and ivory. It was so light that a man could carry it on his shoulders without tiring. Much as he disapproved of the Queen's new warlike craze, Apollodoros had to admit, as she drove into the courtyard wearing her golden cuirass and helmet, that she made a very charming Amazon.

The Governor was indefatigable in his assistance and advice.

"What about elephants?" the Queen asked. "I must have elephants—lots of them. I simply dote on elephants."

"You shall have plenty," Kallimachos assured her. "I have news that elephant-carriers have arrived at Berenice bringing a large consignment of these animals from India. I will have them despatched to Koptos where you may pick them up on your march northwards."

"Indian elephants," said the Queen, "that is excellent, for the elephants of Africa are small and timid and are no good in warfare. It was proved at the battle of Raphia."

*

307

In the midst of all her activities the Queen found time to go and have her fortune told. Accompanied only by Charmion and disguised in menial clothes she went to visit an aged prophet who lived in a cave in the Valley of the Kings. The old man prophesied for her many years of happiness and glory.

"Shall I be mistress of the world?" she enquired, "for nothing short of that will content me."

"You will be mistress of the master of the world," the prophet replied.

"Well, that sounds all right. I wonder if he has guessed who I am," she whispered to Charmion.

"But your life will end in tragedy," the old man added, for he was a true prophet and not one of those professionals who think it necessary to foretell only pleasant things.

The Queen was unmoved.

"Oh, well," she said, "the end of life is always tragic. It's a tragedy to have to end at all. I hope it will be a tragedy that makes a stir."

"It will be recorded gloriously in the annals of history."

"Really," the Queen said to Charmion afterwards, "one can't ask for anything better than that, can one?"

16

There's very odd news from Thebes," said Potheinos. "It appears that she has got together an army. But, what is odder still, I am told that the Egyptians think her beautiful. I questioned the messenger closely. 'Are you sure you don't mean clever?' I asked him. 'No,' he said, 'beautiful.' You must admit it's strange."

Theodotos smiled.

"Perhaps down there they like long beaks. It is true the Egyptians worship things with snouts, jackals, dogs, crocodiles and so forth."

"Kallimachos, I hear, is crazy about her. The old dotard. I thought at least he was a man whom one could trust."

"He's a bit of a highbrow. I expect she got round him with her Greek literature and philosophy."

"I don't imagine she'll be able to effect very much with this band of hooligans. All the same the news is a little disturbing."

Potheinos became still more disturbed when he learnt that the Queen and her army were marching on Pelusium, and for the moment public attention was distracted from the titanic struggle that was taking place in the Thessalian plain where Cæsar and Pompey had at last come to grips.

Achillas was summoned to the Council Chamber. He was inclined to scoff at the eunuch's anxiety.

"I'll soon dispose of the Queen and her rabble," he said. "She shall be brought back in chains to Alexandria."

"Hurrah," piped a shrill voice. It was the little King. Of late he had taken to hanging about the Council Chamber. "I should like to bring her back myself. Can I come with you?"

Achillas patted the youngster on the back.

"If Your Majesty so desires."

The King was delighted. He had a golden cuirass made in which he paraded proudly up and down in front of Arsinoe and his little brother.

"I'll teach her," he cried, "I'll make her sorry she was ever born. I'll pull her nose for her."

"It's all very well to talk big like that," said Arsinoe. "You know quite well you'd never dare—even if she were chained up. And anyhow your cuirass is much too heavy for you. You can hardly stand up straight. You look ridiculous."

The King ran at her and tried to slap her face, but he was embarrassed by his armour and Arsinoe got the slap in first. Encouraged by her success, the younger child joined in and kicked his brother on the shins.

The King took refuge in his royal dignity.

"How dare you do that to my sacred person? I'll have you put in prison, both of you."

Arsinoe slapped his face again and he burst into tears. Both the children danced round him shouting "Cry baby! Cry baby!"

In the palace gardens Potheinos and Theodotos were discussing the outcome of the battle between the Roman giants.

"Cæsar hasn't a chance," was the opinion of Potheinos. "He may have succeeded in driving Pompey out of Italy, but he failed before Dyrrhachium, he has lost touch with Rome and he has no ships. It is sea power that will count in the end."

"But they are fighting on land. Cæsar's troops are of better quality and Cæsar is the better man."

"It is true," Potheinos admitted, "that Pompey's omens have been bad. Thunderbolts fell on the ships at Dyrrhachium, spiders occupied the army standards, and, as he left the vessel, serpents followed him and obliterated the traces of his footsteps."

"Old wives' tales!" cried Theodotos. "The fate of empires are not decided by such nonsense."

"I never said they were," said Potheinos, "but omens are often indications."

"If a thunderbolt fell on my ship, if serpents followed me, I should look upon it as an annoyance rather than an omen."

"You are a sceptic, Theodotos. But I trust you may be right about the omens. For it is to our advantage if Pompey wins. He has always been a good friend to Egypt. Whereas who knows what may happen if Cæsar wins? I mistrust these men of genius."

"Whatever happens," said Theodotos, "we must keep sitting on the fence."

Achillas led forth his army. Potheinos, Theodotos and the King went with him. The Queen was already encamped at Pelusium and the Alexandrian forces took up position on the promontory of Kasion, a few miles distant.

It was here they heard of Pompey's great defeat at Pharsalus. Cæsar's victory had been complete and Pompey had fled from the field of battle.

"There!" Potheinos remarked to Theodotos, "perhaps now you will believe in the truth of omens."

Pompey sought refuge in Cilicia and Pamphylia, but his former friends refused to help him. Finally, in desperation, he bethought himself of Egypt. There, at least, he would be sure to find a sanctuary. He had always befriended Egypt. He had espoused the cause of the late King in Rome and had given him his villa as a residence. His son would undoubtedly take advantage of this opportunity to show his gratitude. He sailed to Mitylene to fetch his wife, Cornelia, and went on with her to Alexandria. Here he learnt that the King was at Pelusium.

There was some consternation in the royal camp when it was reported that Pompey, defeated and no longer great, was on his way to beg asylum.

A hasty council was summoned. Acoreus, the High Priest of Memphis, rose to plead the sacred duty of hospitality.

"Sit down, you old fool," cried Potheinos. "Let Pompey find a refuge elsewhere." And all the others were agreed that it would be dangerous to welcome Pompey in the hour of his defeat.

"Our position," said Theodotos, "is by no means easy. If we receive Pompey, we make an enemy of Cæsar. If we refuse to receive Pompey, we make an enemy of him, and who can foretell the caprices of fortune? Pompey may once more be great—and then we shall be bitten. One thing, however, is certain and cannot be denied. Dead men do not bite."

All, except Acoreus, applauded the wise words of the Master of Rhetoric. Achillas went out to meet Pompey in a small boat. He was accompanied by Septimius, a Roman, who had served under Pompey in former days. Under pretext that the shore near the coast was of little depth and full of shoals they persuaded Pompey to leave his galley. Cornelia, seized with premonition, implored him not to go. But, encouraged by the insidious speeches of Achillas and Septimius, he stepped into the boat. As they approached the shore the manner of these two men changed and Pompey knew that his doom was sealed. But it was too late. The Alexandrian fleet was all around them. Septimius stabbed him from behind and Achillas cut off his head. Cornelia, watching from the galley, gave a great cry that was heard even on the land.

The King was thrilled and clapped his hands with joy.

"That was fine," he cried. "That was something worth beholding. And it made it so much better his wife being there to see it happen. My goodness how she screamed!"

17

Pompey the Great having been disposed of in this judicious manner, Achillas prepared to give battle to the Queen.

"It is a question of a couple of days," he told them at headquarters, "perhaps not even that. I have immense superiority of men, of armaments, of everything."

"Hardly of intelligence," Theodotos whispered to Potheinos.

"That is of no importance," the eunuch whispered back.

It was a constant source of argument between the two men, Potheinos maintaining that military strategy was instinctive and that it was not necessary for it to be based on reason, while Theodotos declared that reason was in all things supreme and that it was essential, even for a soldier.

The trial of strength between the army of Achillas and that of the Queen was destined never to take place. Messengers arrived with the news that Cæsar had come to Alexandria.

There was again consternation in the camp. Theodotus alone was calm.

"You see now," he said, "the wisdom of my counsel. I shall go straightway to Cæsar, taking with me two gifts that will be, I have no doubt, most acceptable to the conqueror. Whatever may have been his intentions in coming here, these gifts will cause him to return to Rome and leave us in peace."

"And pray what may these gifts be?" enquired Achillas.

"The head of Pompey and his signet ring."

But the manner of Cæsar's reception of these gifts was most unexpected. On being shown the head of Pompey he turned away from it and wept. Then, flying into a violent rage, he drove the astonished Master of Rhetoric from his presence.

"I told you," said Potheinos to the crestfallen Theodotos on his return, "that he was a man of genius, and the behaviour of such men is often unaccountable."

"He is also a hypocrite," said Theodotus, "to shed tears over the head of an enemy. Nevertheless he is a man to be reckoned with. I foresee that he may give us a good deal of trouble. He has already established himself in the Palace, in the King's apartments; made himself quite comfortable in fact. He's up to no good I should say."

"I will go myself to Alexandria," said Potheinos.

As the Eunuch was setting out, messengers arrived from Cæsar with a peremptory command that both King and Queen should disband their armies and proceed forthwith to Alexandria to plead their causes before him in person.

"Hoity toity," cried Potheinos. "What gross impertinence. Who does he think he is?"

"I'm afraid," said Theodotos, "he knows that he is Cæsar."

"I will go nevertheless," Potheinos decided, "and I shall take the King with me. It is unfortunate that this message should have arrived before we left as he'll think we are obeying his commands. Have you any idea how many soldiers he has with him?"

"Not more than a couple of thousand I should say."

"A couple of thousand only! That makes his arrogance even more unbearable, but it makes it easier to deal with. Achillas you will follow me to Alexandria with twenty thousand men. It may be well to remind this man of Pompey's fate. Send on Cæsar's messengers to the Queen, and on no account give her a safe conduct. If she fails to put in an appearance so much the better for us. And if she does attempt the journey—well, we shall see!"

Cæsar had come to Egypt primarily in pursuit of Pompey. He had guessed that his defeated enemy, as the avowed friend and patron of the Egyptians, might take refuge there and seek to make a rally with the help of the Egyptian army. He only learnt the truth when Theodotos arrived with his gruesome offering. He was naturally annoyed that his great antagonist should have met with so pitiful an end through the treachery of insignificant scoundrels. It cast a slur on his victory.

He determined to stand no nonsense from the Alexandrians and made a formal entry into the city with a parade of lictors carrying the fasces and axes. This show of state created an unfortunate impression, and was proclaimed an insult to the King's majesty. There was rioting in the streets and a couple of Roman soldiers were killed.

More Roman troops arrived and their total number was now four thousand. Cæsar sent to Asia Minor for reinforcements and barricaded himself in the Palace. He had with him enough ships to guarantee a safe escape by sea should it become necessary.

The city of Alexandria had made on Cæsar a most favourable impression. The climate reminded him of that of Rome. Although it was the height of the summer, it was not too hot, and there were gentle breezes from the sea. The Palace also he thought delightful. As he explored its cool apartments, the terraces and the gardens, he felt that it was a place one might well live in for months without ever wishing to leave its precincts.

The Queen's apartments were of all the most charming. Certainly if she had had anything to do with the decoration of them she must be a young woman of great taste. He was surprised by the quantity and character of the books in her library and he was pleased to find some of his own works there. Strange that a girl of her age should read so much and be interested in such learned subjects! But perhaps they were only there for show.

Alexandria seemed a perfect place for a holiday and Cæsar sorely needed one.

The sight of the books stirred his literary imagination and, after sending out his messengers to summon the King and the Queen, who he heard were preparing to fight one another (ridiculous children!), he settled himself on the terrace overlooking the Great Harbour and started to compose a poem on the tragedy of greatness and the vanity of human aspirations.

18

The Queen was enjoying herself. Camp life was really great fun, and the journey out from Thebes had been full of excitements. Some of the chariots had stuck in the sand; at one point the elephants had run amok, and a slight sandstorm overtook them as they were crossing the desert. In Syria she had made a considerable addition to her forces and she considered that her army was now almost up to Roman standards. But some of the soldiers had a tendency to desert after receiving their pay.

On arriving at Pelusium she had held a great review, and there was wild cheering as she drove past the ranks in her smart chariot, the horses gaily caparisoned in gold and scarlet with tall ostrich plumes on their heads, the Queen herself wearing a suit of armour that glittered with gold and precious stones.

Apollodoros, though he was deeply moved by the spectacle, was beset by misgivings. The pageantry was admirable, but he wondered if it would be of much use in real warfare.

Then came Cæsar's messengers summoning the Queen to the Palace at Alexandria.

"I suppose I'd better go," she said to Apollodoros, "but how the hell am I to get there? I don't suppose Achillas will give me a safe conduct and it wouldn't be worth much if he did. And it appears my dear little brother and that old skunk are already in the Palace waiting to bounce out on me. It's all very difficult, but I daresay I shall think of something. I should like to know a little more about this Cæsar. It is important to know beforehand what manner of man he is."

"I know little more about him than you do yourself," replied Apollodoros. "Among the troops there will be no doubt men who have served under him. I will make enquiries."

An old Roman deserter who had taken part in the Gallic wars was produced and brought in to the Queen's tent so that she might question him.

"Yes, my dear," the veteran began, for he was a rough fellow and had little idea of how to address a Royal lady, "I knew him well. He's a great leader of men. No man can see him or hear him speak but that there comes on him a great desire to do heroic deeds. Cæsar knows what he wants from his soldiers and he gets it too. Assuredly he is a great leader of men."

"We know all that," said the Queen impatiently. "Tell me something—a little more intimate."

The man winked.

"You mean about the ladies, Ma'am?"

"Yes," said the Queen, "I mean about the ladies."

"He's always been a great one with the girls," the man declared, "and with the boys too, they say. There was a marching song we used to sing 'Husbands look out, we bring the bald adulterer.' "

"Oh, dear!" exclaimed the Queen, "is he bald?"

"Well, he's getting a bit thin on the top, Ma'am. But it don't seem to matter. He goes on just the same."

"I don't like that baldness," said the Queen. "However—I suppose you don't happen to know what type of woman he particularly admires?"

"He admires 'em all, bless his heart. Old, young, fat, lean, it's all the same to him."

"Thank you very much for your information," said the Queen and handed him a golden trinket. She was always polite to soldiers.

"I feel more than ever now," she said to Apollodoros, "that my presence in the Palace may be desirable. I hardly think he'll take a fancy to my dear little brother, but it would be maddening if Arsinoe were to get in first. You will come with me, Apollodoros. We'll go secretly and by sea. Just us two. It'll be an adventure. Though I still don't quite see how I'm going to get into the Palace without getting a knife in my back. No doubt I'll think of something on the way."

They took a small sailing boat with two sailors and on the following day at nightfall they anchored in the Royal Harbour under the walls of the Palace.

"I've got an idea," cried the Queen, "I know how we'll manage it."

19

Evening fell on the Great Harbour and Cæsar was still struggling with his poem. At last when all light had faded from the sky and in the lighthouse the lamps were being lit, he rose with a sigh and called for Hirtius, his friend and secretary.

"Tell me, Hirtius," he asked, "why is it that I find so great a difficulty in writing poetry?"

"Our language is not suitable for poetry," Hirtius answered. "You have a pretty gift for prose, Cæsar, so why worry about poetry?"

"I am a poet, Hirtius. That is a thing that no one seems to realise. All my actions, whether in politics, love or war are guided by an inner sense of poetry. In my strategy there is form and rhythm, and creative imagination. You must admit the epic and lyrical qualities of my campaigns."

"That may be," replied Hirtius, "but they are best recorded in prose.

The Latin tongue, I repeat, is not adapted to poetry. That is why we have no poets. Ennius, Lucretius, Varro; one can hardly call them poets."

"I disagree with you, Hirtius. Cicero thinks very highly of Ennius and, although I don't care for Cicero's politics, in literary criticism he is supreme. And what about Catullus?"

"It surprises me that you should uphold Catullus after the things he has written about you."

Cæsar made an angry gesture.

"Have I ever seemed to you petty, Hirtius? Do you think me the kind of man who would let personal opinions influence artistic judgement?"

"Alas, no, Cæsar. But still I do not consider Catullus a Latin poet. His serious poetry is a mere adaptation of Callimachus."

"They say there is a young poet from Mantua who has turned out some charming things."

"I doubt it, Cæsar. I maintain that no Roman will ever write good poetry. So stick to prose, Cæsar, stick to prose."

"If only I had more time for meditation. When I was a captive of the Cilician pirates, I wrote quite a lot of poetry. I read it to them and they very much appreciated it."

"I have always heard you had them crucified for scoffing at it, Cæsar."

"Nonsense. They liked it very much. I had them crucified for very different reasons."

Potheinos and the King had arrived in the Palace and sought audience of Cæsar.

"Now mind you're polite to him," said the eunuch to his pupil, "and don't commit yourself to anything. We shall continue to be polite until Achillas and his army enter Alexandria. Then, I fancy, we may change our tone. Meanwhile I have had assassins posted in the Palace to await the arrival of the Queen."

"Oh, good!" cried the King, "but why can't I have a crack at her myself? What's the use of being a King and wearing armour if I'm never to be allowed to do anything I want."

"Kings never do murder with their own hands."

"Oh, don't they! What about—"

"This is no moment for historical discussion, my boy. Do as you're told and behave yourself."

The King's face began to pucker and Potheinos, not wishing to enter Cæsar's presence with the King in tears, strove to pacify him.

"All right, all right," he said, "you shall have ample opportunity to do murder later on. Who knows? Perhaps the great Cæsar himself? But in the meantime we must be polite."

Cæsar took an instant dislike to Potheinos and greeted him coldly, but to the little King he was gracious in his manner.

"Well, Your Majesty," he said, patting the lad on the head, "I'm glad to see you. But why isn't your sister with you?"

"Why should she be?" the boy answered saucily, "and what do you want with her anyway?"

Potheinos gave him a warning look.

"Do manners," Cæsar asked, "not form part of the education of the Egyptian kings?"

"The Queen," said Potheinos, pushing himself forward, "has unfortunately seen fit to take up a deplorable attitude with regard to her brother, His Sacred Majesty. She has gathered together an army and is proposing to march on Alexandria in order to depose His Majesty and rule alone. This, as Cæsar knows, is in direct variance with the terms of his late Majesty's will, terms that have been dignified by the sanction of the Roman Senate."

"She was potty about the Romans," cried the King, "and that was why we had to drive her out—"

Potheinos gave him a furious glance and he subsided.

"Well," said Cæsar smiling, "that is hardly an argument that you can expect to appeal to me. I have sent for your sister. If you have had a quarrel, you must make it up."

The King was about to protest, but he was again quelled by a threatening gesture of Potheinos.

"I have come to Alexandria," Cæsar went on, "to see that the terms of your father's will are properly observed. If the Queen has been guilty of misbehaviour she shall be reprimanded. Peace must be established in Egypt. When these things are settled I shall return to Rome, but not before. Meanwhile I shall entertain you in the Palace as my guest. I'm afraid I shall have to occupy your apartments as they overlook the harbour. I have no doubt you will find ample accommodation elsewhere." He turned to Potheinos, "And pray make no attempt to leave the precincts of the Palace."

"We are prisoners?" asked Potheinos.

"You are my guests," Cæsar replied.

"You little fool," Potheinos said to the King, as they left Cæsar's presence, "I told you to be polite."

"I hate Cæsar," cried the King. "How dare he speak to me like that? I am King of Egypt, descended from the Gods, and he is merely a vulgar Roman."

"If you don't do as I tell you," said Potheinos, "I shall take up your sister's cause with Cæsar. And we'll see how you like that."

"A nasty pair," said Cæsar to Hirtius, "I hardly know which is the nastiest, the eunuch or the boy. I sincerely hope the sister may be better. What reports do you bring me, Hirtius, of the Queen?"

"Well, Cæsar, they are a little confused. I have spoken with the King's attendants. They are naturally prejudiced, but the messengers who have returned from Pelusium speak differently. They say she is most wondrously fair, Aphrodite in person. That is what they said. The King's people, on the other hand, say she is extremely plain. And some placards I have seen in the streets represent her as certainly not beautiful. It appears her nose is long out of all proportion."

"That is a pity," said Cæsar, "I don't care for long-nosed women. They remind me of Cossutia. But no matter. As soon as I have fixed up this dynastic squabble I shall return to Rome. Although, had she been attractive, I shouldn't have minded staying on a bit. Alexandria is a pleasant city and there's no immediate need for my return to Rome. Indeed it might be better to wait a bit until Pompey's friends have forgotten him."

"There's a younger sister," suggested Hirtius, "she's in the Palace and they say she's quite pretty."

"My dear Hirtius, how can you suggest such things? She's far too young. I may be getting on in years, but I've not yet reached that stage. But it's odd about the messengers. You say they told you the Queen was beautiful?"

"Messengers are often snobs, Cæsar, and perhaps to them all Queens are beautiful."

A soldier appeared in the doorway.

"There's a gentleman asking for admittance, Cæsar," the man announced. "He says he has brought gifts from the Queen."

"What sort of gifts?" Cæsar enquired.

"They're carpets and tapestries."

"Carpets and tapestries," cried Cæsar, his eyes lighting up with eagerness, for he was a great collector of artistic objects, "show him in at once."

Apollodoros entered, staggering under a great roll of carpets. He laid them carefully on the floor.

"Look out," cried Hirtius, drawing his sword, "there's an animal inside!"

The carpets moved and were flung apart, and in the midst of them appeared the Queen.

She looked as elegant and trim as if she had just left the hands of her dressers. Not a hair of her head was out of place. There was not a crease in her silken dress. Her cheeks were slightly flushed, but otherwise she appeared cool and dignified.

"Ouf," she gasped, "Apollodoros, you beast. You nearly dropped me and you've bruised my ankle on the doorpost."

She rose to her feet, as Hirtius said afterwards, like Venus rising from the foam, and smiled at Cæsar.

"Good evening, Cæsar," she said, "I am Cleopatra, Queen of Egypt."

20

———

The Queen sat up in bed and stretched herself voluptuously. She was happy to wake up once more in the pleasant surroundings of her own apartments. The day was already well advanced. She had slept late, for she had sat talking with Cæsar into the early hours of the morning. She called for her breakfast, milk, fruit and honey-bread, and sent for Apollodoros to entertain her while she ate it.

"I am crazy about Cæsar," she confessed to him. "My goodness what a man! Do you think it's a sign of greatness in a man, Apollodoros, that when one meets him for the first time one should feel that one has known him all one's life? For that is how I felt about Cæsar. And there's another thing that's nice about him. He gives you the sensation that you are great yourself. I have never appeared to myself so much to my advantage."

"I've always heard he has a way of getting round women."

"I should say he'd get round anyone. You wait till you've had some conversation with him, Apollodoros. You'll just adore him. It is true that he is no longer young and that he is growing slightly bald. But when you speak with him, none of these things seem to matter. I have the impression that I might fall for him in a big way—but have no fear, Apollodoros, I shall do nothing foolish. I never intend to let my passions get out of control. I am Queen of Egypt and I shall never let Egypt down. If he thinks he is going to use his charm for political ends—well, that is a game that two can play. You might find out, Apollodoros, if you can, what impression I have made upon him."

A few hours earlier, in a different part of the Palace, a similar conversation had taken place.

"Well," said Cæsar, as Hirtius came in bearing a bundle of dispatches, "I have decided to remain in Alexandria for a while. I fancy I shall not be bored."

"She is indeed charming, Cæsar."

"Charming is hardly the word. She is a walking wonder. I have never met anyone quite like her. If the matter ended with her appearance alone, it would be enough. But when combined with such wit, such grace, such understanding—I fancy she might have turned the head even of Diogenes."

"Emerging from the carpets she was indeed a memorable vision."

"Yes," said Cæsar, "one trembles to think what some of our Roman ladies would have looked like after a similar adventure."

"These despatches, Cæsar, require attention."

"They can wait. Hirtius, I feel almost as if I were in the presence of danger, though it's a kind of danger I've never been afraid of. It is perhaps as well that I'm not twenty years younger. Now I have the experience of age and among my many conquests may be reckoned the conquest of my temperament. I shall stay on in Alexandria, but don't imagine that I shall allow myself to be influenced in any way. If this young woman takes me for an old dotard and thinks she can twist me round her little finger, she'll soon find that she's sadly mistaken."

Cæsar examined himself in a mirror.

"You know, Hirtius, I don't look my age. You'd never guess that I was over fifty, would you? There's something to be said for a sober way of living. Drink sparingly of wine, Hirtius, if you want to preserve your youth. Send me the barber, have the Queen informed that I request her presence in the Council Chamber, and tell the King and that foul old eunuch to come along too. The meeting, I fancy, may not be devoid of humour."

Cæsar, that day, seemed bent on making a good impression and he took a great deal of trouble with his appearance. The barber was a talkative man, but Cæsar bade him attend to his business and curtail his chatter. After he had been shaved and pumice-stoned and his hair had been arranged carefully across his forehead, he donned his toga with the broad scarlet stripe and made his way to the Council Chamber. Here he found the Queen, dressed up in her state robes, seated on the throne.

"I have sent for your brother," Cæsar told her, "I hope that we may get this matter settled quickly."

"My brother?" exclaimed the Queen, jumping down from the

throne. "Will you please wait a minute—and don't be surprised at anything you see."

She ran out of the room leaving Cæsar slightly bewildered.

The King and Potheinos appeared, the King looking hot and sulky, Potheinos with his usual oily smile.

"The Queen has arrived," Cæsar told them, "and will join us presently."

"What!" cried the King. "How did she get here? How did she get past the—"

Potheinos hastily put his hand over the boy's mouth. "Silence," he hissed, and pushed him towards the dais. The King climbed on to it and took his seat on the throne.

No sooner had he done so than the Queen returned. Cæsar repressed an exclamation as he saw that she was wearing a most extraordinary false nose.

She went up to her brother with a threatening gesture. "Get out of that!" she said.

"I shant. It's my throne. Potheinos, stop her!" the King cried, as she advanced towards him.

"Now, Cleopatra, you must behave," Cæsar admonished her. "You must both of you take your royal duties more seriously. If, as I am told, you are descended from the Gods—"

"Well, really Cæsar," the Queen remarked, "that is an unfortunate allusion. You know perfectly well the Gods never stopped quarrelling."

Cæsar was unable to repress a smile. She looked so funny in her disguise. Then he turned to her and frowned.

"Cleopatra," he said, "take off that nose and please be serious. We have important business to discuss."

The Queen took off the nose and winked at Cæsar. The King sprang from his throne and got behind it. "Oh! oh!" he cried, "Cæsar is a magician. He has taken away her nose. Oh! I'm frightened." He ran to Potheinos and clung to him. Potheinos rubbed his eyes and stared at the Queen. Cæsar felt that there was something odd about the situation that passed his understanding. He disliked being puzzled.

"Now that we have done with this fooling," he said, "will you all be so kind as to attend to what I have to say. It is the earnest desire of Rome that peace be established in the land of Egypt. This cannot be so long as its rulers are at variance. The strife between brother and sister is causing grave concern. Your differences, therefore, must be settled, your armies disbanded, and you must henceforth rule together in amity. You, Potheinos, appear to have some authority with the King. I myself will answer for the Queen."

"Thank you, Cæsar," said Cleopatra, "that is very kind of you."

"Oh, by the way," Cæsar added, addressing Potheinos, "I understand that you are in charge of the King's Treasury. There is a little debt owed me by the late King, a mere matter of forty million sesterces. Will you kindly have the sum paid into my exchequer. Hirtius will attend to it."

"Forty million sesterces!" cried Potheinos. "That is impossible."

" 'Impossible' is a word I never like to hear," said Cæsar.

"There is not all that money in Alexandria," Potheinos wailed.

"Nonsense," said Cæsar. "You will find no difficulty in raising it. And you," he added, turning to the King, "would surely not wish to see your father's debts dishonoured."

"Papa's debts are nothing to me," the boy replied, "and besides Papa was swindled by the Romans."

The Queen went up to Cæsar and laid her hand upon his arm. "The money shall be paid," she said.

Cæsar patted her cheek and smiled at her.

"Look," cried the King, "how friendly they are. They are in league together. She has given herself to him, the harlot, and that is why he has made her beautiful. Cæsar may be a magician, but everyone knows he is a dirty old lecher."

"Be silent, you foolish child," cried Potheinos.

The King took off his diadem, flung it on the ground and burst into tears.

"I want to go away," he sobbed, "Everyone is against me here."

"There!" said Cleopatra, turning to Cæsar, "do you think a silly cry-baby like that is worthy to rule over Egypt?"

Cæsar raised his hands in a gesture of despair and strode from the room. The Queen made a grimace at her brother and followed him.

21

Potheinos remained for a while in a state of bewilderment. The Queen's transformation had given him a shock that, for the moment, bereft him of his reasoning powers. He was accustomed to deal with the most intricate convolutions of intrigue, but this was something with which he felt himself unable to contend. Although he was not unduly sceptical about supernatural things, the King's interpretation of the phenomenon failed to satisfy him. He wondered if perhaps the Queen, in pursuance of some mysterious ends of her own had adopted, in the past, the travesty of a false nose. But what would have been the point of it? Inclined as she was to strange caprices, she would hardly, he thought, have persisted for so long in this odd disfigurement.

He decided to dismiss the problem from his mind and prepared himself to confront the situation in its practical form, the main points of it being that Cæsar and the Queen seemed to be on excellent terms and that there was little chance of either himself or the King being able to leave the Palace. It was heavily guarded by Cæsar's troops; there were sentries at every entrance, and Cæsar had access to the sea. He knew that if he attempted to escape or too openly caused trouble he would be murdered or despatched to Rome. However, he was not entirely cut off from communication with the outer world and he was able secretly to send out messages to Theodotos and Achillas, who had just arrived in the city with the army of twenty thousand men. Although their presence gave him a sense of security, it would be wiser he thought, for the moment, to go slow. He would continue to allay by a show of amiability any suspicions of treachery that Cæsar might harbour, for the Queen would be certain to put him on his guard. Cæsar should have his money, but it would be contrived that the manner in which it was paid should arouse the anger of the Alexandrians. He wrote to Theodotos long and elaborate instructions on the subject of propaganda. Theodotos replied that he had already started a campaign and that it was going well. Among other things, an obscene Punch and Judy show was appearing in the streets with Cæsar and Cleopatra as protagonists.

Cæsar had decided that a great banquet should be held in the Palace to commemorate the reconciliation between the King and Queen. All the notabilities of Alexandria were convened, with the exception of Theodotos and Septimius. At them Cæsar drew the line.

He spoke with the Queen on questions of policy.

"I shall read your father's will to them," he said, "and announce that everything is now in order, that the Roman Senate will be satisfied. I shall point out to them that the sum I have lawfully claimed is a mere fraction of what is owed me and that I have refrained from levying any tribute, which I well might have done, seeing that Egypt took the side of Pompey."

"Does this entail marriage with that little rat?"

"Certainly," Cæsar replied, "but I imagine you will see to it that it involves no more than a mere formality."

"I most certainly shall," said the Queen, "but I fear that the arrangement, disagreeable as it is to me, will hardly be sufficient to pacify the Alexandrians."

"Well, what would you suggest, Cleopatra? What do you think would please them?

"Give us back Cyprus, Cæsar. That would please them. It means little to the Roman Commonwealth, but it means a good deal to the Egyptians. It was on account of the loss of Cyprus that my father was driven from his kingdom."

"That is an idea," said Cæsar, "I will certainly do that, if you consider it advisable."

"And then," the Queen went on, "you can send Arsinoe and my youngest brother to rule there. It would get Arsinoe out of the way. You have no idea what a little pest she is. It appears she is carrying on nohow with her tutor Ganymede. Of course I've nothing against girls having a bit of fun. But the man's a eunuch. (Oh, these eunuchs!) Can you conceive of anything more insipid? Heaven only knows what she finds to do with him."

"Poor child," said Cæsar, "perhaps in Cyprus she may discover something more robust to satisfy her temperament."

"And her clothes!" the Queen went on. "She has no idea how to dress. She tries to get herself up like a tart, but she merely succeeds in looking, as the Alexandrians say, like a cat in a crocus-coloured robe."

Hirtius came in to speak with Cæsar. His face wore a worried expression. "Cæsar," he said, "there is no gold plate for the banquet. Potheinos has had every scrap of it melted down and converted into money to pay the late King's debt. On the tables are nothing but platters and goblets of wood and earthenware."

"Well, what of it?" Cæsar remarked. "The wine will taste as well in cups of earthenware."

"That is possible," said Hirtius, "but think, Cæsar, of the bad effect it will make. There was no necessity to deprive the King of his golden dishes. The thing was done deliberately by Potheinos to discredit Cæsar in the eyes of the Alexandrians. He has also taken the golden vessels from the temples and said that it was by Cæsar's orders. The priests are in an uproar."

"That's all right," said the Queen, "I have just heard that my luggage has arrived. My golden dishes are finer and more numerous than those of the King. I will have them unpacked and placed on the tables. I have tapestries, carpets and embroideries and there are also bales of artificial flowers from Thebes to deck the banqueting hall. That will be a novelty for Alexandria. Rest assured, Cæsar, your banquet will not be lacking in magnificence. And when the banquet is over I will present my golden vessels to the priests."

Cæsar looked at her admiringly.

"Cleopatra," he said, "you are wonderful. Such resourcefulness, such presence of mind, qualities rare to find in women."

"Oh, that's nothing," said the Queen. "Really, if a woman can't arrange a banquet—"

In spite of the profusion of golden plate, in spite of the rare carpets, the exquisite embroideries, in spite of the garlands and bouquets of artificial flowers, in spite of the excellence of the food and wine, the banquet was not a success. There was a very noticeable atmosphere of constraint. The reading of the will was greeted with no applause and even Cæsar's announcement of the gift of Cyprus fell a little flat. In one corner sat the eunuch Potheinos conferring earnestly with Achillas, in another Arsinoe whispering with the eunuch Ganymede. Hirtius said afterwards that it was like banqueting on a volcano.

The young King, however, enjoyed the feast. He had eaten and drunk copiously and he was a little tipsy. He felt no longer any ill will towards Cæsar and he was surprised and elated by the behaviour of his sister. For the first time she had made no attempt to snub him or be rude to him. She was even gracious in her manner. He had given up pondering on the problem of her nose. Now, all he cared to know was that she was beautiful and that she was no longer rude and disagreeable.

After the banquet, as he wandered through the gardens looking up at the windows of the palace and listening to the distant strains of music, he felt that it was a pleasant thing indeed that she was now his wife.

That night as the Queen lay in bed with Cæsar, she was awakened by the sound of approaching footsteps. Fearing that the sentinels had perhaps fallen asleep and let some unwelcome visitor through, she hastily jumped out of bed. She found her brother standing in the doorway.

"What do you want?" she enquired angrily.

"You know what I want," the boy replied.

"I haven't the least idea. What do you mean by coming and disturbing me at this hour of night?"

"But, sister, I am your husband now."

"Well, really, we heard that piece of news at the banquet. There's no need to come and wake me up to remind me of it."

"I've come to claim my conjugal rights."

"Your conjugal rights indeed! What next. Go away at once."

The King faltered.

"But sister—"

"Go away at once. Do you want me to wake Cæsar?"

The King turned tail and walked away dejectedly. He returned to his bedchamber and flung himself down on his bed in a paroxysm of weeping.

*

While Cæsar was being shaved next morning the loquacious barber dropped mysterious hints.

"Let me warn you, Cæsar. Drink no wine."

"I never do," said Cæsar, "abstinence is the secret of my health."

"And drink no water either," the man continued, "unless it has been tested beforehand."

"And who do you think is trying to poison me?" Cæsar enquired.

"I'm naming no names," said the man, "but there are many in this Palace who would fain encompass Cæsar's destruction. There is danger from within and without. Achillas with his army is meditating an assault on the Palace. I had the news from a serving maid who went into the town to buy some onions."

"Such information is always valuable," said Cæsar.

He dismissed the barber who left with the sensation that Cæsar was not taking the matter as seriously as he should. But that was an impression that Cæsar liked to give. With Hirtius he was less complacent.

"See that the theatre is fortified," he ordered, "and as much of the town as we can hold. Guard the water-supply and have the Pharos island occupied to ensure an open path to Rome. What is the full strength of the Egyptian fleet?"

"There are fifty men of war, twenty-two guard ships and about forty craft of different kind lying in the Great Harbour."

"As soon as there is any trouble send out the fireships and have the whole lot burnt."

"The messengers you sent out to Achillas to bid him disband his army have been murdered. At least, one was murdered and the other escaped in a maimed condition."

"Oh, that looks like business."

"And Potheinos has distributed to our soldiers mouldy corn."

"The fellow is becoming a positive nuisance. Would you believe it, he had the cheek to advise me to cease interfering with the affairs of Egypt and return to Rome. On second thoughts I feel we'd better have the Egyptian fleet destroyed at once before they start any nonsense."

*

"Have you ever read the works of Elephantis, Cæsar?" the Queen asked.

"No," answered Cæsar, "but I've heard about them. Elephantis, if I mistake not, was a courtesan who wrote lascivious verse."

"They're very spicy in places," said the Queen. "That is why they are known as The Shameful Books of Elephantis. There is a copy in the Alexandrian Library. I feel a great desire to read them again. But with all this disturbance going on, it may be a little difficult to get hold of them."

"There's a young fellow in the ninth legion I can recommend for the purpose, the sort of boy who will do anything and go anywhere. If you really want the books I will send him out to get them for you."

"That is very kind of you, Cæsar," said the Queen. "As a matter of fact I do want to read them frightfully. I get like that sometimes about books, especially when they are difficult to procure. At the moment I feel that the only thing I want in the whole world is to re-read the Shameful Books of Elephantis."

"You shall have them," said Cæsar. "Send Rufio to me," he called to Hirtius.

Later in the day, as the Queen was walking through the Palace, she heard a great noise of shouting coming up from the square below. At a window she saw Potheinos haranguing the mob. She crept up behind him and listened.

"Citizens of Alexandria," she heard him cry, "the moment has come to free ourselves once and for all from the accursed domination of Rome. The great Cæsar is in our power. He has but a paltry force at his disposal. We have twenty thousand men and all the citizens of Alexandria. Your King is a prisoner in his own Palace and the Queen has given herself to Cæsar. Let every man, let every woman, whose heart beats with the holy sentiments of morality and freedom, rise up and smite this lecherous tyrant and that foul woman, his mistress."

In the exaltation of his eloquence he mounted on the window ledge. It was too much of a temptation for the Queen and she pushed him over. With a great cry, he fell and broke his neck on the pavement below.

The Queen hurried back to her apartments hoping that no one had observed her deed. She was aware of the curious manner in which Cæsar had received Theodotos when he brought him Pompey's head and she thought it was better he should not get to know of her little escapade.

However she was so amused by the thought of it that she was unable to resist telling Apollodoros. "Only please" she entreated, "say nothing to Hirtius or any of the Romans. I don't want it to get to Cæsar's ears. He is such an odd man. About certain things he seems to have no sense of humour, I mean about things like political assassination and revenge. Of course he doesn't go so far as to take up a high moral line about them. He couldn't very well after some of the things he has done himself, executing poor old Vercingetorix and crucifying those wretched Cilician pirates after having had such fun with them, and massacring the Germans while he was receiving their ambassadors. He seems to think such actions are all right as long as he does them himself, but he doesn't approve of other people doing them."

22

It appears," said Cæsar, "that your friend Potheinos has fallen out of a window."

"That is good news," remarked the Queen, "I hope he has hurt himself."

"He is dead."

"Better still," said the Queen, "we might throw my dear little brother after him. You look displeased, Cæsar. What a strange man you are. I suppose you feel that Potheinos, by dying, has deprived you of your usual act of magnanimity. Hirtius says that nothing gives you greater pleasure than to forgive your enemies. He says that one day you'll do it once too often."

"Oh, has Hirtius been on about that? It is one of his favourite subjects of complaint. He lectures me at times like an old Nanny."

"I think he is quite right," said the Queen. "It is a great mistake to forgive one's enemies. I don't see the point of it. I hope, for your sake, that you'll never make an enemy of me, Cæsar, because, you know, I stick at nothing."

Cæsar smiled and patted her hand.

"Oh, look!" cried the Queen.

Below in the harbour flames were rising and clouds of smoke. The Egyptian fleet was burning merrily.

"Isn't it a lovely sight!" the Queen exclaimed, clapping her hands. "That was a good idea. That will teach them, the silly brutes! I suppose I oughtn't to hate the Alexandrians as I do. But they really are a rotten lot. For the last twenty years they have been growing more and more degenerate. I'm afraid poor Papa's reign didn't do them much good. People take the tone from their rulers, don't they? As for that old eunuch's attempts to run the country. Well, thank the Gods he's out of the way."

"All the same," said Cæsar, "I fear his death is bound to lead to trouble and I wish it could have been deferred until our reinforcements arrive. I don't fancy the prospect of taking on the Alexandrians with only four thousand men at my back. They may be degenerate, but they are ingenious. They have imitated only too well many of our military devices. However, we can defend the Palace and the adjacent buildings."

"You mean there is really danger?" cried the Queen excitedly. "What fun!"

"Yes. It looks as if a nice little war might be starting at any moment. I foresee that it will take place chiefly in and about the harbour, so you will be able to watch it from the Palace roof."

"I should like to do more than watch," said the Queen. "I have a very pretty suit of armour, and I'm always happy when there's any occasion to wear it."

Hirtius appeared in the doorway.

"Well, what is it?" Cæsar asked.

"Cæsar, they say the Alexandrian Library is on fire."

The Queen jumped to her feet and ran to the window.

"Nonsense," she cried, "there is no fire near the library. It is no doubt one of the warehouses where books are stocked for exportation. That reminds me—has anything been heard of that young man who was sent to get the books of Elephantis?"

"He has not yet returned," said Hirtius.

"That is strange," Cæsar remarked, "I trust that nothing has happened to him. He rarely dawdles on an errand. I fear he may have got himself entangled with some fair Alexandrian. He is a little over fond of the ladies."

"He is not the only one," Hirtius muttered.

"What did you say, Hirtius?"

Hirtius was silent and Cæsar did not press the question.

A centurion entered and saluted.

"Cæsar, the troops are embarked and ready for the assault on Pharos Island."

"Can I go with you?" asked the Queen.

"No, my dear. Another day perhaps. Go up on to the Palace roof and watch the fun. I must hurry. I want to take the island while the Alexandrians are occupied with their burning ships. And Hirtius, will you observe the operations and start your war diary."

Hirtius was less interested in the active side of warfare than in its literary aspects. He was a good armchair strategist and he had occasionally supplied Cæsar with some excellent ideas. He went to get his writing materials and made his way up on to the roof. It was already crowded with spectators.

The Queen came over to him. She was in one of her helpful moods.

"I too will take notes of the engagement," she said. "It is often useful to have two points of view. I am farsighted and I am very observant. You will find my notes of great assistance to you in your labours."

"Your Majesty is most gracious," Hirtius answered. But he was not best pleased by the Queen's offer. He preferred his own point of view undiluted.

He smoothed out the sheet of papyrus and wrote on it in his neat scholarly handwriting.

"De Bello Alexandrino."

23

———

The Palace roof had the air of a race-meeting. The Queen and her ladies, a large crowd of attendants and many of the soldiers who had been left to guard the palace, watched the storming of the island with cheers and cries of encouragement. It was a fine autumn day. The air was clear, and although at times the view was obscured by drifts of smoke from the burning ships, it was possible to get a very good idea of the whole proceeding.

By the end of the day Cæsar's troops had occupied the whole of the island of Pharos and the causeway on the western side of the harbour which connected the island with the mainland.

Cæsar returned to the palace that evening in high spirits.

"Well, my dear," he said to the Queen, "I hope you enjoyed the show."

"It was wonderful!" cried the Queen. "All the same I wish you had taken me with you. There are one or two hints I could have given you. You see I know the island well. Indeed I have often planned imaginary assaults on it in my idle moments. I think it was a great mistake on your part not to have secured the bridge on the causeway near the mainland. Its being in the enemy's hands may cause you trouble later on. In fact you ought to have begun at that end."

Cæsar was a little taken aback by the Queen's criticism and said rather pompously, "I am always willing to learn in matter of strategy. However, in this instance I am quite satisfied with the results I have obtained. One can't do everything at once."

"That is where you are wrong, Cæsar," the Queen replied. "In warfare it is essential to do everything at once."

Cæsar was preparing to administer a snub, but noticing a smile on the face of Hirtius, he laughed instead.

"Well, my dear," he said, "if ever we have occasion to fight one another, we can try out our different theories."

News was brought to Cæsar that the Princess Arsinoe and her tutor, the eunuch Ganymede, had, during the engagement in the harbour, taken the opportunity to escape from the Palace.

"A good riddance," cried the Queen, "she'll be no asset to the enemy, I warrant you. That is good news, indeed."

Later in the evening there came in reports of a more serious nature. The Alexandrians had succeeded in polluting the water supply. The Palace and the surrounding buildings were supplied with drinking water through subterranean channels from Lake Mareotis. Into these Achillas had caused sea water to be pumped and the water was growing every hour more brackish and undrinkable.

"These are grave tidings, indeed," said Hirtius. "Without drinking water we are lost."

"That is obvious," said Cæsar, "and what do you propose that we should do?"

"I propose that we should return without delay to Rome, Cæsar. I have always held that it was unwise to dally in Alexandria with an insufficient force at your disposal. You can return later with a proper army and settle the Egyptian question."

"Look here," cried the Queen, "if you think you're going to skip off and leave me in the lurch—"

"There's no question of that, my dearest one," Cæsar assured her, "but there's no doubt we must have drinking water or we shall be done for. There are two means of getting it. We can either send ships to Paræ-tonium—"

"It is much too far," said Hirtius.

"Or cut our way through the town to the lake."

"I have an idea," said the Queen. "Among the Palace servants there used to be an old Jew who claimed to be able to find water by magic."

There was general laughter at this proposal.

"It is an amusing idea," said Cæsar, "but at the present moment we can't afford to waste our time with magic and old Jews. I prefer to put my trust in the valour of my soldiers."

"Have it your own way," said the Queen and left the room with her head in the air.

On returning to her apartments she sent for Apollodoros.

"Find out for me," she said to him, "if that old man is still alive who claims to be a water-finder. He works, if I remember aright, in the kitchens. Papa employed him once to find water in the gardens for a lotus pool. If he found water once he may find it again. We can but try."

After a time Apollodoros returned with an aged hunchbacked Jew.

"Tell me, old man," asked the Queen, "can you find a spring of fresh water for me in the neighbourhood?"

"If water there be, I can find it," the old man replied. "But for the purpose I need my magic wand."

"Go and fetch it," the Queen commanded, "and hurry up."

The old man returned with a bent twig.

"Is that all?" asked the Queen.

"This, Your Majesty," he answered, "is my magic wand. It is cut from a tree that grows by the waters of the Jordan. It has been kept for many years in a casket of salt over which magic words have been spoken. When taken from its resting place into the open air it pines once more for fresh water and when passed over a spot where such springs are hidden it turns in my hand."

"I trust it will not fail us this time," said the Queen. "Let us go. We will start on the beach below the palace."

"Really!" cried Apollodoros, "what an absurd place to look for fresh water springs."

"You be quiet," said the Queen, "you forget that I have studied physiography."

On the way down to the seashore the old man started on a perennial grievance.

"Never a bit of recognition have I had," he complained. "Never anything but jeers and disbelief. 'What's the use of finding water?' they say 'when there's so much about. Find us gold, or precious stones.' I never get a chance to display my magic art."

The old man continued in this strain until at last Apollodoros took it upon himself to reprimand him.

"Let him speak," said the Queen. "It is a good thing to encourage the lower classes to air their grievances. Surely, old man, my father rewarded you for your services?"

"On that occasion," the Jew replied, "His Majesty was forgetful."

"It shall not occur again," the Queen assured him. "If you find water for me now, you shall be rewarded beyond your dreams."

When they reached the shore the old man held out his forked branch and walked forward across the sand, muttering to himself. After he had proceeded about fifty paces the branch suddenly turned in his hands.

"There is water here," he exclaimed.

The Queen sent Apollodoros back to the Palace for men with spades. After they had dug a few feet down, a spring of fresh water came bubbling forth.

"Find us some more," said the Queen.

The old man repeated the process and in a few hours he had found a sufficient number of fresh water springs to supply half the town.

Meanwhile Cæsar's attempts to cut a passage to the lake had met with signal failure. The Alexandrians had barricaded the way with high walls of stone. The defending forces were in great numerical superiority and the Roman soldiers were driven back with considerable losses.

When she returned to the Palace the Queen found Cæsar in a dejected mood.

"For the first time," he said, "I must admit that I am a little perturbed."

"I'm not," said the Queen, "I've found you enough water to wash away all your sins."

"It's not true!" cried Cæsar. "Is it true, Apollodoros?"

"Yes, Cæsar, it is true."

"You see," said the Queen triumphantly, "if you had only put your trust in me and my old Jew with his magic wand, you would have saved yourself a lot of trouble and loss of life. Really, you men!" She leant over him and kissed him. "Ridiculous creatures!"

24

The Alexandrian war dragged on. Several weeks passed without any decisive action on either side. In spite of the urgent orders Cæsar had sent to the commandant of Asia Minor to send troops and ships all haste to Egypt, the reinforcements had not arrived. The Alexandrians, Cæsar had to admit, though lacking in heroic courage, were ingenious and resourceful. In an incredibly short time they managed to equip a fleet to replace that which had been burnt. They rigged out the customs vessels stationed at the mouths of the Nile and resuscitated a lot of old ships lodged in the King's arsenals. In order to supply themselves with oars they stripped the timber from the public buildings.

Disputes that had arisen in the Egyptian High Command ended in the assassination of Achillas, and the eunuch Ganymede now assumed complete control of the operations. As he was a more intelligent man than Achillas, the change was all in favour of the Alexandrians.

At times Cæsar's position was one of great danger. It was often touch and go. If the Alexandrians had succeeded, as at one moment they nearly did, in blocking the access to the sea, he would have been lost. Hirtius, although he was much interested in the composition of his war diary, never ceased to exhort Cæsar to abandon the struggle and return to Rome.

"He practically accuses me," Cæsar told the Queen, "of prolonging the war solely for your amusement."

"It would amuse me more," the Queen retorted, "if you would allow me to take a more active part in it. I am weary of merely observing it from the Palace roof."

"My dearest one," said Cæsar, "I am sufficiently acquainted with your character to know that you would blame me for every defeat and claim every victory for yourself."

"If I were to have a hand in it, there would be no defeats."

"Fond as I am of women," said Cæsar, "I'm not sufficiently fond of them to allow it to be said that any campaign of mine was won by a woman."

"Well," the Queen remarked, "I've no doubt that Hirtius and you between you would see to it that such a thing was never said."

These little altercations that frequently took place between Cæsar and the Queen were, as the reader may well surmise, merely indicative of their affection for one another.

"However," Cæsar went on, "I will admit that you were right about that bridge on the causeway. It has become an infernal nuisance, and I intend to take possession of it to-day."

"In that case," said the Queen, "I advise you to send a detachment round the island in ships and attack the bridge simultaneously from both sides."

"That will be unnecessary," Cæsar exclaimed. "It can be easily taken from the harbour side alone. And anyhow don't you worry about it. All I ask of you is that you prepare a nice banquet for me on my return. Simple fare, mind you. Nothing too rich."

As Cæsar landed on the mole, a young man came forward and handed him a roll of papyrus.

"Here are the Shameful Books of Elephantis, Cæsar," he said.

"Ah, Rufio. So you've returned at last."

"I have had many adventures, Cæsar," the young man declared. "When I got into the library I discovered that the books you wanted had been taken out by the Professor of Deportment. As the man is active in his hostility to the Romans I was obliged to enter his house in disguise, as a servant. Now this professor has a very pretty niece—"

He broke off. The Alexandrians had suddenly attacked in force. They were in great superiority of numbers and they drove back the Roman soldiers in confusion. The cohorts who were guarding the bridge, astonished by the disorder and unable to bear up against the shower of darts that fell upon them, abandoned the defence of the bridge and ran towards the galleys. Some of them, getting on board the nearest vessels overloaded and sank them. Cæsar, endeavouring to reanimate his men and lead them back to the defence of the bridge, was nearly captured by the enemy. Indeed he would have been, had not Rufio with gallant sword play, covered his retreat. Throwing aside his scarlet cloak, Cæsar leaped into the water and swam towards his galley, holding aloft in his left hand, the precious books.

The Alexandrians took possession of Cæsar's cloak and brandished it in the air as a trophy. It was an ignominious defeat for the Romans and over four hundred soldiers were killed, including the gallant Rufio.

Cæsar had but one small source of consolation. The Queen at least had got her books.

Occupied with the preparations for the banquet, she had not been watching the engagement and was unaware of what had happened. She snatched the papyrus eagerly from Cæsar's hands and opened out the scroll.

"Oh," she cried, her expression changing to one of disappointment, "but these are not the Shameful Books at all. This is her manual of Deportment and Etiquette. A most inferior work. One wonders why she chose the subject, for what can a courtesan know of etiquette. Oh dear! This is too disappointing. I could almost cry from vexation."

25

What I like about Cæsar," said the Queen to Apollodoros, "is that he is never discouraged." (They were discussing the disastrous episode of the bridge.) "One might even believe that he is more elated by failure than by success. It seems to put him on his mettle."

"Yes," Apollodoros replied, "and Hirtius tells me that it is the same with his soldiers. Instead of being disheartened by their defeat, they seem rather to be roused and animated by it, so that Cæsar himself finds it necessary to restrain their ardour."

"It must be puzzling to the Alexandrians who are fair-weather fighters and only show courage when all is going well."

"One cannot but admire these Romans," said Apollodoros, "I used to look upon them as vulgar barbarians."

"They are barbarians," said the Queen, "and vulgar too. But they have qualities that one must perforce admire. They are large-hearted and they have a sense of humour that is more agreeable than that of Alexandrians. And above all they are tough. We could do with a little more toughness, I fancy. We must be tough, Apollodoros, we must be tough."

After a time the Alexandrians began to be discouraged by the Roman toughness and they sent ambassadors to Cæsar suggesting a truce and begging him to restore to them their King. They hinted that, in granting their request Cæsar would "pave the way to an alliance and extinguish all the fears and objections that had hitherto obstructed it."

The Queen was very much opposed to the idea.

"Disagreeable as it is," she said, "to have that little rat in the palace, he has a certain value as a hostage. From reports I have received it is obvious that the Alexandrians are getting fed up with Arsinoe and her eunuch and, before long, open dissension may break out in their ranks."

Hirtius and the rest of Cæsar's staff agreed with her, but Cæsar himself was bent on restoring the King. He believed that his condescension in sending him back might prevail on the Alexandrians to make peace.

"You little know them," said the Queen. "As long as they are in numerical superiority, nothing will induce them to give in. Like Pythagoras they have a superstition about numbers."

Cæsar sent for the King and told him that he was at liberty to depart. The lad seemed very much upset and assured Cæsar, with tears in his eyes, that he would rather remain where he was.

"Your company, Cæsar," he declared, "is preferable to a kingdom."

"If those are your sentiments, my boy," Cæsar answered, "we shall soon meet again."

The King left the Palace weeping bitterly, but no sooner did he find himself once more among his people than he seemed entirely to have changed his views and professed the greatest hatred for Cæsar. With the King at their head the Alexandrians carried on the war with greater acrimony than before so that it looked as if the tears the King had shed at parting had been tears of joy.

The Queen and Hirtius manifested openly their amusement at Cæsar's having been imposed upon.

"Well, anyhow," said Cæsar, "it is more dignified to be fighting against a King than with a eunuch and a foolish girl."

"It's no good," cried the Queen, "he'll never admit to being in the wrong. He'll always find a very good reason to justify his mistakes."

"It is a part of his strength," said Hirtius.

Cæsar listened to the Queen's jibes with equanimity. He knew that the reinforcements from Asia Minor were on their way.

26

⟨⦿⟩

Mithridates whom Cæsar had sent at the beginning of the Alexandrian war, to raise troops in Syria and Cilicia, had arrived with a large army at Pelusium, had defeated the garrison in that town and was now advancing on the capital by way of Memphis.

Cæsar, on learning that forces were being sent out from Alexandria to oppose him, determined to set forth at once and join up with Mithridates.

"Now this time," Cæsar said to the Queen, "if you really wish it, I'll take you with me."

"Your offer," the Queen replied, "had it been early, had been kind. But it has been deferred until it is too late, I can't possibly go with you now."

"Why on earth not?" Cæsar enquired. "What an extraordinary girl you are! Ever since the war started you have been clamouring to take a more active part in it, and now when I offer you this opportunity—"

"My dearest Cæsar," said the Queen, "don't you realise? How unobservant you must be. Just take a look at my figure."

"You don't mean to say—"

"I do indeed. As a matter of fact I was waiting for you to notice it yourself. I suppose I ought to have whispered the news in your ear like a coy matron. I'll do it now."

She put her arms round his neck and kissed him lightly on his ear.

"The son of Cæsar and Cleopatra," she said. "What a child it promises to be!"

"My dear, how can you possibly know it'll be a boy?"

"Don't be silly, Cæsar. Of course he's going to be a boy. Doctor Serapion once told me that if a woman wills it hard enough she can always determine sex. You must meet Doctor Serapion, Cæsar. You'd adore him. He's a most remarkable man. He might be able to do something about your hair if you really wish it. Personally I prefer a noble brow and I think low foreheads always give men a mean appearance. When you have settled the affairs of Egypt, we'll make a journey up the Nile to Thebes. You'll enjoy that. But if you admire the Pyramids I shall think poorly of your taste. And what about my little babbikins. Aren't you pleased, Cæsar? Aren't you delighted?"

Cæsar pressed her hand. He was delighted, but he would have been more delighted still if he could have been as confident as the Queen of his offspring's sex.

Cæsar sent part of his troops in ships to the end of Lake Mareotis and he himself, with the remainder, marched round the lake to the west of Alexandria to join Mithridates before the enemy could prevent him. With the joint forces he advanced into the Delta whither the Alexandrian army had retreated and won a decisive victory. The Alexandrians were utterly routed and the King, attempting to escape by water, was drowned.

Cæsar returned to Alexandria in triumph. The citizens came out to meet him clad in mourning and carrying the images of their Gods in their hands. Cæsar took no vengeance beyond inflicting on them a very long speech in which he expatiated on the damage that had been done to their fair city and exhorted them in future to cultivate the arts of peace.

The Queen came out to meet him dressed in her ceremonial robes.

"Have you brought back my little husband in a cage?" she asked.

"No, my dear," Cæsar replied, "I am grieved to have to tell you that he is drowned. He fell into the Nile and was dragged down by the weight of his cuirass."

"It serves him right," exclaimed the Queen. "That ridiculous cuirass! It made him look like a rat in a saucepan. And Arsinoe?"

"She is being sent to Rome to adorn my triumph."

"She'll adorn it all right," said the Queen scornfully. "I should like to be there to see."

On the following day the Queen gave a gorgeous banquet and the town was illuminated.

The Queen sat that evening with Cæsar on the terrace overlooking the Great Harbour. The full moon shone on the rippling waters and on the marble lighthouse. From afar came the sounds of revelry in the town.

"What are your plans for the future?" asked the Queen.

"My plans for the future?" said Cæsar. "Well, there are certain matters in the provinces I shall have to attend to. After that, I shall return here—for the great event, I hope. Then, I fear, I must go back to Rome. You will come to Rome, Cleopatra?"

"It has long been my desire," said the Queen, "to visit Rome. I pine to see the famous city, to make the acquaintance of its famous men. I am particularly anxious to meet Cicero. I feel that we shall get on well together."*

"Yes," said Cæsar, "Cicero is a splendid fellow. A supreme orator and a man of great taste and learning. He has but little love for me, I fear. You may perhaps succeed in making him feel more kindly about me. By the way," he broke off, taking up his tablets, "I must remember to tell Hirtius to say nothing about the library in his commentaries. A rumour has gone abroad that it has been destroyed by fire, and you know that it is quite untrue. I don't want to have it said of me that I am a barbarian and have no love for culture. And also," he added, "I hope you will not take it amiss if very little mention is made of you. I think it is wiser. And, after all, the commentaries deal principally with military matters."

The Queen smiled.

"Your wife," she said, "and the Roman ladies. I don't fancy I shall cut much ice with them or they with me. They will look upon me with suspicion as a foreign interloper. I have heard strange things about their private conduct, yet I shouldn't be surprised if they were to take up a high moral line. I'm very unconventional, you know. Have your women much influence on politics?"

"It depends on the politicians," Cæsar answered. "I myself hold that no statesman should allow himself to be influenced by women. How-

---

*They didn't. Cleopatra promised to get some books out of the Alexandrian Library for him and then forgot about it. Cicero took her forgetfulness very much to heart, and wrote, in a letter to Atticus, "I hate the Queen."

ever, there's no doubt that women have sometimes left their mark on the world's affairs. History is not always made by men alone. But the part played by women is liable to be exaggerated. There is a saying, attributed to Pythagoras 'If Helen's nose had been longer (or shorter, I forget which) the whole face of the world might have been changed.' "

"Was that said of Helen?" the Queen exclaimed. "How curious!"

FAR FROM THE MADDING WAR

(1941)

Far

FROM THE

Madding War

❧

Lord Berners

TO

David and Rachel Cecil

Contents

As every character in a work of fiction is bound to have some characteristic that is characteristic of someone, the author will be obliged if his friends will not attempt to recognise themselves or each other in these pages.

1

—⚬⚬⚬—

Emmeline's War Work

Miss Emmeline Pocock sat, intently bending over a large piece of embroidery, surrounded by good taste and silence. The room she sat in was as elegantly appointed a room as anyone could wish to see, although a highly attuned connoissance of decorative subtleties might detect, here and there, a blemish; a somewhat too deliberate juxtaposition of objects; colour arrangements that envisaged artistic ideals without quite achieving them. But, on the whole, the general effect was one of harmony, discretion, lack of pretentiousness, and there was none of that absence of comfort that good taste so often entails.

The room was also sound proof. Emmeline, when her father took up his residence as Warden of All Saints, had caused the walls of her room to be padded with cork and sea-weed, and she had installed double windows, so that she should not be disturbed by the cries of undergraduates, by their practising of musical instruments (some of which were of a very disagreeable nature), by the distant rumble of traffic and, above all, by the perpetual buzzing of aeroplanes.

The sky, above the old university town, seemed to have become a rendezvous for aviators, a kind of non-stop meet; they were for ever circling, wheeling and diving overhead and the ancient walls never ceased to vibrate with their droning. To many this might be a promise of protection; to Emmeline, the sound was a reminder of the precarious age we live in.

Her dislike of disturbing noises was not, however, due to a love of meditation. On the contrary, when she was alone in her room, she preferred to indulge in complete mental repose. Her faculties of association were perhaps unduly sensitive and insufficiently controlled. The shouts of undergraduates would evoke, in the manner of Gray, a poignant reflection on the exuberance of youth and its impending doom;

the sound of a hunting horn echoing through the quad, an *espièglerie* to which representatives of the higher social strata were much addicted, recalled to her alternatively the follies of the aristocracy, or modern music, which she much disliked.

To her, a place where she could spend a certain portion of her time in the absolute quiescence of her consciousness was a necessity. "Life," she used to say, "is so difficult to cope with that I find I can only do so by fortifying myself with long periods of respite from thought."

People to whom she had made this confession had recommended other ways of banishing thought: games, household duties, gardening, charitable works, or reading her father's philosophical books, which were so difficult to understand that it was no use trying. But she preferred her own methods.

Let us consider Emmeline's appearance in order. The first impression was one of gentleness and modesty. Then you began to realize that she was extremely pretty. Some even considered her beautiful. But her features were too retroussé to conform with the canons of classic beauty. Emmeline herself believed that it was better, for all practical intents and purposes, that a young woman should be pretty rather than beautiful, and made no attempt to assume the airs that so often accompany the fatal gift. She was of rather diminutive stature, but her body was so well proportioned that she appeared taller than she really was. Her hair, as a poetical undergraduate had once said, was reminiscent of a cornfield at daybreak. Her complexion was of that fairness that invites freckles, but as she never exposed herself to the sun that was not a serious defect. Her type was more suggestive of the eighteenth century than of the present day. She looked like a nymph in one of the less licentious pictures of Fragonard. Her manner was aloof and dignified. In fact she was not the sort of girl with whom you might be tempted to take liberties without encouragement. And encouragement in this respect was one of the things that Emmeline never gave.

The war had come upon her as a very unpleasant surprise. The twenty years of her life had been spent in the company of eminently sensible people. Her mother, now deceased, had been a very sensible woman.

Her father, who was a philosopher, had always appeared to possess a fund of common sense, and the few who may have held different views had never betrayed them in her presence. Being neither a keen nor a very conscientious student of politics, she had put her trust a little too implicitly in the words that fell from the lips of some of the eminent statesmen who occasionally came to her father's house. And as such people often speak quite reasonably, however much their subsequent policies become distorted by the exigencies of political strategy, she was deluded into rather too optimistic an outlook. In a phrase so frequently used in the newspapers, she allowed herself to be lulled into a false sense of security. With a naïve faith she had clung to her belief in the ultimate triumph of reason.

After going through a few weeks of dismay and depression, during which she gathered from the conversation and the activities of her friends that she was expected to alter her rather indolent mode of life, she determined to apply herself to some form of war work.

But what on earth, she wondered, was it to be? She dreaded the thought of an uncongenial task. She did not see herself in a munition factory or in a hospital; performing clerical work in a Government office, driving an ambulance or even doling out sausages and tomato soup in a canteen.

Engaged in these speculations, she suddenly thought of an immense and valuable piece of embroidery stowed away in her bedroom. Why it should have come into her mind at that particular moment she could not imagine. The associations of our thoughts, as Emmeline had often discovered, are sometimes so unexpected and obscure that they defy analysis. The connecting links flash by with the rapidity of a cinema reel, so that it becomes impossible for the memory to record their succession. But Emmeline was not concerned just then with analysis. She hailed the intrusion of the piece of embroidery as an inspiration. "That," she said, "will be my war work."

She went upstairs and took it from the shelf where it had reposed ever since, some years before, it had been bequeathed to her by an aunt, an old lady who, in spite of a moderate outlay, had succeeded in amassing a collection of objects of considerable artistic value.

During a visit, at a moment when conversation had lapsed and Emmeline had felt the necessity of making some sort of remark, a contingency that is, more often than, not, fraught with danger, she had expressed an exaggerated appreciation of the embroidery (which as a matter of fact she did not greatly admire), with the result that it had been left to her in her aunt's will in the place of some other legacy that she would have preferred.

It was a very fine piece of work, but, notwithstanding its great rarity and value, Emmeline had found no place for it in her decorative scheme. It was too ostensibly precious, too obviously a museum piece, and would have struck a false, or rather too high a note, in a room which was meant to be lived in agreeably rather than scrutinized by the eye of a collector. Emmeline had often thought of presenting it to some museum, but had refrained from doing so, partly from indolence and partly from delicacy of feeling with regard to a legacy, especially as her aunt had often expressed her dislike for museums and referred to them as "those mausoleums of beauty," a phrase that very exactly described her own house. Similar considerations precluded the idea of selling. It would have been repellent to her to make a profit out of a token of family affection. Thus it had become something of a white elephant, and at moments she was disturbed by the thought that she ought to have it insured.

Returning to her room, she spread out the embroidery over the back of a sofa. It was certainly a remarkable piece of work. An expert to whom she had shown it had pronounced it to be German, probably of the fourteenth century, bearing traces of Byzantine influence. It represented incidents in the lives of the saints, interspersed with lettered scrolls and devices composed of flowers, foliage and animals. It was wonderfully preserved. The colours were still fresh, and glowed with a sombre radiance.

She wondered where and in what circumstances her aunt had picked it up. She knew that the old lady had neither the means nor the inclination to pay a very high price for anything she bought. Emmeline regretted that she had not made enquiries while her aunt was still alive. In view of what she was about to do, she longed to know its history, and she wished she had made investigations while there was yet time.

Focusing a swivel lamp on a corner of the embroidery, she took up a small pair of scissors and, drawing up a chair, she sat down before it and began slowly, deliberately to unravel the tiny threads of silk, offering a mental prayer to God to grant her the requisite strength to persevere in her minute labour of destruction until not a single thread remained of this unique, almost monumental, work of art.

2

A Dinner Party at the Warden's

After toiling strenuously for several hours and finding that at the end of that time she had only succeeded in unravelling about a quarter of a square inch, Emmeline was disheartened by the difficulty and magnitude of the task she had undertaken. When she was obliged to unpick some of her own embroidery she had always found it an unexpectedly lengthy business. But here her difficulties were increased a thousandfold by the fact that time had coagulated the silken threads into an almost solid mass, and she was obliged to excavate carefully with the point of her scissors in order to detach each thread. "I am sure," she said to herself, "it must be like picking oakum, only worse."

She was determined, however, not to evade the minutest intricacy of her work. If she were to do so, the whole point of it would be lost, and she might as well throw the whole thing into the fire straightway.

The views she had now evolved on the subject of war work were very definite. Above all it should not be pleasurable. The proper spirit was

one of austerity; and she disapproved of the way in which some of her
friends seemed to be enjoying their work. Had she herself taken on a job
in a hospital or in a government office, had she applied herself to any of
the more normal forms of war activity, she might conceivably have
come to enjoy them too. She knew that the work she had chosen would
never be anything to her but tedious, laborious and heart-rending.

She found her views confirmed by the speeches of some of the cabinet ministers, an almost gloating insistence upon the nation preparing
itself for hardships and suffering, by the admonition of Marshal Petain,
"Trop de plaisirs," and by the exhortations she read in the newspapers
that people should destroy their asparagus beds.

The more she thought on the matter the more convinced she became
that her choice had been appropriate and comprehensive. The spirit of
sacrifice was represented in the destruction of a valuable possession; the
spirit of self abasement in the fact that she had joined the ranks of
the Great Destroyers and was deliberately courting the same kind of
odium that had been incurred by Herostatus, who burnt the temple of
Artemis at Ephesus, or Lady Burton, who tore up her husband's manu-
scripts. Yet, she felt, she was not quite as one of these. Herostatus had
been actuated by a craving for immortality, Lady Burton by prudish-
ness. Their motives, at any rate, were less elevated than hers.

Temperamentally she was averse to destruction. As a child she had
never pulled the wings off flies or broken her toys. But now destruction was in the order of the day. That the embroidery happened to be
of German origin did not appeal to her as a point in her argument,
though it was one that might perhaps meet with the approval of the ra-
bidly patriotic. It was a pity, of course, that what she was doing could
not possibly help to win the war, but then the same thing could be said
of a great deal of war work that was very much applauded.

As a rule she was not intimidated by unfavourable criticism, but she
was easily fatigued by reiteration. Many of her friends, she had noticed,
did not content themselves with expressing their opinions once and for
all. They were inclined to go on and on about them. In spite of her confidence in the fitness of her choice, she suspected that, by even the most
inveterate of vandals, it would be condemned. Thus she foresaw the ne-

cessity of keeping the nature of her work to herself. She would not be able to boast about it or bore people with it, as did some of her friends. It would be better to incur the reproach of doing nothing whatever in the war than to expose herself to constant recriminations, and possibly to be ticketed with the label of eccentricity. It occurred to her that certain war occupations were of so secret a character that they could not be divulged. That, she decided, would be the line that she would take about hers.

It was nearly dinner time. She remembered that Mr. Jericho had been invited, and that he had a habit of bouncing into her room unheralded. She gathered up the embroidery and stowed it away out of sight. She was not a wink too soon.

It was characteristic of this ebullient personality that you rarely heard or saw him coming. He appeared quite suddenly, like a pantomime demon or a cuckoo out of a cuckoo clock. His departures were equally sudden and, unless he happened to be in a situation from which he could not decently escape, he would, like the cuckoo, after sounding the requisite number of notes, vanish with a snap.

Mr. Jericho was blond and rather Flemish looking. His person presented a strange combination of asceticism and sensuality. A spiritual gourmet, he suggested an inspiration of Fra Angelico executed by Rubens. He wore very large steel-rimmed spectacles, through which his eyes focused you with an alarming intensity. You felt that there was nothing they missed, and, indeed, that they often saw a good many things that weren't there.

He was tutor of modern history at All Saints and was said to be one of the most brilliant exponents of that equivocal science, the philosophy of history. His interests centred also in the less serious weaknesses of mankind, and particularly in those of his colleagues. No intrigue, no drama, no love affair, however recondite, could occur within the precincts of the university without his immediately becoming possessed of its every detail. He seemed to hold a divining rod for anything that savoured of scandal, and it was perpetually turning in his hands.

Emmeline was not particularly interested in college gossip, but she enjoyed hearing it recounted and embellished by Mr. Jericho. The most trivial, the most anodyne item of personal news was transformed by his exquisite artistry into a little masterpiece of psychological literature.

He was preparing to regale Emmeline with an account of the latest elopement of Mrs. Postlethwaite, the only don's wife who had pretentions of being a "grande amoureuse," when the Warden tapped on the door and called out that dinner was ready and that Professor and Mrs. Trumper were waiting below.

"Oh, damn," said Mr. Jericho, for he knew that the presence of the Trumpers was going to spoil the evening.

As they sat down to dinner, Emmeline reflected, as she often had occasion to do before, on her father's peculiar ideas of entertaining. He enjoyed the company of intelligent and amusing people and he liked his dinners to go with a swing. But some strange kink in his nature, some blind spot in his social vision, caused him too frequently to ruin a promising list of guests by the insertion of one or two people who, he must have known, would infallibly wreck the party. There was no lack of such people in the town, but if he felt it his duty to ask them, he could have easily invited them all together and made a holocaust of it.

Mr. Jericho had a theory that it was Doctor Pocock's love of experimental research that impelled him to find out whether certain combinations of people would always go badly. The Provost of Unity, who was also interested in the whys and wherefores of human behaviour, had put forward the suggestion that it might be due to a philosopher's mistrust of perfection, to his belief that no rose should be unaccompanied by a thorn. Emmeline herself was disinclined to discuss the matter with her father. Since the death of Mrs. Pocock, they had reached a tacit understanding never to comment on each other's idiosyncrasies.

Professor Trumper was large and ungainly. His rugged features looked as if they had been carved by an indifferent sculptor out of some very unpleasant species of granite. He was reputed to be one of the rudest members of the university. But it was difficult to know whether his rudeness proceeded from arrogance or from stupidity, a form of discourtesy that sensitive people found hard to deal with. To Mr. Jericho in particular, the Professor's rudeness was an irritating problem. He prided himself on a capacity for encountering any abnormal manifestation of behaviour, whether it took the form of extreme rudeness or excessive politeness. In the case of Professor Trumper he never knew whether his repartee should be inspired by anger or pity.

Professor Trumper was one of the few dons of the higher order (excluding, of course, those coming from Scotland or the Dominions) who was willing, in a purely social gathering, to speak for any length of time on his own particular subject. This habit was deplored by many of his colleagues, who held that your "subject" should only be spoken of in the lecture room, in intimate discussions with colleagues or on rare occasions in order to impress some important guest. An ordinary stranger venturing to probe into the nature of a don's scholastic activities would be viewed with suspicion. One was reminded of the anecdote about a personage of the nineties who, asked by a cabman to what address he should drive him, replied: "Why should I reveal to you the whereabouts of my glorious home?"

Professor Trumper, however, was not a prey to such inhibitions. Indeed, one often wished that he were; that he could be psycho-analysed in an inverse sense and given a few.

The Professor had a powerful voice and a manner of clearing his throat that acted like a mine-sweeper. He was able to talk any one down, and his wife often thought that he resembled Doctor Johnson.

Mrs. Trumper was physically unlike her husband. She was small and fragile looking, and she had an air of faded sweetness, which, however, was soon found to be deceptive. After getting to know her a little more intimately you came to the conclusion that she was like marmalade that had gone sour.

She was an international idealist, and, although she never seemed to be doing anything to further it, she was a great believer in what she called "the nations getting together." "If only," she would lament, "the nations would try to understand each other's psychology! It is because the different countries take no trouble to get to know one another that international security has become imperilled." "Tout savoir c'est tout pardonner" was a phrase that was constantly on her lips. Maddened one day by its reiteration, Mr. Jericho had remarked that it would be truer to say: "Tout savoir c'est tout condamner."

She was crazy about small nations, the smaller the better. She often wrote articles in the more intellectual periodicals. In her literary activities, however, she was apt to be dogged by misfortune. Her opinions and her prophecies were continually being refuted by facts before the article was published. Just before the war she had written a letter to the *New Stateswoman* which ended with the words: "If only Hitler would speak all would be well." It appeared on the day after the Fuehrer had made one of his four-hour speeches and all was not well.

Mrs. Trumper had been connected at one time with the League of Nations. She had spent a year at Geneva and had never quite recovered from it.

Resigning himself to the prospect of not having the kind of conversation he would have enjoyed, Mr. Jericho decided to turn the party into a sort of game in which he would employ his wits in heading off Professor Trumper from one of his customary dissertations on marginal utility, imperfect competition, vertical disintegration, and other weighty aspects of economics. However, the Professor, that evening, seemed to have made up his mind to speak about nothing but the war.

Doctor Pocock did not encourage discussion of the war at his dinner parties. He was at heart a little gloomy as to its ultimate issue, and he did not wish to lay himself open to the charge of being a defeatist. Unlike some of his colleagues, he hesitated to express views that were not sincere, and he had resolved to adopt the same non-committal attitude as an eighteenth century sage had done on the subject of religion. If questioned as to his opinions, he would reply that they were those of every sensible man and were opinions that every sensible man kept to himself.

But he did not enjoy having to be silent, and, when anyone spoke at too great a length about the war, he grew restive. Unlike Mr. Jericho, he did not possess the requisite conversational strategy to circumvent subjects that were distasteful to him.

Mr. Jericho, being once more disappointed in the nature of the game he had prepared himself to play, being confronted with cricket instead of chess, was playing it carelessly and with a lack of concentration that enabled Professor Trumper to rumble on unimpeded.

To Emmeline it was a slight source of consolation that the Professor that evening was not in one of his jocular moods. He was being wholly serious. He gave his hearers to understand that, although nearly overwhelmed by the weight of the world's affairs, he was nevertheless able to deal with them. He had them well in hand. And from time to time Mrs. Trumper would insinuate that, in a modest way, she was of some assistance to her husband; that (as in the oriental cosmogony) she was the tortoise that supported the elephant that supported the world.

It was the Professor's jocular moods that Emmeline dreaded. They reminded her of a placard she had seen on a road announcing a "steam roller at work," and she had thought at the time how much more alarming a proposition would be a steam roller at play.

"When the output of such commodities as civilian clothing for the home market is curtailed, there will be a danger of the vicious spiral of inflation. The Government can either attack the inverted pyramid of credit at the base or withdraw purchasing power by compulsory saving or arrange for a valorisation of prices by the cartelisation of each industry separately—"

Listening vaguely with one compartment of her brain and pursuing her own thoughts with the other, Emmeline pondered on the many conversations that had taken place in her father's house. She reflected that, whether they had been brilliant and witty or laborious and dull, always they had seemed to be impregnated with a curious sense of sterility; they never appeared to lead anywhere. There must, she thought, be some kind of inhibitory influence in the air that prevented people from ever really disclosing their points of view. It is true that Professor Trumper never showed any hesitation in this respect, but then his verbal activities could hardly be described as conversation.

She had once ventured to discuss the matter with her father, and he had explained to her that it was probably due to a code of manners that had become established in the days before dons were allowed to marry, before domestic life had come to disturb the monastic routine of the university. When the same people dined night after night in the hall or the common room, it was found that discussions inevitably led to the same conclusions and frequently ended in great discourtesy, just as certain chemical combinations inevitably produce the same results accompanied by explosions. In order to obviate a monotonous breach of good manners, any subject likely to lead to controversy came to be avoided, and the too naked exposure of a point of view was looked upon as an indecency.

Emmeline did not entirely accept her father's explanation. In her school days she had read much about conversations in eighteenth and nineteenth century salons. She had read Boswell, in which the conversation recorded, although not always polite, was at least substantial and incisive. She had read the Journals of the Goncourts and the novels of Anatole France. She had expected too much, perhaps, from the intercourse of clever men round a dinner table. She began to fear that what people had said was true and that the art of conversation, like that of letter writing, had succumbed to the stress of modern civilization. These are not thoughts, you will say, of a highly original nature, but they helped Emmeline to bear the tedium of the Professor's monologue.

"And there is yet another way in which I consider the vicious spiral may be checked. Those who are responsible for our economic policy must firstly take into consideration—"

Noting the growing symptoms of fatigue on the faces of her father and Mr. Jericho, Emmeline felt it her duty to try and do something to relieve them. She took advantage of a momentary lull in the Professor's soliloquy, which up till then had been running on, like Sanscrit, without punctuation. "What," she enquired, turning to Mr. Jericho, "do you really feel about the architecture of Kimble College?"

Emmeline as a rule did not take a very prominent part in the talk at her father's dinner parties. Indeed, she very rarely opened her mouth. When she did so, and asked a seemingly innocent question in a very sweet voice, it produced the effect of a saccharine bomb, and everyone was startled into attention. Even Professor Trumper was momentarily disconcerted and Mr. Jericho was able to say what he thought of it.

The architecture of Kimble College was a bit of a problem to the small section of the university that took an interest in such things. Built in the seventies of multi-coloured brick, and in the Gothic style, it had been a source of controversy ever since. It had been violently attacked and as violently defended. Of late the balance of taste seemed to be inclining in its favour, and an eulogistic article had recently appeared in the Architectural Review.

"One has only to stand," wrote the enthusiastic critic, "in Kimble main quad when a sunset has drained the colour from the bricks, to see how admirably the chapel and hall and surrounding buildings are proportioned to the sunk expanse of the quad. It is a whole that hangs together, the chapel dominating everything, as it should, in a college which was founded for perpetuating academic education definitely based on the Church of England. Whatever criticisms admirers of the Renaissance may level against Kimble College, they cannot say it is a copy of anything. It is not the product of an antiquarian, but of an architect. Sir Gilbert Scott, whose work is all too prominent in England, was a copyist. The architect of Kimble was an inventor."

The passage is quoted at length, as it will dispense of my recording Mr. Jericho's reply. His view reflected those of the article which he had read.

Professor Trumper and his wife, who were not particularly interested in architecture, had nothing to say on the matter, and the Professor was engaged in summoning up his strength for a crashing return into the conversational field. When he did so it was obvious that his nerve had been a little shaken by this aesthetic digression, and both Mr. Jericho and Doctor Pocock were able to interpose an occasional remark. The conversation drifted to the topic of fifth columnists, and Professor Trumper said that every man of them should be taken out and shot. Mr. Jericho agreed with him, and said that most of the fifth columnists were to be found in the Civil Service, and that the Civil Service was in itself a fifth column and a valuable asset to the enemy.

"You forget," said Mrs. Trumper, "that my son is in the Civil Service."

Mr. Jericho had indeed forgotten, but he was sure that Mrs. Trumper thought he had not. He feared lest Emmeline and her father might believe him guilty of a deliberate error of tact and a lack of courtesy to his host. If Mr. Jericho suffered from any social defect, it was rather from excess of tact than its absence.

Everyone suddenly felt a little tired. Even Professor Trumper's flow of rhetoric was beginning to ebb. The conversation flagged again and again, until it resembled the moribund flickerings of an electric torch. The black moth of somnolence settled on Emmeline. In one last flicker Mr. Jericho turned to the amours of Mrs. Postlethwaite, a theme that was invariably resorted to when all other subjects of conversation failed.

Mrs. Postlethwaite had just perpetrated another of her elopements. They had now become of such regular occurrence that they had ceased to cause the stir they occasioned at the outset of her amorous career, and were only censured by those in whom custom could not stale their infinite morality, or by ladies who feared for the safety of their husbands. In her love affairs Mrs. Postlethwaite took the initiative. Her natural selection, however, did not appear to be governed by a preference for strength and cunning, or, indeed, for any physical or mental superiority. Her choice was marked by a lack of discrimination, and it was said of her that her tastes were so catholic as almost to amount to indifference. To Mr. Jericho she was something of a harpy, a female satyr. "What young men loth! What struggle to escape!" And he would imply that her siren lurings were all too often frustrated by the ear-stoppers of Ulysses.

Though Mrs. Postlethwaite's elopements were numerous they were surreptitious and brief. They never attained the proportions of a major scandal, such as might have become for the authorities a matter of concern. After a week or two of uneasy bliss, she would return to her husband, who was a biologist, and, more preoccupied with scientific many lacunæ. But I fancy this must be at least her third elopement within the last year."

"Nothing of the sort," said Mrs. Trumper, "I saw her only this afternoon, and I think it is monstrous the way people go on about that unfortunate little woman. She has every excuse, I am sure, with that preposterous husband. Personally I am devoted to her, and she feels just as I do about small nations. Even if what people say about her were true, I should consider it my duty to deny it. Besides, if we dons' wives didn't stick together where should we be?"

Doctor Pocock repressed the impulse to assure Mrs. Trumper that, whether the dons' wives stuck together or whether they disintegrated, her own position would remain unaffected.

Mr. Jericho jumped up and made one of his cuckoo-clock exits.

It was a well-known characteristic of the Trumpers that, having established an atmosphere of gloom and stagnation, they seemed to enjoy sitting on in it indefinitely. Emmeline felt they were never going. They appeared to be impervious to silences, yawns and references to the lateness of the hour. At last, as even bad things must eventually come to an end, they left. But their leave-takings, unlike those of Mr. Jericho, were as protracted as the finale of a Brückner symphony.

After kissing her father good night, Emmeline dragged herself wearily to bed. "I must really speak to him about his dinner parties," she thought, as she climbed the stairs, "but I know I never shall."

3

Emmeline's Visitors

Emmeline, hitherto, had never subjected herself to the discipline of a methodical routine. Her daily life had been conducted more or less according to moods and circumstances. In the ordering of her day caprice had reigned supreme.

Now all that sort of thing was going to be altered, and she set herself to draw up a schedule of her working hours. It was not, she found, an easy thing to do. It required a great deal of planning and she was a novice in the art of organization. At last she evolved something that seemed to her workmanlike, the kind of thing one might see posted up in a school or an office.

Rise 9 a.m. for 10.15 a.m.

10.15 a.m. to 11 a.m. Interval for breakfast.

11 a.m. to 12. Correspondence and perusal of The Times.

12 to 1 p.m. War work.

1 p.m. to 2.30 p.m. Interval for lunch.

2.30 to 3 p.m. Rest.

3 p.m. to 4 p.m. Interval for recreation.

4 p.m. to 5 p.m. War work.

5 p.m. to 6.30 p.m. Interval for tea.

6.30 p.m. to 7 p.m. War work.

After some deliberation she cut the last item on the programme. Her friends, when they came to tea, often arrived late and were apt to stay on till nearly dinner-time, and it might be difficult to get rid of them. Besides, she might want to hear all they had to say. Now that she was taking an active part in the war she felt it was important to keep in touch with the outer world. A duty not only to herself, but to her country. She might perhaps one day write an article for the newspapers: "What a Don's Daughter thinks about Peace Aims." Furthermore, she was afraid that her war work might be completed too soon, and she dreaded the idea of having to look out for another job.

"It makes a pretty full day," she reflected, as she pinned up the schedule over her writing-table.

After adhering rigidly to it for a week or two, she began to feel the benefits accruing from a well-ordered routine. She now understood why people found it a cure for neurosis and introspection.

Only an hour, you will notice, had been set aside for recreation. For the sake of her health, Emmeline decided to spend it in the open air. She had never really enjoyed walking in the town, and she disliked having to greet her acquaintances when she met them in the streets. It seemed so pointless. One might just as well nod and smile at any well-known building one passed. The contemplation of architecture was far pleasanter and more profitable than any desultory conversation one was likely to hold in a chance encounter in the streets. In order to avoid this she had, on many occasions, been obliged to rush suddenly into shops and buy things she didn't want. As her father had exhorted her to practise strict economy, she took to walking in the meadows instead. When she did so, she was accompanied by an imaginary dog. Upon the approach of anyone she knew, she would cry: "Toby! Toby!" and plunge into a shrubbery.

Executing one afternoon an evasion of this kind, on seeing someone she thought she knew, she was surprised and annoyed at finding herself pursued. She was preparing, at the risk of considerable personal inconvenience, to make her way still further into the bushes when she recognized the voice of her friend Caroline Paltry (it was unmistakable), and she knew that from her, as from the Hound of Heaven, there was no escape.

Lady Caroline Paltry was one of her old school friends. She had always been distinguished for her great vitality and overwhelming persistence. Even in the face of fearful odds she always succeeded in getting what she wanted, whether it were the friendship of another girl or a motor car.

"What on earth are you doing?" she asked the dishevelled Emmeline as she emerged from the bushes; "and I never knew you had a dog."

"I haven't a dog," replied Emmeline. "I was only trying to avoid you—I don't mean you in particular—just anyone."

"Oh, my dear, I hope you aren't getting morbid. You aren't depressed by the war, are you?"

Emmeline begged her not to continue the conversation. "Please don't speak to me here," she implored. "Come and have tea with me some afternoon, and we can have a nice talk."

"I am only here for a few days. I'm looking for a house."

"But you won't find one here," said Emmeline with a desperate desire to hasten her departure. "There's nothing here, only trees—and, of course, nature in a sort of way," she added, casting a deprecating glance at the laurels.

Caroline disliked being mystified, and began to feel that she was wasting her time. "I'll come and see you to-morrow at five, you quaint old thing," and tweaking Emmeline by the nose, a gesture reminiscent of their schooldays, she hurried away.

On the following afternoon Caroline arrived on the stroke of five.

"Well," she said, "I've found a house. It's about three miles from the town. It's modern and has very nice bathrooms and a good kitchen garden, and it's even described in the agent's catalogue as historical."

"Why historical?"

"It appears the Duchess of Windsor once looked at it and said: 'What an ugly house.' As a matter of fact it *is* rather ugly and it's hideously furnished, but it will suit my purposes well enough."

"What are your purposes, Caroline?"

"Oh, I'm running a canteen, looking after evacuees, organizing work parties and recreations for the troops, and then there's the Women's Guild."

"Stop," cried Emmeline. "You're making me giddy."

"And blood transfusion. Have you given your blood, Emmeline?"

"Now, Caroline, let us make the position quite clear. If you're going to start asking me questions about what I'm doing, giving me advice or trying in any way to run my life—"

Caroline did all these things instinctively and unconsciously, but if confronted with revolt she was disposed to be reasonable.

"I never interfere with people's lives," she protested. "I only try to do good and make others happy. I suppose you think that's silly?"

"No, dear," said Emmeline. "I think it's optimistic."

"Are you doing anything in the war?" Caroline continued. "Oh dear, I suppose I'm not to ask you that. I'm sure you aren't. But I don't care. I'm not taking a strong line about it. I'm too busy just now to bother about shirkers."

Stung by the word "shirkers," Emmeline said, "I'm sure I don't know why you should imagine I'm not doing any war work."

"Well, are you?"

"Of course I am."

"And may one be permitted to enquire what, exactly, it is?"

"Please don't talk like Henry James, Caroline, and I'm afraid I can't tell you what, exactly, it is."

"I don't know Henry James," Caroline replied. "And why ever not?"

"Well, you see, it happens to be rather secret."

"Oh, it's that kind, is it?" said Caroline, a little contemptuously.

Knowing Caroline's persistence in asking questions and what she called "getting to the bottom of things," Emmeline thought it advisable to change the topic.

"How is Nathaniel?" she asked.

Nathaniel, from Caroline's habitual way of speaking about him, might have been a dog or a pet rabbit, but he was actually her only child, aged three. She was bringing him up in her own way. When he was a baby she had taken him about with her everywhere in a dog basket, even to dinner parties, where she would deposit him in a corner of the room, and when the time came, would leave the table to feed him from the breast, a proceeding that some of her fellow guests were apt to consider eccentric. He was now being nourished exclusively on carrot juice and given psychological toys to play with. These consisted of things of different shapes that had to be put into holes, and it seemed probable that, later on, a severe course of psycho-analysis might be necessary. He was already beginning to show signs of phobias and repressions.

"Nathaniel?" Caroline repeated, as though trying to recall him to mind. "Oh, Nathaniel. He's all right, thank you. Francis is taking him to Southampton. I want him to get accustomed to the sound of bombs."

Francis was Caroline's husband. He was a composer; the white hope (thus a critic had described him) of English music. His compositions, though slightly lacking in originality and inclined to be long winded, were very much appreciated by the more serious of the English musical critics. He had originally embarked on a diplomatic career and had abandoned it in favour of music, but in so doing he did not abandon the principles of diplomacy. He set out to get to know all the most influential musical authorities in the country. He professed great humility, sought their advice, listened to their opinions and made Caroline ask them to luncheon. Although Caroline herself knew very little about music there was no greater propagandist of his work. She would run round and insist on music-shops displaying his wares in the window, she would expatiate on his genius to all and sundry, and she would bully reluctant conductors into performing his music. In fact, she took his musical career in hand (she took it in her stride), and the Provost of Unity had once suggested that Francis's compositions should be published under the title "Lady Caroline Paltry. My husband's works."

Caroline's parents, Lord and Lady Otterboy, were not at all like their daughter. They were very quiet people, and they lived in Ireland. Indeed, they were so quiet that Caroline, when she married Francis Paltry, forgot to invite them to the wedding. She afterwards reproached herself with this lapse of memory (as a rule she never forgot things) and wrote them a very nice letter.

The parlourmaid announced Mrs. Postlethwaite. It was this lady's custom, on her return from one of her elopements, to show herself about the town, to pay a round of visits, adapting in each case her demeanour to the character of the person on whom she called. To the romantic and compassionate she would pose as the erring wife who had repented. To the more austere she would speak of her great devotion to Herbert Postlethwaite. With Emmeline she took a rather more intimate line.

Caroline, unaware of Mrs. Postlethwaite's romantic reputation, thought her just a silly little woman and was bored by the intrusion.

"I must go now," she said, "I've got the hell of a lot to do to-morrow. All the goats are arriving and the wagonette and Mamma and Papa and some of the evacuees, and I've got to start planting potatoes on the lawn."

Emmeline put out her hand to ward off the tweak. She feared Mrs. Postlethwaite might be shocked by the familiarity of this farewell gesture.

As soon as Caroline had left the conversation assumed the character of a confession.

"Don't ever have anything to do with men, Emmeline," Mrs. Postlethwaite urged. "They bring nothing but trouble and disappointment into one's life. People call them 'gay deceivers.' They may be deceivers but they are seldom gay. Dreary and egotistic they are for the most part."

"Why don't you write a book about them?" asked Emmeline. "I'm sure you could."

"Oh, but I have, my dear," replied Mrs. Postlethwaite, looking surprised. "I'm always writing about them."

Emmeline had forgotten that Mrs. Postlethwaite was, among other things, an authoress. She had written several novels and a volume of short stories. They were not very good. Although full of dramatic incident, they were apt to be marred by too persistent an undercurrent of nostalgia. She was a woman of varied talents, which she exploited at moments when she was not wholly engrossed in love. Before she married Herbert Postlethwaite she had kept a perfumery shop in Cheltenham. Her business, after quite a brilliant start, had languished and eventually collapsed. She had studied perfumery with the intention of putting some of her own creations on the market. But these, like her novels, were of so nostalgic a character that they proved too much altogether for the retired colonels' wives who frequented her shop.

Herbert Postlethwaite, on a visit to his sister in Cheltenham, had rescued her from the debris of her scent shop. Spiteful people had said that
the marriage had been chiefly due to his biological interest in the lesser
apes. And indeed there was something rather monkeylike about Mrs.
Postlethwaite. She had a spiritual prehensile tail that was always getting
hold of things by the wrong end, and, mentally, she was apt suddenly to
stop and scratch herself. You wouldn't be in the least surprised to find
her hanging from the chandelier, indulging in disjointed introspection.
Now, in the more subtly cultured atmosphere of the university, she was
engaged in making ornamental articles for domestic use, which consisted for the most part in fanciful garments designed for covering
things up: teapot and telephone cosies, embroidered covers for address-
books and railway guides, hand-painted gas-mask containers. She appeared, with regard to inanimate objects, to be inspired with an almost
abnormal modesty.

Recently she and Mrs. Trumper had formed a great attachment for
one another. The friendship was a strange one, and it was difficult to see
what these two women could possibly have in common. Mr. Jericho,
who had an explanation for almost everything, said it was the expression of a secret prurience on the part of Mrs. Postlethwaite for culture
and respectability, on that of Mrs. Trumper for sex.

"Mrs. Trumper is taking me to a lecture on Federal Union this evening," Mrs. Postlethwaite announced. "I suggested she should come
here and fetch me. I hope you don't mind, Emmeline."

Emmeline did mind, but it was not her habit to betray her opinions
about other people's friends.

"I never knew you were interested in politics," she said.

"Oh, but I am, Emmeline. I'm interested in everything. That's why
I'm always so happy. And I'm sure that you, too, dear, would be happier
if you concerned yourself a little more with things of the outer world."

"I'm quite happy, thank you, Mrs. Postlethwaite. I'm sure Federal
Union wouldn't make me any happier than I am already."

"Oh, I don't mean only Federal Union. I meant you ought to go
about more and see more people. You sit all day in your room. You've
become almost a recluse, and it's bound in the end to make you intro-

spective and neurotic. Woman is by nature a gregarious animal. Herbert says so."

"Even though I don't go out very much, Mrs. Postlethwaite, I hear a good many things."

"Yes, indeed. I know you see a lot of Mr. Jericho, and the Provost of Unity, I hear, telephones to you every day. But that's not enough. There are so many clever and interesting people in the town, such thrilling people, dear. You ought to profit by them while you can. And won't you call me Antoinette? We know each other so well now that it seems quite absurd for you to go on calling me Mrs. Postlethwaite."

Emmeline thought that it would be equally absurd to call her Antoinette, especially as her identity card had revealed the fact that her name was really Mabel.

Mrs. Trumper put in her head at the door.

"I've just popped in," she said, "for Mrs. Postlethwaite. I find I have made a miscalculation of the time, and the meeting isn't till half past six. I thought I'd just look in and have a little chat."

Instinctively Mrs. Trumper chose the one uncomfortable chair in the room. Her spartan temperament impelled her always to make herself uncomfortable, and, incidentally, others as well.

"Won't you have a nicer chair, Mrs. Trumper?" said Emmeline, preparing to give up her own.

"No, Emmeline. This one does very well for me. I am constitutionally incapable of lounging."

Emmeline, as she looked at her, wondered on what principle she chose her clothes. It was obvious that vanity played no part in her choice. Knowing Mrs. Trumper's ascetic disposition, she concluded it was the nearest approach she could make in modern times to sackcloth and ashes. It was only in the event of a dinner party or a grand political meeting that she would attempt to decorate herself, and would then appear in a grey silk dress with, poised precariously on her sparse grey hair, a single diamond star that looked as if at any moment it were going to shoot. On these occasions she also wore a mantle of dejected white fur that had been removed from one of her husband's disused ceremonial gowns.

"Your room is so peaceful, Emmeline," she said, looking round her disparagingly; "a real haven of rest, a veritable sanctum."

"It's because of the double windows," Emmeline suggested.

"No, my dear. It's because of your own personality. The Provost of Unity, who, as far as I can make out, never says anything sensible, made a remark about you that for once in a way was quite true. He said you reminded him of the Nereid Gallene, the personification of the smooth and smiling sea."

"That was very kind of him," said Emmeline. "I suppose I am rather lethargic, and mother often used to tell me that I smirked."

"Oh, he didn't mean that," Mrs. Trumper interposed hurriedly. Although outspoken, she never willingly made mischief. "He didn't mean that at all. He meant that you give one an impression of calm and repose. You seem so aloof from this world of turmoil and strife, so wrapped up in your own quiet thoughts."

"I often feel," said Mrs. Postlethwaite, "that she would have made a wonderful nun."

"Nonsense," said Mrs. Trumper. She was a religious woman, but she had no use for nuns.

"Although I can well sympathise with your disinclination to expose yourself to the rough and tumble of an active social life. (I mean social, of course, in the proper sense of the word.) I often wonder if it is good for you."

"It is not always easy to know what is good for one," said Emmeline.

"No doubt," said Mrs. Trumper; "but I always say that we must have something definite to live for, whether it is politics, religion or art. I hope you will pardon me for saying so, Emmeline, but I sometimes feel that your mode of life is just a little—shall I say aimless."

"I suppose it is. I am sorry, Mrs. Trumper."

"Oh, don't apologise to me, my dear child. It's yourself I'm thinking about. I often wonder if you are really happy. I don't see how anyone can be really happy leading the kind of life you do. Perhaps you have spiritual consolations. Excuse me for asking rather a leading question, but have you ever tried to find God?"

"Oh, yes, Mrs. Trumper, I have indeed. At least I did once. But, like the people who looked for the Holy Grail, I felt I wouldn't know what to do with Him when I had found Him."

"Oh, hush dear," exclaimed Mrs. Postlethwaite.

"Now, Emmeline," said Mrs. Trumper, "you're not to talk like that. I won't have it. I know your father is an atheist, but that is no reason why his daughter should be blasphemous."

"Father isn't an atheist," Emmeline protested, "and I didn't intend to be blasphemous. I only meant that I wasn't able to develop a talent for religion. It is possibly the fault of my upbringing, but I don't want to blame Papa and Mamma for anything. I have always had wrong-headed ideas about God. It seems to be in my nature. When I was a child I used to think that the Day of Judgement meant that we were all going to judge God, and I still don't see why not."

Mrs. Trumper was rather taken aback by this curious point of view. She attributed it to an inadequate comprehension of the nature of original sin, and was preparing to explain it. But Emmeline had decided that it was time to put an end to what, she felt, was beginning to amount to religious persecution.

"I think, Mrs. Trumper," she said, "it is wiser for us not to go on talking about religion. It is obvious that our views would not be the same. Besides, it is boring Mrs. Postlethwaite—I mean Antoinette," she corrected herself with an internal giggle.

"Not at all, Emmeline. I always enjoy a serious discusson."

"This is hardly serious," said Mrs. Trumper, looking at her watch, "and in any case it is time to be going."

Mrs. Trumper left with the uneasy feeling that she had been worsted by an inexperienced girl, a thought that was galling to one accustomed to hold her own in debate. She also left Emmeline in a state of uneasiness. "This sort of thing," she thought, "is disturbing to my peace of mind. It will have to be stopped. If people start coming into the house and probing into my soul, life will become unbearable."

Had she known it she would have felt that she was being, at that moment, amply revenged.

On arriving at the Pandemonian, Mrs. Trumper and Mrs. Postlethwaite found that the meeting had been postponed for an hour. The place was dark and deserted, and, in spite of Mrs. Trumper's persistence, remained as impregnable as a mediæval fortress. It had begun to rain. They were far from the houses of anyone they knew and they were unable to find a taxi. There was no shelter in the immediate neighbourhood except a public-house, into which their position in the university debarred them from penetrating. And so the two ladies were obliged to wander about disconsolately in the rain until the doors opened.

4

Two Telephones and an Intermezzo

The Provost of Unity had acquired, a little irrelevantly perhaps, a reputation for eccentricity. A Head of a college, on attaining an advanced age (and the Provost was well over seventy) has only one alternative before him: either to end his life in an amiable dotage or else to assume an aura of oddity. He must either become a "dear old man" or an eccentric. The Provost, with his malicious understanding of human nature, his irascibility and his impatience of bores, could never have settled down into being a dear old man. He was therefore inclined to welcome the reputation that had been thrust upon him, and he knew that eccentricity covers a multitude of sins.

Of late this once almost too prevalent trait has become increasingly rare, and those who lament the preponderance of the humdrum, who are on the look-out for symptoms of crankiness in their colleagues, are apt to clutch a little too eagerly at any straw.

It was said that some years ago the Provost had become entangled in a communist procession in the High Street and had been hailed as friend and comrade by some undergraduates from Corpus Diaboli. After this incident he was supposed to have made a vow never to cross the High Street again and had, ever since, remained immured within the precincts of Unity College.

It was also alleged that he had fired a number of shots from his window at the venerable Dean of Dimchurch.

Like many legends, both these stories had some foundation in fact. It was true that the Provost had been hustled during a communist demonstration, but the reason why he stayed so much at home was because he preferred doing so. When he heard of his supposed vow, he made no efforts to deny it, foreseeing that it would provide him with an excellent excuse to refuse the invitations of certain dons who lived on the further side of the High Street. It was also true that he had fired a gun out of his window, but it was at a grey squirrel in his garden, not at the Dean of Dimchurch, and the Dean, who happened to be in the neighbourhood, had been startled.

Though avoiding the hospitality of others, the Provost was far from being a recluse. He was fond of company. He liked seeing people, but he preferred seeing them in his own house. He was essentially a host.

It has been said that humanity may be roughly divided into hosts and guests. A psychologist has explained the types as representing two kinds of will, the will to power and the will to subjection. In the case of the Provost the explanation is undoubtedly a sound one. In his own house he had people more or less at his mercy. If they annoyed him he could be rude to them and, if their physique permitted, kick them out. In other people's houses he was bereft of the necessary authority to deal with any unpleasantness which, in his own, he was inclined to welcome. And that is why he invariably refused invitations, even to the homes of the grand and the agreeable.

He spent most of his time in his vaulted neo-Gothic study, surrounded by early editions and fragments of Greek archaic sculpture, writing his memoirs in a large volume bound in vellum. It was unlikely that these could be published until after his death, and when they were, they would undoubtedly cause a certain amount of surprise and annoyance to a great many grandchildren.

In spite of a pronounced disregard for the feelings of others, the Provost concealed beneath a certain spikiness the sensitive and kindly nature of the hedgehog. He was inclined even to sentimentality. Of this he was fully aware and he considered it an inappropriate weakness that did not fit in at all well with the character he had evolved for himself. The ruthlessness, of which even his best friends often had cause to complain, was in reality a sort of anti-aircraft barrage against the insidious attacks of sentiment. It was a great tribute to the Provost's charm and entertainment-value, as well as to the excellence of his cuisine, that people put up with as much as they did.

In his youth he had been considered one of the best-looking young men of his day. Now, at the age of seventy-three, his features, though battered by time, still resembled those of the Greek head on his mantelpiece given him many years ago by an admirer "because it was so like him."

He was a man of varied interests. He had a great capacity for enjoyment. Latterly his chief enjoyment seemed to be conversing with his friends on the telephone. He was in the habit of ringing up every day one or two of a chosen group of confidants, and with these he would talk on any subject in which, at the moment, he happened to be interested: it might be Greek antiquities, a question of moral philosophy or more often merely local gossip. He found that conversation was more untrammelled when the people to whom he spoke were invisible. The contact was impersonal and less likely to arouse emotions inimical to intellectual discernment. It was a transaction satisfactory to both parties. Unable to see his victims wince, he was less tempted to wound, and conversation was carried on in a kinder, less provocative tone.

It was to Emmeline that the Provost telephoned most frequently. He was devoted to her. He liked to hear the gentle, drowsily malicious intonations of her voice. She was also the only one of his friends whose feelings he never felt impelled to hurt. Perhaps because he knew that she would be the last person to try and take advantage of any display of tenderness. And, even if she had, he would perhaps have welcomed it. The self-portrait he had so carefully composed would appear all the more realistic if there were in it just one weak spot.

*

Emmeline had not yet quite recovered from her resentment of Mrs. Trumper's catechism and, when the Provost rang her up, she complained bitterly of the indiscreet questionings she had been subjected to.

"Your little controversy," said the Provost, "takes me back to the days of my youth. I so rarely hear His name mentioned nowadays. Even in the newspapers His role seems to have been taken over by Time. In the last war they were always saying: "God is on our side." Now they say: "Time is on our side." No doubt, having been told that He is on the side of big battalions, they feel that nothing much can be expected of Him until we attain parity of armaments. By the way," he broke off, knowing that the topic often led him into a vein of rather facile humour, "I had a visit yesterday from Lady Caroline Paltry and her parents. That is to say she left them with me while she went to do her shopping. They are an amiable couple, but their views, such as they have, seem a trifle out of date and, like the Eminent Personage we have just been discussing, they seem to know very little about what is happening in the world. Lord Otterboy asked me if we had had any visits from the Zeppelins."

"Poor things," said Emmeline. "Caroline never tells them anything and they only read *The Times*."

"I dare say she hasn't the leisure. She appears to be a very active young woman. Indeed all the ladies here, with the exception of yourself, seem to be displaying great energy, and Mrs. Postlethwaite, I understand, is writing another book."

"Oh, dear," said Emmeline. "I hadn't heard."

"Poor William Organ," continued the Provost, "will, I fear, once again be embarrassed by his disciple."

"Her first book was, I remember, dedicated to him."

"And her style was so closely modelled on his that one of the critics took it to be a parody. It is the only literary success that poor Mrs. Postlethwaite has ever had. It is pleasant nowadays, when authors are so conceited, to find such a touching example of literary devotion. Where you or I would have at our bedside a volume of Lucian, Voltaire or Simenon, at hers you will find The Portrait of a Genius, The Fountain-Pen or the Journey of a Soul. I lay no claim to having penetrated into the lady's bedchamber. The information was given me in a moment of abandon by Herbert Postlethwaite. He told me that he frequently found her asleep with one of these volumes open in her hands. A charming picture."

"She doesn't often speak to me about her literary work," said Emmeline, "but she did once tell me that what appealed to her in his books was the refined and spiritual manner in which he handled her favourite theme—and you can guess what that is."

"Oh, good heavens," exclaimed the Provost. "That reminds me. It was really the reason I rang you up. A most astonishing piece of news. So astonishing, in fact, that, as in Madame de Sévigné's famous letter, I ought to herald its announcement with a thousand adjectives of amazement." He paused. "I do hope Jericho hasn't told you already. I don't wish to be the purveyor of a twice-told tale."

"I can't say until I know what it is."

Detecting a note of eagerness in Emmeline's voice, the Provost displayed further hesitation.

"It's such an important piece of news (almost a military bulletin), that perhaps I oughtn't to tell you without further confirmation."

"As you please," said Emmeline. He was being too much like Juliet's nurse.

At that moment a tumult arose in the passage outside Emmeline's room. Caroline appeared, pushing before her an elderly and bewildered couple. "Do you mind my leaving Papa and Mamma with you for a few minutes?" she asked. "I've got to rush round to the Blood Transfusion Office and give some blood. I shan't be long. It's just round the corner. I tried to leave them with your father, but he said he was going out."

The Otterboys seemed very glad to sit down.

"We are not as young as we were," said Lady Otterboy, "and Caroline is always on the dash."

They were rather pathetic, Emmeline thought. Every idea they had ever had about anything seemed to have been, at one time or another, demolished by their daughter. Now they were left with no ideas at all and Lord Otterboy appeared to have lost his memory.

"We are returning to Ireland tomorrow," said Lady Otterboy. "We had thought of making a longer stay, but we find everything here is so very uncomfortable."

"Would you believe it?" said Lord Otterboy. "No marmalade."

"Yes," said Lady Otterboy. "Ever since he can remember, Otterboy has been accustomed to have marmalade for his breakfast, and here there is none to be had. Even Caroline can't get it. We were warned about the butter and we brought a large quantity from Ireland, but Caroline has given it all to the evacuees."

More and more they reminded Emmeline of the Babes in the Wood.

"It seems nice and quiet here," said Lady Otterboy. "It is not so quiet in Caroline's house. I thought I heard some bombs falling last night, but it turned out to be Caroline banging doors upstairs."

"Everything is so different here from what it was when I was an undergraduate," Lord Otterboy complained.

"My dear," said his wife, "you know perfectly well you were at Cambridge."

"I mean to say," Lord Otterboy persisted, "the type of undergraduate has very much altered since my day. A more weedy looking set of fellows I never saw."

Emmeline was debating whether it were part of her duties to defend the undergraduates when Caroline returned.

"They wanted me to lie down after giving my blood," she said. "I told them I never lay down during the day, and anyhow I hadn't time."

"My grandfather always used to recommend bleeding," said Lady Otterboy.

"And really," continued Caroline, "one does meet people in odd places nowadays. I should never have expected to find the 'versatile peer' working in the Blood Transfusion Service."

"What peer is that?" enquired Lady Otterboy.

"Lord FitzCricket," said Caroline.

"Old Puggy's son," was Lord Otterboy's comment.

"Don't you remember, Mamma? He came to our wedding wearing a mask."

"We weren't there," said Lady Otterboy.

"Come on," said Caroline. "We've got to get back before the black-out."

A growling noise was coming from the telephone. Emmeline, at the moment of Caroline's irruption, had forgotten to replace the receiver. She was reminded of the sensational piece of news that the Provost had promised her and was anxious to hear it. She reflected however that, in omitting to put back the receiver, she had probably prevented him from making any further calls for some considerable period and consequently he would not be in the best of tempers. She thought of Mr. Jericho. She was a little ashamed of her curiosity. She liked to be told news, but she preferred not to have to ask for it. At the same time she knew that Mr. Jericho would be very pleased to tell her, and would moreover be able to supply a more comprehensive selection of details than the Provost.

Mr. Jericho understood at once.

"You mean the Trumper scandal."

"?"

"Professor Trumper."

"What has he done?"

It appeared that one day, when Mrs. Trumper was in London and Mr. Postlethwaite had gone to Cheltenham to see his sister, the Professor and Mrs. Postlethwaite were seen lunching together at the Beehive, a small restaurant in an obscure side street to which people went when they didn't wish to be seen, so that to be seen there was almost a confession of guilt.

"It is certainly strange," said Emmeline, "but I don't see that it implies anything."

"Ah, but that is not all," went on Mr. Jericho. "You know that awful little Montmorency boy. He is continually stopping me in the street to tell me some scurrilous tale or other. It is most humiliating and makes me feel as if I had the reputation of being only interested in trivial things. His stories are very often untrue, but what he told me the other day was so strange and fantastic that I don't believe he has the imagination to have invented it. What would you say was the most incongruous, the most uninspiring spot for a lovers' rendezvous?"

"I'm unlikely to know," said Emmeline. "I haven't much experience in such matters."

"Well, you might perhaps guess. For now I come to think of it, given the persons concerned, the place might be considered extremely suitable."

"The pathological laboratory?" suggested Emmeline.

"Very near," said Mr. Jericho. "No, it was the University Museum."

The University Museum faces Kimble College, and had it been of later date might appear to have originated in a determination on the part of its architect to go one better. It is with the interior that we are concerned, and here the architect has fairly let himself go, and given free rein to his Gothic imagination. The visitor penetrates through Venetian mauresque cloisters into a spacious garth, lit from above by a diamond-paned glass roof supported on slender iron columns and arches decorated in the Gothic style. The place is crowded with cases containing fossils and stuffed birds interspersed with gigantic reconstructions of the skeletons of prehistoric monsters. A strong aroma of taxidermy prevails throughout and the ensemble creates the impression of a joint design by Darwin and the Tractarians.

"I will try to make my narration as dramatic as possible," said Mr. Jericho. "One afternoon, Montmorency and two of his friends paid a visit to the Museum. Overawed by the strangeness of the scene, they contemplated it for a while in silence. At first they thought the place was deserted, but hearing suspicious sounds coming from behind one of the fossil cases, they approached stealthily. Peering through the skeleton of the dinoceras, or it may have been the iguanodon, they espied the Professor and Mrs. Postlethwaite fondling one another."

To Emmeline's sensitive imagination the vision was repellent.

"There are some ideas," she said, "that are too preposterous to be entertained—even in war-time."

5

—◦◦◦—

Visit of an Eminent Politician

Saturday night at Cato's Restaurant was always a very jubilant affair. Since the closing down of the dining clubs, it was the only place where conviviality could still be found. Sometimes, however, it was apt to be overdone, and the meditations of visiting journalists were disturbed by community singing or the throwing about of comestibles. It was certain that, within this festive hall, tragedy was never allowed to rear its ugly head and, however bad the news might be, the radiant faces and the shrieks of merry laughter created always the impression of a victory dinner.

Billy Montmorency was entertaining a party consisting of four or five undergraduates and a middle-aged gentleman whose portly sprightliness and very deliberate manner of speaking proclaimed him a personage of some importance.

Billy had come to the university at the beginning of the war with the intention of reviving the spirit of the nineties. It had been conveyed to him discreetly and, in one or two instances, painfully, that it was neither the time nor the place and that, in any case, he did not possess the requisite personality to carry out so ambitious and difficult a project. He had been, for a time, one of Mr. Jericho's pupils, but, instead of availing himself of his tutor's extensive learning, he preferred to regale him with information of rather too personal a nature, and Mr. Jericho had thought it wiser to discontinue his tuition. Billy's efforts to attain social prominence by other methods having failed, he was obliged to content himself with giving dinner parties to undergraduates who allowed him to pay the bill without thinking it necessary to pay any further attention to him in return.

The important middle-aged guest was no other than the famous Mr. "Lollipop" Jenkins. ("Lollipop" was the nickname he was known by in the House of Commons.) He had been invited by Jimmie Guggenheim Junior, an American undergraduate who, though continually exhorted by his parents to return to America, had remained obdurate to their entreaties and was staying on to "see the old country through." He was very much impressed by Mr. Jenkins and indeed Mr. Jenkins had all the qualifications for impressing an American undergraduate.

Mr. Jenkins had been an undergraduate at the university himself and his record had been extremely brilliant. He had gained a considerable reputation by the mock-heroic speeches he was in the habit of making at debates and dining clubs.

On leaving the playground of the university and embarking on the more serious activities of political life he continued to fulfil the promise of all that had been expected of him. In the course of an unchequered career he had been in turn author, journalist and member of Parliament and now he was all three at once. His political novels, his biographies of statesmen ran into countless editions; high prices were paid for his articles, his conversation was listened to with respect at London luncheon parties. In the eyes of the world he was a success. Yet as he approached middle age his more thoughtful friends began to suspect that something was going a little wrong. Although outwardly the rose retained its rubicund exterior intact, they scented the presence of the invisible worm.

It was to be expected, of course, that as he grew more successful and more important he should put aside something of the sparkle and gaiety of youth. He seemed, however, reluctant to abandon altogether the role of *enfant terrible* that, as a young man, he had played in so engaging a manner, and people began to feel that there was something really rather terrible about an *enfant terrible* who was growing middle-aged and slightly pompous. The mock-heroic speeches he had made as an undergraduate he now delivered in deadly earnest. They were still enlivened with little jokes. Formerly designed solely to amuse, their function was now to prove a point and they were sometimes a little laboured.

However, there was one very endearing trait in Mr. Jenkins' character, and that was the sentimental affection he felt for his old college. Whenever his activities permitted he would revisit the place and relive the memory of his undergraduate days. "You can't think what this means to me," he had said to Mr. Guggenheim Junior as they passed through Dimchurch Quad, and the tone in which the words were spoken had given that tough young man a lump in his throat.

It was also to his credit that he seemed to prefer the company of quite unimportant young men to that of many of his wealthy and influential acquaintances. He appreciated the necessity of keeping in touch with the representatives of the coming generation so that when they knocked on the door he would be there to greet them.

It will be unnecessary to describe the rest of the party in detail. It consisted of typical undergraduates such as you will find in the pages of any recent fiction dealing with university life, and nothing very striking in the way of novelty has sprung up since the war. Appearances, perhaps, have had a tendency to grow a little less distinctive. One young man, chinless and rather inane looking, was a pure mathematician. Another, who had the air of a faded debutante, was a rugger blue or something of the sort.

"You can imagine," said Billy, "what a shock I got when I caught sight of them through those bones."

"Cut it out Billy," snapped Mr. Guggenheim. "We've had enough of that yarn."

"Oh, all right," said Billy plaintively. "But you can understand my feeling sore. Before she took up with old Trump I rather fancy she had her eye on me."

Mr. Jenkins gave him an angry look. It was intolerable that, while everyone else at the table was treating him with due deference, his conversation should be continually interrupted by this young man's fatuous remarks.

Mr. Jenkins was not entirely satisfied with the way in which the university was taking the war. His visit, this time, had been made in the interests of mass observation. He was, perhaps, a little over-burdened with a sense of responsibility. He had convinced himself that it was largely owing to his vigorous articles and speeches that his unarmed and apathetic country had at last been persuaded to stand up to the dictators. There was a story in circulation that, on being rebuked by an elderly general in a train for not giving up his seat to a man in uniform, he had exclaimed: "If it had not been for me you would never have had your war." The story was no doubt untrue, but it was symbolical.

He had visited his former tutor, the Provost of Unity, a man he had idolized in his undergraduate days, and had found him a little unresponsive. The evening before, Mr. Jenkins had given a lecture at the Pandemonian to an audience composed chiefly of dons and their wives, members of Cheatham House and people from the various government departments evacuated to the city. Towards the end of his lecture, carried away by his eloquence, he had exhorted them to meet the foe with blazing eyes. The Provost had complimented him on the success of his oratory and said that he heard that so many people were now walking about the streets with blazing eyes that torches were no longer necessary in the black-out.

It was sad, thought Mr. Jenkins, that a man whose intellect he had once so greatly respected should have degenerated into a flippant buffoon. He had met with other disappointments. He had failed to persuade Mr. Jericho that, although the philosophy of history was all very well in peace-time, his talents would be better employed in the army, and Doctor Pocock had firmly refused to discuss politics.

"Yes," said Billy, "I fancy she had her eye on me."

Mr. Guggenheim Junior tried to kick him under the table, but kicked the pure mathematician instead. The pure mathematician, who was getting a little tipsy, suddenly produced a chin and assumed an air of truculence. Mr. Guggenheim Junior knew that on Saturday nights dinner parties were apt to end in dissension, and a large piece of Yorkshire pudding, apparently aimed at Billy, had just landed on the table. "It's getting a bit noisy here," he said to Mr. Jenkins. "Shall we go over to my rooms right now—I mean now?" he corrected himself.

Mr. Jenkins was loth to lose the rest of his audience. "Perhaps some of you fellows will come and join us?" he said, emphasising the word "some" in a way that rather markedly excluded Billy. To reinforce his point he shook hands with Billy and thanked him for an agreeable evening. At that moment the press photographer Mr. Jenkins had ordered suddenly appeared and took a photograph of him in the act. The photograph that was subsequently published in several of the illustrated papers was a source of gratification to Billy, but of some embarrassment to Mr. Jenkins.

6

—⟨∾∕∾⟩—

The Lives of the Saints

As Emmeline progressed with her work she found herself taking a growing interest in the figures of the saints she was engaged in destroying. She knew very little about their lives and habits, and as she examined more closely their sheep-like faces and their stiff byzantine draperies she began to wonder what manner of men and women they had been.

Her interest in them was somewhat akin to the melancholy concern she used to feel for the fine old houses she saw being pulled down in London in the days before the war. Of course, in her case, the destruction was not to make way for some hideous hotel or for a block of modern flats, and it was justified by the fact that it was war work. Nevertheless she was beset by a slight feeling of compunction. People, she thought, so often destroy things light-heartedly, without ever bothering to find out anything about them. However useless her war work might be, she was determined that there should be nothing about it that could be considered frivolous or light-hearted.

She went to her father's library to see what books she could find on the subject of hagiology. They were most of them rather bulky, but there was one, the Reverend Alban Butler's "Lives of the Saints," that was a little shorter than the others, and she noticed on the title page that it had been published with the direct sanction of Cardinal Manning.

Once, as a child, during a slight attack of religious mania, she had been very much taken with the idea of becoming a saint herself. She had consulted a Roman Catholic governess about it and had been told that, in order to do so, at least two accredited miracles would be necessary. This seemed a serious drawback, but not an insuperable one. There would no doubt be witnesses who could be bought. After dallying with the idea for a time she had abandoned it in favour of becoming a political hostess. Later on, when she came to read Shakespeare, she decided, on the advice of Cardinal Wolsey, to fling away ambition altogether.

Emmeline had no very great aptitude for research work, and it was perhaps for this reason that the impressions she gathered from her reading were inclined to be superficial. She also had a tendency to concentrate on the female saints, and she rather deliberately avoided those that were better known, lest she should be unduly influenced by the glamour of their reputation. In her initial investigations she was not very fortunate.

St. Gertrude, she read, although possessed of the greatest natural talents, was penetrated and entirely filled with the deepest sentiments of her own nothingness. She longed for death and spent most of her time sighing. In the author's words, "The Saint, as a chaste turtle, never interrupted her sweet sighs and moans." Emmeline thought she must have been a rather trying woman to live with, and passed on to St. Hedwig, Duchess of Poland. This saint also professed great humility and was often seen to kiss the ground where a virtuous person had knelt in the church. No provocation could ever make her show the least sign of emotion or anger. She, too, must have been a rather irritating woman, Emmeline thought. After persuading her husband to build a monastery for nuns at Trebnitz, St. Hedwig refused to live with him any more and would only meet him in public places. She ate very little and dressed so badly that even the nuns complained about it.

Emmeline turned to an earlier period. Saint Olympias, who lived in the fifth century and was described as "a widow," never had a bath and, like St. Hedwig, was very badly dressed. She suffered a good deal from the gossip of her neighbours and frequently appeared in the law-courts. On one occasion she had the bailiffs in the house. All these things induced a chronic state of melancholy. The only bright spot in her life appeared to have been the nice letters she had from St. Chrysostom exhorting her to cheer up.

The character of St. Jane was a little more spirited. At the age of eight she rose from her father's table on perceiving a heretic among the guests. Emmeline couldn't help thinking that she must have been a nasty little prig and that probably the heretic was very glad when she left. "If I were to do that here," she said to herself, "I should never get a square meal at all." She had a poor opinion of St. Paula, who was in the habit of hiding her inability to argue under the cover of violent public abuse. Whenever anyone asked her embarrassing questions about the damnation of unborn babes and the nature of the resurrection, "from henceforth she so detested that man and all of the same opinions that she publicly proclaimed them to be enemies of the Lord." Emmeline knew of a great many artists, scientists and politicians who behaved just like this and were never likely to be canonized.

Emmeline tried hard not to allow herself to be prejudiced and she feared that she had somehow missed the point of these people's lives. As she made a habit of reading for edification as well as for instruction, she persevered with her studies, hoping eventually to come across some useful example, some helpful rule of life. Mrs. Trumper's reproach still rankled. She realised, of course, that the author had been a little too insistent on certain episodes in the lives of the saints that he would have been better advised to gloss over and that he was more preoccupied with questions of doctrine than with morals and manners. She wondered if it might not have been wiser to have consulted some record that was more direct and less coloured by the author's personal views. Yet the book had been approved by Cardinal Manning and the facts at least must be correct. She thought that it might be more profitable to pay less attention to biographical aspects and to study the main characteristics of saintliness and the qualities by which these men and women had achieved canonization.

Asceticism, she knew, was one of the most important of these and she took great pains to try and understand the difference between the austerities practised by dervishes and fakirs and those practised by the saints. She remembered that St. Paul had said that asceticism was not much good without charity and yet this was a quality in which most of the notable ascetics appeared to be lacking. In many cases mortification of the flesh seemed to her to have been a little overdone and not very different from the asceticism of the fakirs, but she was pleased by the account of a female saint who despised her body to such an extent that she offered it to all comers. If Mrs. Postlethwaite, she thought, were to adopt that line, she too might achieve sainthood. And she was personally encouraged by the description of the Fathers of the Desert who "trained not only to hard manual labour, but to that which was apparently as useless as it was hard, often unmade at night the mats they had plaited during the day." As for mortification of the spirit, she suspected that it was too often a form of inverted snobbishness and led to an inward conceit that was worse than indulgence.

The martyrs, of course, were in a different category. But there had been martyrs on both sides, and those who eventually got the upper hand distributed the praise.

However, at the end of her investigations she had to admit that she had come across one or two characters who answered to her personal conception of saintliness, but there were far too many of whom she wondered how they had managed to be made saints at all. She attributed it to backstairs influence or to a talent for publicity.

She came to the conclusion that the Community of Saints was an essentially Catholic institution, a sort of Upper House like the Senate or the House of Lords, and that there were no conspicuous examples of virtue and courage that could not equally well be found in the annals of secular history. Anyhow, she told herself, in a work of destruction the innocent and the guilty must suffer alike. And she continued, with equanimity, to unpick the column of St. Simeon Stylites.

7

⟞⟋∿⟍⟝

The Professor's Love Story

The "affaire" between the Professor and Mrs. Postlethwaite was, according to rumour, beginning to assume the proportions of one of the great romances of history. References were made to Eloise and Abelard, Numa and Egeria, Pericles and Aspasia. The Provost thought it resembled the story of Hero and Leander, the Hellespont being represented by the Professor's physique.

There were speculations as to whether Mrs. Trumper and Mr. Postlethwaite had any idea of what was going on. It was almost certain that Mr. Postlethwaite had not, and that, in any case, he would not have very much cared. He was more interested in the experimental researches he was carrying out with the assistance of his goats, guinea-pigs and monkeys. It was even said of him that he was more solicitous of their welfare than of that of his wife, and indeed at times they gave him far more anxiety. They were apt to play too prominent a part in college life.

As a special privilege, because he was engaged in work of national importance, he was allowed to keep his animals in an outhouse adjoining Dimchurch College. But the permission was very often on the point of being withdrawn. Owing to imperfect supervision on the part of the scout deputed to tend them, they were continually getting out of their cages. A guinea-pig that had secreted itself in Mrs. Postlethwaite's bicycle basket had nearly caused a serious accident by suddenly appearing while she was bicycling down the High Street, and Mrs. Trumper had been butted by a goat on her way to early communion. But it was the lesser apes that caused the greatest trouble. On one occasion they had managed to find their way into the Dean of Dimchurch's study. Being very short sighted, he had at first mistaken them for a deputation of undergraduates and had been much annoyed at having wasted an unctuous welcome.

The Provost of Unity had decided to give a luncheon party for the Trumpers and the Postlethwaites, together with three observers in the shape of Mr. Jericho, Emmeline and her father. Emmeline had at first declined the invitation (Live and let live was her motto), but the Provost had insisted so vehemently that she had ended by accepting.

The gathering had something of the character of an inquisition.

The Provost was resolved that there should be no lack of material aids to the investigation of truth, and produced for the occasion a rare and heady vintage, with which the glasses of the guests were constantly replenished.

The first thing to be noticed was that the Professor was less talkative than usual. It is true that the Provost was perhaps the only member of the university by whom the Professor was a little intimidated. Too often his monologues had been abruptly cut short by one of the Provost's trenchant remarks. It was also noticed that he avoided addressing Mrs. Postlethwaite and that he displayed an unusual tenderness towards his wife.

Mrs. Postlethwaite seemed a little nervous, and her simian restlessness was very much in evidence. She was dressed more quietly than usual. There were none of the bright colours in which she habitually disported herself. None of the glittering gipsy-like beads and feathered fantasies.

"Have you ever been to the University Museum, Mrs. Postlethwaite?" asked the Provost. "It is a curious place and well worth a visit. I ask because so few people seem to know it. Although I am not an admirer of reconstructions of prehistoric skeletons I am forced to admit that in these Gothic surroundings they acquire a certain beauty."

"I have never been there," said Mrs. Postlethwaite.

"You should go," said the Provost.

"How is your book getting on?" asked Emmeline.

The change of subject seemed more welcome to Mrs. Postlethwaite than to the Provost. "Oh, thank you, Emmeline," she cried with evident relief. "It is very kind of you to ask. It's getting on very well. I've nearly finished it."

"I always enjoy your love scenes," said Mr. Jericho.

"Oh, nonsense, Mr. Jericho. I'm sure you never read anything so frivolous as my poor little books."

"Indeed I do," said Mr. Jericho, "and I certainly don't consider them frivolous. If anything, they err too much on the serious side."

"I find it hard," Mrs. Postlethwaite sighed, "to strike a happy medium."

"That," said Doctor Pocock, "is a difficulty we all suffer from."

"May I say that I also enjoy Mrs. Postlethwaite's books," said the Provost, "and even the earnest Trumper no doubt—"

"He never has time to read novels," interposed Mrs. Trumper hurriedly. "You couldn't expect it of him. And I myself find very little time for light literature, especially now that I am working at Cheatham House."

"Tell us, Mrs. Trumper," said the Provost, "between four walls, what it is you really do at Cheatham House? I know you are bound by the strictest secrecy, but you might perhaps give us some rough idea. I always long to know what goes on inside that mysterious building."

Cheatham House had been evacuated to the university at the beginning of the war. It was supposed to be a kind of sublimated branch of the Foreign Office and was said to be concerned with theories rather than realities. From time to time questions had arisen as to its utility, and letters were written to the newspapers complaining of a waste of public money. The only signs of extravagance that were visible to the outside world were the lorries that were continually seen leaving the building with large quantities of waste paper. Investigations, however, proved that, although the institution did not appear to be doing much good, it was doing very little harm, and it was allowed to continue its activities. Latterly the secrecy that surrounded it had been redoubled. A stockade had been erected outside the main entrance, passwords were required to gain admittance, and the building had become more mysterious and impenetrable than ever.

Mrs. Trumper was torn between the desire to maintain an air of secrecy and at the same time to prove how useful she was being.

"Well," she said, "I can't tell you very much. I have to read a great many foreign newspapers."

"That must be nice," said Mrs. Postlethwaite.

"And of course," continued Mrs. Trumper, "one has the usual difficulty in getting one's views accepted."

At that moment Mr. Postlethwaite, who had appeared to be in a state of coma, suddenly woke up and gave a stirring account of the polemics of his early life. It was interesting, but, under the circumstances, not at all what was wanted. Fortified by the Provost's good wine, nothing could silence him. His narration continued throughout the rest of the luncheon, and all efforts to divert the conversation into more relevant channels were vain.

"Well," said the Provost to Emmeline, who had remained behind after the others had left, "I fear we have got no further than we were before."

"I often wonder," said Emmeline, "if it isn't a mistake to try and find out too much about things."

"Little obscurantist," said the Provost.

8

—⟨↝⟩—

Poltergeist

Doctor Pocock had been suffering from an attack of influenza. He was now convalescent and was sitting in his oak-panelled bedroom propped up on his pillows. Emmeline sat at his bedside, reading aloud to him from a book by Gertrude Stein.

"In sometimes there is always and a little more than Arthur if they are mating and there are exceptions. Rules are not what are not sometimes and always with feathers and parallelograms are longer and not warmer when exceptions are there. A cucumber can be its own father if wanted and not wanted and not not wanted so a cucumber can be its own father if fathers are wanted and not wanted and a father can be its own cucumber if feathers are wanted and not exceptions. Exceptions are circular and have little extremities that shake and are less than more and fewer than something."

"Thank you, dear," said Doctor Pocock. "That is enough for the present. I find I am unable to take in very much at a time."

Emmeline closed the book and was preparing to return to her work when Mr. Jericho appeared. He was very excited about the accounts that had just reached him of sensational happenings at Cheatham House. A poltergeist had broken into the place and was creating havoc there. The most extraordinary and unaccountable things occurred every night and sometimes during the day. All the books in the reference library were found to have been taken out and replaced upside down. Important maps had been defaced by ink. Secret and confidential documents were littered all over the garden and had been picked up by unauthorized persons. Sentences were scribbled on the walls in a language that not even the most erudite professors could understand. Some of the rooms had been rendered uninhabitable by the most appalling smell. The telephones were constantly ringing and, when answered, rude words were shouted from the other end, and when the Dean of Dimchurch (whom Destiny seems to have selected for an Aunt Sally) arrived for purposes of exorcism, he had been struck down by a heavy volume of code. Investigations led to the conclusion that these things could not possibly have been done by any human agency.

Mrs. Trumper had discovered, in a scientific work on the subject, that a poltergeist was nearly always associated with the presence of an idiot child, and had insisted on several junior members of the personnel being removed. Beyond creating a certain amount of ill-feeling this measure had not had the slightest effect. The poltergeist continued to haunt the building and seemed to be doing everything within its power to make the lives of the inmates a burden to them.

Doctor Pocock was very interested. His philosophical doctrines did not preclude belief in the supernatural as long as his own particular theories were not embarrassed.

"Mr. Sacheverell Sitwell," he said, "has recently written a book on the subject. I wonder if they have thought of calling him in."

"I fancy he has only a literary interest in the matter," said Mr. Jericho. "I don't think he has had any practical experience. And I feel that if Mrs. Trumper is unable to deal with the situation, nobody can. In any case I don't suppose they would care to have their troubles settled by anyone from outside. I hear they have refused offers of assistance from the Society of Psychical Research."

"It is dreadful to think of their peace of mind being disturbed in this way," said Doctor Pocock. "I fear it may have serious repercussions on our foreign policy."

"I imagine that poltergeists at the present moment must be suffering from an inferiority complex," said Mr. Jericho, "and possibly Cheatham House is one of the few places left where they can really feel at home."

"It is very trying for poor Mrs. Trumper to have this added to her other troubles," remarked Emmeline. "I hear she seems very depressed. I must say I find it hard to believe that Professor Trumper should be able to make any woman unhappy."

"It may not be entirely on that account," said Mr. Jericho. "I understand she was very much upset at having a contribution to the *New Stateswoman* rejected, an article proving that in no possible circumstances could Italy enter the war."

"I have noticed," said Doctor Pocock, "that Mrs. Trumper, in the architecture of her theories, is more concerned with logical accuracy of structure than with the solidity of its foundations. Her conclusions are correctly derived from unsound premises. And although, in the world of politics and theology, happy results are often obtained in this manner, they do not appear to be obtained by Mrs. Trumper."

"You mean, Father," said Emmeline, "that Mrs. Trumper talks nonsense."

"Thank you, my dear," said Doctor Pocock, "for explaining to me what I mean and expressing it so concisely. You must remember that we philosophers never like putting things simply. Philosophy is concerned with the search for truth, and this does not lend itself to simple phraseology."

"That is no doubt why Pilate left in a hurry after asking his famous question," remarked Mr. Jericho.

"I must be leaving you, too," said Emmeline; "it is time for my afternoon walk."

9

—⊸๑๑๐⊶—

Lord FitzCricket

There had been lately so great an influx of refugees into the town that Emmeline, obliged one day to visit the shopping centre, could hardly make her way through the streets. Czechs, Austrians and Germans crowded the pavements. Chattering Frenchwomen were to be heard complaining in high staccato voices about the black-out and other inconveniences. Corpulent Jewesses in trousers, armed with string bags, descended on the food shops like locusts. Women from Whitechapel treated their perambulators as tanks and mowed down everything before them.

At first this alien population confined itself to the shopping centres and did not penetrate into the streets and sanctuaries of the collegiate portions of the town. Latterly, however, it had shown a tendency to overflow into the meadows, and Emmeline now took her daily exercise in the spacious garden of All Saints.

This, for her, was no deprivation. She loved the garden, with its wide expanse of lawn, flanked on one side by the old walls of the town, on the other by the grey edifice of All Saints, half hidden by the elm-trees, above which towered the spire of St. Ethelburga's. A very pretty picture of it by a Royal Academician, entitled "Haunts of Ancient Peace," with a quotation from Tennyson attached, hung in the Warden's dining-room. But Emmeline was not a believer in Wilde's theory of nature copying art, and it did not interfere with her own impressions of the place. However, she would have enjoyed going there more if the same curious thing had not happened to her every afternoon.

It was her custom to walk several times round the little mound in the centre of the lawn that seemed destined for a temple that had never been built. After a while Emmeline found herself becoming hypnotised by the tranquillity and timelessness of the place. It induced a sort of trance in which her steps were always led, as if by an invisible guide, to a corner of the garden in which there was a gloomy little rockery devoted to the cultivation of Alpine plants. Here she would come to with a slight shock and return to the Warden's lodgings obsessed by a feeling of depression.

That afternoon, on waking up at the rockery, she found a man standing before it in an attitude of despondency. He turned, and she saw it was Lord FitzCricket. She had met him once before in her father's house. She had sat next to him at dinner and had thought him agreeable, if slightly absurd.

"Are you fond of Alpine plants?" he asked her.

"I think perhaps they would be better in the Alps," replied Emmeline. "They might be less in evidence."

"It would be hardly worth while going to the Alps to find out," remarked Lord FitzCricket. "I have never felt the charm of the Alps, even on picture post cards. Though even the Alps just now—" He broke off. The thought of foreign travel seemed to be too much for him.

"Would you mind my taking a turn with you?" he asked. "I feel unusually lonely this afternoon."

"I was just thinking of going home," Emmeline replied. "Won't you come back and have some tea? I am sure Father will be delighted to see you."

She felt sorry for him. He looked so unlike the grinning photograph she had once seen in the *Tatler*.

When she got back to the Warden's lodgings she was told by the parlour-maid that Doctor Pocock was asleep and that the tea had been prepared in her room.

Lord FitzCricket was a stocky little man with a countenance that varied rather considerably with the mobility of his features. Quiescent, they appeared saturnine, but when animated, they took on an air of benevolence. He had now become completely bald, and when he was annoyed he looked like a diabolical egg. He possessed, however, no inherently satanic characteristics, and the impression was merely due to a peculiar slant of the eyebrows.

He was always referred to by gossip-column writers as "the versatile peer," and indeed there was hardly a branch of art in which he had not at one time or other dabbled. He composed music, he wrote books, he painted; he did a great many things with a certain facile talent. He was astute enough to realise that, in Anglo-Saxon countries, art is more highly appreciated if accompanied by a certain measure of eccentric publicity. This fitted in well with his natural inclinations.

He had a collection of strange masks that he used to wear when motoring. He dyed his fantail pigeons all colours of the rainbow, so that they flew over the countryside causing bewilderment to neighbouring farmers. He was always surrounded by odd animals and birds. When travelling on the Continent he had a small piano in his motor car, and on the strength of this he was likened in the popular press to Chopin and Mozart. Someone had even suggested a resemblance to Lord Byron, but for this he had neither the qualifications of being a poet nor a great lover.

Animated by the tea and the atmosphere of Emmeline's room, Lord FitzCricket began to speak of his first reactions to the war.

"For a time," he said, "the war knocked me out. I felt as if I had been pole-axed. I was unable to do anything at all. I offered my services, but I was advised to go on doing what I was doing, and God only knows what that was. I couldn't compose music, I couldn't write or paint. It all seemed to have become so pointless. I believed it was the end of everything and certainly of people like me. You see, I'm all the things that are no use in war. My character is essentially pacific and hedonistic. I like everything to be nice and jolly and I hate to think of people hating one another. I've never been any good at anything practical. I'm an amateur, and fundamentally superficial. I am also private spirited. I have never been able to summon up any great enthusiasm for the human race, and I am indifferent as to its future. I have always led a self-centered, sheltered life, and my little world consists of my hobbies and personal relationships.

"In moments of despair I often take a book, it may be the Bible, or Virgil, or even the Encyclopædia Britannica, and open it at random, hoping to find a message of help or comfort. This time it was the Fables of Lafontaine. I opened it at the fable of the grasshopper and the ant. It was not very encouraging, for I realized that what I am is a grasshopper, and it's now the turn of the ants. The world has no use at present for middle-aged grasshoppers."

"You seem to be suffering from a sense of guilt," said Emmeline. "Have you thought of trying psycho-analysis?"

"That is an idea," said Lord FitzCricket. "Thank you for suggesting it. As it is, I feel better already for having unburdened myself, even to an amateur. You may not believe me, but this is the first time since the war that this has happened. There must be something odd about this room. It strikes me as a place in which one could almost write a sincere autobiography. I feel I'd like to sit here for ever, talking about myself. But I don't suppose you'd care for that. As it is, I fear, I have bored you with my whining."

"Not at all," said Emmeline politely. "I hope you'll come again."

Emmeline did not often proffer such invitations to people she hardly knew, and after Lord FitzCricket had gone and she settled down once more to her work she found herself wondering why she had done it.

10

—◦◦◦—

Potpourri from a College Garden

Some concern was beginning to be felt in the Provost's intimate cir-
cle about the curious attitude he had recently taken up with regard
to death.

The Provost had always confessed that the death of a friend gave him
a secret feeling of satisfaction. It appealed, he used to say, to his sense of
composition. Completing the individual's life, it enabled him to judge
it as a whole. It also, he said, appealed to his predilection for tidiness.
He was pleased to think that the poor fellow's affairs were at last in order and that there would be no further shocks and surprises. He felt as
Shelley had felt about Keats.

> *He has out-soared the shadow of our night,*
> *Envy and calumny, and hate and pain*
> *And that unrest that men miscall delight*
> *Can touch him not and torture not again.*

But now death only seemed to appeal to his sense of humour. When
the demise of any of his friends was announced to him it appeared to
affect him with a malicious glee and was the occasion for an outburst of
sardonic hilarity.

"When he enquired of me the other day," said Mr. Jericho, "whether
I had heard of any funny deaths lately, I told him that one of the things
that kept me alive in these gloomy days was the fear of my death becoming the subject of his witticisms. He seemed surprised and even a little
hurt."

That the Provost was becoming slightly unbalanced was manifest in
other ways. He had, of late, grown more acutely irascible. His rendings
of inoffensive persons had taken on a ferocity worthy of Tiberius or Ca-

ligula, and his rudeness to mild undergraduates reminded one of Jowett. As time progressed he grew more and more misanthropic, and now only saw people whom his official position made it necessary for him to see. Beyond telephoning occasionally to Emmeline or to Mr. Jericho, he seemed desirous of cutting himself off completely from all communication with the outer world.

He was not best pleased therefore when Mr. Lollipop Jenkins appeared, one day, in his study.

Mr. Jenkins was full of a book called "Chronicles of Guilt." It was published anonymously and was a vehement indictment of a number of politicians whom the author considered responsible for the actual state of affairs. It was comprehensive, though there were one or two diplomatic omissions.

He had just arrived with a great many copies of this book, and was busy distributing them among the dons and the undergraduates and seeing that they were properly displayed in the bookshop windows. He had brought a specially bound copy to present to his old tutor, for although Mr. Jenkins considered that the Provost's intellect had sadly degenerated, he could never forget all that he had meant to him in the old undergraduate days.

When the Provost looked up from his writing-table, where he was engaged in composing his memoirs, and saw Mr. Jenkins advancing upon him in sprightly pomp, he felt murder in his soul. A murder had just taken place in his own college. One undergraduate had shot another. He feared that the infection might spread and felt that, at all costs, he must control himself.

"I have brought you a book that I thought you might like to read," said Mr. Jenkins.

"I am not reading very much just now," said the Provost. "What is it about?"

"It's about all the damned fools who have landed us in this mess," replied Mr. Jenkins.

"Are you in it?" asked the Provost.

Mr. Jenkins gave a deprecatory snigger. It was as well to let the Provost have his little joke. "I think it will amuse you. And it puts the case very clearly."

The Provost eyed him with disfavour.

"I don't think the subject is one for amusement. And is there anything to be gained by recrimination?"

Mr. Jenkins was becoming unnerved.

"It's not very long. You won't have much difficulty in getting through it."

"The Imitation of Christ is not very long," said the Provost, "but I have never been able to get through it."

Mr. Jenkins persisted.

"Oh, but this is much shorter."

"Then it can't be very comprehensive. In a case like this we are all of us guilty. I would sooner read the telephone directory. You can keep your book. Goodbye."

Mr. Jenkins failed to realise that he had got off very lightly.

There had lately been one or two cases of war neurosis among the undergraduates. Luckily, except in the shooting affray at Unity, the effects had not been serious. A theological student at Corpus Diaboli had opened his veins in his bath, but had been rescued in time and was now recovering. Beyond a certain annoyance expressed by the Blood Transfusion Service at the waste of good blood the incident had no further consequences.

In a lighter vein, Billy Montmorency had at last achieved the notoriety he had longed for, and had been sent down. Having grown weary of the ingratitude his entertainments seemed to inspire, he gave no more dinner parties. But being full of invention and hope, he had set out to devise other ways of making himself conspicuous. For a while he had taken up religion. Enlisting the services of Father MacOrkney (from the Collegio Beda in Rome), he held theological debates in his rooms, but as these were supplemented by an excessive consumption of liquor they ended either in stupor or horseplay and had to be discontinued. He then attempted to form flamboyant romantic attachments with some of his friends, but desisted on being told rather brutally by Jimmie Guggenheim Junior that sentimental friendships were no longer considered chic. At last in desperation he took to communism. He became a violent defeatist. He went round saying the most malicious things about the war, calculated to spread alarm and despondence. And finally, at a debate got up by Mr. Jenkins on "What Britain is fighting for," he had interrupted that gentleman's opening address by crying out: "We are fighting to put back the clock." Whether it was for this, or for some more serious delinquency, that he was sent down, nobody knew nor cared. He left the university unwept. His father, who was a prominent member of the Ministry of Information, was furious and threatened to disinherit him. Billy thought that, in the present circumstances, it didn't much matter whether he were disinherited or not, and he had the satisfaction of feeling that in one respect at least he resembled Shelley.

"I have a theory about the Provost," said Mr. Jericho. "There is something that has puzzled me for a long time, and I believe I've at last discovered what it is."

"This dreadful searching for truth," said Emmeline. "Why can't we leave her at the bottom of her well, which is her proper place?"

"Don't you want to hear?" asked Mr. Jericho.

"Of course I do. Please go on."

"Well, you see," said Mr. Jericho, "we have known the Provost and loved him, and taken him for granted—"

"Yes," Emmeline assented, "we have certainly taken him for granted."

Mr. Jericho had developed a new gesture. He would suddenly whip off his spectacles, polish them with his handkerchief, replace them, and stare through them with a greater intensity than before. The gesture was accomplished in a single rapid movement.

"Please don't do that, Mr. Jericho," said Emmeline. "I find it hard enough to pursue a consecutive train of thought in conversation as it is. You can do it to Professor Trumper if you like, but not to me."

"I am sorry, Emmeline. You will pardon me for pursuing my own train of thought. We have taken the Provost for granted. We have always known that his eccentricity was a mere sartorial detail, like a funny hat or a peculiar overcoat."

"You must admit that it suits him."

"Everything suits him," said Mr. Jericho. "He has seen to that. He has painted his own portrait with the skill of a Holbein—but have you ever wondered if it is the portrait that nature would have painted if she had been allowed to have her own way? I believe that he has achieved the difficult feat of having altered his predestined character."

"That is certainly a difficult feat. I have never succeeded in altering mine—but then I'm not sure that I ever really wanted to. Where I was at school there was a mistress who used to say that God gave us our character and it was blasphemous to try and change it."

"The aphorism," remarked Mr. Jericho, "seems to me rather inadvisable for a schoolmistress, but on the whole I believe it to be true."

"We had a parrot," Emmeline continued. "Father used to say it hated being a parrot. It certainly looked as if it did. But, poor thing, what could it do except make the best of it?"

"Let us avoid question of free will and determinism," Mr. Jericho urged. "I believe that the Provost was intended by nature to be a man of action and not a scholar. Gifted with great intelligence and will power, he has managed to make a success of the career he has chosen, but I believe it was not the one designed for him by destiny. He was born to be an eagle, but he has succeeded in deliberately transforming himself into a parrot, a charming, wise and fascinating parrot."

"And now he hates being a parrot," said Emmeline.

"Now he hates being a parrot," repeated Mr. Jericho. "But it is too late. The eccentricity that is growing on him is not the case of a fictitious reputation becoming real. It arises from a repressed sense of dissatisfaction and vain regret. Had he been a statesman, a man of business, or a military leader, we should no doubt have lost an agreeable friend—however, we must not only think of ourselves."

"I'm afraid I always think of myself," said Emmeline; "and I prefer him as he is."

11

---⟋⟋⟋---

The Rustling of Wings

Emmeline had hoped that the finicky and laborious nature of her
work would enable her to enjoy at least the respite from thought
that was so necessary to her mental and physical well-being. But she
found that, on the contrary, it often gave rise to the most disquieting
flights of fancy and led to meditations on problems that, owing to a lack
of philosophical training, she was unable to solve. The latter consideration was neither a solace nor a deterrent. Once she started thinking
about anything, she was unable to stop, and her persistence in trying to
reach a conclusion often gave her a headache. She hesitated to ask her
father to help her with her intellectual difficulties because his explanations generally made them more incomprehensible than they were
before.

That afternoon she was troubled by a problem suggested by the design of the embroidery. She remembered having read somewhere that
the world showed incontrovertible evidence of having been designed.
She wondered whether the God or Demiurge who was responsible for
the design was beginning to find that it was not coming out quite as He
had hoped and whether He were not at present engaged in destroying
it bit by bit just as she was destroying the embroidery. It was a disturbing
thought. Nevertheless it was nice to think that her work, humble as it
was, might have so distinguished a parallel.

Her cogitations were interrupted by the arrival of Lord FitzCricket.

Some time had elapsed since their last meeting, and Emmeline was
a little piqued at his not having responded to her invitation more
promptly. In the meantime she had found herself thinking about him,
more often perhaps than seemed necessary. Of course, he was an absurd little man and frightfully futile. Nevertheless, he had aroused in her

a certain interest. He appealed to the motherly instincts which, in spite of an almost militant virginity, she was unable at times to repress. Had she been the Caroline Paltry type of woman she might have felt impelled to look after him, to take him in hand and smooth out for him his muddled difficulties. Most of the people she knew were almost too efficiently capable of looking after themselves, and it was a welcome change to have at last met someone who wasn't.

"Do you find," Emmeline asked, "that when you think about anything for any length of time you always end by taking a personal view or getting back to first causes? It is most annoying."

"I never think about anything for any length of time," replied Lord FitzCricket. "It doesn't suit my temperament. Thinking about frivolous things sometimes gives me pleasure, but when I think about serious matters I get discouraged. The only solution is to have something to do that stops me thinking. Lots of people are like that. They're all right until they begin to think."

"Yes," said Emmeline, "that is what I have discovered, and I thought I had found something that would stop me thinking, but I'm beginning to realize that it doesn't."

She immediately regretted having mentioned her war work and feared lest Lord FitzCricket might become inquisitive.

"You're looking much more cheerful than when I last saw you," she said.

"Yes," said Lord FitzCricket. "I took your advice and am being psycho-analysed. I really think it is doing me a lot of good. Psycho-analysis has the same sort of charm as going to a fortune-teller. You lie on a sofa and talk about yourself for hours and hours. That in itself is exhilarating for the Ego. All sorts of curious things were found in my Unconscious; a stuffed bird, a pair of gloves, a black rubber mackintosh, in fact the whole contents of a jumble sale. No wonder I felt queer."

"And have you got rid of them?" asked Emmeline.

"I hope so. Of course, they may come back, but in future I'll know what to do about them."

"Apart from a sense of guilt," said Emmeline, "I didn't notice that you were suffering from any very serious complexes. But then I'm not very observant."

"It's rather in my family, you know," said Lord FitzCricket. "My grandmother suffered from very bad agoraphobia. She couldn't stand being in large open spaces. She was very fond of travelling, but of course she couldn't go to the desert, or the Savannahs or the Tundras or the Steppes. When she went to Russia her doctor said to her: 'Mind the steppes.' His puns, I'm told, were better than his pills. I used to suffer from agoraphobia myself in a mild way. My psycho-analyst tells me it is a form of the back-to-the-womb complex."

"Good heavens! What is that?" asked Emmeline.

"Oh, don't you know? It's a thing we're all supposed to suffer from more or less. Our first impressions of the world are so disagreeable that we want to pop back again at once. Birth is a shock that very sensitive people never get over. American women have womb-chambers constructed in their houses so that they can shut themselves up in them whenever the complex gets bad. I remember, in the Stuyvesant-Kruger divorce case, one of the principal grounds for divorce was that the wife always found her husband sitting in the womb-chamber when she wanted to go there herself."

"Surely they could have afforded two," said Emmeline.

"One would have thought so. But rich Americans often have very odd economies."

"Tell me more about your psycho-analysis," said Emmeline. "It's very interesting. I'm beginning to wonder if perhaps I oughtn't to be analysed myself."

"Well," said Lord FitzCricket, "another thing the analyst found out was that my death-instincts were getting the better of my pleasure principle, and that it was something to do with my Œdipus-complex. It just shows how mistaken one can be about oneself. When I used to feel like that before I always thought it was my liver."

The telephone bell rang. It was the Provost of Unity. He seemed to be in high spirits.

"Emmeline," he said, "I've got a very funny piece of news for you. Prepare yourself for a good laugh. Mrs. Trumper has hanged herself."

Emmeline was silent. From the other end of the telephone the Provost sensed that she was not taking the news quite in the way he had expected.

"What?" he said. "You don't think it's funny? How extraordinary! Nobody seems to think it funny. I must say I am disappointed in you, Emmeline. I thought that you, at least, had a sense of the comic." And he hung up the receiver.

Emmeline remained standing before the telephone for a few seconds and then returned to where Lord FitzCricket was sitting.

"How dreadful," she said. "Poor Mrs. Trumper has committed suicide."

"It is dreadful indeed," said Lord FitzCricket. "I never met Mrs. Trumper, but it always upsets me to hear of anyone committing suicide. I once thought of committing suicide myself. Have you any idea why she did it?"

"No," said Emmeline; "I simply can't believe that it was because the Professor was carrying on with Mrs. Postlethwaite. I should hate to think it was that."

"In nine cases out of ten," said Lord FitzCricket, "people commit suicide not at all for the reasons one thinks. It may be that she was suddenly overwhelmed by a sense of discouragement. Or perhaps she was merely tired of having to dress every day, like the suicide in Mark Twain, who left a note 'Tired of buttoning and unbuttoning.' "

"You might have thought so if you had seen her clothes," said Emmeline. "Oh, dear, I suppose I shall have to write to Professor Trumper. It will be a very difficult letter. I dare say I had better get Father to do it."

Emmeline seemed very distressed, and Lord FitzCricket, feeling that the incident had put an end to any futher levity in the conversation, withdrew.

12

Lady Caroline's Activities

Lady Caroline Paltry was, as usual, very busy. The evacuees she had taken in at the beginning of the war left after a few weeks. They complained that the house was too far from the town, and Caroline, who was not given to considering other people's tastes, refused to let them have tinned salmon and fed them almost exclusively on fresh vegetables, porridge and rabbits. They found her domineering and altogether too whimsical in matters of diet.

The schoolmistresses who succeeded them proved even less of a success. They deplored the absence of intellectual atmosphere, they were shocked by Caroline's physiological frankness and were annoyed by her discouragement of political discussions during meals. So in their turn they left, and Caroline had now filled the house with poor relations. She charged them very little for their keep, but, in return, she made them help with the housework, look after the goats and the chickens, clean the car and the wagonette, dig in the garden and perform any other useful jobs she could think of. When evening came they were so exhausted that they retired to bed at an early hour and gave no further trouble. Caroline felt that she had at last got a billeting arrangement that was fairly satisfactory.

In the town and in the neighbourhood she had found scope for her usual activity. She had doubled the number of work parties and canteens, she had designed a new uniform for the Women's Guild, and although she did not fully appreciate the sociological value of art, except in so far as her husband's music was concerned, she made Francis give concerts for the entertainment of the troops.

She was now engaged in arranging for a performance of his new symphony at the Pandemonian. The use of the place for musical purposes involved certain formalities, but Caroline had succeeded in browbeating the authorities concerned into acquiescence and, as a work of supererogation, she had forced her parents, who had no very great love either for music or for their son-in-law, to come over from Ireland for the occasion.

Emmeline was now seeing quite a lot of Lord FitzCricket, and he had taken to accompanying her on her afternoon walks.

Lord FitzCricket, since his residence in the precincts of the university, had grown more earnest, and suggested that their outings would be improved if some definite object were involved. And so nearly every afternoon they would visit some architectural feature. But after a time, although there were many interesting and beautiful buildings in the town, they found that the repertory was becoming a little monotonous.

"I'm afraid it's not true," said Lord FitzCricket, "that a thing of beauty is a joy for ever. That is the worst of poetry. One is inclined to believe a thing just because it sounds nice."

"I never did believe it. There was a girl at my school who was a thing of beauty, but she certainly wasn't a joy for ever. I don't think anything can be a joy for ever. That's the trouble about heaven."

"One doesn't want any kind of monotony. Perhaps heaven will turn out to be a sort of sublime variety show."

"I don't fancy the idea of variety going on for ever," said Emmeline. "And if we are going to keep our personalities, how is it going to suit everyone's taste? There'll be just as much boredom and complaining in the after-life as there is in this one. And people who go to heaven are bound to be rather exacting. Things in this world are in a pretty good muddle, but it's nothing to what it will be in the next."

"And theology holds out no hope of a different stage manager. I expect that's why so many people are in favour of annihilation."

"That sounds dull to me," said Emmeline, "but of course there'd be no dressmakers' bills, no Professor Trumper, no war. But one doesn't want to be looking forward to something one can't define, and even Father can't define non-existence. I once asked him if a thing could be non-existent and he said: 'How many non-existent things do you think there are in this room?'"

"And how many were there?"

"I don't know. I suppose I had formulated my question wrong. That often happens in philosophy."

"There's not much to be gained by formulating questions about the unknowable. That's what Kant said."

"I dare say he did. Father says he was a great one for platitudes."

"I think it's a mistake to be priggish about platitudes. Speaking as a man of the world I'd rather be guided by a few honest platitudes than by any amount of metaphysics. Let's leave the unknowable to philosophers and theologians and get on with our work, cultivate our garden."

Emmeline's thoughts grew personal.

"Or destroy it. Wouldn't that do as well? It would keep one busy, I mean."

"It depends on the garden. There are some I know that would be none the worse for being destroyed. And I don't suppose you're advocating indiscriminate destruction."

"No," said Emmeline. "Only things that are out of date and no more use. Museum-pieces for instance. What is the good of having them about? They only discourage people or incite them to make bad copies, and a lot of time and trouble is wasted in keeping them up."

"I'm afraid I'm a museum-piece myself," said Lord FitzCricket, "and I still believe in tradition."

"Tradition is nothing but a graveyard," said Emmeline. "I was told that by an undergraduate."

"Destroying the graves won't abolish the necessity for graveyards. And we seem to have got away from the point."

"One always does here," said Emmeline, "and in any case I must hurry home. Caroline Paltry is bringing her parents to tea. There's a couple of museum-pieces for you, and you had better come and compare notes. Only they're not your period. They're much, much earlier."

Caroline arrived with Lord and Lady Otterboy in a small open car. She had some difficulty in extricating them from among the objects with which it was packed—a bird cage, a gramophone, a sack of potatoes and a number of agricultural implements. She had also brought her husband.

Francis Paltry and Lord FitzCricket did not get on very well. Their temperaments and their æsthetic views were poles apart. Lord Fitz-Cricket was a dilettante and had always been interested in the pleasurable aspects of art, and he thought that a work of art should never be tedious. Francis, on the other hand, held that art should be austere, and he felt that he himself had a mission. Lord FitzCricket said that Francis believed in catharsis through boredom.

Francis had once written rather rudely about Lord FitzCricket's compositions. The article was unsigned, but Lord FitzCricket knew that Francis had written it and Francis knew that Lord FitzCricket knew.

"I hope you're coming to the concert," Caroline said. "Francis's symphony is really magnificent. Don't you think so Mamma?"

Lady Otterboy was evasive. "It seemed very nice, but then I have only heard it on the piano."

"I don't suppose FitzCricket would care for it," said Francis.

"I am sure that I should enjoy it very much," said Lord FitzCricket. "But I am not certain if I shall be able to go to the concert."

"Nonsense," said Caroline. "I'll take you."

"Is your symphony very long?" asked Emmeline.

"Certain people might consider it long. It lasts about an hour and a half, and it's in one movement. If a man has something to say, he must take his time about it. I haven't been able to acquire the modern knack of developing a theme in a few minutes or not developing it at all."

"I think you're wise," said Lord FitzCricket. "If you're setting up to be a national composer. The English have a tendency to judge art by size and weight."

"We aren't a nation of shopkeepers for nothing," said Emmeline.

"Napoleon said that," remarked Lord Otterboy. He would show them that he, too, could join in a highbrow discussion if he chose.

"Why don't you modernize your room, Emmeline?" asked Caroline.

"Caroline, will you please leave me and my room alone. I've spoken to you once before about interfering."

"I like it," said Lady Otterboy. "It's a nice quiet room. Caroline's house is so noisy."

"Oh, don't go on about the noise, Mamma."

"Don't you know there's a war on?" Francis enquired facetiously.

Lady Otterboy thought his remark was directed against herself and was offended.

The atmosphere, though not exactly electric, was becoming a little strained. Lord FitzCricket was not good at coping with dissonant personalities, and although he would have liked to examine the Otterboys more closely, he felt that he would have preferred to do so in the absence of Caroline and her husband.

"I must be going," he said.

"Are you still working in the Blood Transfusion Service?" asked Caroline.

"Yes, that's where I'm going."

"Then I'll come with you. There's a new method of storing blood I want to tell them about. Why don't you marry Emmeline?" she asked as soon as they had got out of the room.

"Why don't I what?"

"Marry Emmeline. She's a very nice girl and she wants taking out of herself."

"But do you think that's necessary?"

"Well, you might try. I'm not coming with you really. I only wanted an excuse to get you alone. Think it over."

"I knew that fellow's father," said Lord Otterboy. "Old Puggy we used to call him. He was a splendid old chap, a fine shot he was and rode well to hounds. Does this fellow hunt?"

"I believe he used to."

"Why did he give it up?"

"I think he took to writing music."

Emmeline's remark was intentionally mischievous. She was anxious to divert attention from Lord FitzCricket and she had taken a dislike to Francis.

Lord Otterboy grunted and glared at his son-in-law.

Caroline turned to Emmeline. "Why don't you marry him?"

"Marry who?"

"Lord FitzCricket, of course. It's quite a good title."

"Oh, Caroline, dear," said Lady Otterboy.

Emmeline flared up. "Caroline," she said, "this is the second time this evening that you have given me ridiculous advice. If you do it again I shall have to ask you to go."

"I'm going anyhow," said Caroline. "And, my goodness, you are getting bad tempered."

"I'm sorry, Lady Otterboy," Emmeline apologized, "but you must admit that Caroline at moments is maddening."

Whatever Lady Otterboy thought, she refused to commit herself.

"She didn't mean it, dear," she murmured in an aside.

Caroline was not particularly interested in match-making. It was a matter of indifference to her whether Emmeline and Lord FitzCricket married or not. But seeing two unattached people in a room together had upset her sense of organization.

13

———⟨⟨⟨⟩⟩⟩———

The Love Life of Socrates

M rs. Postlethwaite's novel, that had just appeared, was a new departure in the way of style and background. The scene was set in ancient Greece, and the story was a love romance between Socrates and a fascinating hetaira. The authoress made no attempt to embellish the physical appearance of Socrates, but she had taken a certain amount of liberty with his conversation, which was not at all like that recorded by Xenophon and Plato. There was also an undue insistence on his "voices"; they were continually making the most improbable suggestions.

The hetaira herself was a lady of considerable charm and determination, and she was inclined to thrust herself into unhistorical situations. She succeeded in persuading Socrates, in spite of his well-known dislike for the country, to go with her and live a pastoral life in a secluded valley in the manner of Daphnis and Chloe. During his trial she burst into the court, made an impassioned speech to the judges and ended by taking off all her clothes. The device did not appear to have been so successful as in the case of Phryne, and although several of the judges were very much affected, Socrates was condemned all the same. She made a final irruption into the cell where Socrates was awaiting his death and, at his personal request, handed him the cup of hemlock.

Xantippe did not figure very largely in the book. It was implied that she was a bit of a drag on her husband, a hindrance to his philosophical activities and, in the description of her exterior, acute observers might detect a slight resemblance to the late Mrs. Trumper. Owing to an oversight on the part of the printer and the proof reader she appeared for the first time in the book as Christiantippe.

The only other event, at the time, that stirred the even tenor of university life was the invention by Mr. Jericho of an important military device. It appeared that, unknown to anyone, he had been working for some time on a weapon of lethal character which, after considerable opposition on the part of the War Office, had at last been adopted and was proving to be of considerable value.

Having achieved a utilitarian act of national importance such as to preserve him for ever from the charge of frivolity, Mr. Jericho gained in self-assurance. He acquired once more his pre-war ebullience, and no longer attempted to conceal his interest in the more trivial aspects of human life.

Mr. Jericho had bought a copy of Mrs. Postlethwaite's novel and was reading passages from it to Emmeline and Lord FitzCricket.

"Overhead was the blue sky, and through the silver filigree of the overhanging olive branches the sunlight fell in dappled plashes on the succulent turf and smote the ripples of the quick-flowing stream into a thousand facets of glittering diamond. Aglaia was sitting on the banks of the Ilyssus and, with one foot, was lazily caressing the water weeds.

" 'You say, Socrates,' she murmured, and her voice was limpid, like the clear-flowing water. 'You say that Nature has no call for you, that you can learn nothing from the fields and trees, the mountains and the many-sounding brooks?

" 'I know a little glade far off from the bustle of the city, far off from the distractions of social life. There we could live for ever happy, disturbed only by the bleating of the lambs, the hum of the bees and the twittering of the birds.'

"And that night, tossing sleepless on his couch, above the lowing of the oxen and the clattering of the heavy wine-carts as they laboured over the marble pavements of the city, above the cries of the drunken helots returning from the dicteria, Socrates heard his Voices calling to him softly: 'Go to the country, Socrates, go to the country.' "

"Read us the part where she takes off her clothes," said Lord Fitz-Cricket.

" 'Do not condemn this just man,' she cried. 'What has he ever done to you or to the people of Athens? You say he is a corrupter of youth. I am young and Socrates has loved me. His teaching has taught me nought but ideals of nobility and purity. Here I stand, a living testimony to the falseness of your accusation.'

"Loosening her girdle, she let fall her chiton to the ground and stood before them, an alabaster amphora of purest design. Would that Pheidias and Praxiteles had been there to see!

"Dazzled by the milk-white radiance of her perfect form, a gasp ran round the court. Meletus, in awe of so much beauty, placed his hands before his eyes, and the face of Xantippe skulking behind a column assumed a sour expression."

"I wonder if she has sold the cinema rights," remarked Lord Fitz-Cricket. "There'll be a good deal of competition, I should imagine."

Mr. Jericho closed the book.

"I am worried about the Provost," he said, "Have you heard anything, Emmeline?"

"No. I have telephoned several times, but there was no answer."

"Ever since my little contribution to the war he seems to have taken a dislike to me, and he never once referred to it, even sarcastically. I heard he was ill and went to enquire. I was met on the doorstep by a hospital nurse. She was like Cerberus in her manners. 'You are the last person he would wish to see,' she said and practically slammed the door in my face. Since then I haven't persisted."

"Oh, dear," said Emmeline; "it's dreadful when one's friends get so queer."

14

—⦿⦿⦿—

All Clear

It now seemed certain that Mrs. Postlethwaite had broken off relations with Professor Trumper and that their romance was at an end. No doubt, after the tragic incident that had occurred they both of them thought it wiser to discontinue their intimacy. It was also possible that Mrs. Postlethwaite may have felt that, like d'Annunzio and Goethe, she had purged herself of passion through literature. When that lady paid her a visit one afternoon, Emmeline guessed it was something in the nature of an all-clear signal.

Mrs. Postlethwaite was dressed in the deepest mourning. Emmeline wondered how she was going to treat the subject of Mrs. Trumper's death.

"For several days," Mrs. Postlethwaite said, "I was simply prostrated. It was, as you can imagine, a fearful shock. You knew, of course, that poor Pixy was my dearest friend."

Emmeline appeared a little bewildered.

"Yes," Mrs. Postlethwaite continued, "that was her pet name. She was always called Pixy by her family. Though you may not perhaps agree, I think it suited her. In spite of her serious outlook on life I always felt that there was something about her that was a little 'fey.' "

Emmeline felt that she had not been sufficiently acquainted with Mrs. Trumper to go into that aspect of her character.

"And Professor Trumper?" she enquired. "How is he taking it? I suppose he is quite heartbroken, poor man. She was such a help to him."

Mrs. Postlethwaite assumed a detached air.

"I really don't know. He has a hard, selfish nature. I never really liked him. She was, of course, my great friend. Poor Pixy! I fear she was never a very happy woman, in spite of all her political interests. Her ideals were too high. It was a mistake, in this cruel, evil world of ours, to have too high ideals. One meets with so many disappointments. Well, she is at rest now. She was buried, you know, in St. Luke's in the West, such a charming, peaceful little churchyard. I like to think of her lying there. It appears she had always set her heart on being buried at St. Luke's, and I believe they had to get special permission as it's practically full up. I wanted to design her tombstone, but that horrid old Professor vetoed the idea. All this has upset me very much, and I should like to go right away somewhere and forget things. But I feel my duty is to stay with Herbert just now. He is working so hard and, although he hasn't much time for poor little me, I know he likes to feel I am there. And oh, he has given me such a wonderful idea for a novel—"

"I liked your last one," Emmeline interrupted. "It was so full of poetry."

"Oh, nonsense. That was just a trifle. This one is going to be really serious. It's all about evolution. May I tell you? I always find if I talk about my plots it gives shape to my ideas. The action takes place in the Darwin period, when there was all that controversy about evolution. My hero is a famous biologist, and I shall make him just a wee bit like Herbert. At first he was very religious and believed in the Bible, but after a great deal of mental wrestling and agonies of conscience he ends by believing in evolution, and it comes to mean everything to him. Then one day, while poking his fire, he finds a human tooth embedded in a lump of coal. You see that would upset the whole theory of evolution and ruin his life's work. It would be too cruel, especially after his having given up religion."

"Good gracious!" exclaimed Emmeline. "What does he do then?"

"I haven't quite made up my mind. I had thought of making him commit suicide, but poor Pixy has rather spoilt that idea. I shall have to think of something else."

"Couldn't the housemaid have dropped it?" suggested Emmeline.

"Oh, no," said Mrs. Postlethwaite. "It was a fossilized tooth, and, besides, it wouldn't be a serious ending."

Lord FitzCricket arrived.

"We were speaking of biology," said Emmeline.

"Oh, hush," cried Mrs. Postlethwaite.

"Biology?" said Lord FitzCricket. "That is one of the subjects I never tried to tackle. I've always had a thirst for knowledge and felt I wanted to get to know a little about everything. But my experience with physics upset me so much that I had to abandon the idea."

"You mean things blowing up?" asked Mrs. Postlethwaite. "No, that's chemistry. But biology's quite safe, except that you're liable to be bitten by monkeys."

"It was not explosions or monkeys that I was afraid of," Lord Fitz-Cricket explained. "It was something more subtle and far more disconcerting. When you're as sensitive as I am, you are liable to get acute inflammation of the sense-data. After studying physics for a while, I began to feel the electrons inside me jumping from one level of energy to another, and I became a martyr to Heisenberg's Principles of Uncertainty. I had a nervous breakdown and was obliged to do a rest-cure. I fear something similar might happen if I were to take up any other branch of science, and that is why I have confined myself to the arts."

From below came the sound of the hall door being closed.

"That must be Father," said Emmeline. "He has been to see the Provost. Will you please excuse me for a moment. I want to hear his news."

She ran downstairs and found her father taking off his overcoat and scarf.

"Did you see him, Papa?"

"Yes, dear," Doctor Pocock replied. "It was very sad, but at the same time I felt slightly consoled. He seemed much calmer than I have known him for many years. He was sitting out in the garden under an ilex tree. It is a nice establishment and the atmosphere is very peaceful. The doctors and the nurses all seem very sensible people. I don't fancy he recognized me, but he talked quite coherently. He seemed to take great pleasure in the flowers. I never knew he was interested in horticulture, but he appeared to know the Latin names of all the flowering shrubs. The nurses seem very fond of him and they told me he gave very little trouble. But they said he grew very agitated at times and kept crying out for a machine-gun."

When Emmeline returned to the drawing-room she found Mrs. Postlethwaite expatiating to Lord FitzCricket on the pleasures of conjugal life.

15

———⟨∿∿⟩———

The Garden of Sleep

Whether it was due to Caroline's propaganda or to the fact that, of late, musical entertainments had been few and far between, on the afternoon of Francis's concert the Pandemonian was crowded. All the musical élite were there, and even Professor Trumper, who very rarely went to concerts, was present.

Caroline was sitting with the Mayor and the Vice-Chancellor. She had invited Emmeline and Lord FitzCricket, but they preferred being nearer the door.

"There's always something a little depressing about musical audiences," remarked Lord FitzCricket. "At a concert I often find myself envying King Ludwig of Bavaria."

"They're no worse than people at race meetings or political gatherings," said Emmeline, "or any other crowd of people who are interested in the same thing. It's seeing them all together."

"Yes, I suppose so. Individually they're all right. There's Mr. Jericho over there. He looks just as bad as anyone. Crowds have a faculty of reducing individuals to the lowest common measure. It may well be that the proper study of mankind is man, and the study of mankind is discouraging."

Fragments of conversation emerged from the general chatter. They were mostly complaints.

"They've made Marjorie a corporal. It's sickening."

"All the windows were blown out, and the doors too."

"The greenfly on our roses this year was something terrible."

"She actually had the cheek to say I was gamma-minded."

There was a sudden hush. Francis had appeared on the conductor's platform and tapped with his baton.

The first item on the programme was Brahms' Tragic Overture. Then came the Symphony.

Pale, watery sunshine falling through the high windows, illuminated Francis as if with semi-official limelight.

"There's no doubt," said Lord FitzCricket, "that he's destined for the Musical-Laureateship."

When the Symphony was over, he suggested to Emmeline that they should not wait for the rest of the concert. "I think we have done our duty by music for the day."

On their way out they met Mr. Jericho.

"It supplies a long felt want," was his comment.

"I'm afraid it does," said Lord FitzCricket. He was a little embittered by the rapturous applause with which the Symphony had been greeted.

"Shall we go to St. Luke's in the West?" Emmeline suggested. "It was where Mrs. Trumper was buried. But that's not my reason for proposing it. I think we may find it restful after all that strenuous music and it's quite near."

"The reason why I dislike Francis," said Lord FitzCricket, as they walked along, "is that he's a prig. Priggishness is the one human failing

I have never been able to stomach. For all I know I may be a prig myself. I don't think I am, but if you're irritated by some characteristic it often means you've got it yourself."

"You are perhaps a trifle conceited," said Emmeline, "but I don't think you're a prig."

"There have been too many prigs let loose on us lately," Lord Fitz-Cricket went on. "It has become almost a public danger. But the English, I believe, are aware of it. The abuse directed against highbrows doesn't imply an aversion for culture, as some people seem to think. It is the old terminological trouble, and when they say highbrows they really mean prigs. All the same, the public is often taken in by them. Priggishness is insidious and, in cunning disguise, insinuates itself into art, politics and religion with disastrous results. There ought to be a Vigilance Committee of Prig-detectors."

St. Luke's in the West is an ancient church, standing in a graveyard planted with rose bushes, Irish yews and a few shady trees. Although situated in the centre of the town and close to one of the main thoroughfares, the place has a rural, out-of-the-world air.

"The Provost used to say he liked walking in cemeteries," remarked Emmeline as she opened the gate. "He said it gave him pleasure to think that so many people were dead."

"The thought doesn't give me pleasure," said Lord FitzCricket, "but it might help to reconcile one to death."

"Don't let us talk about death," said Emmeline. "It is a very dull subject. Destruction is a much more exciting problem."

"It's certainly a very actual one. If it goes on much longer there'll be nothing left except military objectives."

"Oh, I don't mean war-destruction." Emmeline sat down on a tombstone. "I mean something far more universal. I mean the destruction that is going on for all time and is the fate of all created things. It'll take millions of years perhaps, but in the end there'll be nothing left at all—not even military objectives. It makes everything seem so silly. Shakespeare was worried by the problem, too. 'The great globe itself shall dissolve and leave not a rack behind,' but if it was a consolation to him that our little life is rounded with a sleep, it isn't to me, much as I enjoy going to bed. I shan't be happy until I get a really good working theory. Please help me, Lord FitzCricket."

"I'd really rather not think about it today, if you don't mind," said Lord FitzCricket. "I'm a mental coward and I can't face theories."

The wicket-gate opened and a woman appeared. She was dressed in deep mourning and was accompanied by a young man. She was carrying a large bunch of flowers. They saw it was Mrs. Postlethwaite, and the young man was Mr. Guggenheim Junior. Emmeline and Lord Fitz-Cricket had a simultaneous thought that the meeting might prove embarrassing and hid themselves behind one of the Irish yews.

Emmeline peeped through the branches.

"She's laying flowers on Mrs. Trumper's grave," she whispered.

"The Altar of the Dead," said Lord FitzCricket.

After the rite had been performed and Mrs. Postlethwaite and her companion had left the churchyard, Emmeline resumed her seat on the tombstone. Lord FitzCricket sat down beside her.

"Will you marry me, Emmeline?" he asked.

"Oh, no, Lord FitzCricket, I couldn't really."

"I was afraid you might say that. I know I haven't much to offer you."

"Oh, it isn't that," Emmeline protested. "It's not that at all. It's simply that I'm not a marrying woman."

"Well," said Lord FitzCricket, getting up from the tombstone, "perhaps I'm not a marrying man either. And in any case if I marry I suppose it ought to be someone who could look after me. You couldn't do that, Emmeline, could you?"

"No," said Emmeline, "I don't think I could."

When Emmeline returned to her room it was growing dusk. She drew the curtains, turned on the swivel lamp and took out the embroidery. But that evening she had great difficulty in settling down to her work. Thoughts kept buzzing about in her brain like a swarm of flies.

"I couldn't possibly marry him," she said to herself, "but it was nice of him to ask me. I don't want to marry anyone. I shall never fall in love, I'm sure. Passion seems alien to my nature and I really haven't the energy. I just want to be left alone. But if Father were to die, what would become of me? Anyhow, he isn't dead yet, and what's the good of bothering about the future? Anything may happen. And then there's this tiresome destruction problem. I can't get on with my work until I've cleared it up. Lord FitzCricket wasn't very helpful, and it's no good asking Father; he would only make it worse. I shall have to puzzle it out for myself." She made a great mental effort. "Some people seem to think that life is a striving for positive perfection. Perhaps they've got it the wrong way round, and perfection is really negative. All created things are doomed to change and decay and only destruction can give them immunity. And so the impulse to destroy is more reasonable than the impulse to create. Perhaps another day I shall think of something better. It will have to do for the present. I really must get on with my work. Oh, dear!" she cried, as she poked her scissors into the breast of St. Agatha. "If only one didn't have to think."